-Books by Ryan Clark-

The Tech Hunter Series:
Cryogenesis - 1
Warden - 2
Contract - 3

Cryogenesis

Cryogenesis

Tech Hunter: Book 1

Ryan Clark

Published by Ryan Clark
www.ryanclarkbooks.com
Cover design by Ryan Clark
ISBN 978-1-7336702-1-0

Edited by Courtney Andersson
www.elevationeditorial.com

To the numerous people who built my imagination:

From the bedtime stories of adventures, simple truths, and encyclopedias, to the explorations of science, games, and photography, my world took shapes of its own because of what you showed me. I am thankful for the years of bouncing meaningless, pointless, and profound ideas back and forth, and the exposure to movies and music I never would have thought to reach for.

I know this book is just a small start, but I have great hopes for the things to come. I could never imagine any of this without any of you, and I thank you for that.

Table of Contents

Chapter 1: Summons

From across the wide opening of Atrium: 447, Jance Lorège watched the kite hovering over the ventilation updrafts. As the silent minutes rolled by, her own struggle to center her drifting thoughts was much like the kite drone's struggle to stay aloft over the tumultuous updraft; except instead of being controlled by the children in the atrium on the level below, she was at the mercy of her scheduled break. All seventeen damn minutes that remained of it.

Jance rapped her fingernails against the railing and began looking around the room. Images of orange dirt, sparse shrubs, and low-lying grasses shone from a network of screens about the atrium in celebration of the successful colonization of Mars. She stared absentmindedly as the presentation highlighted the steps throughout the years leading to the achievement. The fabled "future for humanity" had been created by the corporate giants operating under the government-funded Mars Contract, and she watched as the early days of small, bunker-like structures gave way to the domed tourist traps built on dead rock. Technological advancements and developments over hundreds of years eventually led to the first flora surviving on the surface of the planet, followed soon after by the current settlement. A large central tower ringed by a spiderweb of sealed passages and outer buildings now stood high over the Martian landscape.

As Jance watched, a number appeared over the images of the Mars colonies as they were now, supposedly highlighting the achievement. Jance just shook her head at the reported population of the colonies under the Mars Contract.

1.4 million inhabitants.

As the people's ambassador of the starscrapers in Section-K, she knew that she had over 1.4 million United World Coalition civilians currently inhabiting the 446 levels below her feet, and that was just half of one starscraper. Jance began to pull up the exact number on the display of the visor in front of her eye when she received a warning message from her counselor.

"Let the work go and find your balance. Focus on yourself, Jance. Fifteen minutes."

Jance let out a sigh and glared past the message to the passenger ship moving down through the middle of the room. As the transport passed her level, a hot wave of air from the gravity repulsor engines fluttered against the angled trim of her dress uniform and rolled across her mixed brown hair, bringing with it the smell of burnt electricity. A small ping sounding from her wrist monitor notified her of an urgent message. Jance tapped on her visor, squinting as the distortion field from the repulsor engines caused the image to flicker.

"Open," she said, watching through the shifting words as the passenger ship landed at one of the docking platforms several levels below. As the projection fell back into place, she looked from the people exiting the ship to the displayed message. It was from the Chancellor's Office. Jance let out a short breath and flicked the document to the side. Every bit of her meticulously packed agenda, including her "recommended" break, had been automatically canceled as soon as the summons hit the system.

As she hastily made her way to the side of the atrium, the publicly controlled images of orange dirt and blue sky suddenly switched to the emergency alert system. In an instant, the calming screens throughout Atrium: 447 changed to a view of flames and the flashing lights of UWC response teams. Even the displays on the side of the passenger ship, which set a low, vibrating hum to the air as it powered on its repulsors, showed the live images from just after the attack.

Jance pulled to a stop as she realized the scale of what had happened not so far away in the world. It looked as if one of the starscrapers along the east coast of North America had become the newest site of Last Edict devastation. Half of an atrium, much like the one she was in, was wreathed in flames.

As the passenger ship turned around in the open space to make its way up the several stories to the interior airlock, Jance noticed that the small kite drone was now drifting to the side; the group of kids controlling it from below were distracted by the images in front of them. The kite tipped beneath one of the engines of the passenger ship and disappeared in a flash of blue flame and smoke.

Jance held a finger up to the thin silver wire of her visor and opened a transmission. "I'm off your schedule, Agatha."

"I . . . I see that," her counselor replied. "We will just do the best we can. Good luck in there, Jance."

Jance gave a grim nod, knowing that she was going to be tied up in the Council's meeting when she could do far more good directing and focusing the efforts of her people. "Thank you, Agatha. I will let you know when I am out."

Jance ended the transmission and started off along the rim of the atrium at a brisk walk. She could have made faster time, but the last thing people needed to see was an ambassador running at the mention of frightening news. She passed by a number of individuals either entirely absorbed by the displayed reports or ignoring them the best they could. Jance approached one of the security doors at the edge of the atrium trimmed with an illuminated yellow bar to signal the clearance level needed. The lights flicked white as she waved the back of her hand over the access panel. After the latch snapped free with a hiss, Jance took a step forward into the security lock, and then into the massive room beyond.

All around, large tubes and turbines moved water and air through the thousands of stories in the starscraper. Four miles of towering metal and glass. Four point seven million people. From here she could feel the vibrations from the immense gravity repulsor engines that helped the building to stand upright.

As of yet, even the most advanced materials could not be used to construct structures matching the sheer scale of the starscrapers without the use of external lifting supports like the repulsor engines. The maintenance areas were equipped to dampen the vibrations of the gravity repulsor engines, serving as buffers to most of the populated areas of the starscraper. Thankfully, the maintenance area was still pressurized; only the outer maintenance decks were open to the weather. She would need to exit through another security lock to actually feel what the air was like a mile up from the bleak waters of the Mediterranean Sea as they swirled against the lowest seventy levels of the starscraper.

Jance made her way to the nearest maintenance elevator and waved her hand over another security panel. Normally she would have taken a public elevator, but she was pressed for time. The schedule placed the meeting of the UWC Council within the hour.

"Five hundred: Airlocks." Her selection was met by the pulling in her gut of the elevator speeding upward on distortion fields. Jance slid the visor out of the way and leaned back against the metal and carbon mesh of the wall. The two rectangular windows in the roof gave her a view of the lighted floors flashing past. If Agatha truly wanted her to take a moment away from work beyond the six hours of sleep she got each night, this would be the place. No public announcement systems railing on about the self-sustainability of the Mars colonies, nor the alerts bringing in news of all the torments of the world.

The elevator started slowing well in advance of its arrival, giving her the nearly weightless feeling that even a lifetime in the starscraper system had not eased.

The doors bolted open, and the motion was accompanied by an abnormal rush of air out of the elevator and into the maintenance ways. For a moment, her hair wrapped around in front of her face as the pressure shifted. She flicked the visor back open. The alert showed a pressure leak in Maintenance: 488 through 511. Jance closed her eyes and took a breath of the thin air. This is why she had such a hard time sitting still. She could check out of the system for thirty seconds and something new would always be wrong when she checked back in.

Jance started to sort her hair into place as she continued along the maintenance walkways. Luckily, a construction crew was already arriving to the scene, and the repair drone was making its way up to where a seal had broken along the edge of the massive, rainswept window. Far in the distance, the other starscrapers of Sector: K stood out of the sea, wreathed in repulsor-generated storms of their own.

Jance pushed through the small security door into the wide hangars of Airlock: 500-11. The room was a massive eleven stories high and filled with platforms extending from a system of walkways on every level of the room. Along the exterior wall were exits for vehicles ranging from the individual transport pods to the larger cargo and waste haulers. Even with the large vents circulating as much air as possible, the room still reeked with the metallic, electric odor of hundreds of transports in the air.

Moving along the lowest walkway, she made her way through the crowd of people. The same news segment played on the sides of transports far above, and many of the civilians had paused to watch it in their own personal display visors. It was only when she made her way up the small set of stairs rising over an intake vent that the general crowd began to thin. Her visor flashed a restriction notice. It was an inelegant solution, but the virtual cordon was set up to designate the section for government-level workers only. She tapped her visor to display her clearance and a few of the security guards eased their posture.

Another tap to her visor showed which transport the Chancellor's Office had reserved for her. *"C-13."* Jance kept moving along the row of transport pods clamped vertically on the sides of the walkways. Most were only big enough for one person.

Jance pulled her visor into full view, bringing the display across to span both of her eyes. She activated the navigation prompts and continued along the artificially projected lines on the path in front of her. A moment later, she received a small notice by means of yellow warning lights on the adjacent strut. A quick glance told her that it was *"Routine maintenance, stay clear."*

Her own assigned pod appeared to be one of the newest models, capable of free flight without an emergency request. She tapped the hologram in front of the pod and the glass of the transport slid open from several different angles. Jance stepped over the walkway and into the pod. As the security latches slid over her legs and torso, the glass panels moved back into place. Her location had already been set, so it was only a matter of confirmation to take off.

Jance grimaced at the slight drop as the clamps of the strut released the craft. The pod drifted backward from the platform, leaving her blind to everything but the display on the glass noting the locations and paths of nearby transports.

Her pod tilted back as it aligned for the flight, leaning back but not flattening entirely. The main forward thrust ramped up, which she watched on a holographic slider to her right. The craft now followed the path displayed, much like the line she had followed across the docks. Everything vibrated as she passed under one of the smaller cargo ships, highlighted through the glass with a collision warning even though the paths would never cross.

A moment later, her transport bolted out of the airlock and into the turbulent skies around the starscraper. All along the structure, shining blue glares from repulsor engines cut brightly through the swirling clouds. Several flecks of water slid down the front glass from the scattered rain showers caused by the turbulence from the starscraper repulsor engines. In the distance, the other starscrapers of Section-K and their surrounding storms rose out of the Mediterranean like the Pillars of Creation.

The next broadcast scheduled to display to the public was actually a historic look at the Eagle Nebula, and specifically the discovery of the Pillars. Some thousand years ago, a prediction had been made that the towering masses of stellar gas known as the Pillars of Creation had long since been destroyed, and the light from the event had yet to travel the six or seven thousand light-years to Earth with the answer. Jance just knew it would be a welcome change from this week's dull tones of Mars. That was, if the scale of the attack did not disrupt the schedule.

A flash from her wrist pulled her attention. The narrow light pulsing yellow meant an urgent connection request. She flipped the request onto the larger display of the transport with a prepared scowl.

"Morris?" she asked when the face of her fellow Council member appeared on the display. "What is it?"

Morris Kannei, the people's logistician of Sector: K-8, was a nervous type of man, always ready to leap to the worst possible scenario on any list. That being said, much of his job was running numbers and creating the lists Jance used in her daily work.

He blinked a couple of times to adjust his special, outdated eye lenses. He claimed that the newer eye devices would be used to watch everything from a remote location, which they could, but he also had the clearance level to know they only used that capability for suspected sectators of the Last Edict or during emergency situations. The slight silver lining around his iris was the only sign that he wore the outdated versions—besides the blinking, of course.

"Morris," Jance said again, "what do you need?"

He finally stopped fiddling with the lenses and wiped a bead of sweat from his forehead. "I, uh, just wanted to let you know I finished the reports on the ventilation systems. Expenses to improve the air quality, uh, on upper levels should be well within budget. If started today, the process should be done in two months or so. September the eighth, to be precise. The inhabitants of the upper floors can easily be moved between Starscrapers K-8a, K-8c, K-8d, and—"

The ambassador let out a sigh and interrupted the man. "What about this is urgent? Morris, I told you to stop using emergency pings for non-emergency messages!"

"You do not answer to anything else!" He wiped a frustrated hand over his sloppy shave. It cost nothing to have it trimmed, or even permanently removed, but that probably had some form of wild conspiracy notion to it as well. "Besides, it is more urgent than you might think, and is connected to the security of our starscrapers. You have to contact me, Jance. Before the meeting. I'll be waiting at the common docks."

She closed her eyes for a moment, then put on a false smile and kindly reminded him that it was, in fact, an emergency meeting, and that she doubted Director Auburns or Military Ambassador Hoffsted would care in the slightest about improving air quality when their cities could be on fire. At that, she flicked the transmission away. If the man had anything else to say, she was sure it would be said, no matter how hard she tried to ignore him before the Council started the session. At least this time it wasn't regarding a widespread conspiracy.

As her transport approached the mainland, she saw the lone starscraper standing amongst the dense cityscape between the long ranges of the French Alps. At four miles high, the UWC Council Starscraper and its cloak of storm-forming engines rose above even the highest snowcapped peaks. The place had been chosen hundreds of years ago as the new Council City of the United World Coalition because of the stunning landscape, though now the vast majority of the area was covered in a thick mat of buildings spread out beneath the starscraper.

She surveyed the rest of the city in the distance through a magnified view field. The massive coastal wall still had its standard assortment of airbases, weapons batteries, tidal dispersion arrays, and, of course, tourists. However, the more she looked around the sections of the Council City, the more she noticed military fighters and gunships on patrol. The security had increased by what she guessed to be tenfold.

As the craft turned, her attention was pulled up to the other form dominating the skyline. Hovering a few miles away from the Council Starscraper was one of the main ships of the UWC fleet. The mile-long dreadnought, the *Nemesis Tide*, cast a great portion of the city below in shadow as fighter crafts poured out of the hangars in the belly of the ship. Jance took a tentative breath, fearing that the news alerts had told only part of the story behind the attack and the emergency session of the Council. Her wrist alarm rapidly flashed orange as her craft continued on into secured airspace.

A communication request soon appeared, and the channel opened automatically. "Ambassador Lorège, this is Comms Officer Hayden of the UWC *Nemesis Tide*. You are clear for docking with Council Starscraper, port A-1-37."

She started to ask about the additional security, but the communication had already closed. The virtually displayed line guiding her craft changed its destination from the common airlocks to those just below the UWC Council Chambers. What she did not understand was why the dreadnought was the one issuing the docking statements. Perhaps the meeting was going to be about something more pressing than an isolated attack. Something could have gone drastically wrong with the Mars colonies, or perhaps a sudden change of stance by the Sovereign Republics Alliance had prompted a red flag in the conflict avoidance algorithms. All manner of thoughts with more likeness to those of Morris Kannei's than her own flicked through her head as the craft sped toward the massive heights of the Council Starscraper.

Chapter 2: Norclave

The glowing lights of a transport dropped down from the night sky with an agitated hum and a series of crackling pops. If the hour had not been so late in the small settlement known as the Rift Outpost, the crew at the landing pads would have been readying to unload the cargo once the lumbering craft touched down. Instead, one old man tried to rub the sleep from his eyes as he pushed out the door and onto the rusted balcony of the watchtower. He grumbled about the unexpected arrival in the dead of night and flicked the data pad to turn the guide lights on at one of the open spaces.

The Rift Outpost received a large amount of traffic during the day, but for anyone other than a lost soul emerging from the outerzones, it was less than remarkable. The scattered buildings were made of metal sheets pulled from the surrounding lands and fixed together with little effort toward enhancing the comfort of those who lived within. In fact, the only real worth found in the settlement was shipped out by the merchants and tradesmen, profiting from the large rift cut into the land.

Stretching for nearly a mile to either side of the settlement, the huge split in the earth brought life to an otherwise dead part of the Rift Hills. Where other places were cherished for their vast forests or green fields growing between the ruins, the lands surrounding the rift kept to the dull brown shades of plants struggling to survive amongst the leveled buildings of the past. The rift itself held wealth in the form of electricity, boiling up from the reactors in the core of the Earth like water from a spring. Long ago, there used to be a station here that distributed the nearly limitless energy to sprawling cities everywhere, but now workers simply climbed down the rift in mech suits—known locally as riftwalkers—with heavy loads of power cells to recharge.

The transport finally crackled to a stop, leaving glowing marks on the landing pads where the engines had hovered for too long. The pilot hopped out of the still-shaking vehicle and stumbled a few steps from a knot in his leg. A quick glance around told him that the Rift Outpost had done little more than leave the light on for his rushed arrival. The man shook his head and set out to find directions for a particular technician by the name of Kenneth. The Overlord of Norclave expected his arrival well before noon, meaning there was no time to waste.

He walked quickly through the dark, partly because he had a tight schedule, but mostly out of nervousness. A soft glow came from work lights down along the edge of the rift, and a deep and droning hum echoed up from farther down than any riftwalker or even any tech hunter dared to climb. He couldn't help but entertain thoughts of the stories of something ancient living miles down. Like any other who had found a childhood in Norclave or one of the surrounding settlements, he'd heard plenty of tales of dangers from underground. But what could come from the very center of the Earth?

He walked up to a wide building some distance from the others. The sides of the path leading to it were littered with heaps of scrap that, at least in someone's eyes, had enough potential use to keep them from being hauled elsewhere. He knocked on the door.

"Excuse me! Mr. Kenneth!" he yelled, hoping someone would hear. "Sorry to wake you, this is Arlen. Well, you wouldn't know me, but I was sent by the Overlord. The Overlord of Norclave, that is, though I'm sure you could have guessed that. Kenneth? You there?"

Arlen knocked on the door and called for a minute or more with no answer. He began to feel as if he had been misled by the soldiers, who had just pointed wordlessly to this seemingly old and abandoned warehouse. If he could not find Kenneth within the next hour, he would likely be forced to take his transport out of the Rift Hills altogether. Running was a better idea than returning to a furious Overlord. Perhaps he could shuttle parts for scrapsmiths in the Steel Valley, or maybe join an expedition for the Kessians. Arlen decided he would at the very least have a look inside before such drastic measures. He pushed through into the dark room.

Most of the lights of the place were off, save for a few glowing panels and wall lamps. He could tell that it was the workshop of the technician because he had no idea what even half of the parts scattered across the shelves and tables were; tech work was hardly his avenue. That was one of the reasons his transport was in rough shape. That, and getting ripped off by the man who had said he would fix the touchy shut-off control.

Arlen tried to step lightly, but the place was in such a mess he knew only someone who worked here could make their way around without bumping into more than a few things. He moved toward a doorway lit with a flickering yellow security clearance light. The light would have been pulled from the ruins and stuck there, like everything else. The next room was larger, and inside were a couple of rusted transports with their insides spilled out like gutted fish, as well as a couple mech suits. The riftwalkers.

He stumbled over something on the ground and bumped into a small table full of power converters. Arlen scrambled to stop them from rolling off, but soon the dark room was filled with the noise of metal clattering across the floor. Suddenly, the deep whir of an engine powering up echoed through the space and two bright lights flared on from about ten feet up. Arlen held his hands up to shield against the sudden shock of the brightness.

"Don't you move!" a voice yelled from behind the lights and the sounds of powerful machinery. "I'll chase you down with this riftwalker if you try anything, and believe me, you will not even make it to the door before I—"

"Okay, okay!" Arlen interrupted, "I will not move!"

After a moment, the voice behind the lights continued. "Who are you?"

"I was sent by the Overlord to find a technician named Kenneth. Have you heard of him?"

"Just you? One pilot?"

Arlen stood straighter, giving a confused look while shielding his eyes from the light. "Just me. Why?"

"Usually, when the Overlord sends an order, it comes with a host of soldiers." The man flicked off the lights of the riftwalker. Arlen blinked past the bright blur in his eyes and saw the man crawling out of the seat of the mech. To his surprise, both legs of the walker were lying below it with piles of parts spread about. The main body and arms of the riftwalker were held up by a hoist from the ceiling.

"And do you have any idea why the Overlord is looking for a particular technician?" the man asked, lowering himself to the floor.

"No idea," Arlen replied, rubbing at his eyes. "Just something about fixing a riftwalker."

The man gave a dissatisfied groan. He looked to be in his early thirties, and like he had gone more than a few days without a shave. His arms were covered in the same grease and oil that made the floors slick. If Arlen had to guess, he would say the man had fallen asleep where he had been working in the seat of the walker.

"I would ask you why you were sent in the dead of night," the man said, walking closer, "but you probably forgot that reason as well. Do you remember who you talked to?"

"Just someone who said he worked for the Overlord." The pilot frowned as the man walked past. "Wait a sec," he said following the man into the other room, "do you know where Kenneth is?"

"Really? I'm the technician you're looking for," he said. "Let me grab some things and we'll be off to Norclave."

At least there would be no punishment from the Overlord for being late. He already had one mark on his arm for not paying the transporter's tax, and in the Rift Hills, a second mark meant the Overlord would decide if you should be executed or not. It had been years since anyone was chosen to live.

* * *

An hour later, Kenneth leaned back in the rough seat of the transport as it rumbled over the treetops. Bright searchlights on the craft shone hundreds of feet forward, illuminating the way over the thin forest. The air of the cool morning rushed past his face as they sped along, bringing a slight bite to his throat as he took a breath in. All along the horizon of the Rift Hills lay the broken shapes of skyscrapers and other ruins that had been reclaimed by the thicker forests hundreds of years ago.

Around the Rift Outpost, most of the land had been all but leveled. But here, miles from the rift, it was almost like flying through hollow canyons of bent steel. Anyone could get lost in this place.

In the sky far above the ruins, the field of wreckage on the edge of space reflected the bright glimmers of sunlight of the day yet to come. Kenneth watched absentmindedly as the broken fleet still held in orbit of the planet slowly drifted, supported on the blazing blue lights of centuries-old repulsor engines. It was a wonder that after more than six hundred years, the twisted and torn ships had not yet fallen upon the remains of cities they had once likely protected.

It was then that Kenneth was jolted sharply forward. One of the repulsors on the craft crackled and shot out a bright jet of orange flame. Kenneth had to raise a hand to shield his face from the heat as the craft rolled to one side, threatening to pull them into the forest below.

"You had better do something!" Kenneth yelled to the pilot.

"Don't worry!" the man yelled back. "This happens at times!"

"Then why the hell wouldn't you tell me that!"

They crunched through the outer branches of a tree, touching down in a clearing with a couple loud bounces as the man struggled to cut the faulty engine. The pilot undid his harness in the welded-on cockpit and hopped out, sliding out a metal pipe from beside the seat. The rusty craft began to spin in a circle as the one repulsor refused to turn off, still popping with orange flame. Kenneth yelled a curse that was drowned out by the loud clangs of the pilot smacking the repulsor with the pipe. The transport finally ground to a halt.

"There, fixed it. We should be good until Norclave."

"What is wrong with you?" Kenneth yelled. More than nearly anybody, he knew what could happen if a repulsor became misaligned. Once, he had worked on one that backfired. It had dropped a glob of metal out of its core, and he'd stepped on it. Kenneth undid his harness and pulled himself up out of the seat. After a quick glance up at the tree they had set on fire, he jumped down off the transport. He still had that chunk of metal where it had welded itself to the steel plate under the sole of his boot.

"It only does that sometimes," the man said. "If I wasn't so close to the trees, I would have just let it sort itself out."

Kenneth stepped over the glowing line the repulsor had cut into the concrete, dirt, and steel of the ground. He angrily grabbed the pipe and ushered the man out of the way. The repulsor had been dented in from a number of nearly suicidal beatings. If the man had bent the inner coils the wrong way, there was a strong chance it would have just exploded, turning the transport into a lump of superheated goo.

He used the pipe to pry open the dented side panel on the repulsor. When he looked inside, Kenneth rolled his eyes. Any idiot who opened the panel instead of beating it with a pipe would have clearly seen the piece hanging down, loose. He reinserted the regulator and pulled his hand back, careful not to touch the outer casing. He used the metal sticking from the bottom of his boot to shut the door, and with a grunt threw the pipe as high as he could into the burning tree.

"Hey, hey! What are you doing!" the pilot yelled.

"Just drive!" Kenneth stepped up onto the back of the transport and sat down in the third seat, careful to not cut himself on the pieces of broken glass that reflected the fires behind him. The sharp edges had once been the part of a windshield. "Hurry up!" Kenneth yelled. He thought about taking the pilot's seat himself, but who knew what other problems this piece of junk had that needed a trick to keep it from crashing to the ground . . . or at least, from crashing too often.

For the next few minutes in the air, he listened to the repulsors and other abnormal sounds of the craft, fearing that each thump was the snapping of a bolt that held the casing on the power pack, or even that the welds holding his seat were breaking away. Kenneth began to wonder if sating his curiosity about the Overlord was worth the risk of dying in a horrible crash.

As the sun continued up into the haze of the sky, the city grew steadily thicker around them. The pilot managed to fly through the tangle of fallen towers surprisingly well, despite his numerous shortcomings. In the long shadows cast from the half-standing ruins, Kenneth saw what looked like a campfire. No doubt tech hunters out looking for the next great find.

"Four people down there!" the pilot shouted back. "Good thing they can't reach us!" There was always an unwelcomed risk of being shot down by an improvised repulsor cannon or some other fancy bit of tech, although he doubted anything happening so close to Norclave. Normally, the patrols kept things as calm as anyone could hope for.

The sound of the craft echoed back to them as they passed under the slant of one building leaning against another. The pilot slowed down and made sure none of the hanging vines were actually power cables. There was a cool spray in the air as water poured out of one of the floors above, falling as a sunlit waterfall hundreds of feet down into a pond that had formed long ago. Sometimes Kenneth was still amazed at how things came to be so many years after the fall of the supercities, though he imagined most others hardly gave any of it a second thought.

The pilot switched off his lights as they broke past the larger buildings. For about a mile stretch, the city had dissipated enough for a sizeable forest to take over. He could pick out several roads cut through the trees, all leading toward a point that could have been just another rise in the land. In actuality, it was a structure toppled on its side. The ruins of the starscraper stretched on for two miles in each direction, surrounded by crumbled buildings and thriving forest. In the center of the shadowed face of the structure were the lights of Norclave.

"Always a sight to see," the pilot yelled back. Lights not only came from the cluster of the city, but from all across the starscraper. Some were steady, while others popped in and out from hundred-foot arcs of electricity.

The bottom layers of the starscraper had been crushed together from the weight of a half mile of metal pressing on them from above. Kenneth guessed the structure was originally a rough mile square at the base. As for the city of Norclave itself, it was nestled in amongst a missing section of the outer skeleton of the building. An explosion like Kenneth could hardly fathom had brought the starscraper to the ground, but hundreds of years later it had also given a home to the people of the Rift Hills.

It was not his first time seeing the city. The Overlord of Norclave had called on Kenneth many times when all the other technicians had given up on what they thought was impossible. Ever since he was no more than a boy, he could bring systems to life that normally would have been scrapped. It was just a part of surviving that he had held on to after leaving the outerzones.

"Put us down on the fourth layer!" Kenneth called over the winds and rumbling engines.

"But the Overlord is on the top! I have strict orders—"

"Just do it!" he interrupted before the pilot could finish.

As the pilot entered the shadow of the starscraper, Kenneth got a good look at Norclave. It consisted of seven chaotic levels of plates of fused metal and suspended walkways. There were separated platforms on each level where a transport could land, and at the lowest level was a large gate for scraphaulers and other ground vehicles.

This early in the morning, only the sounds of a few people in the city echoed through the vast number of steel walkways and suspended buildings. Those that were out and about would be merchants or travelers looking to get an early start on the day. Kenneth gave a nervous glance around, realizing that their arrival would be out of place. Any other transport would be leaving the city at this time.

"What's wrong?" Arlen asked.

"It's nothing," Kenneth said, perhaps not loud enough for Arlen to even hear.

The pilot set the transport down on the fourth level, and Kenneth hurried out of the harness. He let out a breath as he stepped down onto the platform, his left boot clicking with the chunk of metal on the bottom. He glanced up at the city above them as Arlen pulled himself out of the transport. The pilot tried to follow Kenneth's gaze, looking up to the platforms hanging onto the side of the city like metal fungi.

Kenneth finally realized that Arlen was looking openedmouthed up at the city. "Hey, don't . . . Look at me. Eyes here." If anyone had been told to keep watch for their arrival, looking suspicious would rule out any luck to be had with those prying eyes missing them.

"What is it, technician?"

"Follow me. And just keep looking forward." At the end of each docking platform was a station of normally at least two Norclave soldiers. Kenneth stepped up to the mesh gate and tapped his boot on the frame to wake the man leaning against a crate on the other side. How he could sleep through a transport landing at his dock, Kenneth did not understand.

The soldier stretched his shoulders without hurry, not bothering to wake the other guard snoring behind the crates. He wore the standard grey uniform bearing a red stripe painted crossways over the chest, and he had some sort of club or shocklance holstered on one leg.

"Morning to you," the soldier said. "Have you two been to Norclave before?"

"Of course we have," Kenneth said impatiently. He grabbed Arlen by the shoulder and moved him closer to the gate.

"Alright, alright. No need to go over the rules then. Arms."

The pilot pulled back the sleeve on his left arm, revealing a heavy scar several inches behind his wrist. It was a warning mark, a brand that ensured his next crime against Norclave would be his last.

The soldier gave Arlen a firm look. "Best not push your luck." He hit a panel on the other side and the gate slid open, allowing the pilot to move on into the city.

"Arm."

Kenneth wiped a bit of the grime off and held his left arm out toward the man. The soldier took in a sharp breath. Kenneth then handed him several Norclave tokens beyond the payment for the dock and pulled his sleeve back down. Arlen was waiting on the other side with a curious look. He glanced at Kenneth's arm as Kenneth walked past without a word.

"What is it?" Arlen asked.

Kenneth simply replied, "Nothing," and kept walking.

Soon after, they were well into the chaotic walkways and paths Norclave was known for. It was not uncommon for the view below the gratings to show several levels down. Kenneth glanced through the mesh flooring he was walking on. If it gave out, he had a near two-story fall, and if he missed that platform, it would mean a hard landing just behind the main entrance on the bottom level. He glanced at the welds, and even though he had walked over much less stable structures many a time, he put a hand on the railing and continued.

For the most part, the city was well lit. It had to be with the massive shell of the starscraper hanging overhead. Norclave would first see bright daylight just before noon for a time, and then off and on as the city fell under new shadows until the latter part of the day. Cables ran in no particular pattern between the lights on the railings and walkways, and several times Kenneth had to resist the urge to stop and fix one that was off or another that was sparking. It had been a long time since he had been put to helping about the city. He turned sharply and led the way up a narrow set of stairs, barely wide enough for two people to pass each other.

"Where are we heading? Shouldn't we be going to the Overlord's complex?"

"We have time yet. Tell you what, you go up and wait outside the complex, get some sleep, and I will catch back up."

Arlen glanced at the mark on his own arm. "I'll walk with you."

Kenneth shrugged and turned onto a walkway without another word. He had not been on this path before, meaning it had been added some time in the last few years, but it was simple enough to make his way through. He was heading to the trade center of the city, a place that could be heard even at this hour.

Goods from all around funneled their way through the trade center, be it food stores or pieces drug up from the wilderness. Energy cells, power converters—anything considered more than scrap found a place in the market, and the rest went to the smiths down below.

Kenneth took a good look around as the city opened into the wide area of the trade center. It was a freshly waking chaos of trades and services spanning up four levels. All along the sides were shops, and spread about the web of walkways were a number of stalls setting up for the day. A man shouted an "All clear!" to the pilot of a large cargo transport sitting on one of the inner platforms. A deep rumble filled the area as the repulsor engines pushed the transport up on jets of bright blue. The glowing signs above the shops and the nearby lights flickered as the engines passed by.

Arlen gave a low whistle as they both watched the transport lift up and out of Norclave. "I would love to own one of those." He gave a long yawn and held a hand up to cover his mouth. "Someday."

The transport kept going up for nearly a half mile. It moved through an opening in the overarching hull of the starscraper and spun off toward the east, likely taking a shipment to the Steel Valley, or perhaps to the Kessian lands.

Kenneth pulled his attention back and started off again. Metal crates of varying shapes and designs clogged the pathways where merchants had started setting out their wares for the day. They passed by a few stands laying out packs of preserved foods. Like everyone else, Kenneth had eaten his fair share of the readied meals. They were perfectly balanced in nutrition, designed to rejuvenate fully from the powder upon opening, and they even tasted better than most fresh meals one could find. However, there was one thing about the meal packs Kenneth had a difficult time looking past: anything that came out of them was over six hundred years old.

He waved away the merchant who had noticed him looking and kept moving. It had been a long while since he had been to a trade market besides the small one in the Rift Outpost. He knew he could spend the entire day looking around, and that was without watching for the new items that found their way in with the tech hunters throughout the day.

The center began to fill even as he made his way around one edge of the second layer. A couple of prices he heard mentioned were over what they should be, but that was anything but abnormal in a place like this. He almost stopped to ask about a pair of boots, but decided to keep moving before a crowd really started to show. A few shops later, he found a vendor selling what looked like fresh rounds of bread. Kenneth put down a coin and picked up two pieces as they continued through, tossing one back to Arlen. Even with the noise of people trying to budge prices and the racket of the sawing and grinding of steel, the pilot looked as if he was going to fall asleep on his feet.

They passed several scrapsmiths hard at work trying to pull a battery out of a repair drone. Kenneth shook his head, wondering if they would ever figure out that it wasted less time to go in from the other side. At the next spot over, where Kenneth had been heading all along, two men were arguing about a price.

It took no trained eye to see that one was a tech hunter. He had a rough bag and a dark grey cloak, both slung over one shoulder. His tall boots and the bottom edge of the cloak were covered in a coat of dust. Kenneth could see that just under the edge of his sleeve was a bit of tech, and on his hip was some sort of pistol.

Kenneth motioned for Arlen to take a seat on a crate shoved against the railing. Kenneth leaned against the rusting bar and glanced over the edge. It was nearly forty feet to down to the bright flashes of the scrapsmiths working below. He turned back to Arlen. "This may take a few minutes. The old wrinkle of a man hates getting the back end of a deal."

"I would be sorry that I can't help you," the merchant said to the tech hunter with a scowl, "but the price you want me to pay makes it not worth my time!"

Mackelry Norton had been a merchant of collectable goods in Norclave since before Kenneth had arrived as a boy. The man was thin as bones and the shadiest merchant one could find without getting a name beforehand. Up front, he bought and sold items at prices best suited to him, and in the back of his shop he made a hefty profit off of tech banned within the city.

Kenneth glanced at what the tech hunter was trying to sell; it was a pair of gloves made of intricately woven carbon fibers and steel insets. He blinked a couple of times in surprise. They were not scrapped together, nor had they any hint of having been repaired. He had never seen anything from before the fall still in such perfect condition. Even the normal coat of rust-filled scratches was missing.

Kenneth stepped closer. "Where did you get those?" he asked. The tech hunter pulled the gloves back and gave Kenneth a suspicious glance.

"Kenneth! Is that you?" Mackelry said in a hushed voice. "What the hell are you doing in Norclave?"

"I was called here to fix a bit of a problem. Riftwalker, I was told." He tried to get a second look at the gloves the tech hunter had pulled close.

"You mean you came here to help old Mackelry out with a problem," Mack said, giving a hoarse laugh as he grabbed the tech hunters' gloves and slid them back to the center of the counter. A dangerous move for most people. "Tell this man how much these are worth. Tell 'em forty is too high, will ya boy?"

"Who is this?" the tech hunter asked with a deep rattle in his voice.

Kenneth felt a tingle on his neck, as if someone were watching, and he almost turned to look over his shoulder. He fought the urge, knowing the tech hunter would likely take the chance to take the gloves and leave before any trouble started.

"I'm a technician," Kenneth replied. "Soon to be working for the Overlord of Norclave. These just caught my eye as I was passing."

The tech hunter gave him a long glare, weighing him up. Kenneth crossed his arms and returned something of a similar look. The man had dark skin and a thick jaw covered in a rough shave caused by both scars and weeks spent in the outerzones. All the suspicion came from the uneasy transition from the ruthless wilds into the control of Norclave. To that, Kenneth could relate. While the chances of getting in trouble inside the city were limited to fistfights at the bars and scars from the Overlord, in the outerzones there was no one to say if you were killed by a live line, rubble collapse, or a shocklance to the back.

"What do they do?" Kenneth asked, trying to break the man's stare.

"Let him take a look," Mackelry insisted, sliding the gloves over to Kenneth. "I might cut you a deal."

Kenneth made no move to take the gloves and instead waited for approval. While most of his life had been spent in the city, he had lived his early years in the outerzones and knew firsthand that it was hard to earn a tech hunter's trust. After a second, the man gave a small nod. Kenneth then picked up a glove. It did not weigh as much as he had expected. The fingers could move with more ease than he had thought possible, and when he tapped the tips of the fingers to the palm, a small disk popped out of the back of the glove.

"Hey, look at that!" Mackelry called out. "You still got it, boy!"

Kenneth rolled his eyes at the comment. The disk stayed floating in the air, likely held up by a distortion field. A screen was projected above the glove, and when he moved his finger through the slider, the light produced from the disk increased. When he folded the fingers forward with another click, the disk snapped back into place.

"The other one," the tech hunter said, pulling out a thin metal case, "makes a power link with these."

"Now what is that?" Mack asked.

The tech hunter slid a finger over the case and it unfolded, fastening itself to the counter with magnets. The man slipped on the other glove and pulled a device out of the case. It looked to be the same make as the glove and about twice the size of one of the fingers. He waved it over the back of the glove a few times to establish the power link, then took hold of it with the glove. He touched the tip of the device to the counter, causing a bright light as he moved it in an arc. When he pulled it away, there was a clean cut in the metal.

"Well, that is neat," Mackelry said, "but I am afraid I will have to take off a bit for damages."

The tech hunter picked up another device from the case and waved it over the back of the glove a few times until it made the connection. With a motion like before, he mended the metal back together.

The old merchant scratched through his wispy hair in overdramatic thought. "Kenneth, my boy, what would you say a good price is? Don't oversell me, mind you."

Kenneth paused for a moment. He knew his answer couldn't have anything to do with the item's real value. The Norclave technicians would gladly trade an entire transport for the gloves, and the Overlord himself would pay for their pristine quality. However, Kenneth needed some answers from the old merchant before he headed up to speak with the Overlord, and raising the cost to double was perhaps not the best way to keep Mackelry's attention.

"Thirty hundreds is fair," Kenneth stated.

"What!" Mackelry scoffed. "Twenty-five, tech hunter, and I will pay no more!"

The tech hunter pulled the gloves and case off the counter and stuffed them into a bag. Just as he started to turn away, Kenneth tapped his fourth and fifth fingers on the counter. It was a signal Kenneth had picked up from spending too much time at this shop when he was a boy.

"Wait one sec, tech hunter." Mackelry pulled a breath in through his teeth. "Thirty. Both gloves and that box. Thirty."

The tech hunter slowly turned around. "Try five more for wasting my time."

Kenneth could see the red boiling up in the merchant's face. Before the old man started shouting or calling for his strong-arms, Kenneth tapped his fingers again. It was all Mackelry could do to let the word "fine" slip out through his teeth. He started slamming down hundred-mark Norclave tokens. Once the payment was settled, the tech hunter left the sack on the counter and disappeared into the ever-growing crowd.

"I should have called my men on him," Mack said with furious eyes.

"They would be lying on the ground foaming at the mouth," Kenneth said. There was no way to tell what a tech hunter like that was capable of. From the quality of the tech he had just sold, Kenneth knew he was no amateur of the trade. "Besides, I just earned you twice that much in profit."

Even when helping Mack out with illegal trades of explosive devices or light distortion tech, Kenneth had always said a price near enough to fair. Enemies earned by shorting them were the worst, but if shorting that tech hunter would buy him the information he needed to keep from walking into a trap, Kenneth was willing to deal low.

It took a moment before a toothy smile spread across the merchant's face. "So what is it? What do you need from old Mackelry?"

Kenneth leaned closer. "Advice." He glanced over his shoulder to where Arlen sat leaning against a railing at the edge of the walkway. "The man sleeping behind me was sent in the night, alone, no soldiers, with word from a man—claiming to be working for the Overlord—about fixing a riftwalker."

The old merchant frowned and crossed his arms. "That's dangerous info you're dealing in."

"That's why I came to you."

Mackelry nodded, his frown deepening. "Let's go to the back." He picked up the sack and waved to a large man leaning against the building. It was a signal to his guard to let Kenneth through. Kenneth followed Mackelry through the packed front of the shop and into a small doorway in the back.

In the black trade business, secrecy was even more important than contacts, especially with the harsh laws of Norclave. When Kenneth entered the small room, similar to most of the other shops in the trade center, the old man was nowhere to be seen. Kenneth stepped up on a conveniently placed stack of metal plates before ducking through the falsely projected wall. On the other side, a glowing orb hovered knee-high over the distortion generator lying on the ground. It was a beautiful piece of tech, but it was not worth the risk of having in Norclave unless it was being used to hide a thousand other things that could also get the owner executed.

Kenneth continued, stooping down as he moved through the pipe passage. He had always wondered why Mackelry had something so short put in, but at least it blended in more than a stairway on the outside. He finally stood up and rubbed a hand on the back of his neck. Once through, it was no problem to even stretch his arms. The room was nearly twenty feet tall, and with the exception of a crude table and chairs in the center, it was filled with rows of shelves.

To the criminals Mackelry dealt with, the shelves were stacked better than a Kessian armory. To Kenneth, he saw a trove of dangerous and uniquely fascinating devices either preserved from before the fall or scrapped together in more recent years.

"So, someone wants you in Norclave," Mackelry said, leaning against the table in the center. "We know it's not the administrators, though I figure you've guessed as much."

The administrators were the ones appointed by the Overlord to carry out his rules. In recent years, the power had been slowly shifting in their favor. Trade was now governed by the administrators without input from the Overlord, and most messages were sent to them first. Luckily for Kenneth, they had yet to take control of the executions. He himself had quite the reputation in Norclave, mostly for rebelling against the administrators once tasked with watching him. In his youth, not long after he had been pulled from the outerzones, he had stolen a transport and tried to escape. He'd earned a mark for that—his first—at no more than age twelve.

"Then who?" Kenneth asked.

Mackelry shrugged. "If it was somebody wanting you dead . . . well, it would have been easier to do it outside of Norclave. I suppose that leaves either some well-connected individual wanting a pricy bit of tech worked on in secret, or the Kessians think you would make a good informant."

Kenneth scoffed at the idea and turned away. The Kessians were the family that controlled the lands to the northwest. They had always held a tense relationship with Norclave, but as much trouble as Kenneth had made within the city, he would never turn against it. He paced around a bit before turning back to the table.

"And if it was the Overlord sending for me?"

"If the Overlord did arrange to get you here? In secret?" Mackelry almost laughed at the idea until he worked through the thought further. "If that is the case, boy . . . I hate to say this, but your best move would be to bribe a ride from the next cargo transport leaving. You don't want in the middle of a power struggle. That's how you get someone else to finally tally the marks on your arm."

Kenneth brushed a hand along the ridges on his left forearm in thought. The first mark was for stealing a transport in an escape attempt. The second was earned the year after for disabling the cannons of Norclave before another failed escape. The third, for stealing from the Overlord's personal library. The fourth, fifth, and the sixth for various incidents involving the administrators. Each time, the Overlord had decided against his execution, disregarding the opinions of the administrators.

"If you want to find out, best to find the man who spoke with your pilot."

Kenneth tapped his fingers against one of the shelves as he thought. The reason he had agreed to come to Norclave in the first place was to see what this was all about. He knew there were risks, especially if the Overlord was no longer able to protect him.

Mack walked a few steps from the table and turned back to Kenneth. "I'll arrange for a cargo transport to be ready to take you out of Norclave within the hour. You can either be on it or not when it leaves." The merchant picked up the tech hunter's sack from the table and tossed it to Kenneth. "I expect those gloves back, you hear? So you had best stay alive, boy."

He looked at the sack now in his hands with surprise. For someone like Mackelry, handing an investment of that value out on goodwill was far from ordinary. Kenneth clasped forearms with the man in what very well could be their final farewell. Without another word, he smoothed his sleeve back over his arm to cover the scars and started back out to the trade center.

* * *

On the highest level of Norclave, the First Administrator sat at his desk of cold steel and scanned over the reports that had come in throughout the day. He tapped the thin metal of his visor against the data pad as he thought. He had been keeping eyes on a group of tech hunters that arrived in the city the day before, but the report said the soldiers lost contact somewhere on the far side of the trade center. He set the pad down and shut it off, deciding that if they did not turn up again throughout the day, he would send a patrol to look.

A fist pounded on the door to his office, and the First Administrator pushed himself to his feet. He clipped the visor back on to his temple and adjusted it until the display was moderately in focus. It was a great wonder that in the past, every individual had one of these. Now the visor was a symbol of power and control reserved for the highest officials of the Rift Hills. With a quick brush over his uniform—styled after those that appeared in the archives designated as "UWC"—he called for whoever was at the door to enter.

The Norclave soldier stepped in and put a fist to his chest in salute, his arm crossing the red stripe on the torso of his outfit. "Administrator Silas," he said, bowing his head low and pushing his unkempt, frazzled mess of a beard against his chest.

"Have those tech hunters finally been seen again, Gunward?"

"I do not know, sir. I'm reporting in about a transport spotted on the fourth-level pads. It is the same one that managed to slip past us and depart in the night. It arrived back in Norclave just after sunup."

Silas Konrev rubbed a hand over his face.

"No cargo unloaded as far as I could find out, sir," Gunward added.

"Passengers?"

"The soldier said there was only one other besides the pilot. The pilot had a mark on his arm, and the other man he couldn't recall one way or the other."

That caught the First Administrator's attention. Besides a quick look for overtly illegal weapons—no one really expected a tech hunter to disarm completely—the only other requirement was that the scars be checked. Every day, every person, and this soldier couldn't recall the first occurrence of the day?

"Relieve those posted at that dock and set up your own watch. I want to speak with the soldiers and the pilot," Silas ordered.

"Yes, Administrator. Are we to look for the passenger as well?"

The First Administrator paused a moment before shaking his head. "No, that won't be necessary. If it is who I suspect, you will never catch him by just looking. Send a messenger to find Draken on your way out."

"The tracker?"

Silas gave a short nod and Gunward turned and moved out the door. Silas then sat back down in his seat and rapped his knuckles on the thick metal sheet of the desk. Something was at play in Norclave, and if he had any hope of contesting the Overlord, he needed to get ahead of it. Quickly.

Chapter 3: Council and Questions

Hidden in a decommissioned air shaft of Atrium: 447, a pair of nervously scanning eyes kept watch of the atrium from behind the glow of a visor in the dark. Images of recovery teams scouring charred interiors displayed outside the shaft as usual, and even when part of the displays switched to a view of the UWC director at the emergency session, those searching eyes kept their watch. Soon, an ICC security force would pass by. She hovered a hand over her holster, and a small note on the display told Maylee Sharpes that she had over half a magazine of pulse rounds left. She thought it would be more than enough to take out the targets and get away safely.

". . . and as a result," the director's voice echoed about the large room outside the shaft, "EMA-GO, will be allowed to employ extra scrutiny in their selections regarding applicants to the Mars colonies."

Maylee quickly turned her head and pulled the pulse pistol from her hip when she heard a sound in the shaft behind her. She stared into the fading dark, holding her breath as she listened for the noise again. After a tense moment, she leaned her head back against the sidewall. The sound must have just been a shift in the starscraper, or perhaps a noise from the workers in the maintenance ways above. After all, nobody but her knew of her secret path in and out of Atrium: 447. Not even the ICC.

She had found this place sometime after her mother mentioned something about the fresher air in the area. The kids of the nearby decks used the new vents to fly kites, and Maylee had figured out on her own that the old air circulation system hadn't been completely pulled out, leaving her all the passageways between maintenance shafts that she needed to bring the fight to the ICC on her own terms. In a way, this ambush had been a long time coming.

She turned the pulse pistol over in her hand. It put off a soft glow, and its see-through frame made it easy enough to manually check the level of ammunition. She tossed it a few times, spinning it from her hand and catching the weightless weapon with ease. It had cost her a hundred times the credits that a kite would, but each searing round of pulse fire would be worth it once put to use.

"Mr. Director," a man's voice echoed from the other side of the metal grate, "will this new order continue the unlawful prohibition of SRA citizens on Mars?" The displays about the atrium likely showed SRA Representative Lao Weijing speaking with the normal frown he used to address the UWC Council. "The selection process is required to be unbiased!" As a representative of the main opposing world order to the UWC, the Sovereign Republics Alliance, Lao Weijing was often met with disdain during UWC Council meetings.

"I appreciate your concern," Director Auburns said, "however, until significant effort has been made against the terrorist operations of the Last Edict, further admittance of any outside organization to the Mars Contract will have to remain closed."

Representative Weijing sneered at the proposition. "There is not a person within the United World Coalition that has not seen the recently released statements about progress on Mars. Your own public spaces display the message of finally reaching permanent self-sustainability. The SRA formally requests a report from the UWC on the parameters by which the planet will be fully considered habitable land, and under which doctrine the UWC plans to dictate ownership of an entire global landmass with only a few settlements," he finished bitterly.

There was a short pause after Weijing's comment, in which information was filed to the director. Of course, the director likely wanted to snap a remark about the SRA having avoided all involvement in the endeavor of colonization until now. He took another moment to consider his words. "Mr. Weijing, I assure you that Mars is on course for becoming a human habitat; however, extreme care must be taken to ensure that the system maintains this positive trend. Outreach Systems controls the human impact on Mars through precise habitation procedures so that Solstice Consolidated may continue to terraform it into a 'living' planet. If we were to do as you wish and force EMA-GO to lift all restrictions and grant even a portion of the billions of current applicants access to the planet, the entirety of the Mars Contract would fail. We will be working closely with your nations on an amicable solution. In the meantime, I would like to address security issues relating to the recent Last Edict operations in the coastal North American section of the UWC." The director motioned with his hand, beckoning the SRA representative to take a seat.

Representative Weijing gave a low bow. "Forgive me if I have sidetracked the discussion. The SRA fully sympathizes, as we have experienced Last Edict attacks in the Mid-American States, as well as in many other of our other nations. If it would resolve the issue of SRA citizens being barred from the Mars colonization, the SRA will gladly share intelligence gathered against the Last Edict."

Maylee put a hand over her mouth to hide a yawn. She'd already had enough lectures on politics in her government classes. At least with the displayed news on the Mars Contract, she could see something interesting, like vast stretches of orange dust filled with half-dead shrubs. She set the pulse pistol down and tried to tune out the discussion being had miles away in another starscraper. She had the feeling this could be a long wait on her part, and the last thing she needed was boring old people putting her to sleep.

Military Ambassador Hoffsted was announced, and he started in on a long-winded speech of his own. Several other names also spoke, each having something unnoteworthy to say, until Maylee heard a name she recognized.

"And now for the People's Ambassador to Sector . . . let's see, K-8," the communications chancellor read out, "Jance Lorège. What are the concerns of the citizens in your sector of the UWC regarding these proceedings?"

The screens flicked to a face Maylee had seen a few times before. Jance was the ambassador of this entire section of starscrapers, and she even lived in the same starscraper as Maylee. Maylee had seen her in person on several occasions. The ambassador gave an approximate report on the number of people who had been watching the Council meeting, but Maylee's attention was pulled away by a ping on her visor.

Three of the ICC security forces stationed in the sector were making a pass around the atrium. Each of the soldiers wore the standard flight armor used by the UWC; however, it had the same translucent white glow that her pistol did. She felt around for the weapon for a moment, and once it was in her hand took a nervous breath. Ten shots, three men. She wanted to save some ammunition in case her path back through the maintenance ways was not clear, but her first priority was to show the ICC that the occupation was not without resistance.

She narrowed her eyes and lifted the pulse pistol, carefully positioning it so she could shoot through the metal grating. She took a breath in. This was the moment she had been preparing for. She followed the first of the three men in her sights, and decided that once they passed the civilians standing and watching the Council meeting, she would open up.

The second soldier in the group pulled out a data pad and got the attention of the first. They had picked her up on a scan. She only had a few seconds before they opened fire on her position. Maylee twitched her finger back, and a flash of blue shot out of the pulse pistol. She had no choice but to keep firing. Shot after shot of searing blue pierced through the men until the twitching of her finger only prompted an empty signal to light up on the weapon. The three men lay still on the ground, riddled with glowing marks.

Just then, a man walked past the soldiers on the ground to stand next to a couple watching the displays. The two greeted him with smiles and exchanged a round of laughs at some joke. Another group of people walked by, never slowing for the dead ICC soldiers on the ground. Their translucent armor flickered as people's feet passed through the overlay. Maylee wiped a hand on her forehead, bumping the thin wire of her visor. The weapon in her hand and the soldiers on the ground shifted over at the nudge. She readjusted the visor and watched as the credits began pouring into her account from the reality shard.

She had to hold in a laugh as the tense moment passed. Though her father had warned her against messing around in any type of alternate reality, it was hard to argue with the fact that she had just made over a month of his wages in credits at only thirteen years old. That would buy far more than a few of those kites the younger kids played with. She looked down to the displayed pistol in her hand and frowned at the red cross over the magazine. She pinched her fingers by the bottom of the grip and motioned out the empty slide. Then again, it would not hurt to put a weeks' worth of that toward ammo. She could even buy a spare magazine and go after a bigger target next time.

Maylee turned and started back through the maze of air shafts. The program would start to send ICC reinforcements, and she had to escape notice without disrupting her link to the system, otherwise the system would deduct a large percentage of her newly earned credits.

* * *

On the other side of the central opening of the atrium, the attack on the ICC constructs drew the attention of a local supplies coordinator. Avery Thorne spent a good portion of his day ensuring the numbers between the local stores matched with the UWC goods distribution regulations, but in his off time, he enjoyed watching the activities of the virtual conflict. At times, he even made a few spare credits selling information to more active participants, like the type that had just unloaded a flurry of shots on the ICC through the grating.

It was fairly rare to see another person using the system, especially just offshore from the Council City here in Sector-K. The UWC had been pushing harder on the ban of alternate realities, particularly ones such as this, known as reality shards, where instead of full sensory simulation the program was mixed with the real world via visor overlays. The only reason this one had not been shut down yet was that it was a decommissioned military strategy test program, functioning on multiple private systems with connections masked as regular functions. The people running it were very good at keeping it hidden.

Avery slid his visor to the standard position, where the image only projected over one eye. With the UWC notifications often spouting reminders to civilians to report irregular activities, such as pretending to hold something while looking through a full display or running in an irregular and hurried manner, he preferred to be as secretive as he could. A quick check reminded him that he still had his rifle on his back. It had been years since he had used it, though.

He took a moment to search the records of the ventilation system. It was information that did not hurt to know. Avery was quickly met with a dead end. The old system had supposedly been taken out after the new system had been installed. From where he sat, however, it looked like some jerk found a way to cut expenses by leaving parts of the old ventilation system in. Obviously, the shafts still went somewhere. A person had been hiding in them, after all. Avery decided that the best way to figure out was to simply make contact.

He produced a data pad in the reality shard, masking the motion over his hip as if he were scratching. He made his way around the wide ring of Atrium: 447, making sure to stop several times along the glass walkways and watch a bit of the emergency Council meeting. He shook his head every time they mentioned defeating the Last Edict. It was not something that could simply be fought.

After another transport rumbled past, distorting the reality shard data pad he pretended not to be holding, he started toward the ventilation shaft. There was no reason to rush the process, so he stood leaning against the metal grid, watching the ICC forces now swarming the area. They set up a barricade, warning all civilians to stay back. Of course, only Avery could see any of it, and only out of one eye at that.

He waited for a few minutes for just the right moment. He still had an hour until he had to log a shipment to a local clothing store.

It was tricky business, hiding from two worlds at once, but he had experience at it. If he simply turned and slipped something into the decommissioned shaft, one of the passing UWC civilians was sure to notice. That could mean big trouble and large fines. If the ICC forces saw him, they would confiscate the data pad and find out that he was trying to contact the person who killed the soldier constructs. That would certainly drive away the person he was attempting to contact.

When both realities seemed to be looking away, Avery reached behind his back and flicked the data pad into the ventilation shaft. He touched the visor, disconnecting himself from the reality shard. The ICC soldiers disappeared, and if he looked behind him, there would be no way to tell that a data pad was sitting there in the dark, a reality away.

* * *

Jance fought letting out the yawn she had been suppressing for some time; she couldn't let it out, especially since there was the possibility that she would show up, even for just a moment, on millions of displays throughout the world. She had joked about what would happen with Agatha, her official counselor and close friend, but the reality of the situation was that the nature of this meeting demanded an attentive look.

While trying to keep her head facing forward, Jance occupied herself by looking around the Council Chambers. The room was constructed in the general shape of an amphitheater, much like the stone recreation in Arboretum: 153. There, the stones had been gathered from three-thousand-year-old ruins across the world and set in amongst the beautifully tended gardens. Here in the Council Chambers, the shape fit with the more formal modern style. The main members presiding over the meeting were spaced along a large stage at one end, and the rest of the councilors sat in their own seating above the bottom floor. Perhaps the room's most striking feature was the large UWC emblem hanging on the wall. It was nearly fifty feet across and fashioned out of solid metal, like a medallion. The abbreviation of the United World Coalition was written in bold letters above the map of the globe.

She glanced to her right. The other members and representatives from Sector-K sat with blank stares as the communications chancellor spoke. Chancellor Liberty Malcom was a tough figure who presided over all Council meetings, second only to the director during meetings like this. Unlike many others of the Council, she was never afraid to set a point of order straight.

"This display," the chancellor said, motioning to the raised image on the wall behind her and the other key speakers, "shows every attack by the Last Edict in the last hundred years."

It was a scattered spread of points across the globe that had perplexed logisticians and military strategists alike. For the most part, the globe had been long divided into three world orders: the UWC, SRA, and the ITS. The United World Coalition, or UWC, was quite proudly a single functioning unit, divided only by regional lines for organizational purposes. The Sovereign Republics Alliance, or SRA, were, sillily enough, nations banded together to protect their differences, and the Independent Treaty States, or ITS, had been formed to create a world order out of five smaller governing systems with little in common.

What ultimately proved such a great problem was that the Last Edict showed no preference to where in the globe it struck. The most recent attack, in what was referred to regionally as the UWC East Coast, was displayed most prominently. The worry was that the attacks were gravitating toward government targets, as a month earlier there had been a similar strike on a low-level SRA official in the Capitol Region of the Philipeans.

"How can they get away with that?" Morris Kannei said.

Jance glanced to her left at the man. She could only guess what he'd decided on as his next cause to fight for. A few months back, an emergency meeting had been canceled before it began under grounds of reevaluated information, and Kannei had ranted about there being a conspiracy for weeks. If history proved anything, she likely would not hear the end of this new theory of his for some time.

"The core analysis team," he said, turning to her.

"Oh, do not go bringing that up again, Morris!" Jance snapped. He reached for his data pad. "Just leave it alone!" If she could have beaten him to the pad, she would have tried to keep him from signaling to make a statement.

Chancellor Malcom paused just before she was about to speak. She glanced to the director, seeing Kannei's name pop up. The hesitation was understandable after the storm of suspicion he'd raised last time. "Morris Kannei, People's Logistician, Sector: K-8. You are recognized for the standard amount of time for a point of order."

Jance put a hand to her forehead.

"Thank you, Chancellor," Kannei said. "I first would like to ask: Is this map up to date?"

"I can confirm that it is," the military ambassador replied from the seat next to the chancellor. "It has been cleared with military intelligence."

"And what of the deaths of Archa Thompson and Marke Reyson, the engineering officers overseeing a review of the core reactor containment field and authors of the Core Reactor Report? Why are they not on the map? Has it finally been ruled that their deaths were not the work of the Last Edict? Who did you find responsible?"

A murmur passed around the Council Chambers. The two engineering officers had conducted a routine inspection of the core reactors, the power generators built near the core of the Earth that harnessed the geo-turbulence and acted as the main sources of power for the cities of the world. Both officers had died a few days after the report was submitted, and Kannei had raised the nonsensical suspicion that they had been killed for what was in the report. After derailing several Council sessions with his questions, he was finally given the report in full. Thousands of pages of system readouts later, he'd claimed there was missing information, furthering his belief that the engineering officers had in fact been killed over what was in their original report.

"Mr. Kannei," Ambassador Hoffsted said in a cold tone, "I am surprised you are questioning the rationale of my intelligence teams. The unfortunate circumstances regarding Mrs. Thompson and Mr. Reyson show no signs of involvement by the Last Edict, nor any other entity, for that matter. Accidents happen, even in our world."

Chancellor Malcom stood up from her seat after Hoffsted ended his point. "Mr. Kannei, if you are well and finished, I would like to continue uninterrupted." The chancellor sat down and motioned to the large world map displayed behind her. "As Ambassador Hoffsted stated, the map is, in fact, up to date. What it shows is the scale of the Last Edict's efforts to destabilize the world as we know it."

Kannei held his head low and wiped a hand over the reddened skin of his face in anger and embarrassment. "I have to go." He turned to Jance with a look of determination. "I have to get them to search for answers somehow, before it's too late."

"Morris, wait . . ." she said as he stood up from his chair and slung his jacket over his shoulder in a hurry. As he continued down the center corridor and out of the room, Jance forced herself to hide her frustration. The man had just piled a round of apologies onto a schedule that would already be pressed to catch up after the interruption of this meeting.

Chapter 4: The Edge of Plans

"Arlen, wait!" Kenneth called, hurrying to keep up as the pilot weaved through the foot traffic on the walkways leading out of the trade center. "You can't go back!"

The man stopped and turned on his heel to face Kenneth. He jabbed a finger into Kenneth's chest angrily. "I have to leave Norclave. Because of you. If I go to the Overlord alone, I die."

"We would never even make it to him." Kenneth shoved Arlen's hand away. "There are too many eyes watching, eager for any chance to overthrow order in Norclave. Something tells me we would only be giving them that chance."

"What tells you that? How can you even know without speaking to the Overlord?"

Kenneth ran a hand through his hair after getting a strange look from a passing woman with an armload of meal packs. He leaned toward Arlen and in a low voice said, "That is why we need to talk to your man. Whoever paid you to find me, he knows what this is about."

"No. I'm going to the docks. I'm going back to my transport, and I'm going to fly away from Norclave." Arlen turned away.

"At least tell me where he is!" Kenneth pleaded as he followed along behind the man. "Where can I find him?"

"We were not supposed to meet again. As I said, I was supposed to bring you directly to the Overlord!"

Kenneth threw his hands in the air. "Then give me some description of who I should be looking for."

"No!" Arlen said with annoyance.

"I'll follow you." Kenneth grabbed the man's arm and forced him to stop. "You just try to explain why the man who won't leave your side has six marks on his arm." Kenneth pulled his sleeve back.

Arlen's eyes widened as Kenneth twisted his arm so he could see.

"That's what you said was nothing? Six marks? How is that even possible?"

"I showed these to the soldier at the docks. Do you really want me to go back there with you?"

Arlen pulled in a breath, glancing to where Kenneth was adjusting his sleeve back down again. "The man had a silver piece of tech over his left eye. When he put his hand up to it, it gave off a glow and made a little display. Now go away!"

"An administrator?" Kenneth sifted through the possibilities in confusion as Arlen vanished in the tangle of walkways. Perhaps the contact was an administrator, still secretly loyal to the Overlord?

Kenneth felt his hair stand up on the back of his neck and his skin prickle as he got the feeling of being watched again. He forced himself to not turn quickly. While he might catch a glimpse if someone was following him, looking suddenly would only let them know they had been found out. Patience would pay off more. He could lose anyone in the haphazard passages of Norclave at a walk; running would only bring the attention of more soldiers.

Kenneth stepped onto a side stairway leading up to a cluster of houses on the next level. It was an assortment of containers once likely used for hauling heavy loads of cargo, but which were now arranged around a central mesh courtyard. Doorways had been cut into the sides of the containers and pipes for electricity and water had been built in wherever possible. Down below was another setup of housing containers. The pattern repeated all the way down to the first level.

Kenneth gave a quick nod to an old man sitting on a rope bench. The top ends of either side of the bench were tied at odd angles, one to the bent support of his container and the other to a pipe running just below the walkways above. He was using what looked like a short piece of cable looped at one end and tied at the other to scoop sauce out of a meal pack.

"You lost?" the man asked.

"No, just on my way through."

"You trying to lose someone then? What for?" The man took another scoop and gave Kenneth a questioning look as he mashed up the food with his gums.

Kenneth stopped, glancing over his shoulder.

"Let's just say I need to make it back to the trade center before the hour is up."

"Well," the man said, setting his meal pack to the side, "perhaps I could tell them you went the other way." He paused just a moment and held up the crude utensil, rolling it between his fingers. "I'll tell him a few tokens dropped out of your sleeve as you passed through."

"Fair enough," Kenneth said, dropping a few Norclave coins in the lid of the container. He turned and picked one of the stairways leading up. Even if the man gave his path away, after passing a hundred or more ways to veer off in another direction, Kenneth knew his steps could not be followed.

* * *

The old man picked his meal pack up again and began contentedly scooping up the half-rejuvenated powder. A lot of the time, the ones marked with the Ready Packs brand didn't quite work right. Of course, they were sold at only a portion of the price of the Timeline or Cryopair meal packs, but they were still mostly edible enough for him to live on. He glanced in the lid at the coins the man had dropped, and was pleasantly surprised by not only a couple of single marks, but a ten-mark as well. It was the same as earning a good meal for a day. He raked through the powder with the loop of cable. Or this for a week.

Another batch of footsteps tapped against the stairs leading up onto the level, causing the light hanging by frazzled wires at the top of the handrail to sway.

"Dammit!" one of the two men said as they stepped into the open area. "We should have started after him when we had the chance." They both had the red stripe across the chest of Norclave soldiers, though from the raggedness of their outfits, they were definitely of the lowest rank, if that.

"You heard what they said," the other man snapped back. He had close-cut hair and what looked like a freshly scabbed wound on the top of his head. It looked as if he had slipped when shaving with a knife. "Why do you think Gunward was sent for the tracker?"

"We just have to think smart, Darmic," the first man said. He grabbed his forehead and gritted his thick jaw in thought.

The old man smirked and worked another scoop to the edge of the pan with the bent cable. The pair looked as if they wouldn't find their own feet if they weren't stuck in place just below their ankles.

"You looking for someone?" the old man finally asked.

"Uh, yes," the soldier with the nearly scalped head said. "Have you seen him?"

"Would you care to give me a better description than that? There's a lot of people here in Norclave, if you haven't noticed." He held the pack to his face and scooped in a bit of soupy powder.

"A man. He passed through here just now. I know you saw him."

"There was a poor fellow who dropped some coins as he passed by, if that would help."

The soldier with the square jaw stepped forward and leaned over the old man. "Just tell us which way he went."

He set the meal pack to the side again. If they weren't smart enough to work a bribe, it would do them some good to run circles for a while. He pointed off at a different walkway leading down. At that, both men took off running, shaking the loose lights on the rails and making a racket no one could miss if they were trying to stay hidden.

Just as he was going to pick up his meal again, determined to finish it this time, another figure topped the steps. This man caught his eye. Unlike the other two hooligans, he had a sharp gaze and looked as if he knew what he was about. He wore clothing somewhere in between the cut of a soldier's uniform and the make-it-work piecing of a tech hunter. He had a dark cloth hanging from his shoulders down to his lower back, and instead of a red stripe painted on or even sewn in across the torso, he wore a sash of fabric that could be easily removed. His rank, the old man guessed, was undoubtedly something to respect; the silver bit of tech looping around from the side of his head to just above his eye was enough to tell him that.

He pushed himself up from his makeshift bench, careful not to flip it accidentally. For a moment he tried to decide if he should salute, but the ominous figure spoke first.

"My name is Draken. In Norclave, they call me the tracker. I'm looking for a technician by the name of Kenneth."

"Oh, are you? What makes you think he came this way?"

Draken worked his fists in his heavy gloves as he stepped closer and picked up the lid to the meal pack. He dumped the coins out into his hand and gave the old man a level stare as a warning to not protest.

The tracker pitched the lid to the side, causing it to bounce and tumble in a racket across the mesh flooring. He held up a closed fist and opened his hand. The two smaller coins dropped down. One clicked against the metal flooring just before joining the other in falling through the grating.

"These were not dropped. You were bribed." He flicked the last coin up and caught it without taking an eye off the old man. "Tell me which way, or I drop the ten-mark."

The old man let out a sigh, listening to the feint echo of the coins still bouncing off the levels below. He pointed to the stairway leading up and reached for the token.

Draken pulled his gloved hand back. "The trade center?"

The old man shrugged and held out his hand again for the coin. The tracker made a motion as if to give it to him, but instead flicked it to the side. The coin bounced a few times, stopping just on the edge of a gap in the grating. As Draken strode away, he stopped just long enough to push it with the bottom of his boot to make sure it fell through.

* * *

Kenneth leaned on the railing of the top floor of the trade center, looking to make sure no soldiers were at the cargo transport docked a level down. It was the one marked with a blue triangle, the symbol of the Steel Valley. He had finally decided to take Mackelry's advice and hop transport out of Norclave. There was simply too much risk. The merchant was right about getting in the middle of a power struggle between the administrators and the Overlord, and there was no way to get more information without taking a blind chance.

He pushed through the crowds and merchant stands filling the walkways until he found a stairway leading down. The transport would likely be leaving soon, no matter how much Mackelry had bribed them to stay for the full hour. He set foot on the next level and immediately smelled the water vapor and electricity generated by the repulsors warming up. The holographic signs around the area flickered from the distortion, as usual. He moved to where several men were finishing loading crates into the back of the transport.

"Are you Kenneth?" one of the men asked. Kenneth nodded and the man motioned inside the craft. "Mack's already paid your fee. Just keep quiet."

Kenneth walked up the ramp into the cargo vehicle. As the sun started to shine through the gaps in the starscraper above, light also broke into the belly of the hauler through the cracks and rusted holes. One side of the thing looked as if it had fallen out of the sky and since been pounded back into shape. Kenneth edged past the stacks of containers and to a small seat in the back. It should have folded down from flat against the wall, but it seemed to have a support bent and was wedged shut.

Rather than take out the gloves and fix it, Kenneth decided to just find a spot on the floor. The gloves would draw attention, and it would be a sour thing to be robbed thousands of feet in the air. Hopefully they would pay him no mind, and better yet, not drop him off before they arrived at the city of Reclaim. He had tokens to buy his passage if need be, and if he had to, the tech gloves would pay for a place to get settled in the Steel Valley.

Just as he started to work out a plan, the repulsors shut off and the vibrating in the cargo hold stopped. His first instinct was to think of the converters and releases that could have caused the ship to power down, but the voices outside quickly changed his thoughts. It sounded like the men loading the ship were arguing with someone.

"We don't haul passengers. This is a cargo ship!"

"Then explain to me," a commanding voice replied, "why I received an order from a Norclave tracker to search every cargo vessel in the trade center?"

Kenneth bolted to his feet. The only thing between him and capture was a wall of crates. He started looking around for another way out of the ship or somewhere to hide. None of the crates seemed large enough to fit in and there was no other door. However, if Mackelry could bribe this ship, that meant he had wares of his own aboard. Kenneth started lifting the lids on all the crates he could find. Medical packs, batteries, cloth bundles—none of the crates had anything he could use.

"But it has already been inspected," a voice outside argued.

Near the bottom of a stack was a crate locked with a security data pad. Kenneth immediately went to grab the gloves to cut through the container, then stopped. It was obviously the most suspicious crate in the pile, making it the least likely to have something hidden inside. Kenneth put his shoulder against the stack and pulled the bottom container out.

"What was that?" a voice asked at the noise the crates shifting had made. "I'm searching your vessel. Gunward, check it."

The soldier stepped up onto the loading ramp with heavy boots. After a moment, he moved to the side and started edging past the crates with his weapon ready. Kenneth held his breath as the soldier shoved over a crate.

"Hands up! I want to see them!" the soldier yelled.

"Bring him out!"

"I . . ." the soldier named Gunward stammered as he looked around in the empty space. "There's nothing back here, sir. Just some toppled crates spilled out."

Kenneth sat crouched on the floor, holding in his breath even though the pounding of his heart made it difficult. Until the man left, he could not risk moving. He didn't know what the light distortion generator he'd found in the crate could handle.

"Come out, you overexcited clod," his commander yelled.

"Yes sir," the soldier said with a shake of his head. He growled and started shoving his way back, causing a few crates to topple onto Kenneth.

Kenneth rubbed his head and pushed the crates away. He then powered down the device, having no idea of the state of its energy levels. For all he knew, that was the first time it had been activated in years. Possibly hundreds of years, even.

"In form!" the commander shouted from outside.

"Don't salute me!" another voice shouted. Kenneth immediately switched the device back on. He recognized that voice. There was no mistaking it. "I'm here to do my job, not watch you stand around for pleasantries. Well?" the tracker yelled, probably jabbing a finger into the commander's chest. "Where is Kenneth? Did you search the transport, as I asked?"

"I did, sir," Gunward replied.

"Oh, did you?" Draken growled. He sniffed the air a couple of times. "The repulsors were on. Did you have them turned off?"

"Yes, sir."

"Turn them on."

Kenneth gritted his teeth. As he and Draken knew, when the engines started up, any light distortion generators would start phasing and crackling, much like the displays on the storefronts. If anyone walked to the back of the transport now, they would see a flickering and distorted view of the surrounding crates—and Kenneth.

There were a few heavy steps on the loading ramp as Draken moved forward. As Kenneth heard the crackle of the shocklance, he turned to the distortion generator. A press on the side brought up a display holograph. It flickered from side to side because of the repulsors firing outside. Kenneth frantically placed his fingers where the image should have been and started making adjustments. He heard the shuffling of crates again but kept working as quickly as he could.

Just as the light from the weapon's popping electricity rounded the corner, Kenneth got the hologram to fall into place with the new resistance values. Again, he held his breath. The tracker glanced around furiously. He had obviously expected to find a half-formed image of Kenneth in the back of the transport.

Kenneth held as still as possible as he and Draken shared an impossible gaze. The settings should be perfect, but then again, this was the tracker who had caught him on every count before.

Draken grunted and shook his head. He started to step back, but something grabbed his attention. "Cut the repulsors!" he yelled back. "Now!"

As the rumbling engines outside powered down, the folds of light concealing Kenneth began to warp from the overcompensations. As if watching from underwater, Kenneth saw a bright flash of electricity before violent spasms gripped his body. Eventually, he crossed into the dark of unconsciousness.

* * *

The head of the group, Commander Branon, looked on with a scowl as his men pulled the unconscious criminal out of the transport. The order had popped up on his visor not ten minutes ago, telling him to check any transports about to leave the trade center. He had no doubt it was an official command; only those working for the Overlord of Norclave were given working visors.

"Make sure the crew of this ship is accounted for," Branon said in an attempt to maintain some sort of control of his men. Draken always had a way of ignoring rank and stepping to the lead. If it had been any other man, the commander would have put the tracker in his place. Then again, if it had been any other man, he would have been able to.

As the soldiers dragged the body out of the transport, the commander felt a hard grip on his shoulder.

"Next time I tell you to search, Branon," the tracker growled, "you don't quit until you find something." Draken pushed past the commander to where the soldiers had rolled Kenneth out on the platform. "His sleeves. Pull them back."

Even to the commander, who had been informed of the scars, it was still a shock. Only the most ruthless of murderers and leaders of the criminal underground survived with two marks on their arms. And that was only because they managed to escape the Cells. If any were caught, the only course of action was to cut a third mark and continue to the execution.

"This man," Branon said in disgust, pushing his visor out of the way, "this man should be killed on the spot!" He started to give the command to one of his soldiers, but his words were cut short by a gloved hand slamming onto his face.

Draken clawed his hand and pulled the commander in close. "Do that, Branon," he said to the one uncovered eye, "and we'll see if you can learn to fly before the bottom level." He shoved the commander to the side, leaving him to check if the visor he had on was broken.

"This man," Draken said, pointing to the technician, "is to be taken to the Cells at the order of the First Administrator. See that he gets there."

The commander watched with a scowl as the insufferable tracker stalked away into the crowd without a further word, leaving him to deal with the mess. The soldiers started to pick the technician up from the ground, but Branon motioned them to stop. There was no sense moving dead weight when they could afford to wait until the technician woke up.

"What about the crew?" Gunward asked, glancing to the two men who had been loading cargo, and the third who was being escorted out of the pilot seat.

"Give them their marks." Branon tossed the knife from his belt to the man. It was a special blade for carrying out Norclave law. The edge was made to heat up and scald the skin on contact, ensuring that the scar would be well visible. The men gave cries of pain as the glowing edge sizzled through the flesh on the back of their arms.

"This one already has a mark," Gunward said as he took hold of the last crewman's arm.

The man begged, but the commander motioned with his hand to continue. "We'll take him to the Cells with the technician."

* * *

Kenneth drew in a breath despite the pain in his chest. He had to force air in, like the stressful moments after a sharp punch just below the ribs. Kenneth looked up, seeing the overarching canopy of the starscraper shell blocking the sun in the clear sky above. Below that, lights flittered unnaturally around the trade center as Kenneth tried to reclaim focus.

His world shifted, and voices took on the sound of hollow drones as he was pulled to his feet. Minutes passed between each slow blink of his eyes. Kenneth found himself plodding along in a daze as the Norclave soldiers cleared a path through the crowds of people. It was obvious where they were going. The pilot from the cargo hauler had a second bright mark across his arm. Kenneth glanced down at his own arm, where a new jagged burn glistened on the skin above his wrist bindings. There was little effort put into keeping the line straight, though it ultimately did not matter. They were still going to the part of Norclave closest to hell.

The part of the city located nearest to the lifeless interior of the starscraper had been turned into a disposal ground for the doomed of Norclave. Even the lowlife scavengers kept from straying too far toward the Cells.

A sharp hit to Kenneth's shoulder made him stumble forward a few steps. He turned back to see a man with a scraggly beard lowering his club. He growled something, but Kenneth was still in too much of a daze to make it out.

After a few minutes, Kenneth finally began to come to his senses, though his muscles were still tight from the shocklance Draken had used. They were now threading through the back walkways of Norclave. The poor of the city watched from their scattered spots claimed amongst the abandoned buildings. Each one looked for just a moment before turning their eyes. For them, a patrol of Norclave soldiers meant one of two things: either the Overlord was passing out the daily half rations of meal packs, or some poor soul was being sent to have their bones picked clean.

Kenneth had heard plenty of disputes over the subject. Some thought the swarms were the result of genetic test projects mixing with the common species of flies over the past six hundred years. Others argued that there was no evidence that the swarms had not existed before. However, everyone knew what it was when they felt the distinct stinging pinch of a rubble mite.

"Out of the way!" the soldier in front of Kenneth growled, shoving one of the begging scavengers to the side. The soldier's pulse cannon cast an idle orange glow on the scavenger, forcing him to crawl away into one of the many dark corners of the warrens. Most of the lights in the underbelly of the city were broken, never put in place, or had been ripped out and sold in the trade center.

As they moved onto a long path lit only by the lights held by the soldiers and the humming pulse cannons some carried, Kenneth felt a tap on his shoulder. "Is it really as they say?" It was the pilot from the cargo hauler. "Do the rubble mites really burrow into the flesh?"

Most of the cages hanging over the edge of the city were filled only with the bone powder left by the mites, but the criminals contained there would never see the swarms set in. Not for them, at least. The mites never gathered in large numbers for living flesh. Kenneth simply decided to reassure the pilot as best he could in a whisper, "Not while you're alive."

The man took in a ragged breath. "I can't die. I just can't!"

"Shut it! The both of you!" Kenneth nearly tripped forward at the strike to the base of his neck. "If it wasn't for the Overlord's rules, technician, I'd roll you over the edge right now."

"Gunward!" the commander of the group barked back. A bright light shone on them and the column stopped. "We take them to the Cells. If they don't make it alive, you'll take their place."

With the different angle of illumination, Kenneth noticed the power cell on the side of the pulse cannon just in front of him. Just like Arlen's malfunctioning transport, if there was some way he could change the output, he could get the weapon to overload. An explosion that could tear someone's leg off might serve as enough of a distraction to slip away.

Branon turned and the group started walking behind him. He soon motioned them to one side of the walkway as they neared a section missing its railing next to a hundred-foot drop. Water sprayed over the walkway out of a long-unattended leak in the piping system. As they moved in single file around the rusted-out edge of the walkway, Kenneth edged up to the pilot.

"I can get us free. Do you have a knife?"

"Stay back, you," the man hissed. "I'm keeping it for the mites."

Surprised the man actually had something hidden away, Kenneth gritted his teeth to keep from yelling at him. He needed something sharp to alter the output without the soldier noticing. Kenneth decided that he would just have to take it one step at a time. First, he had to take the power pack out. Then he could get the knife, make an incision in the power pack, and drop the pack on the walkway as if it had fallen out.

The group turned out of the long passage and started up a narrow flight of steep stairs. The steps were uneven, scrapped together out of an array of metal. Kenneth pretended to catch his foot on one of the steps and shouldered into the soldier in front of him, causing him to drop the weapon. He reached forward and unclipped the power pack as quickly as he could.

"He's trying for a weapon!"

Kenneth felt a heavy thud on the back of his head and watched as the pulse cannon slid over the side of the steps, falling onto the floor far below. As the soldier shouted about his weapon, a hand pulled on the back of Kenneth's collar and jerked him back to his feet. "Keep moving! I can break everything but your skull and still be within my orders!"

"You're not smart enough to know where that is!" Kenneth snapped back before he could think twice.

"You're dying as soon as you get there anyways," the man growled. "The both of you."

As he was shoved up the remaining steps, Kenneth kept a tight hold on the power pack in his fist. At the moment, it was all he had. As they passed the level under where the scrapsmiths worked, showers of sparks danced down through the walkways. Watching the flickers of ignited metal gave Kenneth an idea. All he needed was a distraction. He could just overload the power pack itself. In theory. He just needed that knife.

"I thought the standing order from the Overlord," Kenneth said, speaking through the water in his eyes and another sharp jab into his back, "was that he decides all executions."

The commander shook his head. "It's been years since a two-mark has walked from the Cells. The Overlord has no say in it anymore. You don't get out this time, technician."

Kenneth had pieced together as much already, but he was hoping to scare the other prisoner. Perhaps he would start thinking about escape a little harder.

A few minutes later, Kenneth felt the cargo pilot bump into him and a small knife slide into his hand. The man said nothing, but Kenneth knew what it meant. The only problem was that he could give no guarantees this would work. With that last thought, he started prying into the power pack.

The blade eventually slid deeper in and immediately began to heat up. Kenneth took a breath and glanced down. It took all he had to keep from dropping it or yelling in pain. The blade of the knife started to turn red, and the only thing masking the sizzling of his fingers was the grinding from the scrapsmiths at work on the level above.

His arms started shaking from pain, but he knew this was the most critical part. It was going to rupture. When was only a guess, and he had to hold on long enough that the flash would catch their attention. When the heat became too great, Kenneth tossed it into the air in front of the group. The pack fused itself to the bottom of the walkway above with a glow bright enough to draw everyone's attention.

"What the hell is that?"

He closed his eyes, avoiding the blinding flash that felt only a few inches from his nose.

While the shouts started up, Kenneth shoved to the side, toppling him and the cargo pilot over the edge. They landed along with a section of the railing onto the walkway ten feet down, missing a fifty-foot drop by only a couple of feet.

"Get up!" Kenneth said, pulling himself up with a side railing. He turned to help the man but stumbled backward as pulse rounds hit from above. The first melted through the railing, and a second blasted a white-hot patch on a nearby wall that slowly dissipated into a heated orange. A series more tore through the walkway in several places. As the pilot let out a dying scream, Kenneth turned away and started running as fast as his knotted muscles would allow.

He tried to make as unlikely of a path as he could, occasionally pulling himself over one railing and stretching with a groan over to the next walkway where the lights below were at least a hundred feet down on the bottom level. At one point he thought of pulling off his boots to stop the clanking from the chunk of metal on the bottom, but each time he stopped, more piercing cracks rattled off, sending sparks skittering by Kenneth as he moved down the walkways and narrow passages.

He pulled himself up a set of stairs and tried wrapping his hands around a pipe to swing over to a different walkway. Kenneth sucked in a breath and eased his weight onto his shaking fingers, but they gave out and he crumpled down onto the steps. He stared for a moment at the torn boils on his skin before forcing himself back up.

Kenneth slowed to a stop a few minutes later to pull off the rough bindings around his wrists. Taking a deep breath, he remembered what Mackelry had said to him during one of his attempts to escape the city. "You can run from anything at a walk, but you will never get away running." Kenneth tucked his hands under his arms and started off again. A few minutes later, he made it to the bottom level of the trade center.

Here, materials with no immediate purpose were the center of trade. Where Kenneth could take a piece of tech and bring it back to life, a good scrapsmith could take piece of nothing and make something new. Carbon heat paneling, plated wiring, alloys from repulsor engines, and much more traded hands here. For the moment, the trade had slowed down on account of the commotion spawned out of escaped prisoners and weapons fire throughout the lower levels. All of Norclave seemed to be buzzing with soldiers moving about, and here seemed no exception. Kenneth kept on forward at a walk, but his skin started prickling as whispers whirled around him. It was clear that he was still drawing too much attention.

He then glanced up and had to fight the urge to run. Two men with red stripes painted over their shirts were walking in his direction. One of the Norclave soldiers pointed at Kenneth and spoke to the other.

"Kenneth?" a voice said from the side.

He turned away from the approaching soldiers and toward the person that had said his name. He had never seen her before, but she was obviously a tech hunter. She had the typical dusty greys for hiding amongst rubble, as well as enough hanging bags and pouches to be ready for anything. A reddish sweep of hair was tucked beneath her hood and a lengthy but thin scar pulled over one cheekbone.

"Should I know you?" Kenneth asked.

"Now more than ever." She reached out and pulled Kenneth's hands into her own. He flinched and tried to pull back, but a surprisingly iron grip held him tight. Her tone of voice switched to that of a lighthearted encounter. "Tomman! Our friend said you would meet me here a half hour ago!"

Kenneth was gritting his teeth too hard to think of a reply.

"Oh, never mind that," she continued. "I have something I wanted to show you. It's not something I can do anything with, but I was told you would love it."

Kenneth fought to make up a reply that wouldn't come out as a shout. "Thank you," he finally managed.

She rolled her eyes but quickly hopped back into the ruse. "Oh, don't thank me yet. We just have to hope it is still there when we . . ." the tech hunter trailed off as she saw the soldiers lose interest and move on. She took her hands off his and stepped back, glancing at the fluids on her hands that had come off of Kenneth's burns. "What the hell did you do?"

"I had to overload a power cell. It was the only thing I could think of."

She shook her head and wiped her hands on her thighs. "I was told you knew your way around tech, but I suppose that says little else about you."

Kenneth looked at her for a moment, trying to think of whether to ask a question or argue against that statement.

She reached into one of the pouches and pulled out a small red tube marked with a double-barred cross. "Hold out your hands."

Kenneth hesitated, but she grabbed his wrist before he could pull back. She pushed out a foamy paste onto the burn and he immediately felt the prickling of the regenerative salve. He closed his eyes, trying to suppress the thought that the paste was many centuries old. However, the numbing immediately began to set in, and he could not help but admit relief—to himself, at least.

When Kenneth gave her a questioning look, she started to mirror his hesitation. She looked him over with a narrow-eyed curiosity. "When you asked if you should know me . . ." She leaned forward and stared at him as if the answer were written behind his eyes. "You have no idea who I am. You never even spoke with the Overlord, did you?" She took a step back and cursed under her breath. "I knew this was a lost cause."

"What cause?" Kenneth asked, still holding his hands in front of him as if the fading burning sensation was a real fire. "I've been shocklanced, pummeled by Norclave soldiers, shot at and . . . Look, all I want to know is know why I'm here. Why I was brought to Norclave."

"Answer me this: Are you Kenneth, the technician?"

"That's what I've been told."

She narrowed her eyes, obviously not liking his casual response. "Well, Kenneth, let's all hope you are as good as they claim. You will follow me, and you will keep as silent as you can."

"And what tells me that I would not be better off with them?" he said, nodding in the direction the soldiers had walked.

The corner of her mouth twitched up in what might have been a smile. "You're not going back. You cross me, and I'm throwing you off the edge myself. I have enough people trying to stab me in the back as it is."

From her level stare and the dangerous reputation of tech hunters, Kenneth normally would have taken the threat to heart. However, after today, he simply gave a shrug. "You and me both."

* * *

The heavy thud of First Administrator Silas slamming his fist on the desk caused the messenger to take a step back. Silas looked up from the reports streaming in from officers about the city. Three other administrators stood in the room along with a couple of ranking Norclave officials and the officer who had had failed to get the prisoners to the Cells. For the time being, Branon's blistered skin from the explosion had been pointedly left untreated.

"Speak. Now." Silas gave a demanding look to the messenger.

"Yes, sir. The tracker is here, along with the pilot you asked for."

"Send in Draken first."

The messenger ducked a quick bow, forgetting to cross his chest with a fist, and exited the room. A moment later, the tracker walked into the room ahead of the accompanying guards, as if they were his own escort. From the indifferent glance he shot toward the administrators, Draken did not seem worried. Silas motioned for the two guards and the messenger to step outside, wanting nothing said here to leave the room.

"All this commotion for one man?" Draken said with a smirk. "What was so important this time?"

"That is none of your concern, Tracker." Silas stepped out from behind his desk and leveled his gaze with Draken's. The First Administrator stood nearly a head taller than him, though that didn't seem to intimidate Draken in the least. "Your orders were to find him and—"

The room stiffened as Draken cut him off. "I did my part." He gave a nod to Commander Branon. "It was your man that let him escape."

Silas formed his need to shout into a cold tone. "And how many times have you pulled that technician from a hiding spot amongst the rubble, or knew which transport to watch for his escape?" Only silence met his questions. "You know Kenneth, and you know exactly what he is capable of. Why did you order Branon to take him to the Cells without accompanying the group?"

"Are you accusing me of wanting him to escape? That's an awfully bold position, Silas. What would the Overlord think?"

Unsheathing knifes and warming pulse cannons would have been just as much of a threat. So far, the events of the day had been kept from the Overlord. It had been weeks since the Overlord had left his library, but accusations of acting against him were still dangerous.

Toward the top, allegiances had been swayed from the Overlord, but many in Norclave still supported him.

Silas decided he had no choice but to push the question. "Why did you have Branon take Kenneth to the Cells, instead of to me?"

"Because as you said, I know Kenneth. When I left, he was unconscious, and I knew the only way he would make it to face the Overlord's judgment was to wake up in a steel cage."

Silas frowned. There was too much of an accusing tone in Draken's voice for comfort. Draken obviously suspected that the technician would not have been given a chance at the Overlord having a choice in his fate. For a tense moment, Draken watched the First Administrator with narrowed eyes. The tracker even moved his hand dangerously toward a pocket, as if for a weapon.

"The pilot did not look Kenneth on his own accord. He was contacted by someone under the false pretense of carrying out the orders of the Overlord," Silas said. He watched carefully to see if Draken flinched. When he saw no movement, Silas reached a hand to his visor and signaled to the soldiers outside.

Arlen was shoved into the room with his hands bound. Silas watched intently as Arlen eyed the tracker moving over to the side.

"Describe the man who first contacted you, pilot. The man who posed as a servant of the Overlord."

The pilot glanced to the side but immediately closed his eyes and looked to the floor. "I can't remember. I'm terrible at giving descriptions," he said in an attempt to avoid answering.

"You will never get the truth here," one of the other administrators said. Terrus Fenton. Generally a reserved man, he was in charge of overseeing trade deals on behalf of Norclave. "This cheat got that scar trying to avoid paying for using the Norclave docks. Perhaps given time—"

Silas held up a fist in a signal for him stop. Keeping his eyes locked onto the pilot for the slightest change in expression, he ordered, "No one leaves."

"Yes, Administrator," Terrus agreed from the side.

"Arlen," Silas said quietly, "let me make this very clear. A second mark on your arm will be the least of your problems if you do not tell me who you spoke with. Immediately."

The pilot drew in a ragged breath and looked to Terrus. "I'm sorry. I never meant to give you out."

Silas let out a breath. "Everyone leave." He slowly turned to face his own man, who looked perfectly surprised. At least Terrus was replaceable.

* * *

Arlen was pushed out of the room and shoved to the unforgiving floor of worn metal. What he had just done was not right, but he had been instructed to keep it all secret. The meeting, his trip to the Rift Outpost, all of it. It was supposed to be a quick run, a way to get back a life ruined by one lapse in payment. Instead, he had been dragged into the middle and forced to give up a name.

He did not try to get up. Arlen instead pulled his head down and felt the heavy breath he let out bounce back from the cold floor. Terrus Fenton definitely deserved retribution for the extortion commonplace at the docks, but setting him up as the Overlord's informant was too far. The man might die for a secret Arlen knew next to nothing about.

Chapter 5: Edict

After the emergency Council meeting had been called to an end, there was a quick regular session that followed immediately afterward. After the grim briefings to the world about the continued activities of the Last Edict, it seemed hardly appropriate to voice concerns about air quality, regulation changes, or any number of routine Council subjects. And given the short length of the second meeting, it seemed many of the others agreed, or at least mirrored the somber tone for political reasons.

It was only after the Council broke session and when the world's view was cut from the chambers that the work actually began. Jance glanced one last time at the empty seat beside her before making her way to the front of the Council Chambers, threading through the trenches of greetings, conversations, and political workings.

Once the official session ended, the blast shutters had been opened and the large window on the side wall let in sunlight as well as gave a view of the sweeping city. The *Nemesis Tide* still hovered miles out, creating storm effects from the repulsors keeping it in the sky. As she found herself hoping the strengthened military presence would deter any acts of violence, a military fighter blazed past the window. At least the Council Chambers were under a protective watch.

Jance made her way down the steps to the main platform where the key speakers were taking questions from reporters and other councilors. She found a spot outside the cluster of people and waited patiently for the director, the communications chancellor, or the military ambassador to break free.

"And what of the comments made by Logistician Kannei?" one of the reporters asked. "What did you make of it, Mr. Hoffsted?"

"Perhaps another time?" the ambassador said, dismissing the question with a pat on the reporter's shoulder as he started to move past. "I am due back to make an inspection on a ship over the Atlantic in a few hours. I thank you all for your questions and concerns and will be glad to take more at a later time."

"Ambassador Hoffsted," Jance said to catch his attention, "If I could have a quick moment."

"Ah, Ms. Lorège, of course," the man said. For looking every bit the part of a forcefully retired soldier, he had a well-groomed manner of speaking, as if he had always been meant for politics. "Walk with me, I have a transport to catch."

They walked through a passage in the back of the room that led into the inner workings of the Council, where smaller meetings would be had in the rows of rooms off to the side. "So, Ms. Lorège, what is it you need?"

"As the people's ambassador, I figured it was my place to make an apology for the behavior of Logistician Kannei on the behalf of Sector: K."

Hoffsted nodded. "Though no apology is necessary, I shall formally accept. I admit, I perhaps reacted too strictly on my part. It seems with the Last Edict attacks and the SRA trying to force their way into the Mars Contract, the stress of it tends to spill over."

"Thank you, Ambassador."

"Call me Jonithan. All this formality is every bit as stressful as defending a planet barely able to function on its own. Every time Weijing speaks, I want to throw something at him and yell at the stupid SRA symbol on his coat. A good thing Klemmeth Auburns is the one who has to speak to those outside UWC."

"I am sure Director Auburns has many of the same notions," Jance said.

Jonithan Hoffsted laughed and shook his head. He flicked a hand to his visor, casting an image in front of his eye. They turned down another one of the passages and soon passed a second-story balcony that looked out over the Council atrium. It was filled with assorted waterfalls gliding over glass flow ways, and numerous seating areas were nestled into the natural gardens and artistic displays on various levels. Jance could never make herself stay there for too long. She felt odd about hiding away in the back rooms of the Council as a people's ambassador.

"The director was selected for his ability to manage under pressure, as I am sure you know." He flicked to a different image on his visor. "My strengths come from an extensive run in military intelligence, definitely not in politics. You on the other hand, Ms. Lorège, expertly manage daily communications with the citizens of your sector, as the records strongly support."

She gave a short nod of thanks. That was likely the information he had pulled up just now.

"That brings to question," he continued, "and please, stop me if I step too far, but I am simply curious about your friend, Morris Kannei. Some details elude a quick review."

"I'm not entirely sure 'friend' is the correct phrasing, Ambassador Hoffsted, but I have worked in conjunction with him for a number of years."

"Is that simply a clash in personalities, or a professional decision?"

She rolled the question in her head. "Perhaps a bit of both. He's a rather suspicious man by nature, oftentimes running probabilities on elaborate conspiracy scenarios and other such nonsense." Jance quickly moved to lighten her words. "They are harmless inquiries, simply fanciful notions, but I have always tried to keep his ideas to the side."

"And he acts as a UWC councilor?"

"Yes, but mostly to present data to the sub-councils during precursory planning. Or, at least, that is what I thought we had come to an agreement on. You said of yourself, Mr. Hoffsted, that your strengths lay outside the Council Chambers. The same goes for Kannei. Under his watch, all materials and resources for repairs have been accounted for. And when the population in the starscrapers needs to be shifted for one event or another, no schedule of any citizen in or out of Sector: K has been interrupted by incorrect location assignments. He is the best logistician in the UWC, and only his personality holds him back from obtaining a higher ranking in the Council than my own."

"I can say the same of many officers who once were under my direction. Perhaps I could speak with Chancellor Malcom about the matter. She may be able to create a special non-Council position for Kannei, enabling him to keep his work without the interruptions of Council matters."

As they crossed over to the other side of the room, Jance started to formulate a question regarding his suggestion, but was interrupted by the ambassador motioning to the soldier waiting at the door. "This is my personal pilot, Officer Rigel Weyburn. He takes me wherever I need, which usually entails trips all around the globe at any hour of any day."

The soldier took off his helmet and bowed his head, holding a fist crossways over the military stripe on his chest piece. The man was tall and had a rigid posture that was only further enforced by the flight armor he wore. He had a hint of darkness below his eyes from a lack of sleep, but he still had a dangerous, well-trained alertness.

"It has been a pleasure to speak with you, Ms. Lorège," Ambassador Hoffsted said, "but my duty to the Council and UWC, as I am sure you can well empathize, does not end with the meetings. I wish you and those of your sector luck."

Jance started again to protest the shift in position for Morris Kannei, but the military ambassador turned and stepped through the security door. Officer Weyburn stepped out of attention and followed the ambassador's rushed exit, leaving Jance alone. She uncharacteristically cursed under her breath, fearing that she may have unintentionally pushed for the removal of Kannei from his position as the logistician for Sector: K.

She flicked her visor back across and over her eye and attempted to contact Kannei through a secure connection, as he always requested. After several failed attempts, she pulled up the flight path data logs. Either he was still in the building, or he was avoiding showing up on the system by using any of the number of ways he had come up with to avoid detection. After looking into any usages of his clearance code and coming up empty, Jance pulled aside her visor in frustration.

If she could not contact Kannei before he got word of a possible position change, it could lead to some hard misunderstandings. Just today, she had essentially ignored his proposal to improve air quality for the upper levels. Combined with his easily suspicious nature, he would think she was trying to get rid of him. Then a thought gripped her tight. He was already trying to expose something about the UWC, and if his Council clearance got revoked, there might be nothing to rein him back from his public inquiries.

Jance pulled her visor back across her eye and retrieved the quickest route to the transport bays. As of now, she could only guess where he might be, but if she got any sign, she wanted to be in the air and ready to travel to his position. With luck, she could keep her schedule for the next couple of weeks from being reorganized to allow for administering apologies. She still had to speak with Chancellor Malcom and Director Auburns, and there was no telling how many more people he could manage to offend if she didn't find him first.

* * *

After the majority of the councilors, their working staff, and the swarms of reporters finally left the UWC Council Chambers, Director Klemmeth Auburns stood alone in the center. For years, he had been involved with the great process of maintaining the United World Coalition, and ever since he'd worked as an assistant for the associate coordinator of global commercial services, Auburns found this particular place to be like no other in the world. When the large hall was emptied of all but a few quiet conversations and the passing of distant footsteps, the chaos of the world was briefly overshadowed by the simple view of transports racing out over the city.

It was that tranquility, surrounded by the grand form of the Council Chambers, that Auburns always imagined to be the closest symbol of what they were striving for. Not just peace. Not just unity. A protective frame in which fluid choices could be made by anyone. A system designed to support the greatest achievements of humanity, whether they were as grand as the room he now stood in or as simple as a personal connection.

Those unrealistically pure ideals were forced into the back of his mind as a confirmation request flashed on his wrist and a blip on his visor notified him of the arrival. This meeting was not scheduled; the director knew better than to allow that information to get on any server. Auburns tapped his visor to override the security protocols.

He heard an echo from a set of side doors and a hint of the conversation between the man he had called to meet him and the security personnel outside. The director looked around the room at the few other individuals through the guise of his visor. There were only pockets of councilors talking with reporters or representatives crossing the chamber to get to their next meeting. A laugh echoed out of one group, but as far as he could tell, no notice was given to the entrance of the supplies coordinator aside from the brief checks by security verifying his now elevated clearance access.

Avery Thorne knew the meaning of secrecy as well as anyone. His job negotiating the supplies for the localized businesses of Sector: K hardly fit what he was capable of. He was a man of average height and build and had short black hair; perhaps the only thing that stood out about him was that he was here in the Council Chambers to negotiate between the UWC and the Last Edict.

The sectator gave a brief look behind Director Auburns toward the massive UWC seal as he came to the center of the room. It was a metal disk with the letters raised from the golden surface. Further illumination was added over the disk with a holographic overlay.

"This is the last time you contact me, Klemmeth," Avery Thorne said, still looking at the seal. He glanced to the director. "I suppose you knew that, calling for me here."

Auburns nodded. Out of nearly a half year of clandestine contact with the Last Edict, he knew this was the end. "Our deal was for complete secrecy. But at the moment, the risk is too great."

"You could have avoided this months ago, Director." Avery brushed a hand through his hair. "Even still, the Last Edict could do with your full support."

Auburns had known they would strive to sway him ever since he had worked for contact. He needed information, they needed access, but now it had turned into a half-uncovered mess. "Morris Kannei. He openly used his Council clearance for several information requests. He has stepped too far."

Avery looked out toward the city and waited.

After a moment, Auburns finally made the decision. "If he disappears now, no one else will raise the same questions again. I need you to take care of Kannei."

Without another word, the sectator took off on his new mission. The director took in a breath and looked at his schedule as Avery hurried out of the chamber. While the world seemed to be silently collapsing around him, he had to go prepare for a blasted meeting with the ITS.

* * *

"Emmen, would you make sure Maylee gets to her Literature Communications course today?" Agatha spoke to her husband through the visor as she was preparing to leave. "I can drop her off at your office if you need, but I have to get to an appointment."

Maylee sighed and tried to get her mother's attention.

"Just a second, darling," Agatha said to Maylee before returning her attention to the call. "Yes, the Council meeting is over." She paused for a moment as Maylee's father asked a question. "I do not know. Jance just asked to see me. She sounded worried."

"Mother!"

"No, I don't think it is about the attacks; Jance has never been upset about them before. Hold on one moment, Emmen." Agatha set down her handbag and turned to Maylee with a sharp look and paused for explanation.

"It's canceled today. The course. Mr. Larkson went to speak with the families affected by the last attack."

Agatha let out a short breath. "Really?"

"That's what I've been trying to tell you." Maylee rolled her eyes.

"Emmen, are you there? Yes, that's what she said. Sorry to bother you at work. Yes, I know. Love you, I have to leave, bye." Agatha turned to her daughter. "I don't know how long I will be gone, so find yourself something to eat." She touched a finger to her visor, transferring some credits to Maylee. "Just stay on 448, understand?"

After her mother gave a quick goodbye kiss to her forehead and moved out the door of their pod, Maylee looked at the pending credit transfer. She was surprised for a moment at the amount, but just before she accepted the payment, her mother corrected the numbers. Maylee let out a sigh and fell back into the seat suspended by a distortion field.

For being the personal counselor to the people's ambassador, her mother held onto money worse than an SRA transferee. Sometimes Maylee even wished one of her parents had been pulled from cryogenic hibernation. She had a friend whose grandfather was born in the 2,600s. Given three hundred years, a small fortune could build itself. Then again, there were people who were defrosted and put back into the workforce on a weekly basis because their accounts could no longer pay for the storage fees.

Maylee stood up and grabbed her sling bag, zipping out a length of string to loop over her shoulder. She flicked her visor to display over both eyes and double-checked that the new magazine of ammunition and the pulse pistol were still in the bag. Thankfully, everything seemed to be syncing properly with the program. The only thing more frustrating than her internal tech courses was having to use what she learned in them to reroute connections to make the reality shard function again. Normally the connection errors happened after the UWC authorities uncovered one of the hidden reality shard servers.

She made her way out of their living pod and into the wide halls lined with info displays and location numbers. Constant replays of the Council meeting flickered past as Maylee moved beyond several sets of elevators. The elevators linked the blocks of living pods vertically in a large grid, though it was just as quick to make her way through the halls first before heading down.

Several minutes later, Maylee stepped out along with a group of people into Atrium: 446.

The massive room reached up and down several levels, and if her intentions were only to walk around and enjoy the space, she could have done as her mother had asked on level 448.

The problem was that to enter the ventilation shafts, she had to go to a particular spot, because everywhere else needed a priority maintenance clearance to enter the maintenance ways. Apparently, when they updated the ventilation system, they had cut corners and simply manually sealed the entrance ports. Luckily for Maylee, one port, still obscured by a large garden display, had been overlooked.

The heavy fronds of the wide bushes hung out over the edges of the display, so much so as to make the nearby benches unpleasant to use. Maylee walked to the small circular entrance port behind the leaves and looked around. Once sure no one was watching, she tapped the control panel next to it. It flashed orange for priority clearance, but the inset panels slid open anyway.

Maylee gripped the top of the entrance ring and pulled her feet through first. Most likely, it was a port for a drone to make repairs to the interior of the air shafts. An adult would have an uncomfortable time fitting, and doubly so when equipped with tools. As she braced her back next to the ring of the entrance with her feet pressed against the opposite side of the air shaft, the door snapped shut next to her, and she was left in the dark. The only light coming in was through the grating nearly twenty feet down.

She began to shift her feet and shoulders to slowly slide up the shaft. She had to work her way up ten feet before a grating on the side could be used as a ladder. Just before the shaft widened into an impossible climb, there was another access panel and a port to open. There had been no security reason for any of the ports within the maintenance ways to be resealed, as no one was supposed to get this far in the first place. The seal slid open and Maylee pulled herself out of the vertical shaft.

The deep humming of the back workings of the starscraper now reverberated all around her as she landed as softly as she could onto the suspended walkway. There was always a chance that the maintenance crews would be working on something. She hurried along the walkway and moved up a set of steps when it split. One hop through another access port and she slid into a flat section of the ventilation shafts. She was now back on level 447. If she was lucky, she could take out a few more of the ICC before they became too alert for any further operations.

Maylee readied her artificial pulse pistol and used the faint glow of her visor to light her way as she crawled through the shaft. Eventually it turned and the grating at the end became visible, letting through the light of the atrium and the echoing sounds of Council meeting replays. As she neared the end, she happened upon the curious sight of a data pad lying just inside the vent. Maylee slid her visor all the way to the side to get a better look, but data pad disappeared. It was part of the reality shard.

She slid her visor back across her eyes and looked around, hoping that this was not some kind of ambush. There were humans that worked with the ICC, and after her attack they could be trying to weed out the rest of the resistance. Taking a breath, she quickly took hold of the data pad and pushed herself back into the darkness.

"To whoever finds this," the data pad read, "it is imperative to the efforts against the ICC that this data pad be deposited in a reality shard bag at the displayed location. Your efforts will be well rewarded with 100,000 credits. —Waypoint added—"

Maylee nearly dropped it in surprise, though the fall would not have affected the virtual device. Was this one of the randomly installed missions she had heard about? And a hundred thousand credits? That price made the ambush earlier seem like child's play. Maylee had heard that more extensive operations greatly increased both the risk and the reward, but she hadn't thought by that much. A quick look at the location showed her even more stunning news. The bag was sitting just ten feet away, on the outside of the vent.

She quickly made her way back out of the shaft and into the maintenance ways. There was no need to stay for an ambush against the ICC. In fact, there was no need for her to ever enter the program again once she'd transferred the money to her account, and no need to ever ask her mother for money again. Maylee hurried down the steps and slid herself back through the narrow entrance, then forced herself to slow down. Unlike the data pad and pulse pistol on her hip, the shaft that she was about to climb down was very real.

She reached the access door and tried her best to slide out quietly. Once she was standing behind the overgrown display, it was hard not to simply run toward the drop location. Whoever had built the parameters for the mission system had seriously messed up with this one. Maylee would have expected to at least have to make her way to a different starscraper in the Sector for half that many credits. No, definitely less than half. She started off and immediately passed a group of ICC soldiers as well as a group of UWC security. Neither could tell she was doing anything wrong.

When Maylee reached the outside of the same vent that she had originally waited at, she noticed a small virtual duffle bag in a corner behind a holographic map display of the starscraper.

Maylee flicked the small metal figure she always carried toward the virtual bag. The figure was a piece from an old board game, probably from the pocket of a person out of cryostasis. The only marking was the word *"Warden"* on the edge of the base. Nevertheless, it fit her purposes perfectly, and she picked up the small knight while simultaneously placing the data pad in the virtual bag. Any onlookers would have been fooled by the simple game piece and should have no suspicion about her illegal activities.

Maylee stood up and watched her visor display closely, waiting to see the credits shift into her account from the reality shard. Unlike her previous dealing with her mother, the number stayed the same as it was transferred over. Maylee could not hide her excitement as she began to skip back toward the elevators. She could buy anything she wanted: new clothing, devices, even a vacation. She'd have to come up with something so her parents would not wonder where the money came from. Just out of curiosity—she told herself—Maylee found herself looking through her visor at the armor, weapons, and tactical gear within the reality shard database.

* * *

Agatha followed Jance into her living pod on level 447. Unlike many of the other Council members, Jance had insisted on standard living conditions. Everything about Jance's living quarters gave the notion that no one actually lived there, and most of the time that assumption was right. The people's ambassador spent more time working than could ever be considered healthy. Often, Agatha had tried to forcefully limit her schedule, but even during forced free time Jance would make herself seen about the atrium and continue to gather her own data. Agatha's last round of attempts at using the councilor's visor to monitor rough thought patterns had proven that it would take a great deal more work just to get her to relax.

"Please, have a seat, Agatha," Jance said, motioning to the chairs hovering about the room. She touched her visor and a table rose out of the floor. Another touch and a display dropped down. It was showing a review of the Council meeting.

Agatha set her small bag on the table and began to set up her recording device. It picked up sound, body motions from the patient, and if linked properly, rough neural scans for further review.

Jance held out a hand in protest. "In this case, I would rather not."

"Nothing leaves my confidence without a Council clearance override," Agatha reminded the ambassador with a smile.

"Please, just put it away."

Jance had yet to take a seat.

"As you wish," Agatha said, putting the device back. It was easy enough to recognize that something had her distressed. "If you would take a seat as well . . ." she said, motioning to Jance, but the ambassador started pacing.

"I have tried everything to contact him, but I've only come up with dead ends."

"Who?"

"Morris Kannei. The logistician."

Agatha nodded. His name had come up on plenty of occasions, however none before had sparked any need for alarm. "And what is it you need to draw to his attention? Why—" Just as she was about to ask another question, the security light on the door blinked, and it opened without a confirmation request.

The people's logistician stepped into the room, red in the face and eyes twitching about nervously.

"Morris? What are you doing here? Where did you—" Jance started, but the man cut her off.

"Who is this? Jance, who is this woman?"

Agatha stood up and smoothed the wrinkles of her outfit. She started to introduce herself, but the man frantically turned to seal the door behind him. He started about the room holding a device in his hand as if he were scanning for something. His search led him to Agatha's bag, and he quickly upended it. She started to protest, but he just moved into one of the other rooms.

"Get out of there!" Jance barked, taking off after the man. "What are you doing?"

Kannei moved back into the center room and began to fiddle with one of the off-colored lenses in his eyes. "Take them out." He looked up at the other two with a furious gaze, more red flushing into his face. "Your lenses, take them out now."

Jance gave Agatha an apologetic look and motioned for her to follow his lead. For both of them, the blurred vision was a strange feeling.

"Jance, you have to listen to me." Kannei touched the display above the table and adjusted the video feed until it was at the part of the emergency Council meeting when he spoke. "Watch this. This is supposed to be the full version. Here I am asking about the validity of the report, yes? Now look. The military ambassador confirms it, and then Chancellor Malcom continues on without me ever saying anything else."

"That is what this is all about, Morris?" Jance asked. "Surely you are not worked up over a small bit of censoring?" She started to retrieve her lenses.

"I pulled the personal records of the mechanics that inspected the craft—the craft that the two engineering officers responsible for the Core Reactor Report were killed in. The numbers on the recovered gyroscopic brackets were different from what the standard model should have been, but the part is never recorded as having been changed!"

"The Core Reactor Report again?" Jance sighed.

"Not only that, but I found major inconsistencies with the timeline of the Mars Contract."

"Morris, we were given the reports. The Mars Contract is within days of the schedule given to us years ago! Agatha, can you help calm him down?"

"Both of you, perhaps if you just sat down . . ."

"Just one moment, hear me out," he continued. "EMA-GO. Emergency Medical Aid and Genetic Observations. For years, they've selected a specific genetic variation for the populace of the Mars Contract that would allow it to continue long after contact with Earth has been severed."

"It's not like we're supposed to lose contact with Mars, it's just meant to be self-sustainable!" Jance said as the man continued.

"Just today, EMA-GO has been given full preference on whom to allow onto the Mars colonies. However, I looked at the existing lists. No Sovereign Republics Alliance, no Moja Africa or India or any other ITS. Only UWC."

"Perhaps that is just an error. Or even if it is bad policy, what does it matter?"

"Because it is only the beginning of something bigger."

"Morris," Jance sighed, "what could you possibly think the UWC—"

"I have data," Kannei interrupted, "that supports frightening trends. What we think of as Last Edict operations, I believe instead are actually someone using the scattered attacks as a smokescreen to get rid of people. Let me just access . . ."

Kannei suddenly had a stunned look as he focused on his visor. Jaw hanging and hand shaking, his face went from being flushed with frustration to pallid with beads of sweat. "Jance, check my clearance."

She pulled up his data. "Oh no," she said quietly. The change had gone through. Kannei had lost Council clearance.

"They are after me. They are trying to cut off my means of escape."

"Wait a moment, Mr. Kannei," Agatha said, holding up her hands to try to calm the man. "Jance spoke with the military ambassador. You remain a logistician for Sector: K, the only change being that you no longer need worry about Council matters."

"Hoffsted?" Kannei whispered. "Him?" He drew in a sharp breath. "Signal for security! I have to get a transport ready!"

"Mr. Kannei, if you would just—"

"I'll do it myself!"

Just as Kannei raised a hand to the side of his head and touched the visor, all the displays and lights in the room began to distort, much like the effects from a repulsor engine. Everything flickered violently until all but the chemical-powered emergency lights went dark. Agatha gave a surprised scream as her seat dropped to the ground under her. Everything else in the room held up by a distortion field toppled just as Agatha had in the now eerie yellow light.

"Morris?" Jance asked nervously, looking at him over the tilted table in the yellow glow of the emergency lights.

"I was too late," Kannei whispered.

Agatha shared a quick look of worry with the ambassador. The security light over the door slowly pulsed on. It flickered rapidly until the yellow switched to white, as if the security had been overridden. The door was pulled halfway open, and a figure pushed through the gap.

"Thank goodness!" Jance said to the man entering. "Officer Weyburn, what is . . ."

A bright flash and a loud crack sounded filled the room. Agatha pulled her hands over her ears, wondering who had enabled the use of a firearm. Several more loud shots rattled off and Kannei fell backward. Agatha rolled to the ground from her collapsed seat and turned to see the man moving the weapon toward her. There was no mercy in his eyes. No hint of the UWC crest on his shoulder holding him back.

Just as suddenly, a deep pulse sounded from the rooms behind them, and a searing ball of heat struck Weyburn. Weyburn let out a yell and dropped the weapon as it began to melt away. Agatha covered her head as he drew a pistol from his hip and leveled a piercingly loud barrage of shots toward the threat behind him. He moved the pistol down for the distortion field to reload it, but whatever had affected the lights had the same negating effect on the weapons belt.

In his brief moment of hesitation, another bright ball of heat pulsed forward, taking Weyburn in the chest. He dropped the pistol and grabbed a disk from his belt. With a flick of his thumb, all the lights and displays flickered on again, the chairs and table lifted back up, and the door snapped the rest of the way open. He twisted and took another shot in the shoulder, and Agatha could hear as his flesh pop and hiss underneath the armor.

Weyburn pulled something else off his belt and tossed it into the center of the room before stumbling out the door.

"What is that?" Agatha screamed, pointing at the orb as it rolled off the collapsed table. A line down the side of it started to blink rapidly, as if on a timer. She looked to Jance, but there was no answer in her terrified eyes, only the reflected flashing in her teary glaze.

Another man stepped out of the back room holding a weapon in one hand and gripping a wound on his arm with the other. He let go of his arm and pulled a disk similar to Weyburn's out of his pocket, causing all the lights in the room to flicker out once again. The man lifted the toe of his shoe to stop the grenade from rolling past where Kannei lay motionless on the ground.

"Who are you?" Jance asked, sounding as if her mind was as numbed from the chaos as Agatha's was.

He lifted his foot off the grenade and tossed his own makeshift weapon to the side with a wince as it started to spit scalding liquid through heat-cracked metal.

"I'm Avery Thorne." He knelt down and unclipped Kannei's visor. "Sectator of the Last Edict."

"A sectator?" Agatha said in shock.

Avery looked at the visor for a moment before responding. " I would suggest you clear out." He tapped the grenade with his foot as he stood, causing it to roll a few feet off to the side. "This thing goes off when I stop the distortion."

Agatha pushed herself up, feeling her stomach reel as she looked at the logistician. "Then who . . ." she said, pulling her eyes away. She wanted to speak, wanted to run, but a heavy breathing started as panic began to build. She knew all the signs, knew the chemicals and neurological pathways that triggered the response, yet she was powerless to control her fear.

The sectator turned to leave, and Agatha started to back away, now staring intently at the grenade slowly rolling through the red pooling on the floor. "Jance!"

"What are you doing with his visor?" Jance snapped as Avery slipped it into a pocket. "How did you get in here, and why are you here?"

The man dabbed a finger at his arm and looked at the blood on his hand. "I was sent to save Kannei. Now I'm just doing what I still can."

"But the Last Edict . . ." Jance said.

Avery held up the disk and looked at Agatha as shouts echoed down the hallways. "Run."

A moment later, Agatha was stumbling out of the doorway and into the strangely lit hallway. Without the chemical backup lights, it would have been completely dark. There were several startled faces watching in fear and confusion. She should have said something, should have reached for her visor out of instinct, but instead she just ran as fast as her legs would carry her through the unfamiliar darkness.

Chapter 6: Symbols Past

Norclave's reputation for being a city only a shade more forgiving than the outerzones held true as the tech hunter led the way through the tangle of the South Corridors. Where Norclave soldiers avoided the Cells because of the lack of life and the infuriating rubble mites, the South Corridors were more often than not free of Norclave enforcement because of the trouble their presence caused. Mercenaries, freelance trackers, and thugs that had been turned away from joining as Norclave soldiers all found a place amongst the backdoor bars and fighting clubs. More than that, though, the trade here preferred staying clear of a lawful watch.

Kenneth kept his head down as much as possible. Not necessarily to avoid uncalled-for attention—most people tended to mind their own business in the South Corridors as a rule of thumb—but to avoid long overdue attention. He owed money to a number of dangerous people here, and Kenneth had no wish to draw their attention.

The tech hunter started down one of the corridors, glancing back occasionally to make sure Kenneth was following. He ducked his head as they passed under a low stretch of pipe crossing above. At most places, he could reach up and touch the metal grating serving as the floor for a similarly crowded section just above.

"A tall man, you are!" a merchant called from the side. He sat on the ground with a replacement leg stretched out into the walkway, surrounded by piles of clothing. The man was missing a part of his jaw, and he waved a crooked finger at Kenneth. "Some of the finest clothing to fit!" He gestured to the pile of rags of clothing from a bygone age mixed in with some pieces clearly marked as part of a Norclave uniform. Kenneth said nothing as he walked past.

Similar stalls and shops lined the walls, most with goods not worth enough to appear in the trade center, and the others would never survive frequent Norclave inspection. It took quick eyes, but on more than one occasion Kenneth spotted bits of tech that he knew had been smuggled in. One owner primed a grenade of some type for a moment to show that it could still be activated. He also saw the lesser-quality meal packs trading hands, some of which Kenneth could see had their seals broken already. Not that he would say anything. It was not his business, and the tech hunter had been clear about avoiding anything that would slow them down.

A couple of strong-arms eyed their passing. From the bar slits embedded in the wall it was easy to tell it was a debtor's prison. It was not so much a prison on the inside as the deals being passed out to the streets would hang like chains on any who accepted money from here. One of the men flatly told Kenneth to keep moving after he stared for a moment too long. He watched as a small amount of Norclave tokens were slid out to a kid no older than fifteen.

"Where are we headed?" Kenneth asked when the crowd thinned enough to move up beside the tech hunter.

She did not look at Kenneth, but instead kept a constant watch for anything that could amount to a threat. Kenneth liked to think he was aware, but spending the latter part of his youth and the years since in Norclave meant he could not compare to the tech hunter. If he had to wager a guess, Kenneth would have bet she'd moved outside of any claimed territory early in life.

"Just keep close," she said quietly, "and avoid drawing attention. The administrators have been trying to track me and my partners since we arrived in Norclave. It will not be long before they think to find you here."

Kenneth had no choice but to follow. How she was planning to make it back to the transports from here, Kenneth had no idea. As far as escape was concerned, they were running through closed-off rat ways.

"You there!" a loud voice shouted from the side.

Kenneth tried to keep his attention forward, but when the man yelled his name, there was no avoiding it. The large man took hold of the grate above and lifted himself over the counter, landing on the metal below with a heavy thud.

"Karzon! What a—" Kenneth started, but a large hand gripped the front of his shirt and stopped him cold.

The man pulled Kenneth to him and looked down from his extra foot of height. As always, he kept his head shaved to the skin, and he might have put on even more pounds of muscle atop his shoulders than before. "I'm not sure what would make me more happy, Kenneth: the money you owe me or the chance to finally break that lying smirk off your face."

Kenneth tried to push away, but he would have to rip through his shirt before breaking free of the vein-laced muscles holding him tight. He looked to the side for the tech hunter, but he could not spot her in the crowd passing undisturbed around them. Kenneth lowered his eyes. He did not blame her for simply moving on. The attention he had attracted would only make escape all the less likely.

Karzon put a hand on Kenneth's other arm and pulled back the sleeve. "Another new scar and you're walking free. I can't believe it, you slimy son of—"

"Let him go."

In the South Corridors, one man threatening another was a regular part of the day. However, when a tech hunter involved themselves in a matter, it was enough to pull the attention of everyone walking past.

The brute bared his teeth. "This is not your business, tech hunter."

"This one is mine," she said.

Kenneth raised an eyebrow. "Now I wouldn't say that, but—"

A hard shake from Karzon cut him off. "You be quiet." He turned back to the tech hunter. "He doesn't look like one of your people. Try again." The man shifted which hand he was holding Kenneth with and pushed him against a support beam. Kenneth tried to pry himself loose, but another hit against the wall made him give it up.

"Last warning." Her threat hung in the air like a grenade about to be dropped. Even against the likes of Karzon, her words had weight. Tech hunters had a reputation that brought about a mystic fear, not because of what they had proven they could do, but because there was no way to tell. Kenneth guessed she at least had a hidden weapon or pulse emitter, but Karzon was forced to work his mind through all the exaggerated stories. If nothing else, he had to decide how far she was willing to take the threat. Pulling a bad reputation in Norclave mattered little when she could simply disappear into the outerzones.

The grip holding Kenneth slackened for a moment. Then, as if in the hands of a riftwalker, Kenneth was thrown forward toward the tech hunter. As Kenneth hit the ground hard, the tech hunter reached behind her short cloak. However, when she saw the brute pull a pipe from behind the counter, she changed her motion and instead jumped up and touched the ceiling, causing a spark and a sharp hiss.

Karzon rushed forward as she landed with a knee on the ground. He took a swing at the tech hunter with the pipe, but just before the metal rod crushed into flesh and bone, it rebounded as if it had hit a support beam. A silvery blue wire stretched from the floor to where she had touched the walkway above. As Karzon stared in confusion, she spooled out another loop from her sleeve and tossed it at the man. Out of instinct he caught the loop of flexible wire and pulled. She then touched her wrist to the floor with another bright hiss, and the wire turned rigid. Karzon tried to pull, but the now unmovable metal wrapped around his hand only dug in to his skin.

The tech hunter stood up, rested an arm against the vertical wire, and watched as Karzon tried to pry his hand loose.

"You can either cut off your hand," she advised, "or wait several hours." She then motioned to Kenneth. "Get up. It's time we left."

Kenneth pushed himself up and gave Karzon the smirk he hated so much before following the tech hunter through the marveling crowd. The people wasted no time in shuffling to the side as she gave them hard looks. As if the stories were not enough, a fair number had likely heard of Karzon or had run-ins with him themselves. The fact that she'd rendered the brute completely helpless, unable to move and shouting furiously at anyone passing by, was more than enough reason to convince them to stay clear of her path.

As they continued, Kenneth tried to get a glance at the tech she had used. He had never seen anything quite like it, but he assumed it would have been used to hold things together long enough to make permanent repairs.

"Where did you find that?" Kenneth asked as they passed a section dealing in rough-made breads. "I can think of more than a few occasions I could have made use of that wire."

The tech hunter turned to him with the same unyielding look she'd leveled at the passing crowd. "I have my secrets, you have yours. You would do well to let them stay separate."

Kenneth frowned. "Why is that?"

She stopped in the middle of the corridor, forcing people to move around her. "I do not know you. I do not trust you. The only reason I am helping you is because of thin promises and dangerous agreements."

"Helping me?" Something about that sparked wrong with him. "It may only be those damned promises and agreements that got me here in the first place! Do not say you are helping me. Dragging me along, maybe, but not helping."

She scoffed. "That was not my debt or my fight back there."

Kenneth crossed his arms. "Just give me a straight answer or I turn around."

The tech hunter reached a hand under the cloth around her neck, likely gripping a hidden knife. "Remember my warning."

Kenneth rolled his eyes. "It's the same as every other one I've lived with all of my life. Do as you are told or die. Well," Kenneth said, motioning with his arms, "I'm still here."

She glanced at the scars on his arm, and Kenneth hurriedly adjusted his sleeve back down. For a moment, her expression changed. It was if she was just now realizing something she had been told about.

Kenneth continued, "I was kept alive by the Overlord for the same reason you cannot kill me now. You need my help, tech hunter, and I will not be ordered around."

Her attention moved past him for a moment, toward a commotion behind him. A quick look showed Kenneth the patrol of Norclave soldiers trying to make their way through the corridor. There was a chaotic scramble as merchants began hiding anything they thought the soldiers would be after.

"We have to go, now," she said.

Kenneth shook his head and stood his ground. "Even up. If you want my help, you tell me what this is about."

"There is no time, Kenneth." She glanced both ways to ensure they still had an escape. "I will tell you once we are out of Norclave."

Kenneth fought the urge to run away from the advancing soldiers, but this might be the only time he could get the information that would keep him from walking into another trap. "Give me something first."

She gritted her teeth and watched as the soldiers struggled through the commotion. "We found . . . something. Tech the Overlord would pay well for, but we cannot risk trying to open it on our own. That's where you come in."

"Open it?" Kenneth asked. What container could bring all this attention without knowing what was inside? His chance for more answers passed when she turned away and started into the crowd. Kenneth almost had to run to catch back up.

"One more thing before we leave," Kenneth asked as he shoved his way to her side. "Do you have a name, or should I just make up something to call you?"

She said nothing and dodged down a perpendicular walkway. Just around the corner, Kenneth nearly tripped over a spilled crate of burnt-out power packs. He pulled on several cords draped above to keep his balance, causing the display of lights above the next spot over to rattle sharply. Ignoring the shouts trailing behind, he followed the tech hunter down a set of stairs.

Immediately to the left, Kenneth recognized a particularly rough bar. There was no sign above the entrance, and the entrance itself was nothing more than a panel removed from the wall. In fact, the place had never even been given a name. Kenneth had heard it called a number of different things, as everyone who knew about it had a name of their own for it. It often served as a meeting place for some of the darkest deals in Norclave. He'd gone there with Mackelry once when the old man brokered a deal with some Kessians, though he was never told what they were trading.

"Are you sure this is where you want to go?" he asked.

"Kara." She watched a group of Norclave soldiers farther down the corridor ransacking the shops in their search. People on the streets made use of the commotion to pocket anything that fell onto the walkways and out of the attention of the owner.

Kenneth gave her a confused look. "Kara?"

She took a step toward the doorway. "It is the name I picked up, somewhere along the way. Now stay close and walk lightly." At that, she turned and stepped through the rough doorway in the wall. Kenneth ducked his head under the metal and followed her in. Whether it was real or not, it was the first time he had ever heard a tech hunter's name.

A strong odor immediately grabbed his attention. Resting on crates and other makeshift seating were a few dull figures, and several more were sleeping off the previous night in corners or under tables, but for the most part the bar was empty. Even the man who would have been serving drinks was instead leaning against the back wall fast asleep.

Kenneth looked around again. He had expected to see the other two tech hunters waiting for their arrival. Instead, the only life to the place was one man slowly filling his bowl with the broth left on abandoned plates and with any forgotten drops of alcohol left in the cups strewn about.

"You look familiar," the man said to Kara as she passed by. "There was two like you come in here, a yesters' day, I think." He looked to Kenneth with his bloodshot eyes. "And you, I remember . . . well, no I don't. But you . . ." He said, turning to point at the tech hunter again.

Before the man could continue, Kara held a finger to her lips to get him to be quiet. She reached in a pocket and pulled out a small silver square. It was marked with the same double cross as the medical paste. The man crossed his eyes as she moved it toward him and touched it to the side of his head. "Close your eyes, just a moment."

With a confused look, the man blinked a couple of times before following her order. Kara pushed the side of the medical device and the man stumbled. Kara plucked the bowl out of his hands before he collapsed completely to the floor. She set the bowl on the table with a shake of her head and wiped away the oil and grime from his skin off her coma-inducing tech.

She motioned to Kenneth to follow as she moved on through the room, disappearing into a back doorway. When Kenneth passed through the door, he found her pulling a panel off the wall. Without a moment of hesitation, she stepped out onto a small pipe running across the open space between the corridors.

Kenneth stuck his head out and looked to either side. The back ends of the small buildings stretched on for a staggering distance, made only more intimidating by the open space below. If he were to fall, he would bounce from several cross-running pipes before dropping out of the bottom of the city.

"Oh, don't tell me the heights get you nervous," the tech hunter complained as she turned around and started walking backward across the pipe. It was a foot wide, at the most.

"No, it's not that," Kenneth said, watching as she paced backward over assured death.

"Well then, hurry up!" Kara flipped back around and pushed in another panel on the next building. She moved inside, not waiting for Kenneth to start across.

He cursed under his breath and set a foot on the pipe. Almost immediately, the piece of metal on the bottom of his boot slid an inch. Kenneth gripped the side of the wall and let out a breath touching upon a curse word. He made his way out onto the pipe with his feet sideways, sliding one foot over at a time.

"Hurry on with it!" the tech hunter appeared again and urged to him. "Did you forget Norclave is after us?"

"And you think they will find us here?"

He kept sliding one foot to the next until he neared the other side. A quick pull from the tech hunter sent him through the removed panel and roughly onto the floor of the dusty storeroom. Empty shelves and broken crates were scattered about, looted long ago. Kara started through the room, looking through the gaps in the metal flooring. She stamped a foot in several spots until she found the one section that shook more than the others. Kara worked her fingers underneath and flipped it to the side.

Kenneth immediately had a bad feeling as Kara produced another piece of tech. She turned on the magnetic clamp of the device and fastened it to a support strut just under the floor. A blue ring pulsed around the device as she pulled a length of cable out of it. She then produced a small handle from one of her many pockets and clipped it to the cable.

"You can go first." She passed the handle over to Kenneth, who hesitantly took hold. "I will watch up here in case Norclave soldiers start looking."

Kenneth peered over the edge and felt as if the span of the room had shifted to an incredible size, leaving him feeling helplessly small as he looked down the hundreds of feet to the floor of the starscraper. He took a step back. "How will we get to a transport?"

She took his clenched fist and held up the handle. She tapped one end and brought up a projected display. "It only recognizes inputs from the back."

"That's a simple fix," Kenneth said.

She took the handle back from him before he could continue stalling. Kara tapped through the back of the screen, causing the tech to flash blue several times. "You can work up your nerve while I go." Without a moment lost, she jumped and vanished with no more sound than the whirring of the cable.

* * *

Arlen stared blankly at the chair across from him in the small room. The two guards standing outside the room would have their orders—from the First Administrator, not the Overlord—to keep him from leaving.

He rubbed a hand over his face to wipe at the tiredness and other mixed emotions. Terrus, he reminded himself again. That was the name of the man he claimed he had met with. Arlen could not shake the feeling that the lesser administrator would be disposed of quietly and without the Overlord's approval. He would just be one more person who went missing, like so many others. Arlen leaned back in the warped and blackened seat, listening to the muffled and agitated voices on the other side.

A moment later, the door swung open and gave way to a rough man. It was the tracker, Draken. He slid the silver wire of his visor and its projected image out of the way and took the seat across from Arlen. The man looked everywhere about the small room and patted his hands on the chair to transition himself from yelling at the guards.

"I suppose I should thank you," Draken finally said.

Arlen merely pulled his gaze to the floor as the tracker continued.

"I know you did not do it for me," Draken said. "Whether it was for the Overlord or some ploy of your own, I will stay alive because of it."

Arlen rolled his gaze toward the dim light on the wall opposite the door. "So you came here to cover your secret? You here to kill me?"

There was a heavy moment of silence before Draken spoke again. "It crossed my mind." The tracker pushed himself up from the chair and stretched his arms over his head. "That wouldn't help Kenneth, though."

Arlen then looked angrily up at the man. "You were the one who led the soldiers to him in the first place! And you were there when they dragged me off the docks!" Arlen clenched his fists. As much trouble as Kenneth had brought him, he knew the technician was more clueless about it all than he would have ever admitted. "You sent him to the Cells to die."

Draken spun a loose nut on the light. "I had to stop him. Kenneth was leaving Norclave before he ever met with the tech hunters. The Overlord made it very clear where he is needed, and stowing away aboard a cargo transport to Reclaim is not that place." Draken pulled his hand back and crossed his arms. "As for the Cells, even an idiot like Branon would not execute Kenneth without an order from Silas. Kenneth only made things worse by making his own escape. Now everyone is after him."

Arlen wiped a bloodshot eye. "If you are not here to get rid of me, and you actually want to help the technician, then what are you here for?"

Draken held up a small data device. It was no larger than a one-inch square, but a tap of the finger on the side made a larger display flicker into place. "Read this, memorize whatever parts you think you need, and keep it in a pocket." The display distorted and flicked off as Draken tossed it to Arlen.

"What is it?" he asked, turning it over a few times.

Draken took a few steps toward the door. "The First Administrator will soon figure out you gave him the wrong man. That may come back at you, but for now this false information on Kenneth's location may give you leverage. And that will give me time."

Arlen stopped Draken just as he reached for the door. "Time for what?"

Draken let out a frustrated breath. "Time to see that Kenneth gets to where the hell he is supposed to be going before anyone else beats us to it."

The tracker pulled open the door and cursed at the soldiers as he exited, leaving Arlen with nothing but the false data and questions. He slid his finger down the side and opened it. He immediately saw the potential. According to this, Kenneth was making his way to Reclaim, where Draken had stopped him from going in the first place.

* * *

Karzon gave another hard pull on the cable, gritting his teeth as it dug into his hand, though he could have sworn this time there was a flex in the line. He growled and swung his other hand around behind him, hoping to knock the lowlife trying to empty his pockets with a solid hit under the chin. At the moment, he had a lot to swear about. As the pickpocket scurried way, Karzon had no doubt that another would try before he could free himself.

Karzon pressed a boot against the cable and shoved as hard as he could, though he gave up when he felt the thin wire cutting into the sole. He gave another curse, this time not directed at that damned technician or his tech hunter, but at the Norclave soldiers that had left him like this. As he glared down the confused looks from passing faces, Karzon doubled down on his musings of getting hold of Kenneth. There would be no hesitation, no reveling in the moment or drawing it out; if he saw the technician again, he would put two hands around his neck and keep squeezing until he felt bone.

He gave another sharp tug. This time it cut in farther than he had wanted, causing blood to drip from the skin under his small finger. He gave a frustrated kick, tripping an unsuspecting passerby. He was forced to realize that if he kept fighting it as he was, he might be left with only the one hand. Karzon resigned himself to fending off pickpockets and waving the steel pipe at any thieves looking to enter his shop. He was a feared enough man that his swings had threat beyond what the damned cable would allow him to reach. After all, they saw him as a vicious hound on a thin chain.

A man passing by eyed him with particular interest, looking along the lengths of the steel strand. Karzon felt his blood surging again with anger, though he managed to keep himself restrained enough to hold the pipe at his side. The dull greys of worn cloth hanging over pouches and belts marked the man as a tech hunter. He was dark-skinned and had a web of scars from years of a rough life, and even if Karzon had not been strung up he would have given this man his space in passing. Whereas the small woman had caught him by surprise, this tech hunter looked as if he knew his way around a fight.

"What do you want?" Karzon asked the man.

The tech hunter walked a slow circle around him. He ducked under the tilted vertical strand and eyed the loop that held Karzon. "Who did this to you?"

"Get me out of this and I'll tell you," Karzon said.

The tech hunter snapped a hand up and set the glowing edge of a heated blade against Karzon's wrist. Karzon tried to jerk back out of instinct. He was about to swing the pipe with the other hand when the tech hunter spoke again. "You had better watch what you put up for trade."

"Wait, that's not what I—"

"If you want to decide how I free your hand, you will speak. Now."

"It was a tech hunter. She was with the technician Norclave is searching for." While the tech hunter nodded in approval, Karzon made special note that the blade had not moved. He could still feel the heat painfully close to his skin.

"Who was this tech hunter?"

"I don't know," Karzon said. "I've never seen her before and I didn't get a name."

"A name?" he asked condescendingly. When Karzon tightened his grip on the pipe, the tech hunter only glanced at it. "Perhaps you really are that stupid if you're thinking about using that. Drop it, and we will continue to talk."

The pipe made a hollow ring as it bounced off the floor.

The tech hunter took a breath. His abnormally glass-blue eyes showed that he was fighting a violent urge of his own. "I know that this woman did not bind you up and then stop to chat about political balances and the damned weather. Just tell me what she looked like. Did she have a red tint to her hair?"

Karzon nodded. "She had a hood and kept it tucked in about her neck, but I would say her hair was a reddish color."

The tech hunter stood there for a moment before letting out a chuckle at some irony Karzon was ignorant of. "Close your eyes. This might sear, but there is no need to lose your sight." Karzon did as he was told and gritted his teeth yet again. The tech hunter grabbed his hand, and he could clearly imagine the glowing edge of the heated blade sliding through the metal wrapped around his fingers. There was a pop, and Karzon felt his arm drop, now free from the binding that had held him for far too long.

He opened his eyes just in time to see the wire drop from the ceiling like a wet string. If there had been a flash, it was no brighter than a normal light. As the tech hunter put something away, he nodded to Karzon. "Can't have you knowing too much, now can I?"

Karzon tenderly cupped his hand and looked over the wounds. He had some medi-seal in his lockbox, but some simple bandages might do instead.

"I have another deal in mind," the tech hunter said. "Come with me and help find Kara, your tech hunter, and you can do what you will to the one I can only assume is named Kenneth."

Karzon's attention was pulled away from his hand as he looked up at the man. He tried to weigh his intentions. The promise of finally getting even with the technician was almost too good. He tightened his fist and let the pain build up his arm.

"How do you know Kenneth?"

"He sided with a merchant in the trade center."

Karzon grunted, trying to work his hand. "I'm in, tech hunter."

"The name's Mallec. Now clean your wounds and get ready to go."

* * *

Kenneth sat on the edge, waiting for Kara to complete the trek down. He could hear the shouting and confusion spreading outside the abandoned storeroom, and on several occasions he heard a fight break out between mercenaries and the Norclave soldiers. A string of curse words came to mind as he waited for them to burst through the far door.

The pitch of the cable changed as it started back up. Kenneth leaned forward and watched as the handle with its glowing display was pulled up from the vast space below. As it clicked against the support of the storeroom, he took in a deep breath. He leaned across the gap and grabbed the other side, holding his weight over the middle of the hole in the floor. He tried not to think about the empty space below as he reached down with his left hand and took hold of the handle.

Suddenly, his right hand slipped, leaving him gripping the small handle and holding to the edge above with the heels of his boots. He started reaching in a panic to pull himself up, but forced himself to stop. In trying to claw his way back up, he would lose his grip and fall. With a relenting breath, he tapped the back of the handle's faulty projected display, and his boots slipped from the edge as he started in an upside down freefall.

The spooling cable kept just enough tension to pull his arm above his head and let his legs drift back under him as he plummeted downward. Pulling the handle and its projected display back in front of his face, he tapped through it with his other hand, then gripped the handle with both hands as the rubble below neared. Like easing his feet into water, the ground below softly pressed onto the soles of his boots.

Kenneth opened his eyes and murmured a few choice words as he looked around. The city of Norclave was a chaotic hive far above, its ever-present hum of noise contrasting heavily with the dead silence surrounding the immediate area. Thick moss clung to the wide slopes of metal and small plants grew from layers of soil that had collected within the wedges and hollows over the centuries.

He started making his way up a nearby slope to inspect his surroundings, feeling the dirt trapped underneath the moss trying to give way as he moved. Once he reached the top of the small rise, he could see out farther into the heart of the starscraper than he had expected.

A forest of twisted steel and light-starved trees stretched out across the inner impact valley. With the exceptions of the titanic pillars of steel arching into the distance, the interior floor sat well below the ground level of the surrounding lands. Kenneth could see through the gash in the large plate he was standing on into the other half of the crushed starscraper with its cavernous openings below that had yet to be filled by decaying plants or the dust of the winds. Some pits would be just under the top layer, while others might stretch down hundreds of feet.

He knew that there once was a settlement in the center of the starscraper, before Norclave had started its rapid growth under the Overlord's direction. The settlement, known as New Solace, was founded by tech hunters, scavengers, and anyone else looking for a safe place in a dangerous world. Kenneth also clearly remembered the warnings to stay far away from it. New Solace had been a dead settlement since he was a child.

He turned around to see Kara reaching out to catch the cable as it swayed from the winds pulling at it from high above. A shiver traveled between Kenneth's shoulders as she unclipped the handle and sent the cable zipping up into the distance. He watched for a moment, realizing that the path back had truly been severed.

"We have disappeared for now," the tech hunter said, "but they will soon think to expand their search once they cannot find us in the city." She stepped past Kenneth and hopped over a gap between the metal. "Follow my steps. I will tell you everything you need to know while we make our way to the north side, to the Wraith Steel Slopes."

Going all the way around the starscraper meant traversing several miles of rough landscape, but if anything, traveling on foot would be an unexpected move.

Kara stopped with one foot on a band of steel and the other on a small patch of dirt covered in green sprigs. After a quick adjustment, tucking her hair underneath the cloth about her shoulders, she looked to Kenneth. "We are going through the center."

Kenneth looked past her to where pillars of light fell through the starscraper onto a pale forest of withered trees. An entire settlement had been wiped out in there, and any who had investigated it in the years after had disappeared as well, seemingly hunted down by . . . something. That included the only remaining members of his family, and it would have included him had his parents not hidden him away in the rubble. "You do realize what happened out there, don't you?"

Kara sent a patronizing smile toward him. "Reactivated hunter drone? War mech? Rubble mite swarms?" She shook her head. "Crossbred descendent of genetically altered experiments? What about a Cryo, who upon being reawakened decided to mercilessly slaughter every person not from its own era? Kenneth, why would there be so many different options if one was actually the truth?"

Kenneth shrugged and kicked at a patch of dirt. "If only there was somebody left alive to ask."

"If it makes you feel better," Kara said, "this is the same way we came into Norclave." She turned and pointed ahead. "It is hard to see, but the New Solace road is ahead. The shifts in the rubble have not claimed it yet. Not entirely."

He started forward, meaning to go just far enough to see the so-called road. Kenneth had looked out into the starscraper on many occasions, but his earliest memories—and nightmares—had been enough to keep him away. As he neared, Kara started down a slope of rough steel. Kenneth almost called for her to stop, but he figured it was no use. If she was not lying about taking this path in, they might actually make it through. Not that it would be a comfortable journey, but perhaps whatever danger was ahead had finally passed after all these years.

"You keep talking as if there are more tech hunters than yourself," Kenneth commented as he followed her over a half-twisted beam. "Or did they die in here too?"

"Their names are Randin and Comar, but we used to be more. Not that our searches were always together, but each of us eventually decided that a simple trust in each other was worth the risk." Kara hopped off the end of the beam and looked around for a moment until Kenneth finished his way across. "You don't feel quite so surrounded if you have a corner you can back into."

"That's a different mindset than any tech hunter I have heard of." Kenneth followed as she started through the narrow crack in a fallen support. Having to turn his shoulders and walk sideways was better than the alternative of climbing the twenty feet of smooth steel on either side of the opening. "With a profession like yours, I'm surprised you can trust anyone else."

Kara stepped out of the split and searched while Kenneth tried to unwedge his foot. "Many would consider it a weakness. And it is." She glanced back to Kenneth. "A group slows you down."

Kenneth gave a final heave and pulled his boot free. "Fair enough."

The tech hunter started again into a small swath of land covered in more plant life than twisted steel. She skirted a puddle surrounded by pale, slender stems and carefully moved through the thin grass. Kenneth spent more time looking into the surrounding area than watching his step. Following her path would be safe enough, though any of the ridges or spires of steel around them could easily have prying eyes. The only thing worse than the feeling of being watched was that he knew there was nobody there. Nobody came this way. Not anymore. Not even the most desperate scavengers.

The deep shadow cast by the steel of the starscraper above finally set over them. Ahead, the uneven terrain was lit by lights scattered throughout the dark. Kenneth knew that down here, nothing as fragile as functioning lights would have survived when the building fell. Much of the steel had fused itself together in the crash. The only explanation was that the lights had been placed there by someone.

"Look," Kara said, pointing just ahead off to the right. "I remember that. The path is just on the other side."

The slope to the right had a different color from much of the rest of the steel. It was as if a dull honey had been poured over it. Odd shapes rose from the surface of the metal, forming large, sweeping curves and sections of lines about waist high. As they stepped up onto the bronze-colored surface, Kara produced a light and pointed it up the slope. The overall shape of the bronze surface was once some kind of large oval or circle. It was only when Kenneth pulled himself up behind Kara onto one of the raised lines that he stopped to wonder what the sweeping protrusions in the metal had been for.

"What is this?" Kenneth finally asked.

Kara stopped and tried to find what he was looking at. When he motioned in an arc at the large, raised curve they were standing on, she started to look as well. Shining the light forward showed the next raised section was made of several straight bars joining at sharp angles.

The tech hunter tilted her head and slowly turned around, surveying the area. She pointed to the arc they were standing in. "This is a . . ." Looking to the next of the large shapes for a moment, she continued, "They are letters. UWC."

Kenneth gave a nod. "The same markings are on plenty of the riftwalkers."

"And on tech," Kara added. "Mostly weapons."

For a moment, the two stood looking at the great metal emblem. They both could imagine the importance once given to the icon, but to them it was nothing more than a relic of a bygone age, half-buried in a part of a world they had always known. Kara decided that they had spent long enough and started moving, shining her light across the huge letters to better see the way to move past them.

"What is it we are looking for?" Kenneth asked, this time with more curiosity than frustration.

Kara stopped on the edge of the *C* and turned to face him. "Nothing," she said. "Randin, Comar, and I already found it. We just needed a technician we could somewhat trust."

"Alright. I'll try to manage that. Would you at least tell me what this 'it' thing is?"

She nodded, though her expression hinted that she had a stipulation.

"Go ahead," Kenneth said with his palms open at his sides.

"You do not tell this to anyone, do you understand? It will be more than just the administrators hunting us if others know."

Kenneth rolled his eyes, growing impatient again. A tech vault or a store of activated weapons did not warrant this much secrecy, even from a tech hunter. "We're in the middle of the starscraper. Who else could I tell?"

Kara swept the light over the large symbol again, seemingly lost in thought. When she finally settled her gaze back upon Kenneth, she spoke. "We found a Cryo."

Chapter 7: Chasing Images

As they wedged themselves through the small port of the ventilation shaft over her bed, Jance felt the raging glow of the fires they'd left behind. Though the searing brightness pulled at her skin, it felt as if the heat reached her very core, forging a sudden anger deep within. It was an unfit ceremony, a rushed cremation of a man who had been killed for what he might have discovered. The sectator helped pull her up into the narrow shaft and ushered her to hurry. She caught him saying something about the UWC reinforcements being on their way, but her mind had retreated from the moment.

It was not that nothing felt real. Far from it. In one instant her world had flipped on its head and, rather than struggling in disbelief, she was left only with questions. After all, it was Weyburn, the UWC soldier the military ambassador had introduced her to, that killed Kannei.

"Keep moving!" Avery yelled back to her. "The entire UWC will be after us now. Not just me, do you understand? Before you think of going back, remember what just happened. Kannei was of the Council, same as you."

"What about Agatha?" Jance almost paused to go back. "What happens to her?"

"Once we reach the maintenance ways, we keep moving."

The way he skipped the answer caused a sharp pull in her chest. "And where to then?" Jance asked, wiping her eyes the best she could as she continued to crawl.

"I take you to the SRA." The sectator leaned against the wall at a bend and slammed the flat of his fist on the terminal. The small port opened just as it would have from a simple touch.

"You work for the SRA? If you expect me to betray—" Jance started.

She was cut off as Avery shut the exit in front of him and turned a red-eyed look on her. A mixture of anger and grief shone in the light of Kannei's visor, which he'd pulled from his pocket. "You don't know the last thing about who I stand for."

"The Last Edict are terrorists. They stand for terror and are hell-bent on bringing chaos and pointless bloodshed to Earth!" Even though she meant what she said, she still did not see the same cold eyes in this sectator as she had in Weyburn when he'd looked down his sights. This man was driven by more than an order. "Who are you, Avery? What is the Last Edict?"

"The Last Edict . . . it's not just an organization. It is an idea. Some believe it is divine in origin, others simply take it as the next logical step for humanity."

"What? What is that supposed to mean?" Jance asked. "Why would you even become a sectator?"

Avery paused for a moment.

"I'm just a supplies coordinator. I grew up in a UWC starscraper, same as you. But I fight for the final judgment." He took a breath, seeing the look of confusion on Jance's face. "The only permanent solution, the final end, the *last* edict that will be placed on humankind— is our ultimate destruction. There is nothing beyond the final ending. We may live on until the collapse of the sun, or the breaking of the universe, but our end will come."

Avery looked down. When he met Jance's questioning look again, his tone had softened. "It will always be beyond our control to fight against the end, but it *should* be beyond our ability to cause it. That is what I fight for."

After a moment, Jance asked, "And what exactly are you trying to stop? What was Morris going to find out?"

Avery held the visor up. "That secret is buried along with his Council clearance. All I have to go on is the last image."

Before Jance could ask what it was, Avery pulled himself through a small opening. She could see no other option but to follow him. They soon hurried along the long maintenance walkways, passing row upon row of turbines and stabilization brackets. Avery finally stopped at an elevator and waited impatiently for Jance to catch up.

She reached for the terminal to open the door, but Avery grabbed her wrist. "If you do that," he said, "you tell Weyburn and the others where we are."

As Avery produced the circular distortion device again, Jance asked, "How many others like Weyburn can there be?"

He activated the disk once again, causing the visor in his hand and the light on the elevator to flicker. "Only about half of the points on that map you were shown in the meeting were strikes by us." He wedged his fingers into the lip and pulled the door open. Once they were both through, he stopped the distortion and hit a level on the elevator. Airlocks: 500.

"Procedure states that all exits will be sealed," Jance reminded him. "The airlocks will be a dead end unless you think you can pry open a blast door by hand." Jance had never seen anything like his device, but if she had to guess, she would say it was a technology banned by the Inhibition Protocols. Not that the Last Edict cared anything for protocol.

Avery noticed her looking and tucked the device away as the elevator sped upward. "It can only disrupt electrical systems."

Jance looked at the visor he still held in his hand. "Why not use Morris's visor to find out what he was on to?"

Avery gave her a judging look. "The only useful data on this," he said with a motion of the visor, "is the display. Everything else is locked away on a UWC data server. Unless, of course, you want to tell the world where we are by using your own clearance."

The elevator stopped at level five hundred and the doors opened. This time, she was not met by a pressure leak. The maintenance crews had all but moved on to the next project, having left only a couple tables with tools and a bit of machinery at the base of the massive window. From here, she could see several other starscrapers of Sector-K scattered out across the sea. Avery walked past the repair drone to a large mechanical suit sitting powered down against the window.

It was a caretaker exosuit, designed to carry heavier loads than what a simple repair drone could. Large magnetic pads on the feet and hands of the caretaker allowed it to climb effortlessly wherever needed. Beyond making repairs, they were often deployed by fire defense crews and military construction outfits.

Avery pulled himself into the seat and made the suit stand up, putting his head nearly ten feet in the air. Jance began to worry. This model of caretaker unit had a second deployable seat.

"Grab that drone controller," Avery said as he picked up the repair drone in the magnetic grip of the exosuit. Jance moved to the table and picked up the controller, already not liking the idea of taking the drone with them.

"Activate the glass welder," he said.

Jance reached up to her visor and quickly linked with the controller. She pulled up an overlay and found which control to use. When she flipped the switch—a rather curious input method—the front of the drone lit up with a bright, sparking light. "Now what?" she asked over the noise.

The motors in the caretaker fired up to full as Avery pulled the drone back. In one titanic motion, he swung the drone downward into the window. The broken heap of the drone screeched across the glass and scattered over the floor in pieces. Jance watched in astonishment as Avery brought the foot of the caretaker forward against the newly formed crack in the glass. Jance could feel the slight pull of air through the gap as he moved to dig at the hole.

As the thick pieces of glass slid back around the legs of the caretaker, occasionally colliding with the destroyed repair drone, Jance could see the reflective absorption layer normally visible only from the outside. It was a thick gold laced with an amber-colored grid of conductive material. The color varied from building to building, but the function was the same. Since the glass only produced less than a fraction of a percent of a starscraper's overall power usage, they were essentially for aesthetics. After all, the starscrapers had to rely on the massive gravity repulsor engines on their exteriors to remain standing, and that meant utilizing far greater means of power.

Once Avery seemed satisfied at the destruction he had caused and they had a gap big enough for the caretaker suit, Jance dropped the controller on the ground next to a bent piece of the drone's outer shell. She pulled herself into the seat that deployed from the chest of the machine and activated the harness to close around her.

"Just keep breathing," Avery yelled from above as he started moving the suit backward.

Jance held onto the straps over her shoulders and pressed her feet down into the foot cradle. As soon as Avery backed out of the window and onto the exterior of the starscraper, her hair began to whip around. The thin air caught her by surprise.

"We are going down now!" Avery yelled. There was a hiss from the arms of the caretaker as the magnetic pads lessened, allowing the suit to start sliding down the side of the building. Jance looked down and was greeted with two miles of carefully designed architecture, dotted with relief windows and sleek, five-story gravity repulsor engines. Jance began to scream as the caretaker gained speed in its controlled fall. As one section of the wall flowed into a longer curving strut, Avery released one of the arms.

Jance felt a jolt of fear as the mech shifted, thinking that one wrong move from Avery could leave them falling alongside the building with no way to latch back onto it. The magnetic pad squealed as he pressed it against the other side. There was a hard pull in her stomach far worse than the elevators as he tightened the other grips, causing them to slow suddenly. She let out another scream as one of the feet let go to shift over to the other strut.

"Are you going to do that the entire way down?" Avery yelled angrily. "We still have two miles yet!"

Jance closed her eyes and bit into her lip as he pulled the caretaker the rest of the way over and started to drop faster again.

"I thought you said you were a supplies coordinator!" she yelled back.

"I have the controls displayed in here!" he replied.

Jance nearly fainted as they continued rocketing down layer after layer of the starscraper's hull.

* * *

Rigel Weyburn gritted his teeth as the medical attendants of 447 peeled sections of the flight armor from his skin. A large burn pattern stretched across his chest from where the first shot of the improvised weapon had hit the heat-resistant material. A woman ran a scanner over his shoulder, but he did not need a readout on a screen to know the burn had reached deep.

"Close that door," one of the medical staff said. Just outside the main entrance, a squad of soldiers hurried past. The UWC military was pushing to replace the local enforcement. Before the wide door was sealed off, Weyburn could see a group of civilians being ushered away from the section.

"Apply the medi-seal, type 5-C, while I calibrate the regeneration formula."

In the back of his mind, he knew they had survived. The grenade somehow went off far too late, meaning there were three individuals who knew the truth of the matter. The only thing that had gone correctly about the operation was keeping Morris Kannei from joining the Last Edict. However, that still left room for SRA suspicion and questions from more of the Council.

He let his head roll back to look up at the ceiling, knowing that the cover-ups would increase tenfold. The only thing he could do was hope that Hoffsted would not have him die of his injuries in a military medical facility. Weyburn looked over to where the woman was accessing the databases for his medical records. She tilted her head in confusion, then turned to the others with a nervous look.

"His records are missing."

The assistant about to apply the medi-seal took a step back. Weyburn then noticed that the wristband of the woman at the terminal was flashing red. She had signaled for security. Moments later, the main door to the medical station opened and a squad of UWC soldiers entered. They had the red mark across the chest as well as an additional gold X on their shoulders. They were of a different company than those in the halls, and they immediately started their work about the room.

Weyburn's equipment, including the distortion generator, was gathered into a lockbox, and on the other side of the room another pair of soldiers worked on the terminal. One accessed the logs while the other pulled open a side panel. The monitoring cameras in the room were scanned and their data stores erased at the same time Weyburn was pulled up from the table.

"You cannot take him! I have medical custody, that means priority clearance. He can only be released to another equivalent medical unit." The woman moved to stand in the way, but the officer in the group held up a data pad. It was marked with command clearance. She threw her hands in the air and stepped to the side as the soldiers at the terminal moved to reopen the main door. Within thirty seconds, the group had entered the room, cleared it, and were already finishing the last touches and moving out.

As the door closed behind them, the soldiers made a formation around him and began making their way through the chaotic halls of the starscraper. Atrium: 447 had been locked down and checkpoints established at all of its entrances. The public transports had been grounded and their passengers were being vetted as they exited. Several military transport ships hovered between the walkways, having already deployed their soldiers. Weyburn was led to one of the docking platforms and rushed into the back of a ship.

Before the ramp had even closed all the way, the transport pulsed upward, making its way up through the tunnels intended for civilian passenger ships. Scarcely a moment later, they entered Airlocks: 500, where all traffic had been momentarily halted. With the same urgent speed, the transport scraped through an airlock and launched into the open sky.

Weyburn unclipped the restraints and pulled in a heavy breath as their speed leveled off. He could feel the tightness of the skin on his chest as he tried to catch a full breath. There was also a rasp to his breathing that had never been there before.

"Officer Weyburn," the commander of the group said with his hand to his helmet, "I am in contact with Ambassador Hoffsted. He requests your report. Was the target eliminated?"

He gave a quick nod at first, though he knew better than to disclose everything. "Kannei is dead, but a sectator escaped with Ambassador Lorège."

The soldier nodded and closed the transmission, looking at the large burn across his chest. "We will drop you off at the *Nemesis Tide* where you will receive medical attention."

"No. If Hoffsted has you following another connection, I cannot slow you down. Just get me some medi-seal."

"You will only slow us down by being here, Weyburn."

"Get me the damned medi-seal!" he shouted.

One of them opened a latch along the wall and tossed him a small tube. Weyburn leaned back in his seat and smeared it under the edges of his half-burnt undersuit. "You will need me to take this sectator down."

"The sectator? He's not the objective."

"If you are going to eliminate a target tied to Kannei, he will be there."

"How?"

"He nearly beat me to Kannei. Plus, the logistician's visor was undamaged; I don't think it will take the Edict long to figure out who we are after next. As for dealing with the sectator, I'm the only one who knows his face."

* * *

Agatha cursed at her visor and the inability to find an available transport. She turned to her daughter. "Maylee, I told you to stay on 448! I told you to stay!"

"Mother, what happened?" With all the UWC military dispersed amongst the security personnel, Maylee was reminded of when the ICC had first taken control of the starscraper. "It's not like I was far away. And you were on the same level! I just wanted to see Ms. Lorège."

"Maylee, that is besides the point." Agatha tapped a fingernail impatiently on the visor and looked around as if the power failure earlier had allowed captive animals to escape from the sanctuary on 217. Even then, pretending that the tigers *had* figured out how to use elevators, Maylee was not sure her mother would be as nervous as she now was.

"Emmen!" Agatha barked into her visor. "Drop everything, get a transport out."

Maylee's father likely tried to console her, which only brought a sharp response. Maylee watched as a large UWC fighter hovered above the landing pads in Airlocks: 500. As far as strategy went, it was a bit much to give the heavily armed soldiers at the checkpoints aerial support. If their intent was to stop a person from leaving, they seemed to think that person had a gunship of their own to escape with.

Maylee tugged at her mother's sleeve. "Where is Jance?"

"Quiet, dear." She kept tapping furiously on the screen. "She made a choice to leave with him. I only have time to look after you and your father."

Agatha gave her a confused look as Maylee reached up and pulled her mother's hand away from the visor. "Mother, stop fidgeting. I don't know what happened, but you are only going to draw attention. If you want us to leave, you have to calm down." Maylee spoke out of experience, as taking part in a reality shard meant masking your actions constantly.

Agatha took a breath and smoothed down her skirt. "Alright. You're right." She touched her hand to her visor, but this time her nervousness looked more like all the others standing on the walkways. After she received a ping, they started toward where a large passenger transport was touching down on a docking platform. UWC personnel motioned for the surrounding people to board as soon as possible. It then hit Maylee that this looked like an evacuation.

They, along with the hundreds of others, were ushered to take seats amongst the many rows. She looked to the screens at the front, but there was no destination displayed. After all the seats had been filled, as well as most of the standing room, the doors were sealed. Out of the large side windows, she could see more of the overpacked three-hundred-passenger vessels touching down or flaring off from the docks.

There was a low rumble and they started to lift up off the platform. It was only then that their destination appeared on the screens.

Maylee stood on her seat to look over the packed crowd. "Secured Orbital Staging Facility: K-4. What is that?"

Her mother slowly covered her mouth in alarm. "They are sending us off planet. To wait out a pending conflict." She held a hand up to her visor and got back in contact with Maylee's father. "Emmen, are you—okay, good. What's your destination? We are K-4."

Maylee tried to listen, but the crowd drowned the conversation out, even with her head basically pressed against her mother's. The UWC forms, barely visible in the distorted view of her mother's visor, looked to be a transfer order. Her father would have to be rerouted from some other staging facility.

"Mother, is this about the power failure? And what happened with Jance?" Maylee asked.

Agatha gave her a very sharp look. "You don't say another word about that."

It was a tone far from what she had ever heard her mother use. If the flat stare was not close enough to a death threat, hearing her mother completely break from her normal composure scared the hell out of Maylee.

* * *

"Just get outside the airlocks!" Avery shouted above the wind rushing past. They had slowed, but the pads on the caretaker suit had been smoking for the last mile of sliding down the starscraper. Jance watched as one of the feet actually started to set off a flame. "I am yelling," Avery continued into his visor, "because we will be there very soon!"

It did not take long until the friction and flames consumed the pad, leaving a shower of sparks trailing above them as they continued the descent. Avery yelled through his visor as they shot down the last half mile. They had already passed the ships pouring out of several airlocks, and for the first time in as long as she could remember, the ocean at the base of the starscraper had her worried. She had always thought of it as something to look at, a backdrop to fly over. As another pad caught fire, the waves foaming under the lowest repulsor engines before the tower continued to the seabed seemed to take on a dauntingly physical presence.

"You are here?" Avery shouted again. "Be more specific!" The engine of the caretaker exosuit roared as he pulled tighter to the wall.

Jance felt multiple times heavier as all the magnetic latches screeched horrendously against the starscraper. After a few seconds, their descent finally stopped, leaving glowing metal and blackened score lines reaching hundreds of feet above them.

Jance looked back as best she could and saw Avery unlatch his harness. "What are you doing?" she yelled, her voice now suddenly echoing back without the drowning noise of scraping steel. Avery stepped out onto one of the arms and held onto the cockpit bars with only one hand.

"I can see you! Fly up!" he yelled just as loudly into his visor. "No, that is what I already told you!"

After a moment, a small hauler flew up beside them. Avery yelled further instructions and the craft turned around to put the loading door up next to the caretaker. When the time finally came, Jance freed herself and climbed on top of the exosuit, trying to not look at the side of the building stretching down into the turbulent water below. The hauler bumped into the caretaker, and the slight jolt caused Jance to latch on tight to the exosuit. It was all she could do to make herself let go enough that Avery could drag her into the back of the transport.

Avery slammed a fist into the control terminal next to the door in his usual manner and the door folded shut. He reached a shaking hand to his visor. "We are in. Go."

For the first time, Jance could hear the voice of whoever Avery had been yelling at as her visor synced with the ship's communications.

"You sure picked a hell of a day, Avery. You wouldn't believe the game I had to walk away from! Two more rounds and I actually would have broken even from the last time I had to help you."

"Shut it, Lance." Avery put his back to the loading door and slid down to the floor. "Can you get us past Gibraltar?"

The pilot of the craft laughed. "I don't know if you have heard yet or not, but now is not the best time to be trying to move between any airspaces. We would have better luck heading straight through Moja Africa."

"Then do it," Avery said.

"Woah, hey," Lance said in protest, "I was joking about that. They are tighter than the SRA. Hell, even the UWC are lax compared to them."

Avery turned Kannei's visor over in his hands several times. "I do not care how you do it. Just get us to the Drake Passage and then to Brabant Island."

"Arctica?" Jance asked.

The craft tilted as they veered off in a different direction. There was a short pause as Lance leveled the craft back out. "We'll have to head over some of the more independent of the ITS. I'm thinking the Arabic States."

"Just get us there."

They flew in silence for some time. Avery had made it clear she should cut any contact to systems beyond the ship. Even so much as searching for anything about the evacuations Lance had described could be traced back. Eventually, Jance had to break the silence.

"What was on Kannei's visor? Why Arctica?"

Avery looked over the thin piece of metal in his hand before tossing it across the floor of the transport to her. She held it up and squinted. It was a manifest of the population of the UWC on Brabant Island; however, access had been restricted when looking for a more detailed report on an Alexander Hale, the lead engineer at the UWC data archives. It took a great deal of strength from Jance to not simply use her own clearance to unlock the data to find out what Kannei had been trying to say.

She sat for a long while, thinking about the thin glowing device resting in her hands. Kannei may have not been the most respected member of the Council—he was even a nuisance on many occasions— but Jance knew she held in her cold and fearful hands a fragment of his last effort. She gripped the visor tight, causing the image to flicker between her fingers.

Instead of feeling crushed by the pursuit of corrupt UWC forces or lost in uncertainty with all the many unanswered questions, Jance felt resolve; she knew she had to bring this to light.

It might weaken the UWC, give the SRA the political edge to disrupt the Mars Contract, or even cause a level of instability around the world not seen for centuries, but she would uncover everything. Then she would bring the threats to her world to an end.

Chapter 8: Silent Paths

Kenneth was astonished, to say the least. A Cryo was an unimaginably valuable find. It was the type of discovery that sparked wars and marked the rise of new orders of power. Cryos were the harbingers of forgotten technologies and valuable historic information that could shift everything they thought they knew. It was a living person from a time before the fall of Earth.

"And that is the truth?" Kenneth asked as he and Kara continued up the slope of the UWC seal. They stepped off onto a hill covered in a wide layer of moss. Vines spiraled up cables hanging from a beam above. "You and the others truly found a Cryo?"

"As far as we can tell, it is alive and still in the pod." Kara pointed to one of the lines hanging down that was covered in leaves of a peculiar blue. It was one of the types of plant life that had either evolved or had been engineered to utilize electricity for various functions. It was a clear sign to watch for live cables. Kara glanced back to Kenneth. "The thaw sequence had a security lock on it. We need you to bypass it."

Kenneth drew in a breath at the enormity of the task. It was one thing to pull wires and switch them around on a riftwalker, but to work on a container where you could not disrupt the contents . . . He rubbed his forehead but nodded a few times. There was always a way. He would just have to see the pod to figure it out.

As they continued though the small grove, he looked up through the thin leaves and the starscraper to the orbiting wreckage above. He had always wondered what that fleet was, and how it came to its destruction. The thought of being able to actually find out was thrilling. "What was the year? Did you look for it?"

"Twenty-nine ninety-four."

Kenneth followed Kara around a patch of blue leaves on the edge of a pool of water. "That date," he said, "should be very close to the fall. I have never seen anything marked from the third millennium."

Kara shone the light off toward the right. "Here we are." The high ridge gave way and the plant life faded into barren sheets of steel. Kara led the way down to where a twisted piece of metal had had been placed over a gap leading deep below. As they continued, he noticed similar additions that had once aided travelers along the way. Kenneth gave a nervous glance around as the path dropped down beneath a large strut, forming a sort of tunnel.

"Stay to the center," Kara advised. The tunnel had an eerie patterned glow from all the lights overgrown with an array of blue-tinted leaves on the walls. Kenneth noticed multiple crates resting along the passage. Just like the lights, they had been added in a time long after the starscraper fell.

Kenneth felt a pull in his chest as a hollow shift sounded in the distance. As his now racing pulse sped his breathing and the hair on his arms prickled upward, the queasy notion of faded memories started pulling him inward. It was underground, and the same echo of shifting steel had come first. He started looking around in panic at the walls, waiting to see which one would cave in on top of the others.

A reverberating screech of sliding metal rang out from behind them. Kara shouted back at Kenneth, but her call was drowned out by the crash of metal dropping from above. Kara switched on her light as a cloud of dust poured into the tunnel. It all matched the edges of the dreams that had pushed him awake so many times in a cold sweat. Kenneth slapped a hand over his nose and clamped his eyes shut. He could feel the hot cloud of debris pushed by the impact rushing past him, pulling at his clothes and even testing his balance.

He then felt Kara grip his shoulder and she pulled him forward. The thick cloud finally settled as they emerged from the tunnel. The first thing he noticed was rough debris covering the path in front of them. He turned and looked up. There was now a new layer of scrap heaped up on top of the strut.

"At least luck is on our side," Kara said from behind.

Kenneth turned back to find her digging through the debris on the ground. Instead of concerning herself with the tons of steel that had landed directly on top of them, she held up a meal pack that had been rusted through even before it fell. Kara ripped the small display off the mealpack, dropped the rest to the side, and continued her search along the path.

Kenneth let out a breath and put his hands on his knees. This place was part of the outerzones he could barely bring himself to remember. Dangerous. Immediate. Few people could truly prepare for the broken road ahead.

When Kenneth finally opened his eyes, he noticed a small square of silvery metal between his feet. Seeing that Kara was still kicking through the scrap, he knelt down and traced it with a finger. The etched lines formed a portrait of a young woman. Moving his finger over some of the finer marks that had not been worn away over the years, he began to realize it must be handmade. Someone at some point in time had carved the image. He took one last look before standing back up, leaving behind the memories of someone else's past in the rubble. He started forward in attempt to keep pace with the tech hunter as she continued her search along the path.

"Take a look at this," she said, tossing something over her shoulder.

Kenneth caught a small crushed piece that resembled some sort of bracelet. He looked it over for a moment to make sure it had none of the characteristics of a weapon. After popping the back slide and looking for damage, Kenneth decided to try turning it on. A touch on the side, a swipe across the face, and multiple combinations he had seen work before were all ineffective.

"There's no tech in this. Just parts to scrap." Kenneth moved to toss it to the side.

Kara glanced over her shoulder. "I thought you could fix anything."

"Of course I can. I just need the right tools, parts, and enough time."

"That had better not be the answer when we get to the Cryo," Kara said.

Kenneth clenched the worthless scrap in his hand. "If somebody would have told me what to be prepared for, maybe I could have been. Tell me this, tech hunter. Why did you not come find me yourself in the Rift Outpost?"

She stopped and turned around. "Do not think that I orchestrated this. I am just trying to make something of the aftermath. I went to the Overlord and told him what we found; he set up a well-equipped expedition team to accompany us, and that was supposed to include you."

Kenneth wiped a hand across his forehead in frustration. "You mean to tell me that instead of going with the Overlord's plan, we are walking through this?" Kenneth motioned to the twisted pillars of shredded metal hanging down around them.

"I never trusted their plan in the first place, and I was right. The Overlord's people are split, and the expedition wouldn't have been different. Oh, and you got yourself captured, so there is that."

She turned and started walking again. Just beneath the scrap metal bridge they were crossing, a small stream of water dropped off into the darkness below. "More than that," she continued, "the three of us were being followed throughout the city ever since we arrived. That is why I sent Randin and Comar out as soon as we met with the Overlord, even though Draken said we had to wait for him and the others."

This time Kenneth stopped. "Draken was to be part of the expedition? When he found me, he practically handed me over to the administrator's people himself!"

Kara scoffed. "When he found you? Draken was the one who was supposed to get you onboard with the whole thing in the first place. He sent the pilot to find you. If he had been working for anyone but the Overlord, you would have never set foot off the docks."

"No, no, no," Kenneth said quickly. He distinctly remembered telling Arlen to set the craft down on a different level than they had planned. "If Draken knows we are after a Cryo, that means the administrators know as well."

She shook her head in disbelief. "Even if it is as you say, Draken does not know where it is. Only three people know where the cryopod is, and two of them are waiting in Kamriek's Grove." She glanced up through the starscraper at the shadows shifting with the moving sun. "And that means we should keep moving."

* * *

Draken tossed the sack Branon had confiscated from the damned technician into the back of the transport. The three waiting soldiers gave each other worried glances as the tracker paced in and out of the expedition craft. One of the technicians onboard simply gave them a smug look. Their departure had been delayed for much longer than anyone had counted on, and that was because they were not only missing Kenneth, but the tech hunters as well.

Draken stepped outside onto the platform once again. He looked across the face of Norclave at the multiple scout crafts taking off. The First Administrator was throwing everything he had into finding the blasted technician, regardless of having the Overlord's approval. Perhaps Silas wagered that the Overlord could no longer do anything about his insurrection. It seemed that despite all his efforts to bring together the history and lost technologies of the Earth, the Overlord had caused his own downfall by not retaining control of a single city.

What would this wild chase for a Cryo even be for if Norclave simply shifted hands? Draken shook his head slowly as he looked out over the city.

If he turned on the Overlord now, it was possible he could still make a deal with Silas by leveraging information about the Cryo. A man like the First Administrator could be persuaded to forgive, especially in exchange for the one thing that could expand his power and influence over the Rift Hills. It might even be under the rule of the new Overlord, Overlord Silas Konrev, that the Kessian Lands and Steel Valley would fall under Norclave control. Hell, if it meant keeping his head, Draken knew he could stretch the pitch to as far south as the Shattered Coast.

Draken let out a small chuckle as the winds pulled at his rough clothes. Silas Konrev to become Overlord of Norclave, Reclaim, Carvanhold, and possibly Bleaktide? After a moment of thought, he mused over simply destroying the Cryo and starving the insufferable man of the chance. He was about to start pacing again when he revisited the idea. If Silas controlled the entire region, it would force any who had not switched loyalties from the old Overlord into the outerzones. To Draken it suddenly became simple: keep Norclave from getting the Cryo and the other cities would be safe havens from Silas's vengeful reach.

Draken turned and entered the transport for the final time. "Get ready for takeoff," he commanded.

"What about the others? The tech hunters?" Sora, one of the Overlord's researchers, asked.

Draken picked up Kenneth's sack from the floor. "When we find them, we find the Cryo."

* * *

The first signs of the dead city of New Solace started to appear along the path as they continued the long walk upward. The settlement was centered atop a debris-covered hill, and as they climbed over a newly shattered section, it became clear that eventually all signs of the city would fade under the rubble.

There was no mistaking the empty feeling to be had in walking through the rows of buildings. They had been hastily abandoned, evidenced by the crates scattered about and the scrapsmithing projects left unfinished along the road. Kara motioned toward the tools covered in several inches of dust. When Kenneth hesitated, looking over his shoulder for the watching eyes that were not there, she moved to the table and stuffed a few things into her bag.

Neither had spoken since they'd entered the lost settlement. Caution was at the forefront of their minds, even in this lifeless place. Something had created the scars in the buildings, and the weapons lying at the edges of discolored patches were last used by the people rubble mites had long since cleaned away. Kara nudged a few scrap blades and worn pistols with her boot before moving on. The weapons under the dust must not have been worth scavenging.

Perhaps what made the scene even more nerve-wracking was the dead silence of the scattered trees sprouting up through the structures. No wind brushed through the pale leaves, nor anywhere in the entire area. Even the dust their boots stirred up hung lazily in the air behind them. Kenneth swore he saw figures in the slow plumes created by their steps.

Kenneth tapped her shoulder and motioned downward. Just in front of them were several sets of footprints following a cross-running road. Kara crouched low and pulled out her knife, causing a wavering red glow as the dust slowly folded around them. At first she looked as if she was ready for someone to jump out at them, but then she suddenly relaxed and held the knife down to the track, using the glow to look at the boot prints. She looked around at the surrounding buildings before rolling her eyes at Kenneth, then turned and set her own boot next to one of the prints. When she pulled away, it was an identical set. Kenneth nodded in understanding. These were the prints from when she and the other two tech hunters had traveled to Norclave.

Even with the only sign of recent life in New Solace being from the tech hunters, Kenneth still kept as sharp of a watch as he could. It was only a little farther when they happened upon a large building rising out of a pocket of trees. It had a gaping hole in its wall, and just in front of the door, dozens of discolored patches and bits of armor were scattered about. This was where a number of people had tried to make a stand to protect the center of New Solace.

Bits of amber-colored points sparkled at the base of the building beneath slots for windows. Something had shattered them out from the inside. Kenneth slowed, and Kara motioned him to hurry on. It seemed this place was getting under her skin as well.

As a deep shadow was cast over the ruins from the shifting sun, it all took on a different tone. Areas became lit by dust-shrouded lights, making the dim outlines and dull illumination the only means of navigating until their eyes adjusted to the dark. Kara did not use her light, though she had never said what she feared it would bring. Instead, they continued on, and if wandering thoughts could be heard, they moved with even more silence than before.

As the path started sloping down, signaling their crossing onto the far side of New Solace, Kenneth was surprised when none of his nervousness faded. Perhaps he had been so certain that something would happen that nearing the end brought a new encroaching fear. His foot slipped an inch forward down a slope, which was enough to send him into a moment of panic. He feared the slightest mishap would cause the situation to finally devolve into sudden violence.

It was only when a pillar of light broke through onto the fading edge of New Solace that Kenneth finally let out a full breath. They waited until they passed the last of the desolate buildings before breaking their silence.

"I told you," Kara finally said, "that there was nothing to worry about."

Kenneth glanced back to the hill behind them. "We can go back if you want, then."

It was at that moment that a wailing call cut through the dead air. Kenneth spun around, trying to pinpoint which direction the chilling noise had come from. Much of their view was obscured by the rising mounds of rubble to either side.

"What was that?" he asked.

He then felt a sharp sting on his neck and slapped at the small humming rubble mite. Kenneth gave it a confused look as the berry-size bug spiraled off and hovered a few feet away.

"I don't know," Kara said, pulling her hood over her head to keep away a mite of her own. "We should keep moving. I do not like being trapped in a pass like this."

They pushed on as more of the pestering insects gathered in the air around them. The narrow gap in the rubble eased out into a wider area; however, they were still surrounded by high ridges along the curving path. Kenneth brushed away at least three more mites biting at his arm, and another that tried at the back of his neck.

"Why are they swarming?" Kenneth asked. He remembered getting bit before on plenty of occasions, but he had often been told that the rubble mites would not start to swarm unless it was for dead flesh.

Kara motioned for Kenneth to stop. "Perhaps they know something we do not."

Another chilling scream made Kenneth's hair stand on end. This time it was closer. The sound echoed around until it faded into a chuckling growl. Kenneth looked to the high ridges that surrounded them, but he could see nothing more than the occasional patch of clinging grass shifting in the wind. It was only when a series of low clicking hums sounded from multiple directions that Kenneth realized that the grass should not be moving. There was no breeze.

He heard a shriek from behind, and the area lit up with a crackling blue. The shriek turned into a clicking gurgle as a creature about the size of his boot fell short of its target, still popping with arcs of electricity. Kara spun and held her weapon ready. The two prongs that stuck out from either side of her closed fist still crackled, casting a blue light on her determined face. She shot another writhing bolt forward, and a dying shriek sounded from a patch of grass.

Kenneth looked at the creature lying dead on the ground. The several long legs still twitched, and the large, fly-like wings slowly shifted the insect back and forth.

"That's a damned big . . . is that a rubble mite?" Kenneth asked, nudging it with his boot. The shape seemed a bit wrong for being the same species. Just as Kenneth was imagining how deep it could sink its powerful jaw pincers into flesh, he felt an explosion of pain in his back. It felt as if someone was pinching a large fold of his skin, but their fingers had not stopped and instead continued on deep into the muscle. He swung a fist around behind his back and felt a thick exoskeleton crack. The creature dropped off and started to fly away, but was met by a searing strike of blue.

There was more skittering from the crevices and grass patches as the other creatures moved away. Kenneth turned around to the twitching insect that had jumped on him and stomped a boot on it. The body of the creature was the size of his sole, and the twitching legs curled up and over the top of his boot. He hurriedly shook it off and tried to reach a hand around to feel at the sharp pain below his shoulder blade.

Kara spun a slow circle, ready to shock anything else that jumped from the rubble. After the rubble mites decided no meal would be given to them by the larger creatures, the swarm started to fade. "How bad are you hurt, Kenneth?" she asked. She let the glow fade from her weapon but still kept a watchful eye out.

"It is not pleasant, I can say that much." The muscles around the area seemed to draw stiffly in, as if forced into a cramp by something in the bite. He grunted and tried to roll his shoulder forward. He was forced to quit, as the contraction was too tight. If he had been bitten by more than one of the creatures, he might very well have been unable to fend any others off.

Kara glanced his way. "Are you bleeding?"

Kenneth raked the back of his hand over the spot, feeling a hot numbness but nothing else. "No blood." A look to his fingers confirmed as much. For as deep as it felt like it had punctured, he was surprised.

"If you can still walk, we had best—"

"I know. Keep moving." At this rate, Kenneth figured he would be missing half of his limbs before they ever found a transport.

* * *

Karzon glared at the second person to walk by their table. While the tech hunter, Mallec, seemed to be enjoying wasting time sitting at the corner table of the bar, Karzon rapped his knuckles on the table in anticipation. To make it even worse, the drink in a place like this was as weak as the timid-footed patrons gossiping about trade and happenings in Norclave. Not a one of them could offer a fight demanding enough to take his mind off the question of why they were still sitting here when Kenneth and that woman had likely left the city by now.

"You look like a fighting hound in a cage," Mallec commented, absentmindedly spinning a small bit of tech on the table. The display screen stretched as it flipped around rapidly. "We'll be on our way soon enough."

Karzon jerked the handle off the small mug and used it to start creating a deep score in the wooden slat of the table. The last place he had spotted Kenneth was in the South Corridors. Now they were sitting in a bar several levels up just outside the Norclave docks, listening to the worried grumblings of merchants talking about the administrators and the Overlord.

"What are we wasting our time here for?" Karzon finally asked. "We should be following Kenneth."

The tech hunter took his time in drawing a slow drink. When he set the cup back down on the table, he gave Karzon a heavy glare. "There is no following Kara, and if the rumors hold any truth, Kenneth is just as elusive when he wants to be. All of Norclave is still searching, and they have found nothing *after* he already escaped them once. We wouldn't have a chance."

"Then what?"

"Draken, the tracker. I was in the trade center when he pulled Kenneth out of the transport. He happened to pick up a sack that belonged to Kenneth. In that sack is a pair of gloves that belonged to me." Mallec gripped the piece of tech and shifted it to the center of the table. The display shifted from blue to orange as the marker alert sounded. In the distance, they could hear the rumble of another transport lifting off. "Something tells me that Kenneth will be reunited with my tech soon enough. We track the gloves, trail the tracker, and follow him and Kara to whatever tech is important enough to send Norclave into chaos."

Karzon thought it all over for a bit. "And then what? After we find the tech, what happens?"

Mallec took a final drink, stood up from the table, and surveyed the room. "You level your debt with the technician. That was the deal."

Karzon set the handle down next to the wood dust and the heavy furrow he had made. He looked up to the tech hunter. "What do you get out of it all?"

Mallec clipped the device on to his wrist and shot Karzon a glance. "I sell Norclave to the highest bidder."

* * *

As Kara and Kenneth neared the towering north face of the starscraper, a gentle wind picked up. It brushed across them at odd angles, spreading amongst the chaotic walls of steel to pull at the thin grass sprouting beside a small stream. The murky, rubble-lined flow appeared from under a large mound off to their east and meandered along a haphazard path until disappearing into a cluster of sickly trees farther to the northeast. Oftentimes, life was not only difficult for the humans scratching out a living beyond the cities, but for anything else trying to survive off the land as well.

"Have you ever traveled to Kamriek's Grove?" Kara asked. She held a hand to her wrist and shone a light forward. Hundreds of scattered orange reflections flickered amongst the rubble. Even if the looming edge of the starscraper was not enough, the shards of wraith steel were a clear sign that they were close to the mines of Kamriek's Grove.

Kenneth shook his head. Of course he had heard about it; the mines were nearly as valuable to Norclave as the energy wells of the Rift Outpost. Starscraper glass, or wraith steel, as it was often called, was a special kind of glass made to be nearly as strong as steel and laced with solar-absorption particles. Kamriek's Grove was situated near where a massive amount of the material had been deposited during the fall.

Kara pointed into the tangled wall of the starscraper. "There should be a passage through there, not far ahead."

Kenneth had to strain his neck to look up at where the jagged layers of the interior clung along the massive curve of the wall now towering over them.

As the New Solace pathway faded into mounds of fresh rubble, Kara veered off, now guided by memory. The pass she'd pointed out was little more than the crinkled underside of a walkway, arching over some of the larger gaps in the titanic structure. The uneven slopes of the upturned walkway were not fastened to the massive pipes it snaked between; it simply rested where it had fallen. Kara continued, shining her light into the nearly complete darkness in front of her. She only stopped once to shine it back on a split in the walkway for Kenneth.

The daylight finally started to seep in from the other side, and eventually the passage opened up, giving them a grand view of the impact valley.

Other large buildings jutted up into the horizon at the edges of the forest, and in the distance beyond was a clear view of the band of orbiting wreckage. Off to their right, a section of the view was distorted by a glimmering, translucent spire of wraith steel sticking up nearly ten feet out of the ground. Kara walked toward it and used a hand to wipe away the dust. From the transparent side of the wraith steel, Kenneth could only faintly see the lattice grid buried within the glass. When he walked to the other side and looked into the reflective surface, the deep-set lines of the solar absorption grid were easy to spot. However, he could only see the faintest shadow of Kara standing behind the glossy amber layer.

Kenneth turned and looked out along the slope of the hill. Dozens of similar shards jutted up from the ground, either reflecting a soft amber glow onto the areas in front of them or distorting the images of what lay behind, depending on their orientation. Around a few of them were mats of vines that consumed the electricity the shards produced.

He rolled his shoulder and twisted his torso, trying to work out the tightened muscles. Farther along the hill was the settlement of Kamriek's Grove. The buildings of the lower portion of the settlement were nestled between large sections of wraith steel arcing up out of the ground, while nearer to the starscraper the rest of the settlement's structures rose up the sheer face of the metal cliffs like a trail of clinging fungi. Even from where he and Kara stood, they could hear the noise from the mines. The workers would be gathering the glass and dividing it into small enough chunks to ship, with most of it going to Reclaim.

Above the starscraper, a transport flared its engines to slow its descent into the city. Kara cursed, seeing the clear markings of Norclave on the side of the craft. They watched as two more Norclave vessels appeared high above them.

"The others are waiting for us in the city," Kara said. "How many do those transports hold?"

"Ten seats a piece, not counting the ones up front." Kenneth watched as the vessels started down into the city.

Kara shook her head and started forward. Kenneth rolled his shoulder, trying to get the muscles around the bite working again. There was something unnerving to him about walking into a city that they just saw reinforced by Norclave soldiers. Not that he expected anything less in following Kara, of course. After all, they had just walked through the center of the starscraper.

As they weaved their way through the standing shards of wraith steel, Kenneth got a better look at the city. There were several large, partially buried sections of the starscraper's glass windows stretching hundreds of feet throughout the lower section of the settlement. Thick cables ran between the tightly packed container houses and other scrapped-together buildings, all pulling power from the wraith steel. In the center of it all was a crashed cargo hauler, nearly ten times the size of any of the other buildings and reaching higher than all but the tallest of the shards.

After spending so much time in Norclave, where every person was checked before they entered the city, it was an odd feeling as they simply walked in. Streets of packed dirt snaked through Kamriek's Grove, worn down to the concrete and steel underneath in most places. Most of the paths were wide enough to drive a scraphauler over, and a surprising number had nothing but clear sky above. Kenneth watched as another transport's repulsor engines popped into full power to slow its descent. This one was marked with the blue triangle of the Steel Valley and had the look of a civilian cargo hauler.

"Look!" a girl from the side said to a young boy who must have been her brother, "a tech hunter!"

Before Kara could think of how to cover their tracks—hopefully not like she had back in the nameless bar—the two children ran off down the street. They passed by a number of people going about their business, a few even carrying fresh food supplies.

"You look new to Kamriek," a man said as they passed by. He was wearing pieces of flight armor ground down to where all but the thickest of rusted patches had the shine of renewed metal. One arm had a brace on it lined with power cells and a rail of magnets. The shoulder piece, made out of a chunk of starscraper glass, marked him as a mercenary hired by the mines. "There is a medical post up on the hill if you need that limp looked at."

Until now, Kenneth had not noticed that the muscles tighting themselves in his back were causing him to walk leaned to one side. "I think I'll be fine, but thanks anyway."

There was a loud crash to the side as the two kids knocked over a pile of crates. The mercenary barked at them to settle down as they rushed off down another street.

Kara gave a small nod to the side and they started back into the city. Kenneth glanced back to see the man helping to pile the crates back up. This place was nothing like Norclave, to say the least.

"Keep a watch out for any Norclave soldiers," Kara whispered to Kenneth as they passed under a wide glass arch that served as a bridge for an upper level of the city leaning back toward the starscraper. A second mercenary of the mines was passing by overhead, though the man would have been unable to see them as more than shaped blurs through the reflective surface underneath his feet.

They were steadily nearing one of the large divides in the town made by a sweeping shard of starscraper glass. Without asking for directions to be sure, he could only guess that the roadway they were on would snake through the town between the blocks of wraith steel and clumps of buildings until it ultimately reached the large vessel in the center.

Kenneth felt a tug on his arm and turned to see Kara disappearing down a side path. He glanced forward to see soldiers wearing red stripes ahead on the road setting up a checkpoint. The Norclave soldiers were stacking crates and panels to make a partial block in the road. It did not look as if they were paying any attention to the people moving past, but it was clear Kara did not want to take that chance. He turned and followed the disappearing end of her cloak as she rounded a second corner.

When Kenneth finally caught up, he was not surprised to find her climbing the side of a building.

"You expect me to be able to get up there?" Kenneth asked, gritting his teeth and pulling his shoulder to remind her of the bite he had suffered.

Kara pulled herself up the edge and looked back at Kenneth with a smirk. "If you had been watching your own back instead of ogling my tech like a falling piece of the orbital wreckage, you never would have got bit."

"Ogling?" Kenneth laughed. "If I had been that distracted by looking at you, it wouldn't have been your tech that I—"

"Just wait here," she interrupted with a roll of her eyes. "I'll find us another way around." At that, Kara disappeared over the edge and into the second level of the city. Kenneth shook his head and took a seat next to the wall. It might have been simple enough to find another street, but Kenneth had the suspicion that her answer to everything was to disappear into a back alley and start climbing. He pulled the small wrist display out of a pocket and popped the back off once again while he waited.

Kenneth took the pieces out the best he could with nothing more than his fingers to work with. He examined each part with an experienced eye and missed the footsteps entering the alley.

"Where is the other one?"

Kenneth looked up to see that the mercenary they spoke to earlier had followed them down the side pass. The man walked with a stance ready for a fight, and he held a hand to his forearm, ready to flip the magnets and launch whatever bit of metal he had loaded out like a bullet if need be. He eyed the tops of the surrounding buildings as he edged toward Kenneth. "You wouldn't know anything about the sudden appearance of soldiers from Norclave, would you?"

Kenneth made one last adjustment on the device and clicked it back together. A new pip of light appeared on the side.

"They are setting up blockades in all the major chokepoints in the city," the mercenary continued. "I asked myself what they could be hunting," the man said, sending a sudden glance to the top of another of the buildings. "Criminals, traitors, it could be anyone."

"I suppose it could," Kenneth said. He flicked a finger over the device and a small screen popped up, though it was too distorted to make out any of the information.

The pieces of the mercenary's armor shifted as he quickly turned from scanning the skyline to see what Kenneth was doing. "But then I saw you turn away from the Norclave soldiers. Where is the tech hunter?"

Kenneth set the device to the side. He wasn't sure if he could adjust the display further anyway. "If this is about not stopping to talk, I can apologize."

The man gave Kenneth a stiff look. "We could go talk with those soldiers if you like."

Kenneth ran a hand through his hair. "You mean to tell me that you start harassing people *before* you find out what they are here for?"

"Get up." The mercenary leveled the rail on his arm toward Kenneth.

Kenneth pushed himself up with a grunt and started walking. He gave a quick glance to the weapon the man had before he was pushed out of the alley.

"Why are you really in Kamriek's Grove?" the man asked, putting a hard, gloved grip on Kenneth's shoulder and forcing him forward.

Kenneth simply let out a sigh. "The usual, it seems. Now if I may ask, what is it you think I have done?"

"Does it matter? All I have to do is run you past the Norclave checkpoint. If they recognize you, good, if not, we go to the containers and see what we can find out about your dealings with the tech hunters."

"You know," Kenneth started, looking back as far as his tight muscles and the hand shoving him forward allowed, "if I did have a bounty—not saying that I do, of course—but if I did, there wouldn't be much of a reward for you for turning me over to Norclave."

"You just keep talking," the man said, making it clear he could not be persuaded.

Kenneth shrugged, then winced at the pain in his shoulder. "Nobody would ever know it was you that found me. No reason to pay for that. So let me ask you: Why are you doing this? Suspicion and goodwill?"

"I get my fair pay from the mines."

Kenneth scoffed. "And how would it be fair pay if those jokers got the reward?" He gestured ahead to where the soldiers gave no mind to the passing people and instead were welding their barricade of scrap together. When the man did not hesitate, Kenneth decided to adopt another strategy. "To be honest," Kenneth continued, "it's just like this city to bend over backward to serve Norclave and get nothing in return. Did they even ask if they could move in and start setting up barricades?

Just before they drew the attention of the soldiers, with one last shove the man released his grip on Kenneth's shoulder. As they passed through the checkpoint, they received little more than a second glance.

"There is your one favor," the mercenary said to Kenneth on the other side before slapping a hand on his shoulder. "Now tell me why you were so eager to avoid Norclave for the sake of Kamriek."

Kenneth gave the man the smirk that Karzon and so many others had learned to hate. Recently at the Rift Outpost, Kenneth had heard a merchant from Kamriek's Grove complaining, giving him the perfect ammunition. "After months of the administrators stealing from the mines, I decided to finally demand the price the wraith steel is really worth. But leave it to Norclave to keep prices down by hunting merchants like myself."

There was the slightest pause in the mercenary's step as he took in what Kenneth had said.

Kenneth offered a hand over his shoulder in introduction. "Name's Tomman. Glad to have your help."

The mercenary ignored the hand and continued pushing him along. "Iren. Mercenary for the Nuand family. And we will just have to see about that story of yours."

* * *

Arlen waited in front of the heavy door of the First Administrator's office. He honestly had no idea what to expect. Something was odd, simply based off the casual actions of the soldiers in the hall. One leaned next to the doorway, watching another pair sitting at a small table playing a game of dice. If he was walking into a meeting that would end with the Cells, this was not how he'd expected it to start.

As one soldier laughed and the other started to hand over a few coins, the door to the First Administrator's office slid open. Arlen could now clearly hear angry voices from inside, and though their argument sounded far from its end, the soldier leaning next to the door motioned for Arlen to enter.

He stepped in and was directed to a seat in the corner. The First Administrator sat stiffly behind his desk and was speaking with an old man who leaned to one side in the chair. Arlen glanced to the side, where a pair of thick-armed men looked as if they wanted to be outside gambling with the Norclave soldiers. Arlen recognized them as the hired strong-arms of the merchant Kenneth had spoken with.

"The Overlord left my business alone, and you know that," Mackelry said.

"What exactly is your business, Mr. Norton?" the First Administrator pried. "I was always curious."

"That, Silas, is what he did not ask about." Mackelry leaned forward and spoke softly, though in the quiet room Arlen could still make it out. "Our unspoken agreement was that he need not look too hard, and that I do nothing to make any of you start with these questions."

"But why? It seems that you are practically stealing from Norclave with this deal."

The merchant let out a cackle and flopped back in his chair. "Silas, I understand you are looking to be the big shot around here; however, if you think you're just going to step into the Overlord's shoes and take control, you are making the mistake of believing that he had control in the first place." He tapped his bony fingers on the armrest. "Let me spell it out for you. Norclave has laws, and it has exceptions. The laws are what keep the common man safe and the good trades pouring in, and the exceptions are what give the city the power to keep the laws."

"It is no stretch of the imagination to believe you are a man of many exceptions of the law," Silas said.

Mackelry bowed his head. "Do not discount my reputable business as well. I live on both sides, and that is why the Overlord trusted me to understand. If you do not allow me my exceptions, backwater business will eventually leak out somewhere without your knowledge or permission."

"Your point being?"

Mackelry stood up and pointed a crooked finger at the man. "What starts as a leak can end up as a break in the pipe. And when there is unfavorable trade running rampant on the streets without your control, fear of Norclave law will wane. That is when the supply of meal packs, and wraith steel, and even scrap for the common smith start getting siphoned away by thieves."

Silas nodded for a moment as he thought. "And why is it that only you can save the city? Mr. Norton, keep in mind that you tried to skirt around a part of the law not given to my exception once already. You bribed the transport pilots that attempted to smuggle the technician out of the city." Silas stood up and motioned to his soldier by the door, calling the meeting to an end. "I will weigh your offer, but you must tread lightly if you wish to continue to be prosperous through the transition, Mr. Norton."

Mackelry turned and stomped out of the room, followed by his two large guards. The First Administrator sat back in his seat. He motioned for the soldier to leave, and only once the door was fully closed did he address Arlen.

"I was told you had a meeting with the tracker." Silas skimmed through the reports on his data pad. "I'll not ask what it was about; you have already proven able to dance around the truth."

Arlen kept his head down and said nothing in reply.

Silas sighed and slid the data pad to the side. He folded his hands together and leveled his gaze at Arlen. "I expected this silence. Draken's secretive meeting with you and his sudden disappearance mark him clearly as the Overlord's connection. But that puts you in a tough situation, doesn't it?"

Arlen scratched at the irritated prickles around his hairline as the room began to feel oppressively hot.

"You clearly suggested one of my men, Terrus, was your informant and the Overlord's man."

Arlen felt the blood drain from his face and cold wrap around his hands. The First Administrator knew he had lied. That could only mean one thing.

Silas stood up and leaned on the desk. "I had him disappear anyway."

Arlen looked up at the First Administrator. "Why?"

"Two failures in one day? The day I begin to claim control of Norclave?" Silas moved to the side and unclipped the visor from its spot over his temple. He stared at one of the blank walls of his office and flipped the thin metal between his fingers. "There must be no questions about my ability from the other administrators. My rise is due to the lack of control the Overlord has exerted over Norclave and the Rift Hills. It would be suicide for me to make the same mistake. Thus, he is my example of what happens to those who do not follow, no matter their influence. As you can see, even those in control of the majority of the black trade in Norclave come scraping to my feet, firm in their belief that I am already the Overlord."

He clipped the visor back on and drew in a breath. "I suppose that leaves you wondering where you will come to stand." He sent a sly glance Arlen's way. "As far as the others are concerned, you told me who the informant was. Your wrongdoing only comes from being a pawn caught in the influence of the Overlord himself. I know differently, but that is why we must come to terms."

"Whatever you need," Arlen said. He was visibly shaking, but if there was any chance of hope, he would take it.

"Draken knows where Kenneth is heading, and you were the last one to speak with Draken." Silas moved around and took his seat again. "I know he will have given you orders to keep up a misdirection, otherwise he would have found a way to permanently silence you. Is this true?"

Arlen slowly nodded. "He gave me this." Arlen fished in his pocket and produced the small data device. "It claims Kenneth is heading to Reclaim."

Silas took the flat square and shifted the information to his visor. "If not the Steel Valley, then . . ." Silas trailed off as he read the false plans. His expression changed, and the corner of his mouth twitched up. "One wrong step, and I have you, Kenneth."

Chapter 9: Infinity

"As thousands of transports packed with UWC civilians now arrive at the orbital staging facilities across the world, tensions between the global orders are on the rise. These images are from just outside the OSF in K-4."

Maylee slid a bit farther down into the seat next to her mother, away from the main crowds being ushered into the orbital ships. She watched a scenario very similar to what was on the display happen outside the large window overlooking the transport docks. Hundreds of ships flew through the sky in a massive effort to bring the civilian population to the staging facilities, though she was still confused about why.

"Following allegations regarding the murder of one UWC Council member and the disappearance of another, the SRA has entered the preparation stages for an internal discussion of possible reprimands or hostile actions toward the UWC." The display switched feeds and Maylee noticed the same pair of transports shown were landing just outside.

"A statement from the military ambassador points to a possible SRA connection, contrary to the initial reports of a Last Edict attack in Sector: K."

Maylee pulled herself up in the seat. She nervously bounced her legs, not needing to ask her mother to confirm that it was Ms. Lorège that had been taken. Even still, she glanced to the side for just a moment to see her mother looking forward with a pale face.

"A statement from Admiral Brakka has confirmed a UWC military presence within ITS airspace in the search for the missing UWC Council member."

Maylee touched a finger to her visor and pulled up additional information relating to the transmission. Brakka was in command of the *Nemesis Tide*, a ship she had seen before. She heard it was the real-world equivalent of the *ICC Carosa*, the capital ship that had begun the takeover of her starscraper the year before. It was actually surreal how that week in the reality shard mirrored what was happening now.

"While the UWC's search may be seen as hostile to the other world orders, Chancellor Liberty Malcom continues to push for bringing back the people's ambassador by any means necessary. Resistance to the Chancellor's call to action was shown by Director Klemmeth Auburns in his attempts to evoke caution with a statement before his orders at an unprecedented second emergency meeting in the Council Chambers today. As we can see with the boarding of the Orbital Armistice Fleet, caution is at the forefront of UWC operations. No information is available at this time on whether the fleet has been issued a time of departure."

Maylee looked around at the worried faces in the observation wing. It was a gathering of nervous and frightened individuals, replicated again and again on the floors above and below where they sat. The woman standing at the edge of the railing next to the observation window had been there long before Maylee and her mother had arrived. Another elderly man held his hat in shaking hands while he looked around for his family, who had yet to arrive.

Maylee and her mother were both tense as they waited for her father to be cleared for transport to them, to Orbital Staging Facility: K-4. She looked behind her, where a similar window gave a view of the inside of the massive, circular building. She pulled up the overlay of her visor and looked out across the sections. There were hundreds of observation and docking areas visible in the circumference of the five-mile-wide staging facility. In the center of the ring-shaped structure was the main ship, over three miles long, along with its support craft.

In essence, it was an evacuation of the planet for the duration of the tension between the world orders. If there was a war, they would be forced to helplessly watch the destruction from the safety of the edge of space.

She stood up, walked over to the interior window, and watched as ground shuttles hurried back and forth to the massive ships. Even the smaller ones were a half-mile long and capable of temporarily holding millions. The largest ship, showing on her visor as the *Solstice Dawn*, emitted a slowly building glow from beneath it. When Maylee reached out and gripped a seat tightly to watch, she could almost feel the vibrations from the colossal ship feeding through the superstructure.

"When are we leaving?" she asked her mother. "How much time do we have?"

Agatha let out a sigh and looked over her shoulder to watch some of the smaller transport ships in the distance lifting up above the line of the cityscape. "I don't know." She rubbed a hand on Maylee's back to reassure both of them. "We will get him transferred. Or we will sit on the edge of the planet, several ships away from him, and see him when we return."

Maylee turned and leaned into her mother's shoulder. There was nothing to do but watch the incoming transports, just the same as the many other worried souls all around them.

* * *

"This is madness, Hoffsted, all of it!"

"Calm yourself, Director Auburns," Ambassador Hoffsted said in an attempt to placate the director. "This meeting has become necessary. Just looking at the news reports shows us that."

Klemmeth Auburns drummed his fingers on the wide table. "And what will the world see of this? Right here—me, you, and Chancellor Malcom—sit in perhaps the only secretive meeting between the highest UWC officials in two hundred years. What will they think?"

The chancellor, Liberty Malcom, folded her wrinkled hands together and set them on the clear surface of the table. "Director Auburns, recent events have dictated the necessity of our convening. The quicker we can come to a conclusion, the fewer assumptions will be made, both by the civilians of the UWC and the other world orders."

"They already prepare for war, I can guarantee you that," Auburns said, stopping the nervous dance of his hands on the table. "Your demand, Hoffsted, that Representative Weijing not be admitted to this room saw to that."

The military ambassador gave a combative smirk. "And what of the Orbital Armistice Fleet? You called for their departure, Director Auburns. Surely that calls for war just the same."

"The evacuation is not a militant action," Auburns stated. "The SRA has been clearly informed of that on numerous occasions. It is based on clearly outlined protocol that the appointed director must order the temporary evacuation of as much of the civilian population as is possible in the case of possible intentions to discuss hostilities."

"And here we are." Hoffsted slowly moved around the table. "Possibilities of war. I need not state that the SRA will look for any way to muscle into the Mars Contract. To assure the future of humanity, the system must not be compromised by irresponsible outside sources."

Auburns scoffed. "Then open discussions on how to grant them access. None of this would have happened if we had not been using the excuse of the Last Edict attacks to blockade the SRA from Mars. Not only are we monopolizing interplanetary expansion, we are accusing them of organizing the terrorist attacks that continue to block them from it." He gave the military ambassador a hard look, knowing where this conversation was likely to lead.

"And should we not accuse them?" Chancellor Malcom stood up from her seat. "May I remind you that one of our own was murdered by the Last Edict, and another currently is their hostage?"

Auburns looked down at the table. Avery Thorne was supposed to take Kannei and transport him to safety somewhere. Somehow, Kannei had ended up dead and the ambassador taken in his place. He could not say if the reports on how the events unfolded were accurate, but there was no way to contact the sectator to find out.

Chancellor Malcom continued, "I vote we remove Ambassador Lorège's security clearance."

Auburns shook his head. "We cannot do that. The only way to find her is when she accesses her Council clearance."

"She has yet to make contact," the chancellor said, motioning to a data pad in front of her on the desk, "so it is safe to assume the Last Edict has control of her, and in turn, her clearance."

"We only need one activation to know her location," Auburns argued.

Malcom leaned forward with a scowl. "And they only need one activation to cause untold chaos. That is not something we can afford while on the brink of war."

"The Last Edict seems to be effective even without it," Auburns bit back. After all, they had been in contact with him, one of the heads of the UWC, for months. He turned to the military ambassador. "How would our movements into ITS airspace be seen if they found out we had discarded the best chance of finding her? If you cancel her clearance now, you have to pull back the search from their territories or risk infuriating another major portion of the planet."

"Pulling back is not an option," Malcom said.

Hoffsted nodded slowly. "We must wait until we know where she is being held to strip her Council privileges. Or until the Orbital

Armistice Fleet is in the skies. We must wait until it is safe enough to back up our threats of war."

* * *

As the transport rumbled through the turbulent air over the South Atlantic, Jance wrapped her arms around herself and pulled her feet up into the seat to fight against the cold air. For hours, they had been listening to the news reports in silence. Everything pointed to a rapid global escalation of hostilities, much of it propelled by her own disappearance.

"Lance," Avery called over the comms to the pilot, "how much farther do we have yet?" He rubbed his reddened hands together and looked toward the front of the small craft.

"Oh, it's beautiful. The ice walls are coming into view just now. I'll send it back to you." A small display lit up with the frigid blues of the polar south. Lance pulled the craft low above the sharp waves of the Drake Passage. In the distance, massive walls of ice jutted out above the turbulent ocean. They had been set to grow under the careful watch of Solstice Consolidated for hundreds of years to help normalize the planet's climate. As they neared, Jance could make out the hundreds of observation beacons blinking on the high edges of the cliffs.

"Welcome to Arctica," Lance said. "Home of the great forgotten experiment of the UWC."

A small city stretched out over the inland ice of Brabant Island. It was home to the Drake Discovery Mission, a scientific endeavor of Outreach Systems. They had used the extreme environment as a test ground for the colonization of the hostile red planet. But after hundred years of research—which eventually resulted in the establishment of a successful sister colony on Mars—the Drake Discovery Mission was abandoned to the ice and winds of the Antarctic.

Her teeth clicked together as the ice-covered towers grew larger. They were built in an older, simple style, much like the wide-ranging continental cities, and the largest building was only a fraction of the size of a starscraper. The patterned glow of exterior lights between support struts continued far down, even illuminating the ice that had built up high along the steel base. The lit passages running between the buildings looked like spiderwebs buried under the ice. At least, that is how her sister, an intercontinental reserves agent, would have described it.

"Do we have clearance to enter the city?" Jance asked, her breath fogging out in front of her.

"Don't you worry," the pilot said. "I've been here a few times. Know the perfect way in. Back entrance, if you will."

Jance did not like the sound of that, but if it meant keeping her from freezing to the seats of the transport, she was willing to go along for the ride. Lance flew past the main docking rings of the city and made for a low building on the far side, where the walls of ice had pushed up hard enough to break through the steel many years ago. He slowly approached the opening between the ice and the structure. Jance felt the harness bite into her nearly frozen skin as the ship jerked around twisted supports and ice-covered cables. She heard a creaking as he touched down next to a few ramshackle transports. A few had already been consumed by the weather.

"You might want to take a breath," Avery advised. "No telling how cold it is out there."

Jance stood up, feeling a brittleness in her bones. There was a pounding on the back and Lance shouted through the door.

"Ready in there?"

Avery pulled a hand from under his arm and waved it over the door control. They were met by an immediate swell of cold air circulated by the lowering ramp. Even though they could hear the wind howling above, it was a stagnant freezing down between the walls of ice and the twisted sheets of metal.

"Get them coats," Lance called out, breath billowing through the cloth on his face. His command echoed under the distant howl of the wind.

Jance immediately noticed that Lance stood a full head taller than her and the other two people walking up to the craft. They were all bundled up in full suits to protect against the cold, and they held out spares for both her and Avery. It took no convincing to get Jance to pull her arms through the heated carbon-laced environmental suit. Though she could not work her hands enough to get it to seal properly, it was enough to keep her walking as they crossed the hidden landing port.

The door, which was not originally an exterior entrance, swung open and the group made their way in. Jance leaned against the wall and began to pull breaths of air into her stiff lungs. Even if it was still cold air, the contrast was enough to make it feel like the heat of a repulsor.

"Let me help you with that, dear," a woman said, her voice coming from an external speaker on her facemask. She slid her mask up and folded back the gloves before starting to work on Jance's suit. The woman had dark eyes and a smooth tone to her skin, as well as a welcoming smile. A few presses of the display on Jance's suit adjusted the fit of the heavy cloth and started a heating sequence. "No sense in you freezing now that you're inside." She moved to help Avery, but he waved her off.

"Lance Gyven?" the woman asked, continuing down the line. "Is that you? Take that silly thing off your head so I can see."

"Leave him alone, Feyn. The message said this was business," the other suited man said.

She still gave the pilot a twinkling glance and smile when he took off the wrap. She took it and started winding it around his hands to warm them up. "Don't get anxious, Welnn," she replied, "I've seen the news, same as you. But not every moment has to be for the Edict."

"Come," the somber man said with a motion over his shoulder as he started walking.

Jance noticed that Lance gave Feyn a wink and Avery a nod before turning to go back out into the frigid waste.

"He'll keep the transport ready," Avery explained to Jance as he motioned for her to follow the other two.

"Who are they, Avery?" Jance asked.

"Sectators, contacts, old friends. This is about the only place where someone can go to truly hide and still technically be within the UWC." Jance pulled her arms tight to herself with a shiver and started walking close beside Avery. As they started to catch up with the other two, Avery added in a lower tone, "While here, I recommend you stick with me and trust nobody but these two."

The hallway soon opened up into what Jance imagined a slum might be like. Even the topmost floors of the starscrapers were neatly organized in comparison to the chaotic array of crates and makeshift housing in the wide cargo storage area. There were even a few fires lit to help against the intermittent cold of fluctuating life-support systems.

They moved along the edge of the room, through a door, and down another hall, stopping at a door at the end. Welnn produced a card and passed it in front of the latch on the door. Jance looked for a moment at the aged technology before she was ushered in. The room was a smaller storage area that had been repurposed into a living pod. By the way Feyn leaned back on the loose covers of one of the beds, Jance knew it was where she and Welnn lived.

"Avery," Welnn said, pulling off the helmet of his suit to reveal oddly pale skin, a wide nose, and many small scars, "it has been a long time."

"Ah ah!" Feyn teased. "No time to start that, you said business!"

Avery's expression hardly changed. "If you insist. I need your help. We," he said, glancing at Jance, "need your help."

"Are you really the ambassador?" Feyn asked, tossing a small curled wire ball between her hands. "A member of the UWC Council?"

Jance glanced to the floor before answering the woman. "Yes, but for how long I can't say. My clearance has yet to be revoked, but it will happen. I know there is no going back."

"Council clearance?" Welnn said in surprise. "Avery, that is what many of us were after. Think of what the Last Edict could do—"

He was cut off by a ball of wire bouncing from the side of his head. Feyn gave him a scolding look and quickly turned a caring gaze to Jance. "It's not all over. The reports everywhere say you have been abducted by, well . . . by us. I'm sure that we could get you back with plenty of time to spare."

"The only way I am going back," Jance said with a furious quiver in her voice, "is if I have the information I need."

"And how do you plan to do that?" Welnn asked. "What is it you think you will find here?"

"Alexander Hale," Avery said. "There is something in the old data archives Kannei was after. Hale is the one who manages them."

"Ah, so you need to break into the rest of the city complex." Welnn reached behind him, opened a small box, and pulled out a pistol. It was covered in wires in an obvious attempt to override the mandatory remote activation. Something told Jance—and it might have been the menacing chuckle—that it was functional.

"We can help you get wherever you need."

* * *

High in the central tower of the Drake Discovery Complex, the director of the facility looked out over the icebound city and the surrounding polar wasteland. There was a serene beauty in looking out at what could truly be called the edge of the Earth.

"Sir?" his second in command asked. The director did not turn from gazing into the endless desolation to address the assistant director. The only thing visible beyond it were the glowing points from the

Solstice Consolidated monitoring probes. "Mr. Rulari," she insisted, "Observation sent me with the details of an unidentified craft landing in the decommissioned area."

"Yes, yes," the director said absentmindedly. "I saw it. Just another lost soul wandering the edge, no doubt." Looking out was a semblance of the same feeling he had often dreamt of having, of standing at the edge of the solar system and knowing there was nothing beyond for an eternity. Perhaps, one day, he could go to the Mars colonies and look out into the oblivion.

"But, Mr. Rulari, sir, we were told to be on heightened alert."

"What for, Ralena?" the director asked, rolling his hand slowly against the backdrop of endless tides of ice.

She sighed and continued with all the reserved temperament she could muster. "The ambassador. The one captured by the Last Edict. Based on various readings, Observation is concerned she might actually be here."

The director spun on his heel and turned his blank stare on her. He blinked a few times and seemed to drift back to reality. "Send a ground team in. I want reports of their progress, and alert me of any transports leaving from the docks or the decommissioned section."

Ralena pulled in a breath, relieved to get actual orders from the man. "Shall I alert the UWC?"

The director shook his head. "I will take care of that. Just begin the search."

He watched until the woman left before he waved a hand to secure the lock on the heavy door. Only after moving back into the room and stopping next to the permanent ice sculpture did the director put a finger to his visor. The display flickered for a moment as it cycled through the encryption sequence.

Before the connection with the Council completed, he pulled the visor free. He watched as it pulsed off, severing the connection. "Perhaps," he said quietly to himself, tapping the thin wire against his lips.

Rulari clasped the visor behind his back and slowly made his way back to the window. He had been refused admittance to the Mars colony by EMA-GO, even though they'd offered no explanation as to why. His only hope of experiencing the expansion of humanity firsthand was if the UWC could be forced to dismantle their needless regulations and prejudice. Perhaps misplacing one of their Council members would be enough to cause the other world orders to finally stand up and intervene. To force the UWC to break the exclusivity of the Mars Contract.

He moved a finger gently over the thin layers of sculpted ice and sighed. The artwork had been given to Outreach Systems as a gift from Solstice Consolidated at the start of the Drake Discovery Mission, and had sat in this very room for hundreds of years. Both companies had known full well at the time that the scientific test was nothing more than a demonstration to the governments of the world. The goal had always been to secure a contract for the eventual colonization of Mars. Director Rulari watched as the heat from his finger caused a droplet of water to slide down the intricate, flowing edges of the sculpture.

Movement, after centuries of stillness. Rulari kept that thought circling the edge of his mind as he moved back to the large window, resuming his watch into the precipice of infinity.

Chapter 10: Tech Hunters

Kara moved quickly behind the buildings built on the ledge of the starscraper glass. A quick look at the outside of Kamriek's Grove had fooled her. Instead of an unplanned array of houses around the crashed transport and the huge shards of wraith steel, the town was designed to where access into the center of the city was limited to only a few key roads, all of which were now blocked by Norclave soldiers.

Kara ran across the roof of a building below to cut over to another section and, not for the first time since Draken had suggested they wait for the technician, wondered if it was even worth it to drag Kenneth along. All the risks they'd taken would be wasted if he could not get the Cryo out, and the only way she and the other tech hunters would come out ahead was if everything went perfectly.

But it had already been a disaster since the start.

Kara walked for a while, passing by a few mercenaries with their bits of flight armor ground down to a rough shine. When Kara finally returned to where she left the technician, she felt a tingle on the back of her neck. He was nowhere to be seen.

Kara dropped down and spun a frantic circle. The ground here had not yet been worn to the steel underneath, and there were no signs of struggle in the dirt. Perhaps he had just taken the moment to flee from it all. From what she had heard, Kenneth had tried to get away from Norclave all his life. Maybe he'd taken this whole hunt for the Cryo as just another way to make his escape.

Kara then noticed a small device on the ground. It was the bit of tech she had picked up after the rubble collapse in the starscraper. Kenneth had known just as well as she that it was just scrap, but now a small light glowed on its side. Kara scooped it up from the dirt and bounced it in her hand for a moment as she looked around again. "Alright," she said quietly. "You've bought yourself a chance." Kara stuffed it into a pouch as she started out of the alley.

A warm wind filtered through the town. Kara adjusted her hood, though not because of the rift air pushing across Kamriek's Grove; there were simply too many watching eyes. She hated the feeling of not knowing who had been paid for information or who was just looking for a bit of tech to steal. A couple of young girls passed with small crates filled with woven cloth and an older man laughed at something someone had said. A woman, closing the windows on account of the winds, called out to the girls with the crates. A group of kids ran around. Kara simply ducked her head and continued on.

She headed toward the barricade the Norclave soldiers were finishing. If they had a description of what she looked like, they obviously cared little for the search.

Kara continued on to where she believed the Norclave transports had first touched down in the city. A wide area opened up between the two massive arcs of starscraper glass, providing enough space for quite a few transports. Cargo was being unloaded and taken through a large building at the opposite end of the open area. They were likely supplies for the mines. Her attention, however, was on the three Norclave transports sitting along the edge. They were guarded by only a couple of men who looked very entertained by a game they were scratching into the dust at the bottom of one of the loading ramps. Hopefully they would stay that way.

She moved to the first transport and carefully opened a panel on one of the repulsors. It was simple work to jerk on something inside to disable it. If the Norclave soldiers did get hold of Kenneth, she wanted to make sure it was impossible for them to leave. She glanced around the edge to make sure nobody was watching and then closed the panel.

In only a few short minutes, she'd worked her destructive way around to the last of the transports. When she pulled on the panel, instead of opening, it just fell off and made a loud thump against the side of the ship. Kara immediately started pulling herself up onto the transport. She rolled onto her back, heart racing, and forced herself to wait.

Eventually, her curiosity overcame her nerves and she moved to the edge to find the soldiers sprawled over their drawings in the dirt. Above them stood a man looking up at her with a raised eyebrow.

"I thought I would find you here," Randin said, wrapping his club back up. He gave her a smile as he tucked it back into the belt running diagonally across his sleeveless shirt. He had a square jaw, short hair, and the scars to prove he enjoyed a fight even though he was no hulk of a man. "I take it you ran into some trouble after we left?"

Kara lowered herself off the transport and glanced at the soldiers sprawled about. "The plan was shot to hell from the beginning. The technician was with me until now. That is why I was disabling the transports."

"You were making sure they can't get him back to Norclave." He gave a small frown as he looked at the transports. "Was he willing or captured?"

She glanced at some of the passing cargo merchants. "We cannot risk it either way."

Randin simply shrugged. He knelt down to adjust the distortion generator sitting on the ground. The glowing orb seemed to show it was working properly at least. To all the others in the area, Randin would still be there talking with the soldiers.

"Comar spotted him," Randin said as he grabbed one of the soldiers by the hand and started dragging him toward the transport. Kara used a boot to lift the man's head over the lip of the loading ramp as Randin continued on in.

"A Kamriek mercenary had the technician," he said, "though with all of the Norclave soldiers about, we were not sure what was going down. We split up to prepare for what we could, hoping you would show up."

"Are you sure it was him? You're sure it was our technician?" Kara asked as Randin went back for the other man on the ground.

"Matched the description Draken gave us." The soldier on the ground rolled his head from one side to the other and murmured something. Randin grabbed his foot and started pulling. "I would guess they're headed to that large ship on the hill."

The soldier groaned as—without Kara's help—his head bumped hard into the lip of the ramp.

"So how much begging did it take to let Comar give you his distortion generator?" she asked.

"Not as much as you would think," Randin replied. He gave a final heave and slid the man into the transport. "So this technician, is he worth the trouble of saving?"

"Only if we can get him to the pod."

Kara fell in step next to Randin as he picked up the device from the ground. A warp formed around them as reality collided with the collapsing field. They could only hope the others in the landing field would think twice about questioning a pair of tech hunters walking away from the Norclave transports. With luck, they would have Kenneth and be on their way before the hour was up.

Randin led the way toward the center of the city, past the chaotic commotion of the markets and the noise of the craftsmen scraping away at chunks of starscraper glass. A short while later, they stepped onto the area near the massive cargo hauler. Its broken form had long since been turned into a multistory cluster of residences and offices for Kamriek's Grove, and a system of walkways had been constructed to weave through the gaps in the hull and lace around the exterior.

Kara took note of the several guards standing at the center entrance, which consisted of a large gap between two crinkled cargo pods. The flow of people moving in and out of the structure as a part of their daily routines showed that there were many ways through, making the entire complex more like another section of the city than a fortress. She tapped Randin's shoulder and started moving away from a group of Norclave soldiers arguing with the local mercenaries.

"Our order is from Norclave! We are to secure the city and post a watch at the major entrances."

The man wearing pieces of burnished flight armor shook his head. "I'll not have you patrolling here and disturbing things as you have in the streets of Kamriek."

Kara found herself feeling glad that someone else had a problem with Norclave as they stepped through a side opening onto the open ground floor of the massive transport. The inside was a market square with tiers built over the slanting floor of the ship.

Unlike the claustrophobic mess of stacked levels in Norclave, the overlap of the platforms here left a good portion of the area open. The top of the room had been mostly torn out, evident by the tilted doorways lining the walls above. Close to them were a few partial stairways that were now being used to support the walkways and platforms ringing the chamber. Randin nodded to a path leading up. That's where they would have taken Kenneth—to the offices of the settlement's ruling family.

She made her way through the thin crowds amongst the half-circle platforms. With the entire bottom level clogged with trade, the tilted paths of the old ship would provide the best means for escape if this went bad, though they would be in the open too much to evade weapons fire for long.

"Sorry," a Kamriek mercenary said, blocking the stairway. "Access to the upper levels is limited. Business of the Nuand family only."

Kara could see Randin balling his fists out of the corner of her eye. She took a step forward to block Randin's path. "We come looking for a friend."

The guard nodded slowly and sent a leery eye toward Randin. "And I don't suppose that friend is another tech hunter such as yourselves?"

After a moment, Kara shrugged. If Comar had managed to get by him, it was possible they could follow his lead.

The man frowned at her. "I turned him away."

"For what reason?" When she got no answer, Kara reached into a pocket and produced a Norclave ten-mark.

The guard looked it over thoughtfully. "Looked like he was trailing a merchant being taken to Nuand."

"Who was this merchant?"

"I'll have you know that we are not allowed to—"

Kara slid her fingers to the side and revealed a second token.

"Some fool grumbling about his trouble in Norclave." The guard reached for the coins, but Kara pulled them back with a raised eyebrow. "I heard the name Tomman. My guess is that he was found shorting the mines. Now I suggest you go look somewhere else for your tech hunter."

Kara tossed him the coins and turned away, pulling Randin along with her. She leaned on the railing overlooking the staggered slope of the market. "You think Comar will get Kenneth out of there, or will he need help?"

"Depends on how much he wants this Cryo."

"We doing this like Reacher's Hale?"

Randin nodded in satisfaction. "How big of a distraction do you want?"

Kara started walking back toward the old set of stairs. "Just don't kill him."

Randin went through the routine of popping knuckles, rolling shoulders, and crackling his neck from side to side before he turned to have a chat with the mercenary.

* * *

Kenneth and Iren made their way through the top passages of the ship down a twisted hallway. Kenneth kept on complaining about the injustices of trade using phrases out of Mack's book, but even with his persistence, Kenneth knew Iren still held strong suspicions.

"This tech hunter you were traveling with," Iren said, adjusting the rail on his arm, "where did you meet?"

Kenneth tried to use a hand to rub the tightness in his back. "Norclave. After they took my transport, I hired the tech hunter to get me back here. I needed to speak to someone in charge about the injustices of trading in Norclave."

"If Norclave took your transport, then how—" Iren started before Kenneth interrupted.

"This is the one, isn't it?" He pointed forward, to a large door at the end of the hall. The two mercenaries standing guard in full sets of flight armor ground down to a rough shine marked this as the head Nuand's office.

One of the two standing guard stepped forward, flicking a switch to activate the automated rifle he carried. "Ms. Nuand is not expecting anyone at this time. Give your reason."

Kenneth turned to Iren. "Looks like I will just have to try another time. I doubt you want to get on her bad side any more than—"

"Trouble between the merchants and Norclave," Iren interrupted. "You can tell her to just shut down the trade, or let us in so we can start sorting this out."

The guard pulled in a breath and stepped to the side. It was clear from the look on his face that *nobody* wanted to step between the Nuand family and the wealth they pulled up from the ground. The other hit a panel on the wall to open the door. Kenneth felt a hard shove on his shoulder as Iren forced him inside.

The Nuand family had ruled over stretches of the Rift Hills long before Norclave ever rose to power. Even though Norclave had outgrown Kamriek in terms of wealth and size, the strength of the Nuand family was never a question; the large glass dome of the room was a testament to that. Starscraper glass had been used to replace the large windows that shattered when the transport had crashed. The bridge of the vessel was now the office of Olana Nuand.

Kenneth ran the lump of steel on the bottom of his foot across the new floor that had been constructed to level out the room. It was a mixture of well-polished tiles of metal and the amber glass. Kenneth then looked to the side, where the floor shifted up another layer to pass over the top of the tilted control stations beneath. The entire room was separated into three levels of the ornate flooring, the lowest being off to their right. In the center level was an ornate desk made of heavily lacquered wood and inset glass. It was flanked by two mercenaries much like those standing guard in the hall. Kenneth weighed their distrusting looks as he stepped forward.

Iren gave a low bow to the woman, who slowly moved around to the front of the desk. Kenneth followed his lead and ducked as far toward the floor as his tightened back would allow. There was no mistaking Olana Nuand. She wore a fine dress with angled cuts, styled after the dress uniforms from before the fall, though it was possible it had actually been recovered in perfect condition. She had her hair pulled up tight into a grey bun, but for the most part age had only put wrinkles around the corners of her inquisitive eyes.

"I would like to know," she said with a measured breath, "what information or event should be so drastic that I should be interrupted?"

Kenneth started to reply, she held up a finger to silence him.

"Before you answer, I would like you to keep in mind that Norclave has moved into *my* city without the slightest attempt at gaining my approval. My patience, as you may guess, is less than thin. Now, speak."

"My apologies," Kenneth began, as near to the end of her words as possible. The last thing he wanted was for Iren to have the first word. "Trade with Norclave may soon be in jeopardy. There is definite tension between the Overlord and the administrators, and the result is Kamriek's Grove being shorted."

"Tomman, if that is his name, claims Norclave stole his shipment," Iren explained. "I have my doubts about his story. He was avoiding the Norclave patrols."

Olana folded her hands behind her back. She looked Kenneth and Iren over firmly. Even the two guards standing to either side of the desk seemed on edge at the silence.

"You, what is your name?" she asked, looking at the mercenary.

"Iren, of the Markay family."

"Markay . . ." Olana said with a glance upwards. "That puts you toward the South Rise. Your family lost a member recently, is that correct?"

"Yes, Ms. Nuand. My brother, about three years back. He was killed by a tech hunter while on the night shift."

Olana sighed. "Now, why do you say this man was avoiding the Norclave patrols?"

Iren shot Kenneth a glance. "The tech hunter he was with disappeared in one of the alleys."

Kenneth knew he had to get control of the conversation. "Just a bit of protection I hired, hoping to get here to warn you," he said. "I paid the tech hunter upon arrival, concluding the deal. That is when, if I remember right, Iren agreed to help me get past the Norclave checkpoint."

When Olana raised an eyebrow in question to Iren, he stammered a few words as he searched for the correct reply.

Kenneth used the chance to push his side further. "I might add—"

Olana held up a hand to silence Kenneth. She turned away and walked back toward her desk, which was covered in elaborate glass engravings.

Iren gritted his teeth. "I felt it better for Kamriek to have control of the situation than simply shifting the matter over to Norclave. This is our city; we should have say before Norclave."

Olana nodded slowly, picking up a small cube of glass from her desk and turning back to face them. "My city," she said in a pointed correction to Iren. "Even still, you did well to bring him to me, regardless of your logic." Olana gestured toward Kenneth, and the two soldiers raised their weapons. "This is Kenneth. I heard that Norclave's First Administrator has called a hunt for him."

Kenneth pulled in a slow breath. He looked at the two weapons pointing straight at him, but it was the small glass cube that made him the most nervous. It caught the light at odd angles as Olana rolled it slowly along her fingers.

"Kenneth, it looks like we have a deal."

He did not like the sound of that. She made it seem as if the bad choices were already made for him.

"Your part of our agreement is cooperation. I want to know what the First Administrator wants from you." She raised an eyebrow at his silence, expecting an answer.

Kenneth pulled back his sleeve to reveal the marks on his forearm. "He thinks he can seize power and make Norclave more secure. That means getting rid of the criminals like me."

"I would have been told if it was a standard manhunt, but I had to rely on spies in Norclave to get the message about you." She motioned to a data pad on her desk. "Silas is trying to hide his intentions. He risked untold conflict by moving soldiers in without reason. Try again, Kenneth."

Kenneth paused for a moment, hoping his searching for another excuse would be seen as reluctance to tell the truth. "Silas's reason for keeping it from you could stem from his fear of fraying any longstanding alliances before he takes control."

Olana rolled her eyes. "Silas knows I despise the Overlord and, more importantly, Norclave. Where do you think he is getting the supplies to fund his little overthrow? You no doubt have overheard my merchants complaining in some hole-in-the-wall about unfair prices. In reality, that was the mines paying for the new soldiers throughout Norclave. I am not one to simply give bargain shipments at a whim."

"Why would you give Norclave to the First Administrator?"

"Silas has the same deal with me that you do. Cooperation. You should know that wealth comes after power, and I am perfectly willing to sacrifice a bit of the profit from the mines for a secure grip on the Rift Hills. Now, Silas withholding information from me, that is . . . expected. But as for you, I can only assume that you have some importance in what happens *after* he takes Norclave. Something that may allow him to break away from my influence. That is why I am giving you exactly one more chance to tell me what you know."

Kenneth motioned to the weapons still trained on him. "You can threaten me all you want, but you need me to earn the trust of the tech hunters."

Iren clenched his fists to the side. "A tech hunter does not know trust."

She leaned back and motioned with the cube for her men to lower their weapons. "So a pricy bit of tech it is." She tossed the cube up a few inches. "The Overlord sent you to help recover something a scoundrel of the wastes found, and Silas thinks whatever it is will help him take control of the Kamriek Mines after he has Norclave. I suppose your next excuse will be that only the tech hunters know where, or what, it is?"

Kenneth nodded. "That's right."

"Well then, I suppose that leaves me to simply . . ." A loud crack sounded from the ceiling above, drawing the attention of everyone in the room upward. Another loud pop caused a section of glass to shatter, forcing Olana to duck forward as amber shards spilled onto the desk. Just as the mercenaries stopped covering their necks, Kara hit one with a bright flash. Glass still bounced across the floor to either side as she landed from above and slammed the other's head onto the desk.

Iren started to raise the rails on his arm, but Kenneth hit him hard across the jaw. A quick backhand caught Kenneth under the chin, and he stumbled back from the metal-clad blow. Iren tried to raise his arm toward Kara again, but Kenneth lunged forward with both hands and quickly pulled the power pack tied to the rails free. Iren shoved Kenneth to the ground and pointed the disabled weapon at Kara.

"Stay your weapon!" Olana yelled, ducking as another chunk of glass fell to the side. She glanced toward the door as if wondering what was keeping her other guards. "You are the tech hunter, are you not?" she called, hand reaching out to Kara.

Kara kicked one of the mercenary's weapons off the desk and onto his unconscious and crumpled form and stepped down onto the shard-covered floor. "Get away from my technician," she said, moving past Olana without giving her a second glance.

Kenneth tapped the power pack against his own head with a smirk. Iren glanced at his arm and cursed. He gave Kenneth a spiteful glare before backing away off to the side as Kara neared.

"You will never get your payment from the Overlord." Olana took a step toward Kara. "Norclave will fall any day now, and you will be left without reward for your efforts."

"You hurt?" Kara asked, still ignoring Olana as Kenneth held a hand up to the split on his chin.

"Nothing new."

"Listen to me," Olana Nuand said again, shooting another glance behind them at the entrance. "If you return to me with your tech, I will double whatever price the Overlord has offered."

Kara rolled her eyes, finally turning to face Olana Nuand. "Nobody is coming to get you out of this. Just stop talking already."

Just then, the door behind them popped open with a shower of sparks. A man with his hood pulled down stepped over one of the many mercenaries lying outside. The lenses in his eyes made a silvery ring around his pupils, adding an ominous feeling to his quick look about the room. He glanced up at the shattered window. "Looks like I am late."

"My offer stands," the head of the mines said again. "I will pay you double whatever the Overlord is offering."

"I'll keep that in mind," the second tech hunter said, stripping Iren of his arm rails before pushing him to the side. He took the power pack from Kenneth without a word as he continued forward.

"Comar, make a way out," Kara said, pointing toward one of the side windows. There was a sharp hiss as the tech hunter loosed the mercenary's weapon, punching a hole through the window and making a large crack. A shove from Comar's boot split the panel and sent it falling.

Moving to the new exit, Kenneth picked up Olana's small glass cube from amongst the shards and spun it in the air before happily stuffing it into a pocket. He glanced back to Kara before ducking through the window.

"So, you are the key?" Comar clicked a device beneath a warped panel. The device was very similar to the cable spool Kara had used to escape Norclave. He gave Kenneth one last look with his eerie lenses before dropping down over the side. Kenneth set a knee close to the edge and peered over at the uncomfortable height.

"We have to go, now." Kara said, glancing back to the mess they had left behind. She handed Kenneth a strip of cloth as she wrapped another around her own hand. "Make it tight."

"I do not—" Kenneth started, but a shower of sparks rained over them as the deep thrum of a pulse cannon smashed through the glass. Kara vaulted over Kenneth and grabbed the cable midair. The shouts of Norclave soldiers pushed Kenneth to wrap the cloth as tightly as he could around his hand. Another shot got him to kick his feet over the edge.

He landed at the bottom and tossed the smoking cloth to the side, stamping his foot and yelling through a clenched jaw at the pain. Kara grabbed his arm and pulled him as a series of flashes pulsed down from above, sending chunks of smoldering dirt spinning into the air. The soldiers were finally forced to cease their desperate attacks as Kenneth and the two tech hunters moved into the crowds, eventually disappearing into the streets of Kamriek's Grove.

* * *

"Orders, sir?"

Commander Branon stood with the pulse cannon still emitting a rippling heat up his arms. He'd missed, making this yet another time he had fallen short of catching Kenneth. He shoved the weapon back to Gunward and stepped back inside. His boots crunched over shards of the fallen glass as he moved across the room.

Olana Nuand gave a sharp scowl to him and the other Norclave soldiers lining up in the room. Only a few of the Kamriek mercenaries were left able to stand next to Nuand.

"Get back to the transports," Branon ordered to his own men.

As he followed the drumming of boots in the tilted hallways, Branon held a finger up to his visor and started to connect with the relay mounted atop the starscraper. The Overlord was said to be the one who discovered how to use the visors, but years had passed since Norclave benefited from his leadership. A long walkway stretched over a broken section of floor, looking deep into the inner workings of the ship. His visor flashed and he pulled the image across one eye.

"Report, Branon," the First Administrator said.

"Kenneth and the tech hunters were spotted in Kamriek's Grove. Due to friction between us and the controlling families, they were able to escape from the Nuand headquarters."

Branon expected a torrent of shouting, but instead was met by silence from the First Administrator.

"Sir?" Branon finally asked, reaching up to his visor again. He winced as he brushed a finger against the burn left from Kenneth's first escape.

"Get your men to the transports," Silas finally said. "Start toward Carvanhold and wait for instruction."

"Carvanhold?" Branon said in confusion. "Surely you don't mean to stress relations with Norclave and—"

"If he is truly working with the tech hunters, that means they are taking him to whatever they found, which is somewhere within the Kessian lands."

"If I may, sir," Branon started, "they are still in the city. We could keep them from leaving."

"No," Silas said. "Between the technician and a group of tech hunters that we could not even track through our own city, you would only lose them again. Head north and wait for them to reveal their destination."

The connection was terminated by Silas as Branon continued through the market platforms centered in the wreck. Minutes later, he stepped into the wide-open port.

"Load up!" he yelled to the formation. As the soldiers began piling into the transports, Branon started looking around for the two men he had posted to guard them. He spotted scratches in the dirt from a game they had been playing, right next to the trails of their dragged bodies.

"Sir, you had better look at this! It's Hallen and Nals, sir!" Gunward motioned from inside.

It was then that Branon noticed that a panel on one of the repulsors had fallen off. His pulse skipped at the realization. "Everybody out, now!"

He yelled as loudly as he could over the repulsors now firing on, but down the line of the three ships, the far craft had already closed its ramp, and only a few of the second stepped out to see what the shouting was for. "Kill the repulsors!"

Gunward relayed the order inside just as the first transport exploded. Branon waved the rest of the men out as quickly as he could as the second transport flipped onto its side from the blast. Its own repulsors began to superheat metal anywhere near the agitated and furious jets of orange. With a thundering crack, the second gave way, ripping into shreds with a torrent of flame that wrapped around the final transport.

Branon turned away from the blinding heat. For the moment, he was glad that the noise of the ripping fire and collapsing metal drowned out the shrieks from inside. He fell to the ground, shielding his face with an arm as secondary bursts sent showers of shrapnel piercing through the pillars of smoke.

* * *

Kenneth held a hand over his mouth to help against the rolling walls of black smoke pouring from the burning Norclave transports. He could not say what had happened to them; perhaps it was the workings of some resistance group or other outlying force. Kara kept pushing him to stay close behind the other two tech hunters. He caught a glimpse of a riftwalker spraying a thick foam on the fires to no avail.

"This one!" Randin yelled from a few yards ahead. The tech hunter shoved a coughing merchant over the back of a pile of crates he had been sitting on. "Hurry aboard!" he yelled back.

As soon as Kenneth and Kara stepped on the loading ramp, Comar hit the lift to close the door. Kenneth started to the front as he heard Randin cursing about the controls.

"Move over," Kenneth said to the tech hunter. His voice was hoarse from the smoke. "I'll fly."

The man looked as if his temper was going to flare, but Kara put a hand on his shoulder.

"Kenneth, just get us up in the air," she said.

After trading places, he flicked a few switches on the manual panel and a rumble sounded from outside. He could see very little but thick smoke through the front glass, and it was starting to seep into the cockpit through various cracks and long-eroded seals. He pulled a makeshift lever on the side and popped two cables together with his other hand, making the craft jolt into the air. The display projectors looked as if they had been ripped out long ago, leaving him to hope the needed systems were on. Kenneth moved his hands to the control rods and started flying over the city, heading through the towers of smoke and away from the massive wall of the starscraper.

"Just keep a straight course," Kara said. "We will touch down after the Northern Rift."

Kenneth settled back into the rough seat the best he could. It would be a while before they reached the northernmost edge of the Rift Hills. As the waves of forest and overgrown rubble slipped underneath, Kenneth took to listening to the tech hunters in the back. He heard crates being moved about, either being rummaged through for tech and supplies, or being shifted to make room to sit. When Kenneth glanced back, he saw them pulling the tops off the crates.

"Comar, catch," Randin said, throwing him a tube of medi-seal.

"Next time," Comar said, opening the small tube, "you can follow the technician. I'll do the distraction. And give me back my light distortion generator." He pulled back his hood and rubbed a thin line of the paste into a gash along his forehead. From the quick glance, Kenneth could see he had a heavy layer of unshaven stubble across his uneven jaw, and a thick scar ran down the side of his chin to leave a notch in his lower lip.

"With luck, we will not have to chase after Kenneth again," Kara said, popping the lid off a container. She raked through the wires before deciding they were nothing but parts.

Randin gave a short laugh as he tossed a crate to the side. "And what happens without luck?"

Kara shrugged. "We end up like those Norclave soldiers. The world suddenly goes all to hell."

"Sounds just about normal." Comar tucked the paste into a pocket and leaned back against the wall. "I'm willing to gamble if it means we get paid for the Cryo. Then we could be done with it all. No more collapsing tunnels, no more crap deals."

"I don't buy that," Randin said, placing a lid back on a crate with little care. It slid off as he moved to the next crate. "You could never give it up."

"What more would there be to find?" Comar asked. He thought it over for a moment. "If anything, I might join an expedition team. We all could. Once we recover the Cryo, guarantee our living, we could move on to something a little less reliant on luck."

This time, Kara weighed in. "You two go for it. If you want to trust a city's clueless expedition volunteers to not set off war machines or missile pods behind your back, that's your choice. I, for one, would feel safer trusting myself. Alone."

"Same here," Randin commented. "But now that you mention it, that's a bit like what we are doing with the technician, isn't it?"

Comar adjusted his hood back low over the tops of his eyes. "Except he was hand-picked by Norclave to open the pod. Something tells me the Overlord wants the Cryo for information, not frozen meat."

"But can he open it?" Randin asked.

"Here we go again," Comar said under his breath.

Randin continued. "If he can't get in, what use is all of this? I don't want to return to Norclave after torching a bunch of soldiers, whether they were the Overlord's or not."

Kenneth frowned, hearing it was Randin who had sabotaged the Norclave transports. It was one thing to make lies and take what you could, but there was something different about destroying ships full of men. Kenneth pulled the transport around a tree-covered hill growing out of the base of a building. Then again, this flight would have been a lot more interesting with three Norclave transports shooting at them.

"He can do it."

Kenneth was surprised to hear Kara say anything in his support. Perhaps she was just hoping that their only option would work.

"Our job now is to just get Kenneth there," she said. "And to make sure he has enough time to get it open."

Randin nodded. "Are we going to find a way to make contact with Draken?"

"As far as I am concerned," Kara said, finding her own place to sit atop one of the crates, "the fewer people who know where we are, the better. Draken, the rest of the expedition team, the Overlord—I don't care. We are best on our own."

Kenneth pulled the craft back in the direction they had been heading. He knew Silas would not give up the hunt over a few torched transports, and if years of personal experience meant anything, Draken would also be close behind.

Chapter 11: Discovery

Jance kept close to Avery as they followed Welnn and Feyn through the storage rooms of the Drake Discovery Complex. It was a curious thing to see a place like this so cut off from the rest of the world. There was no possible way the habitat here was up to UWC standards. There was no reasonable level of freedom with such isolation, and the raw living conditions were appalling. Shelters had to be created inside the building so that when the power fluctuated the heat of the small fires would not dissipate. The power inconsistencies were all because the installation ran off its own power grid for the sake of a grand experiment now rendered long obsolete. If it had been connected to the core reactor grid, there would be no fluctuations and the entire section would have been reasonably habitable.

Hopefully the sister facility of the Mars Contract would fare better. She could only guess at how many years had passed since the UWC had declared this section defunct. It should have at that time been declared uninhabitable by regulation, then enforced as such.

"How long have you lived here?" Jance asked Feyn as they moved between two stacks of containers. She eyed a mother and her two young kids in the doorway of one of the containers. The woman had what seemed to be a perpetual look of worry, but the two children seemed perfectly content playing with their makeshift toys over the tops of rough blankets.

"Years," Feyn replied, giving a small wave and a smile to the mother and kids. "Ever since I completed my task for the Edict, I settled here. The SRA was too close on my trail for anywhere else to be safe."

"What was your task?" Jance asked.

Feyn rolled the answer around for a bit. "It was a trade coordinator, almost like Avery. I always assumed he had ties to criminal shipments. Something more than smuggling alternative reality equipment into the UWC, though there was no way to tell."

"And you?" Jance asked, looking over to Welnn as they stepped out into the open. As soon as she asked, the thought occurred to her that she might not want to know.

"Enough, Jance," Avery said. "We are not part of the information you're looking for. Don't confuse yourself as to which side you stand with. Not now."

Jance was about to bull up and stand her ground, but Welnn held up a hand for them to stop. "UWC soldiers."

Jance peeked around the corner to see a group of eight soldiers taking up positions around the door leading through to the other sections of the complex.

"What the hell are they doing here?" Feyn asked as another wave of UWC soldiers moved into the large area. The second group split into two and started searching the room.

"They are looking for us," Avery said. He sent a pointed look to Jance. "For you." He gestured to Welnn and the man pulled out the pistol.

Jance shook her head. "No. We will find another way in. They have done nothing, and there is no way past them. They will find us soon enough, but, if we head back to Lance and the transport . . ."

"This is the way in," Avery stated. "Your answers about Kannei and Hoffsted are here."

Welnn and Feyn paid her no mind as they both took off through the stacks of containers toward the second group. Avery pulled out the distortion disk and adjusted the settings, bringing much of the area into a flame-shadowed darkness. All of a sudden there was a series of loud pops from the other side of the crates. The UWC soldiers started shouting through their comms for their weapons to be unlocked. Avery then threw his disk toward the door, plunging the immediate area into darkness.

"We have to move," Avery said as the field shifted away from the first group. The room echoed with chaos as the UWC soldiers fought back against Welnn and Feyn. Jance had no choice but to follow Avery as he ran directly toward the door and into what would have been the line of fire from the second group if the distortion generator had not blocked the fire confirmation from being received.

Feyn momentarily appeared through the crates on the side, holding a UWC rifle in either hand. She tossed one to Avery before disappearing again, returning to help Welnn.

"Stand down!" Avery yelled as he and Jance continued to the door. Several of the UWC soldiers pitched their locked weapons to the side and rushed at him with knives, but the distortion field stopped even the heat from being transferred to the blades. Several quick bursts of fire from Avery dropped them to the ground.

"Pick it up!" he yelled to Jance as they walked over the disk. She bent and took it lightly in her hands as Avery kicked the door and shouldered his way through.

"What about the others?" Jance asked as they stepped into a long hallway. Avery held out a hand without taking his attention off the doorway. She gave him back the device and asked about Feyn and Welnn again.

"They know what we fight for."

"And Lance?"

Avery fired a few shots back through the doorway to keep the UWC soldiers down. "No way to contact him now. We move in the dark."

They started down the hallway in an eerie half-light that seeped through the icebound windows of the passage. With the distortion generator blocking even the heating systems in the crossway, it did not take long for fog to start puffing out with their hurried breaths. She looked back to see the lights flickering on back toward the soldiers.

"Just keep moving," Avery urged.

* * *

"What happened?" Assistant Director Ralena barked over the shoulders of the people at their stations. Only half the displays showed the transmissions of the soldiers. "Why did we lose contact with Anchor Group?"

"Fire confirmation order has now been received by Anchor," one of the people in the command room said from the side. "Connection will be live momentarily."

The sound of a firefight continued over the main displays. "Two hostiles using UWC weaponry!" one of the Blade Group soldiers yelled into the comms. "Request immediate cancelation of—" A voice from Anchor Group overlapped the Blade Group soldier, reporting that the secured exit had been breached and that the ambassador had been spotted.

"Terminate fire orders!" Ralena yelled. Within seconds, the locks on all the weapons were reinstated, bringing the fight to a lull. "Blade Group, secure wounded. Anchor, retrieve the ambassador." She held a hand to cover her opposite ear as she received a direct command from Director Rulari. "New orders: Blade Group, secure wounded. Anchor, hold position and secure wounded."

Ralena stepped back and paced in a circle. She would have never guessed that they would be immediately engaged, but she was going to bring hell down upon the tech teams for losing contact. A disaster was the polite way of describing how the situation had unfolded.

"Can we get visual confirmation on the ambassador?" she asked the observations team. As she waited, she looked around the room at the people working at the terminals. Only half of them were in uniform, and most were breaking code with the layers of clothing on top to stay warm. This team was a disgrace, and she would be the one reprimanded for it.

"Director Rulari," she said into the comms angrily, "do you have any additional orders?" Ralena's jaw dropped as he answered. It must have been his condition showing again, and perhaps at the worst time.

* * *

Avery led the way as they moved along the bottom level of the next building. Wide observation windows showed only the foggy insides of deep layers of ice. The construction of the facility showed its date in a number of ways, and from the lines of rust clinging to metal panels along the floors and walls, he knew nothing here was starscraper-grade. The aged quality was further accentuated by the protruding support ribbing along the halls.

"I see nobody," Jance said, looking around the corner. Avery stepped just far enough to see the opposite way. Everything was clear.

"If you would turn your distortion generator off for just a moment," she argued, "we could read the displays and see where we are supposed to be going."

"The data archives will be in the central tower." He started across the intersection. "Based on the view on the ride in, I think we have at least one more tunnel to go through." He jerked the gun around at the sound of movement. It was a group of civilians hiding in the dim corners.

"Avery!" she gasped. He lowered his weapon and Jance held her hands together apologetically. "I'm sorry we frightened you. Don't be afraid. You have nothing to worry about."

Avery started away and she pressed a finger over her lips, hoping they would stay quiet for at least a few more minutes.

"Where is the security?" she asked quietly, sliding next to Avery behind another pillar.

He nodded toward the next intersection, where a group of officers were looking up at the flickering lights. They glanced around nervously as they tried to get their visors and flashlights working. Avery drew in a breath, as if debating what to do next. The only thing that could stop him from taking them all out was the amount of ammo left in his weapon. He moved forward alone in the shadows, his footsteps masked by the creaking of ice shifting against the building.

He finally stepped out into the eerie lighting of the ice-bound corridor. "Don't bother trying for your weapons." The officers all turned toward him. "They will not work."

In the pale light, it was easy to see the fear in their eyes, though it surprised both Avery and Jance when one man crossed a fist over his chest and stood at attention. "We have orders to cooperate," the man said grudgingly.

"What orders? From who?"

"The director of the facility. Director Rulari. The safety of the ambassador and the civilians are our primary concern."

One of the men shifted to the side and Avery flicked his attention toward him. "I'm not buying it," he said. "Stand aside."

He motioned to the others to move away, though he did not move himself. "Sectator, you are the poison of this Earth, but I have my orders. The director has ordered our cooperation for the safety of everyone here. I do not like it, but there is nothing else to be done."

"I don't like it either," Avery said. All it would take was for one of the weapons to receive fire orders, and it would all be over.

Jance moved from behind the pillar and stepped uneasily into the pale light. "If you actually are trying to help, give us directions."

The officer gave her a surprised look. "Ambassador, are you—"

"Wait," Avery interrupted, shooting a quick glance at the others lined up against the walls. "We tell you where we're going, what is to say that as soon as we leave you don't tell this Director Rulari?"

"We don't have another choice," Jance said.

Avery watched the officer suspiciously.

The officer looked as if he shared the sentiment.

"Avery," Jance said harshly. "We need to know. We don't have time to wander around in the dark." It was simply too late to ignore the opportunity.

"Alright," he gave in. "How do we get to the data archives?"

"They are in the central tower. Keep walking down this hall."

"And what level are they on?" Avery asked.

"Seventy something. Three, I think, and a few levels above that as well."

Avery turned away from the man and gave Jance a glance before beginning the uneasy walk down the hall. Jance kept looking back to make sure they were not being followed, but surprisingly enough, everything remained clear.

They arrived at another door leading out of the building and into another long hallway. Looking through the layers of ice atop the glass ceiling, Jance could barely make out the blurred shape of the central tower.

Avery pushed the next door open and they stepped through into the bottom level of the central tower, into what looked like a large gathering room. The words *"Drake Discovery Mission"* were framed on one of the walls, and displays showing where the other passages led flickered from Avery's distortion device. Pockets of security officers stood throughout the room, probably twenty people in total, but there was no attempt to stop them as she and Avery made their way to one of the many elevators. Avery motioned for Jance to step into the elevator and he followed soon after, leaving the onlooking security behind.

Avery lowered the field of the distortion generator just enough to maintain his weapon and pounded a fist on the control panel. The pull against her stomach as the elevator rocketed upward came as a welcome relief. At least now they were moving.

Avery knelt down and pulled a section from the bottom of the controls, exposing a chipset. There was a spark as he pulled a wire, likely in an attempt to stop their elevator from being shut down remotely.

"If we cannot find Hale to access the archives," Avery said, "I am going to need your Council clearance to get in."

"Of course," Jance replied. "After that, take me somewhere in the facility where I can make contact with the Council."

"And then we go separate ways."

Jance nodded. "Of course."

* * *

Weyburn double-checked that the distortion generator on his hip was ready for use as he stepped out into the breathtaking cold. Clouds of freezing steam drifted from the transport as the powered-down repulsors were overcome with the subzero temperatures. Any other metal would have cracked from the quick exchange of energy. Repulsors were different, much like the distortion generators. However, with distortion generators banned by the world orders, there was no way to know exactly how.

Hoffsted's group followed behind with their weapons ready. Weyburn had warned them that the sectator may still beat them to the target, as he nearly had with Kannei. He glanced back just before leading them into the facility. He said nothing as they checked the area for heat signatures and electronic emissions. Their reliance on the technology would prove a weakness if they actually did run into the sectator, as it had been during his first encounter.

He pulled in a ragged breath as they stepped into the airlock. The air pulling in felt searing hot against the bitter cold before, but a few moments of acclimating revealed almost normal living conditions.

"Several forms on the other side," one of the men reported. They moved to the sides of the door, ready for a firefight, but Weyburn simply put his hands behind his back, ignoring the cold sting of the flight armor against the tormented skin of his chest and shoulder.

"Hold your fire," he told them just as the doors began opening. Four UWC soldiers stood at the ready on either side of a man in civilian clothing.

"I am Errence Jalimed, coordinator of this section. Tell your men to stand down."

"That is not going to happen," Weyburn growled.

The coordinator glanced to the side at one of his soldiers as if unsure what he should do. "We are experiencing an emergency situation. I request that you return to your ship so as to not interfere in the operations of—"

"What situation?"

"I am not at liberty to say. Please, return to your vessel and wait for—"

"We are here under orders from the military ambassador. If that is not a good enough reason, you are also outnumbered and our weapons are armed. Step aside, point the way, or become a casualty in the mission."

The coordinator wasted no time in stepping to the side.

Weyburn ordered his men forward, and without giving the coordinator a second glance, he continued down the hall.

Hoffsted had been monitoring all of Kannei's transmissions for several weeks, and the defensive analysis team had been surveying him off and on for years, but when he started asking questions about the core reactor analysis team, EMA-GO, and the Drake Discovery Mission, Hoffsted had decided to assess Kannei more carefully. The last non-secured transmission the logistician had made was to Alexander Hale, here in this wasteland. Weyburn and his team just needed to beat the sectator to the mark to starve the Last Edict of information.

* * *

Jance and Avery continued upward unhindered. Once the elevator opened, Avery leaned out, aiming the rifle to where he expected resistance. He motioned Jance to follow him out. He pulsed the distortion generator and shouldered through the security door. The place had the look of a research lab, though it was deserted. Tables were lined with disassembled information cores and tools were left where they had been last used. Not even the security alert lights were activated.

"Come on," he said with a roll of his hand. Avery continued forward, using a short activation of the distortion generator and the butt of the weapon to pry open another set of security doors. They stepped into a decontamination chamber, where loose particles would be eliminated so as to properly preserve the data archives. Layers of light flicked about as the automatic sequence purified the environment. Avery simply continued through, paying close attention to the row of windows along the top of the hall. They moved across without any problem, but this time the door opened before Avery reactivated the generator.

"We are walking into a trap," he said to Jance as he took up a position close to the doorframe.

After so many empty halls and abandoned rooms, Jance simply walked forward past Avery. "We already knew that."

The next room was a wide circular chamber stretching several stories above and below where they stood, and filling the room's center was a massive supported pillar of data cores linked in matrices. Walkways reached out to the center in even spacing for maintenance.

She could see patches where the pillar had been stripped of the glowing cores, and along a few of the walkways were carts full of the things. Straight ahead, a worker hunched over by age was taking out flickering data cores and replacing them with ones from a small cart.

Avery kept his weapon lowered, but he looked prepared to use it should he need to. "Have they been stripping the information?" he asked Jance.

She slowly made her way out onto the walkway, looking up at the multistory complex designed for mass data storage. It would have the structural sensor data of the facility stored for the past two hundred years and the information of every person that had lived here during that timeframe. However, there was now the possibility that the information Kannei had been seeking was now cleaned out of existence.

"What are you doing?" Jance asked the worker.

He turned around and adjusted his glasses, forming the suspended semi-fluid for his desired focus. The old man frowned, causing his wrinkled skin to droop lower. He lowered his hand from the long-outdated technology and looked through at them inquisitively. "Replacing the cores," he said. "It had to be done. Now, who are you?"

"Was there information on them?" Jance asked.

He looked down and opened his mouth several times, as if trying to decide what to say. He eventually set the core he was holding next to the others on the little cart pushed against the railing of the walkway. "The information is transferred to a new core before removal of the cores undergoing repair. Now, I assume you are here because of Kannei?"

"We are," Avery said bluntly. "Is the information he was looking for here?"

"I will tell you the same thing I told him: go look somewhere else. This is not the place for your world secrets."

"What was Kannei looking for then?" Jance asked in a softer tone. "Surely you at least have the early research timelines stored here?"

He looked down again before taking another cube from the cart and inserting it into the frame. "I never should have even talked to the man. Some things were buried for a reason."

"What was it? What was buried?"

He shook his head and blinked heavily, bringing the bags under his eyes up to shut with the sagging lids. "I . . . was buried."

Jance gave Avery a confused look as the old man slowly continued whatever he was working on.

He pointed up toward the tower of cores after pulling out another cube. "Outreach Systems designed it to hold incredible amounts of data, and to be easily maintained for millennia. I was alive when this was first built," he said grimly. "I was near thirty years old. Alexandar Hale, the so-called 'genius of my generation.' Born 2768." He let out a sad laugh and looked to Jance. "That makes me a two hundred and twenty-six year old man."

"You are a Cryo," she said with a bit of surprise.

Hale nodded. "I wanted to see more, much like you." He picked up one of the cores and placed it into the frame. "Do you want to know what I found?"

Jance looked back to Avery, but he simply shrugged and glanced over the edge of the rail into the pit below.

When Jance looked back, Hale continued, "I found that my purpose was lost, and I was damned to spend my final years maintaining this system. A mere side project I declined to work on in my time. It was designed to hold nearly infinite amounts of data, but meant only to impress the global orders into funding Outreach System's bid for the Contract of humanity's expansion. Now, the Drake Discovery Data Archive is no more than a vastly empty tower of building blocks, a forgotten prototype to the duplicate still in use on Mars.

"You said you declined to work on this project? What did you do before . . ."

"I was the head of another project, *the* project, at Tech-5 Industries for thirty-three years."

"Gravity repulsors?" Avery questioned. Tech-5 Industries had been the world-renowned manufacturer and researcher of gravity repulsion technology for nearly four hundred years.

Hale shook his head. "Nothing so simple. My work was more groundbreaking than even the design of the core reactors. Nearing the end, I posed a system of theoretic design, but after long and painful years of research, it became clear that I would never see the beginnings of the results. Age sixty-seven, I decided to live a different future."

He squeezed another cube, causing the tendons in his age-thinned hands to bulge. "When I woke, all traces of my project had been hidden by the UWC government. It took years of digging just to confirm that I even existed before my cryogenesis." He looked up into the dark room, at the glowing lights of the cubes in the tower. "My search led me here. Same as Kannei, same as you."

Avery motioned from his half flickering visor to the display amplifiers inserted along the railing of the walkway. An image of what Avery was looking at appeared on the amplifiers for the others to see. She gave it a curious look. It was a communications log for the Mars Contract, labeled *"Tech-5 Industries, Charon Deep Space Research Incident"* with the year 2835.

"That date cannot be correct." Jance did not need to access the UWC database to know. "The Contract was first established years after that."

Tech-5 Industries, Charon Deep Space Research Incident 2835-4-7;

Emil Forge: "It will be another three months before the reconnaissance team arrives at the research facility. Has the analysis team come up with the odds yet?"

Niola Willebrit: "Of survivors? Considering that three mandatory contact intervals have been skipped, as well as the orbit of the body itself being skewed by upwards of 1,250 percent in orbital eccentricity, I think your team is on course for an empty rock. Provided that we can calculate the changing orbit of Charon for them sometime within the next couple months."

Emil Forge: "Were there any signals that made it out before the test that could help explain what happened?"

Niola Willebrit: "Only preparation procedures. The team here is scrubbing through the input data as we speak, but they will only see an anomaly if there was an actual oversight in the setup stage."

Emil Forge: "Like hell Alexander Hale would have let that happen . . . has he been informed?"

Niola Willebrit: "No. Hale went through with it. I have the form here. Entered cryostasis on the third. You would have to sign off to wake him back up.

Emil Forge: "Damn it. He should have waited . . ."

Niola Willebrit: "Perhaps he knew it would fail. Maybe he hoped that someone else could sort out all the difficult parts of his theory for him.

Emil Forge: "Yeah, but now I am the one who has to deal with the effects of the explosion of the whole thing."

Niola Willebrit: "Just speaking technically, if it was an explosion that moved Charon and the station, we would have seen it here on Earth."

Emil Forge: "I am pulling the project."

Niola Willebrit: "Calm down, Emil. We both know you have said that before. There is no turning back if our funding is diverted away. As soon as you send the Council the message, you know it is over for good."

Emil Forge: "As far as I am concerned, Solstice and Outreach can have our share. I would settle with having Mars on the map before another failed attempt by Tech-5."

Niola Willebrit: "You should consult Hale on that decision. Bring him out of cryo."

Emil Forge: "He would just say no. I say it is over, once the recovery team returns from Charon. Hale can just hope someone else picks it up years after our lifetimes. We have done all we can. I'm sorry. I can submit a transferal request for you to another of Tech-5's research teams. Hopefully the switch will not impact your family too much, Niola."

-End Coded Transmission-

"They did not wake you?" Jance asked, holding her fingers lightly to her lips.

"No. I never even saw it all disappear. It was gone the moment I looked away."

"Just imagine . . ." Avery said quietly. "The havoc it could have caused if they had tried that test on Earth . . . Jance, this is exactly the kind of weapon the Last Edict is concerned with. If it was enough to move a planetoid—"

"It is no weapon!" Hale spat, turning slowly to face Avery. "Just because you see an explosion, you immediately think of war. That distorting device in your pocket is the perfect example. My test on Charon could have resulted in so much more than military tricks to shut off the lights. So much more! For all of us, and forever! It was the very edge in the—" Hale bit his own words short and turned back to his work.

Avery accessed another file. The words *Tech-5 Quantum Recalibration Project* and *"project lead Alexandar Hale"* appeared on the display for just a moment before the information disappeared.

Jance looked from the blank display to Avery. "What happened?"

"I don't know." Avery frowned. "It just seemed to . . ." He glanced from the display to an empty space where a data core had been removed from the tower. "Jance, Hale is removing the information."

Jance gave the man a horrified look as he pulled out another cube and set it on the cart.

"What are you doing?" she asked.

Alexander Hale looked back with tears rimming his eyes. "I was told to remove it all. The forgotten logs of my failed experiment, the rushed conclusion of the Drake Discovery Mission in order to join the Mars Contract. Kannei found out before the cleanup was complete only because I tried to hold on. Perhaps I just did not want to face the fact that my life's greatest work had been destroyed. I lied to Hoffsted to keep it from being removed . . . to keep it from being forgotten. Forgotten just as I was."

He lowered his eyes and rested his hands on the handle of the cart. "But some things *must* be forgotten." Hale started to tip the cart.

"No!" Jance cried. She rushed forward and grabbed the cart, but not before it had tipped too far. She looked over the edge with a gasp. The dull thuds ringing from walkways below seemed an echo of the hollow despair she felt as the data cores gave their final flashes before shattering into pieces.

"Let it go. It is finally gone." Hale said.

Avery frantically searched for something Hale might have missed, but found nothing left of any value in the archives.

Those cores . . . the answer had been right in front of her. It was everything Kannei had tried telling her about. Pieces of the evidence, parts to a conspiracy. She knew something was there, but everything was so twisted and hidden away that she still had no idea what it was, and the last dying flashes of the cores were the last whispers worth following.

Jance dropped to her knees and looked up through watery eyes at the glimmering spire of infinite and now practically empty storage. In following the path Kannei had left, she had been trying to bring evidence against something buried where only the proofless shape even hinted at its truth. Jance knew she stood close to the grand shape Kannei had nearly discovered, but she was powerless to give it so much as a name.

The end of Tech-5's Quantum Recalibration Project sparked the end of the Drake Discovery Mission and the beginning of the Mars Contract, though she could not say why it had concerned Kanni. He had also raised alarms over the EMA-GO controlling access to the Mars colonies, but how any of what he said related to the core reactors and the cover-up that ended the lives of two engineering officers, Jance had no idea.

She felt Avery's hand press down on her shoulder. She gripped his fingers tight, holding on to the surprising bit of comfort. A sectator for the Last Edict. She paused a minute, just trying to wrap her head around everything.

"Jance, we have to go," Avery said. She reluctantly let him help her up. "The UWC will not hold forever."

"Wait," Jance said, turning to Hale, who was looking off the edge into the dark. "You said the project . . . that your work was more groundbreaking than even the design of the core reactors. Do the reactors use this quantum recalibration as well?"

Hale frowned. "They always have. My project was not the first usage of the science, just the boldest."

"What is it?" Jance asked sharply. "What is quantum recalibration?"

Hale gripped the railing. "In simplest terms? We alter the pieces of sub-atomic particles and rebuild new forms of matter. This is nothing new, though the specifics have always been kept a secret. The support structures for the core reactors, for example, would never hold up if constructed with materials of natural physics. And Tech-5 Industries found long before my time that they could produce gravitational anomalies with small generators—gravity repulsors—that were manageable for consumers."

"And your project? What change did you try to make that was so important?"

"I found . . . a new layer. A new combination."

Without warning, the room fell into darkness. The flickerings of the few data cores left only provided the most distant lights to cast shadows throughout the room. She felt Avery pull at her shoulder.

"Avery, wait! There has to be something I can bring back to the Council!"

"This is not me," Avery warned. "Someone else is here."

Jance quickly turned to Hale in the darkness. "This is the last chance we will get. It might very well mean the fate of the world. If you know anything, please, tell me now."

He turned slowly, looking at the dim light shining through the flickering cores high up in the room. "The world chose its own fate in the age of my past. We are bound in the solar system, to wait until the end."

Jance gasped as a flurry of sparks suddenly leapt around them to the sharp echoes of gunfire from above. The harsh pings of bullets punching through steel were mixed with the few that gave off vibrating shrieks as they whirred down into the pit of the archives below. Avery pulled Jance back as Alexandar Hale fell forward. As Jance tried to fight her way back to Hale, a shot tore through the handrail next to her.

"Leave him! We have no choice!" Avery pulled her back again and forced her to start along the walkway as more shots popped around them.

Jance finally made it through the safety of the half-open doors of the decontamination hallway, followed soon after by Avery stumbling with an arm pulled to his chest. A bullet had torn a gash into the sleeve of his temperature regulation suit, and the exposed layers underneath were quickly becoming darkly saturated.

"Avery, you are—"

"Help me," he said, holding his weapon out to Jance. He tried to adjust the suit to block off the wound, but the distortion field causing the lights to flicker the length of the hall made the display jump violently around. The only option was to push forward away from the distortion. Finally, with enough distance between them and the data archives, the material of the suit was stimulated to squeeze inward above the tear, hopefully slowing down Avery's bleeding enough for him to continue.

"Lance!" he shouted into his visor as they continued down the hall away from the hostile distortion field. "Do you hear me?" Avery tried again, glancing over his shoulder back down the hall. "If you can hear me, I am going up."

"Up?" Jance asked, still clutching the weapon tight. "But the nearest docking bays are at the base of the tower."

"Someone has shut down the communication relays. The only way to get a message out will be through the director's office."

"You might be able to get a transmission out in time, but that would be it. Down is our only hope of actually getting out of here!"

Avery shook his head. "Your only hope. You can still walk out. We are being hunted, but you still have a chance. Find a local group of UWC soldiers or get aid from some of the civilians. Disappear. Travel to the SRA if you have to."

"Avery, you will not get out of here alive if you do not come now!"

"My life, to assure that humanity will always continue? That is not even a choice." Avery motioned through the elevator's controls and set the lower levels as the destination. "I mean nothing compared to those who will stand after I am gone." He nodded for Jance to enter the elevator. "Go, before the distortion blocks it."

"No, Avery," Jance said, pulling the weapon farther away as he reached for it. "I will not let you send me away."

"Go," Avery argued. "You can buy time for yourself, to explain to the Council."

Jance stood for a moment in indecision, but as Avery jerked the weapon from her hands, she knew what she had to do.

"You need the relay active. Your illegal tech will not help you break through the communication protocols, and we both know there is not enough time to hack through before we are blocked off." Jance switched the direction of the elevator. "You need my Council clearance."

Avery tucked the weapon under his arm and hesitated as he weighed his options. Finally, he nodded and they both stepped in without a word. Avery closed the door behind them, and a rattle of bullets struck the door just as they were lifted upward into the tower of the Drake Discovery Mission.

Chapter 12: Purpose

Kenneth pushed the machine as fast as he thought the worn repulsors and the rattling front glass would permit as they continued away from Kamriek's Grove. The land morphed underneath as the open fields and forests stretching out into the impact valley were slowly dominated by sheets of ruins and the bare steel of splintered buildings.

A flow of thick and murky air pushed up from the east as they passed over several container houses wedged up against an exposed overhang of concrete. The smoky fog that filtered in through the long-eroded seals of the transport had the taste of warm ash and acidic vapors. Of course, tainted air was far from abnormal in the Rift Hills. Tech hunters frequently explored ruins for days with it hanging over them, and often the Rift Outpost billowed fumes that the riftwalkers had to work through. Kenneth looked to the side as Kara pointed out a spot where she had once found a single-person transport in near-perfect condition.

Finally, after several miles, a chunk of the ruined city gave way to the Northern Rift River. A long crag had formed where the land pulled away from itself, and over the years the flows of water had found their way into the crag. There was no easy way over the river for nearly twenty miles in either direction. Eventually, along the western edge of the Rift Hills, the river disappeared into the depths of the Earth at the Hollow Falls.

"How close into Kessian lands do you expect us to get?" Kenneth asked. He kept close watch on the skies for any patrols near the border. While he hoped they would still be in the uncontrolled zones between the two, the last thing they needed was more people hunting after them.

"That building." Kara put a hand on Kenneth's shoulder and pointed past his head with the other arm. "Put us down next to that round section." It was a wide concrete disk that could have been some sort of landing platform. It was missing a support underneath to keep it level, causing it to stand steeply upon the portion buried deep under the small copse of tangled brush.

Kenneth leaned forward and took a closer look. "I could probably get us under it. That would keep the transport concealed."

"No. It is risky enough as it is. No guarantee the area will still be uninhabited, and I would rather not fly directly into a kill zone." Kara pushed away from Kenneth and told the others that they would be landing soon. The crackling of Randin stretching his neck nearly matched the noise of him checking weapons.

"How good of a pilot are you, technician?" Comar called forward. "Can I trust you to slow up enough for me to jump before you reach the landing spot?"

"How far out do you want to be?" Kenneth asked. "There aren't many spaces for a transport between the steel jutting up around here."

"Just find me someplace to give you cover."

Kenneth eased up on the makeshift engine control and started their descent earlier than he normally would have. At their speed, any bit of a collision would jolt them into the razor tips of sheared pillars. Kenneth edged away from a wall of dangling concrete and steel and gritted his teeth as the dead limbs on the other side scraped against the craft. He swung the nose of the ship to the left and then back to skirt around another beam.

"Ready?" Kenneth called back. There was a small trench of collapsed ground just between the thicket and the open area. He looked back over his shoulder and saw the door of the craft opening. He was farther from the ragged tree line than he had thought, but Comar should still be able to drop into the dip for cover. Kenneth slowed their forward speed, getting as close to the ground as he could.

"Take us in," Kara called after Comar jumped. Moments later, the hot smell of repulsors cutting through the browning undergrowth rolled in through the open loading door. He kept gently decreasing the power until he felt the vibrations of the bottom scraping stone.

"You are down!" Kara called back. She stepped off the end of the transport before Kenneth had completely ended their forward motion. Kenneth quickly went through the improvised processes installed to power down the repulsor engines. He patted the rusted wall, pleased that they had both lifted off and touched down in one piece.

Kenneth stepped out of the transport into the cold air and warming winds. He had the same small feeling looking up at the surrounding ruins as he had while in the center of the starscraper. The lowest point of the horizon he could see was where they had entered the area from above.

Kara and Randin stood for a long moment, observing the surrounding ruins for unwanted watchers. The only movement Kenneth could make out was the rolling sway of the thin and tangled branches under the shadows of the huge walls. Kenneth looked to the large round structure Kara had directed him to. Over several hundred feet in diameter, it could easily conceal a small settlement underneath.

Out of the corner of his eye, Kenneth saw Kara tuck a small display into a pocket. It must have been some sort of heat signature detector, based off the relaxing tech hunters. Comar was still nowhere to be seen, but Kenneth felt sure the man could have them in his sights if he wished.

"Once we get the signal from Comar, will you want me to bring the transport under the ruins? It might hide our tracks."

"I think we should bring you to the Cryo," Randin said. "Get it over with. Quicker is better."

Kara glanced back for just a moment before continuing her survey of the area. "Even if Norclave knows which direction we went, I doubt that they are making good time. If anyone can find our transport, it would be the Overlord's tracker, and he might have the tools you need to get the cryopod open. If you think you can do without, well, then I suppose we would be better off if you hid it."

Kenneth rubbed at his brow. Draken might have the tools, but Kenneth had more than enough bad experiences with the tracker to feel like risking it now. Then again, looking under the edge of the circular structure and at the few lights underneath it, Kenneth felt a strong urge to run as fast as he could to finally see a cryopod. If someone gave him the choice between putting the finishing touches on a fully functioning war mech or looking through the frozen glass at a living human from before the fall . . . Kenneth could feel the ends of his fingers going cold from anticipation. He did not even know if the pod would have glass, or if the process actually included freezing or not.

They waited for another few tense minutes, looking into the surrounding shadows for the third tech hunter. Kenneth caught sight of him a few times as he shifted in and out of the rubble edging the clearings. Finally Kara nodded, seeing some signal from the man that Kenneth had missed with his own thoughts pulling at his attention.

"You moving the transport or not?" Kara asked.

Kenneth shook his head. At the moment, all he could think about was making the discovery of hundreds of lifetimes. "Show me to this Cryo."

* * *

Commander Branon was shoved into the large room at the hands of the Kamriek mercenaries. Gunward growled at one of the men holding their weapons trained on him from behind. Another shove on Branon's burnt shoulder made his knees buckle and he fell forward onto the shattered glass. Branon looked up as Olana Nuand stepped from behind her large and over-decorated desk. Above her, the bitter winds made a low hum as they passed over the hole in the glass ceiling.

Olana wrinkled her nose as she neared him and the few other Norclave soldiers that had survived the explosions of the transports. The smell of smoke and boiling metal likely hung on them as tightly as the residual light behind his eyes. Every time Branon blinked, he saw the fires.

"How does it feel?" Olana Nuand asked, leaning over the top of Branon. "The glass digging into your hands and legs. The same shards you strode over when you blindly chased the tech hunters out of my office. This would have ended differently if you had not been playing Silas's games!"

Branon coughed as he pushed himself back up. He set one foot underneath him, but could not lift his other knee off the ground. "You expect me to listen to you? The one who ordered your mercenaries to sabotage my transports?"

Gunward fought briefly against the men holding him, but a touch from a shocklance held him in check.

"I gave no such order," Olana said with narrowed eyes. "The death of your men puts me in no better position over the administrators than if they were alive."

Branon pulled in a slow breath to calm himself. His words took a quiet and dangerous tone. "Then who was it?"

"I think you know. The same group the First Administrator ordered you to hunt for, even though he knew you could never catch them. You were only sent to find which direction the tech hunters were headed. He gave no regard to what would happen to you when you failed."

"Are you saying the First Administrator is at fault for what *they* did?"

Olana reached for the glass cube that always sat on her desk. She paused before simply picking up a glass shard. "I am saying that if you let me give you the aid you need, you will not run into these tech hunters ill-prepared again."

"You want me working for you?" Branon asked. He pushed up hard with his leg but fell short of getting up.

Olana tossed the shard of starscraper glass to the side amongst the hundreds of others. "You will keep your command. I will provide the equipment, transportation, and any further manpower you require."

This time Branon pushed himself all the way up to stand. "And what do you get?"

She leaned her head from side to side in thought. "Does it matter? You get to continue your orders, and you get to take another shot at Kenneth. Maybe this time I'll supply you with a target-locking rifle, instead of those limited pulse cannons."

That comment was enough to set Gunward back to struggling, though not as strongly as before. Branon finally nodded. The First Administrator would not tolerate this latest failure, even if the man had known it would happen. He simply had nothing else to lose.

Olana pecked a few things on her data pad. "You will meet one of my mercenaries by the name of Iren in the second landing zone. He has history with tech hunters, as well as experience with the technician's evasiveness."

* * *

Kenneth stepped forward underneath the large slant of the disk-shaped structure propped above. Concrete and steel nearly twenty feet thick was supported where it dug into the land on one side and against the half-toppled tower on the other. Inside was a surprisingly large opening above the maze of rubble along the bottom. There were containers scattered all about the area, though most had been smashed under rockslides.

Kara led them deeper into the room, to where the ground sloped down farther into the tower's side. They passed the most intact cryopod he had ever seen. It had a front made almost entirely of glass, and he was surprised how much the rusted scratches on the exterior reminded him of some of the more intact transports. The main difference was the pile of bones in the bottom of the container that were half eaten away by rubble mites. From the few still buzzing inside, Kenneth guessed that the long crack near the base of the glass was a recent formation.

"Down this way," Kara said. She took long steps down a steep face of rubble until it met with a smooth floor.

"This must have been a storage facility," Kenneth commented, looking at the twisted steel of more pods off to one side. Light filtered in through the mangled fingers of the ruins above, though it was still mostly the scattered status lights and the pockets of undestroyed interior lamps that lit their way. Kara stopped and turned back to Kenneth. Along one straight wall was a row of three cryopods. Bits of rubble had been pulled away from them, most likely by the tech hunters on their first trip here. A heavy beam of steel that had entirely crushed a fourth looked to be the only thing keeping the weight of thousands of tons of ruins from shifting down upon them.

The two cryopods nearest to the beam were warped to the side with the glass in each shattered. The third pod had something Kenneth had not seen yet: the reflective shine of ice on the inside of the window. He pressed his hands against it, and just as he had hoped, it was no colder than the surrounding air. He leaned forward to try to look inside, but the only thing he could make out was the dim shadow of a hand pressed against the inside of the glass. He shared a glance with Kara, but she simply shrugged.

"Alright, let's see what the problem is here." Kenneth stepped to the side and activated the control system. The projectors seemed perfectly intact. He tapped through the hologram with as much precision as his cold fingers would allow, bringing up the general data of the pod.

"2994, Sequence Activation Date," he read aloud. "Name: A01. No interruptions since activation. Required Clearance: Priority Command." Kenneth shook his head.

"What do you think?" Kara asked. "What does that mean?"

"It sounds tough. I have heard rumors from Carvanhold that the weapon systems of any large military ships are under Command clearance. Not sure what the hell this Priority Command clearance is though."

Randin pushed a bit of stone with his foot off to the side. "You had better live up to your reputation, technician."

Kenneth smiled at the comment as he searched a bit more in the terminal. "You're just mad you can't do anything more to be useful."

The tech hunter picked up a hand-sized chunk of concrete and threw it offhandedly at the splintered glass of a pod along another wall. "That's a damned straight remark."

"And don't break any more of those than you have to," Kenneth said, not taking his eyes off the terminal. "I might need to try some things on them first before breaking into this one." Randin grumbled something in reply as he found a place to sit along the back wall to watch Kenneth work.

The confirmation message seemed to pop up around nearly every corner that Kenneth tried to take. Active logs on life support were blocked, functional data on the cryopod's logs were barred away, and most troublesome of all, the activation of the cryogenesis needed a clearance long since buried. That was the main problem of getting the Cryo out in the first place; he was trying to skim his way into a lockbox with the access code inside.

"Is there anything we can do to help?" Kara asked.

"Meaning speed the process up," Comar explained, just now following them into the area. He stopped at the top of the ridge Randin was sitting at the base of and dropped down a meal pack. "The quicker you move, the more likely I am to see my pay. That is, if the administrators have not already taken Norclave."

Kenneth crouched down and ran his hands over a panel on the side of the pod. "If you want this done, look around for a container that is mostly intact. Preferably one that did not have an occupant."

The tech hunter moved off, tugging his hood against a few pestering rubble mites. Kenneth knew he would need to take one of the pods apart to see how it functioned. Often he could see how things would fit together when they were apart, whereas when it was all together as a whole it simply seemed to function.

Kenneth picked up a small chunk of concrete and hit it against the access port on the side a few times. The pod was not undamaged, to say the least. He knew as he shoved the plate in and to the side that it was only a matter of chance that this one had survived amongst all the others. As he looked into the shadowy inside, Kara held a light over his shoulder. There were a number of glowing displays on the inside, but they were nothing more than indicators.

"Careful," Kara said just as he started to reach farther into the access port. Normally Kenneth would have ignored any comments and continued his own way. This time, however, it was a more delicate matter than normal.

Kenneth pulled his hand out of the access port. "I'm going to look at some of the other pods."

Kara glanced around the room. The sunlight coming through the overhang was starting to fade into the dim red of sunset. "Do what you need. We are not leaving until it is open."

* * *

Kara watched Kenneth pull wires out of the side of a smashed pod. She could not figure out what he hoped to learn from something as devastated as the one he had picked.

"When is he going to get to the one we want open?" Randin asked. He sat with his knees hanging over the back ledge of the room. "What is he looking for?"

As Kenneth pushed himself away from the twisted heap, Kara simply shrugged from the base of the ledge. "He never said."

"I bet he doesn't even know," Randin growled.

Kara absentmindedly rolled the small wristband between her fingers. She looked at the distorted words for a moment before tucking it away.

The technician moved on to another spot amongst the rubble and tossed a few loose chunks back. It would be quicker if he told them what they could do to help, but it was clear that he preferred to work alone. Then again, perhaps he simply couldn't work with anyone. It would explain the tenuous relationship he had with Norclave.

"Reminds me of Mallec," Randin said.

Kara nodded grimly. The three of them hardly ever talked about Mallec if they could help it. He had once been part of their group, though he'd mostly kept to himself. Things quickly changed when he saw an opportunity with the Kessians. Instead of keeping with their normal practice of dealing with Norclave he . . . Kara let the painful thought fall short and continued watching the sparks jump around the technician.

The faint rumble of a transport echoing into and throughout the chamber caught everyone's attention. She set a foot in a divot along the wall and pushed herself up, giving one more kick with the other foot to get high enough to grab Randin's outstretched hand. He pulled her up and they wasted no time in moving toward the entrance to meet up with Comar.

After making their way across the bottom of the chamber, they moved up a natural ramp in the ruins to where Comar was hidden by the light distortion field. The small rise was positioned to where it was still under the cover of the leaning disk, but they were high enough to overlook the open landing site, where a second transport was touching down.

"Norclave markings," Comar commented as the expedition team began to unload from the transport. One soldier with sunny yellow hair stood watch as another two Norclave soldiers unloaded crates. Another two unarmed people pointed where they wanted the crates, although half the time the two were distracted with staring up at the surrounding ruins. They were spinning too many circles to be looking out of caution; they were probably the workers.

Just as she was about to ask about who led the group, the distinct figure of Draken stepped out of the craft. He was a peculiar man, looking halfway between a soldier and tech hunter from the outerzones. He was followed out by the pilots of the transport. She quickly noted that they were armed as well.

"Eight in total," Comar said, half to himself. "The three of us and Kenneth would have made it a full transport." It was clear that this was the expedition team they were supposed to have taken part of. "Still trust them to get it to the Overlord, and us paid?"

Kara adjusted her hair back down beneath her hood. "I do not see that we have a choice."

"There is always a choice," Randin said just before he stepped out of the distortion field. "Not always the easiest to make it, though."

As Kara and Randin made their way down through the ruins, they took special care that none of the weapons were pointing their direction. People had a habit of getting jumpy at movement in the outerzones, and for good reason. That was half the thinking for leaving Comar up and concealed.

They passed by a large pillar just as the tracker was leading the group under the edge of the disk. He held up a fist and his group stopped. The five with weapons spread out and took positions on the edge of nearby cover. In response, Kara held up an open hand toward them as she and Randin neared the base level. Already uncomfortable about the arrangement, Kara was put more on edge by the few tense moments when Draken made no move to call his soldiers to stand down. Only when he eventually opened his hand to call them off did she feel the tension of the encounter ease a bit. Draken was lucky that the confusion of this Cryo business had made Comar a bit more hesitant to take a shot.

"Where is the technician?" Draken asked.

"Tell me who they are," Kara asked in return, nodding toward the only other two not in uniforms. Kara recognized the woman from their meeting with the Overlord. She had mostly kept to the side.

"Another technician and the researcher, just as planned," Draken said. "This is Sora, and he is Aarol." The researcher had her jet-black hair tied back tight, and her shoulders were cocked to one side as she struggled to carry a large bag with her slender frame. The other had dark rings under his eyes from a lack of sleep, and despite a narrow jaw, his hands, clenched around the ropes of his bag, looked like they had seen plenty of work.

"What kept you from the docks?" Draken continued.

Kara was more focused on getting answers of her own. Giving information to Draken did her no good. "What about these soldiers? We have been hunted since Norclave by the same uniforms. Can we trust them?"

Draken nodded slowly. "Handpicked by the Overlord. Now is Kenneth here or not? If he is not, then you might think about if you *should* be hunted."

"Don't think you can take anything away from us!" Randin bit back.

Before things turned dangerously close to a feast for the rubble mites, Kara pointed back into the interior. "Your technician is looking at the empty cryopods now, trying to learn about them before he tries to open it."

She noticed looks of surprise pass over several of the loyalists. They had to have been told by now what they were after, but it was likely different hearing it in this environment; it made them fully realize what was about to happen.

"Is there actually a living Cryo?" Sora asked. She pulled on the rope of her bag, though there was little use adjusting a bag of that size.

"Come see for yourself," Kara said, turning to head back toward the Cryo. While she'd made an effort to piece things together, the group was far from earning any more of her trust than was necessary, and by that same token, she knew Draken would be holding something back as well.

* * *

"Any of this feel right to you?" Aarol asked Sora quietly as they were led farther into the ruins.

Sora shook her head. Ever since the meeting between the Overlord and the tech hunters, nothing had seemed right. For years, she'd worked in the Overlord's collection, searching through recovered records and piecing them together with reports from the other cities and the outerzones. Something about the controlled environment and her systematic research had made Sora think that finally finding a Cryo would not be the unstable process it had proven to be over the past few days.

She rolled her shoulder under the weight of her bag as they started making their way down a larger slope. The actual preparation for the mission had happened during the span of only one night. With the pressure from the administrators and the location of the Cryo being on the edge of Kessian land, moving quickly was their only option. That speed was also why her bag was overly full of all the data pads and encryption devices that she could quickly grab.

When they heard a distinct string of curses echo from the partial darkness ahead, Aarol gave her a resentful glance. She had kept from mentioning that they would be working with Kenneth until they were already on the transport and under Draken's command.

"You owe me for this one," Aarol practically growled.

"I had to put forward a name. And out of all of them, I trusted you the most." Sora swung the large bag around to her other shoulder. She had heard that Kenneth and Aarol had an uneasy history, but when the Overlord had asked for the name of a second technician to join the mission, she'd had to think about loyalty to Norclave first. Old grudges would simply have to make way for the good of the Rift Hills.

The Overlord had asked only for a second technician; a backup in case Kenneth decided to be unreliable, as he often did. If it had been an option, she would have brought Laila, one of her fellow archivists. Possibly Tenan as well, but he did have a grating attitude similar to Aarol's.

"Just do not think about killing him," Sora said, "and we will get through this." It was not the answer Aarol was looking for, but it was all she could give.

Draken passed an order to the soldier on his right. Marice was her name. Sora had picked it up while they had waited for Kenneth and the tech hunters to arrive at the docks. Marice stopped the group to set up for the night as Draken continued forward with the two tech hunters.

Sora looked in the direction the tracker and the tech hunters were walking. It almost felt wrong to come all this way and not even be able to look around, but not having slept for close to a full twenty-four hours was just as good of an argument the other way. She kicked a few pieces of stone to the side and dropped her bag with a flat thud. It was not until she believed she saw a figure moving on the edge of the shadows that she realized her thoughts had started to act more like dreams.

As the others started to find their own spots to settle in, she swept a few chunks out of the way with her foot. Sora set one of the data pads with a timer for four hours before leaning back against her bag with a sigh. The Cryo had been there for over six hundred years, possibly many hundreds more. The prospect astounded Sora, but if it could wait at least a few more hours, so could she.

* * *

Deep into the night, Kara listened to the sounds of sparks and bitter remarks flying through the air. Both of the technicians had different thoughts on how to do things, and with Draken siding with Kenneth, the one named Aarol was put to retrieving tools and scavenging for parts. Kara looked at the mess of pieces spread around the locked cryopod. Just like the others, she had no idea what Kenneth had planned. And he was so absorbed with the work that he could not justify wasting the time to explain his process to anyone.

"You cannot divert that line of power!" the Overlord's technician argued.

"I am not diverting it, I am splicing off of it." Kenneth used the pair of gloves Draken brought to pick up a piece of metal he had been heating in the center of a coil of wire. He plunged the glowing piece forward into something under the pod and pulled his hand back from the sparks that spit off the heated metal.

"You could very well overload the system and shut down the cryostasis like that! Sora's records warn against a rapid thaw."

Kenneth ignored the man and wrapped a few wires around the new piece of metal. "What is the terminal doing?" he asked Sora.

The researcher tried to move through the menus with careful taps of her fingers. "I still cannot access any system information," Sora said.

"I know! Look at the display, see how sensitive the inputs are, is it pulsing or turning off?"

"I see nothing different," Sora said, fighting off a yawn at the end. "Whatever you did, it did not work."

"It did work because we are not trying to access anything!" Kenneth shook his head and grabbed a different tool from the pack magnetically held to the side of the pod. He waved it over the back of the glove, and it pulsed as the power signature synced. "For the last time, there is no way through the lock. Just keep poking about the terminal and let me know if anything changes. It will be the first system to be affected if I overload the power."

Kara glanced to where Draken sat on his heels, leaning against a pillar. Though he looked asleep in the uncomfortable position, he might as well have had one eye still open. Kara felt uneasy with him around, and she knew Kenneth felt the same with how he had accepted the gloves. The pointed silence still held between Kenneth and the tracker, though at the moment she could not say that was the cause of her nervousness.

Kara let out a short breath, waking Draken. She turned and started up the steep steps to the ledge only a few yards from where the Norclave soldiers had been trading their watch throughout the night. The one on guard jolted upright from his standing sleep as Kara topped the steps. The rest of the soldiers and pilots were sleeping, scattered about the rubble in the immediate area.

Kara then frowned, realizing she only counted another three from Norclave, besides the one supposedly on watch. With, Sora, Aarol, and Draken down by the pod, that put their number one short. Kara walked over and nudged Randin twice with her boot. The man was awake before she was within the last few steps, but they had made a habit of trying to appear less on edge than they actually were. One nudge meant to get up. Two meant something was wrong.

She nodded back toward the noise of the work. Randin stretched his shoulders as he got up to take her watch over Kenneth and the pod. Without either, they had no leverage to ensure their payment.

She stepped away from the lights they had set up around the area and moved silently into the dark of the ruins, using the lowest setting on her wrist lamp to cast faint shadows ahead. Draken would soon figure out that she had gone without a word, but part of leaving Randin behind was to act as a deterrent against any sudden actions. The last thing she wanted was for Draken to attempt to overthrow their dangerous balancing act before she could react.

Once in the darkness, Kara stepped over a set of crushed doors and ducked through their bent frame into a small room with several passages away. One passage was a rip in the wall leading back to the main chamber, and the other two dead-ended deeper into the rubble. She snapped her fingers once, causing the click to bounce around the half caved in room in and amongst the damaged cryopods along the walls. It served both as a place for the technicians to scavenge parts from and a place to give Comar a point to look out over the main room.

He dropped down from a ledge above, appearing as little more than a shimmer until he touched the ground beneath the distortion field.

"I need to know which direction she went. The soldier. Marice," Kara said.

Comar motioned for her to follow. "She started off toward the transports. I was just about to follow, but I did not want to break cover if you knew."

Just as they started off, Comar's transmission detector started blinking at the edge of his hood. Kara pulled her wrist light up to full brightness and they took off at a sprint across the ruins. If Marice had powered on a distress beacon in one of the transports, not only would the administrators be able to find exactly where they were, but any passing Kessian patrols would see them as well.

They stepped out from the cover of the ruins into the warm and swirling winds of the night. Kara pulled her hood around her mouth as a cloud of dust washed over them. When they neared the clearing with the transports, Comar pointed to the Norclave transport on the left.

Kara followed Comar into the open bay of the transport.

"Alive, Comar!"

The soldier looked over her shoulder in surprise just in time to see Comar running up and over the few crates still onboard. As she pulled for a weapon, he threw her back out of the pilot seat and into the pile.

Before Marice could sit all the way up or raise a weapon, Kara was on top of her, letting the sparks of electricity from the shocklance jump dangerously close to her face.

"Turn the signal off," Kara ordered to Comar. She forced the Norclave soldier back flat to the ground by pushing the shocklance closer. "What are you trying to do?" Kara questioned.

The woman winced at a sharp pop from the device in Kara's hand.

"You need to give me one good reason not to end you right here and now," Kara said dangerously.

"The Cryo, it will only be killed if you bring it back to Norclave!"

"How?"

"Either by the Overlord keeping it from the First Administrator, or the First Administrator keeping it from the Overlord. You cannot let that happen!"

Comar stepped back from the front of the transport. "The beacon is off."

"The Kessians are the only way to save it!" Marice pleaded.

Kara used the heated blade of her knife to cut the straps of the soldier's weapon. She kicked the weapon to the side as she stood up. "Draken brought a damned spy."

"Yes," he said darkly. "But we owe the Overlord nothing."

"What?" Kara asked. She glanced over to him and did not like the look he gave her.

"The Cryo is ours, Kara, but nobody is going to simply give us our payment. I've been saying it from the beginning."

"Then what are you suggesting? Go to the administrators? We killed three transports full of their men. Or do you think Olana Nuand will help? I can't think that breaking into her office and setting fires in her city will be taken kindly." She glared at the woman on the floor before continuing her argument with Comar. "We have to deal with Norclave. Our options have been shot to hell ever since Mallec stole the Kessian's shipment and sold it to Reclaim."

"Mallec betrayed us," Comar said, "but we knew he was ruthless long before he killed Zac."

Kara forced herself to take in a breath. Unforgiven ends had a way of stinging more than just about anything.

"Comar, Carvanhold will not care. Their deal was to pay us as a group. That means they blame us all for what happened. I am not willing to just show up with the Cryo and hope that they will forget what we want them to."

"I expect they would start a war to have a Cryo." He held his hands out to the side. "They would at least give us the payment we deserve."

"He is right," Marice said at Kara's feet. "And I can help you contact the right people."

Kara turned to the woman. "Speak again and see what happens." She let the threat hang for a moment before turning back on Comar. "Just who exactly do you think they would start a war with to get it?"

"Right now? Norclave." Comar raised an eyebrow.

"And who did we bring the information to first?" Kara said pointedly. She let the thought hang. "In their eyes, we took sides long ago."

Comar looked away in a measure of submission. Dealing with something of this importance meant taking chances, but defecting to the Kessians was more of a blind gamble than any of the other options.

"If we do decide to stick with Norclave and the Overlord, what do we do about her?" Comar glanced down to where Marice was slowly trying to edge her hand down toward the scrap-pistol on her thigh.

Kara reached down, sliced the holster free, and kicked the second weapon away. "I'm interested in what Draken has to say about this. It might force his cooperation."

* * *

Kenneth heard a bit of a commotion behind him but did not let himself get distracted from his work. He had already tried switching out the second control terminal with no success. The main system board Aarol had brought over from one of the damaged cryopods was not registering the inputs as it should. He now was carefully shifting all the cables to a third board that Randin had found several hours earlier.

He glanced over to see Sora standing asleep at the primary terminal with her forehead leaning against the pod. She pulled up straight and continued looking at the terminal. She likely thought she had only dozed off for a few seconds. A few moments later, Sora glanced at what Kenneth was doing. "Is that a name?" She looked between the display in front of her to the one Kenneth held. It was attached by a thin wire to the second control board where a mess of cables ran into the side of pod. "You made it through?"

"No," Kenneth said. He was almost impressed at how much they did not believe he was not trying to get through the unbreachable lock. "Ernest Doilif was in a cracked pod in the other room. We can only hope that he lost power before the vitals went dark, unlike Charence Beaklin, Sula Mombeck, or Oriel Marenday." Those were just some of the names on the pods he'd gone through that were incompatible with the pod he needed to open.

Kenneth draped the cord across his legs and sat the new terminal projector as evenly as he could on the ground. He accessed the system. This time there were no warnings about critical system failures. He accessed the medical logs, and it was no surprise when it flashed up a number of errors; it was imposing the medical profile of Ernest Doilif and comparing it to the readings it was getting from the pod.

"I think we are ready," Kenneth said. "We tell it to unthaw Ernest here, and it will hopefully impose the thaw sequence onto our mystery pod." Kenneth poked his way through the confirmation protocols.

Sora looked over in surprise at what was now showing on both of the controls attached to the pod. "Cryogenesis. Process estimate: six hours."

Kenneth leaned back from the mess of cables spilling out of the cryopod and felt his hand touch someone's leg. He looked over his shoulder and was glad to see Kara standing there, arms crossed. "And you doubted I could do it," he said to her.

She gave a small smile. "Not since Kamriek's Grove. Now all we have to do is hope that nobody received the distress beacon."

"What beacon?"

"Draken brought a Kessian friend along for the ride."

Kenneth gave her a surprised look. "Who was the agent?"

"One of the soldiers. Name of Marice. Comar and I stopped the signal, but we will just have to see if it was before anyone could pinpoint our location. Draken and the others are still debating what to do with her." Kara reached down a hand to help Kenneth up. "You might as well get some overdue rest. Your part in this is over."

* * *

Mallec sat awake in the open-topped seat of his small, two-person transport. The blowing dust from the rising winds caused the blinking light of the tracking device to flicker. He heard Karzon shift in the back, likely trying to find a comfortable spot for his large frame in the tight seats. They had waited for hours in the dark, and it had been quite a while since the distress beacon had flashed on.

It was a waiting game, there was no getting around that. The only information he had were the location of the gloves and his own guesses. He watched as the dot on the scanner slowly shifted to a second location, where it stopped. Five minutes . . . ten minutes . . . after a half hour had passed and there was no further movement, Mallec decided it was as good a signal as any. With luck, that would mean that the technician had finally gone to sleep.

"Karzon," Mallec said, nudging the foot propped up by his shoulder. "About Kenneth, do you know him to work late into the night?"

"I couldn't say," the large man said, pulling his foot back from Mallec's seat and stirring from his slumber. "I know that I wish he worked half as hard at paying off debts as he did at fixing things."

Mallec scratched the stubble growing between the scars on his chin. The pause could very well mean one thing: that Kenneth's work was done.

Chapter 13: Distortion

Jance watched as Avery leaned against the wall of the elevator and looked at his arm with a grimace. As he adjusted the suit again to clamp tighter, Jance knew it was bad. That was the second time he had tried to stabilize the wound since they started up. Jance crossed her arms and looked up at the levels quickly moving past.

"What can we expect up there?" Jance asked.

"A warzone? Possibly the UWC standing at attention? It all depends on if Hoffsted has taken full control or if we are still dealing with this Director Rulari."

"We can hope," Jance said, just loud enough to be heard over the hum of the elevator.

Avery went to pick up his weapon from where it leaned against the handrails, then noticed that the fire confirmation order had finally been redacted in the absence of his distortion. He simply shoved it over with a boot. It would not go off, even if he tried.

"You will need to access the communications relay as quickly as possible. Any terminal in his office should do with your clearance." Avery glanced up as the lights flashing past started to slow. "Then, re-enable connections with the UWC system."

The elevator slowed to a stop at one of the highest levels of the complex. Avery took a breath and stepped out into the large hallway with Jance close behind. The structure had the same reinforced pillars as in the lower levels, but here the gaps in between were decorated by thin slabs of white slate with additional illumination to highlight the rough-cut edges of the stone. What stood out the most about the large hallway was the absence of any person, UWC or otherwise.

Avery gave a suspicious look around saw that there was no option but to continue forward toward the heavy doors at the end. The engraved plate to the side of the entrance was marked with the director's name. Avery held up the distortion disk, but before he could even activate it, the doors shifted open.

She looked around as they entered the large room. The first thing that immediately caught her eye was the massive window stretching around the outer arc of the room, giving a clear view into the expanse of the polar south. The room was decorated with artistic furniture and revolving holographs of the Drake Discovery Complex. In the center of the room, just at the top of a small series of steps leading up to a separate rise, sat a large ice sculpture of complex intertwining loops and circles. A few of the ice rings were supported by magnets embedded within. The plaque at its base marked it as a gift from Solstice Consolidated to Outreach Systems, two of the three main companies in charge of the Mars Contract.

On the half level above, Jance noticed a man looking out the large window with his hands folded behind his back. Jance held a hand up to her visor, and the name on the overlay showed that he was the director of the facility. She sent a questioning glance to Avery. The only permanent terminal in the room was on the desk that the director stood by. Avery gave a slow look around the rest of the room. The pointedly clear atmosphere was decorated with the occasional illuminated stone slab and suspended banners showing the Drake Discovery Mission symbol. As far as either Jance or Avery could tell, the room was empty. Almost more so, with the director just staring out at the frozen wilds.

Avery slowly led the way across the floor to where the steps flowed up to the secondary level. Even as they moved past the sculpture of ice, the director did not appear to notice they were there. It was only when they neared the thin, levitating curve of the desk that the heavy door to the room opened behind them.

"Director Rulari, what the hell is going . . ." the woman who entered the room stopped short when her attention shifted from her visor to Jance and Avery. "What is going on?"

The director turned around and blinked a few times before he seemed able to focus on anything. "It is all right, Ralena. Do not jeopardize the situation. Lower your hand; I am sure the sectator has no wishes for anyone else to get involved."

Ralena looked as if she was biting her tongue when she pulled her hand away from her visor.

"Come here, easy now," Rulari said with a glance to her. He turned back to Jance and Avery. "This is not quite what I expected, I have to say."

"We need the relay brought back up," Jance said. She gave Ralena a cautious look as the woman slowly moved to stand beside the director.

Rulari nodded but made no move toward his desk. "I have given you considerable aid thus far, and I intend to continue doing so as long as the safety of the ambassador, as well as everyone of this facility—"

Avery pushed forward past the man and motioned the desk up to standing height. Rulari obviously was not going to do anything, meaning their only threat at the moment was from Hoffsted's men following them. The lights on the doors switched to red as Avery used the controls to lock the room.

Ralena gave the director a pointed glare. "What were you thinking? Does this look like control of the situation to you? I left the control room when the archives went dark, and now here we are, watching the sectator using your terminal. Are you intentionally trying to sabotage the UWC?"

"Jance," Avery said to interrupt Ralena. "Your clearance."

She moved over next to Avery and motioned from her visor to the confirmation request Avery had pulled up.

"Communications are now up," Avery said.

Jance nodded in approval.

Both Ralena and the Director Rulari looked to Jance in confusion. She then realized why. They had been told Avery had murdered Logistician Kannei, and that Jance herself was being held as a hostage.

"Ambassador Lorège?" the director asked carefully. "Are you working with the Last Edict?"

Jance turned to them, finding a directionless anger in that they did not know the truth. "Logistician Morris Kannei was killed in front of me. By the UWC. The one other person he contacted, Alexandar Hale, shared the same fate here in this complex. If it means cooperating with the Edict to prove to the rest of the world who was actually responsible, that is what I will do."

"We need to work quickly," Avery reminded her. "This could be the last chance you get."

Jance raised a hand to her visor, ready to pull on an old favor.

* * *

Weyburn rolled a shoulder, feeling his skin sticking to the inside of the flight armor. He followed Hoffsted's group as they made their way to the airlocks. Their primary mission of eliminating Hale was complete. They had been told that Hale had crippling information regarding the UWC and that the only option amidst the crisis was to take him out. Weyburn knew better than the others, though. In tracking Kannei, Hoffsted had informed Weyburn that Hale was a Cryo, and that the projects he had worked on were beyond classified. The UWC had spent nearly a century trying to erase the last traces of it all.

Of course, Hoffsted's dark operation team was trusted, but as the workings of the Last Edict showed, true secrets could only remain hidden for a short period of time once shared. Weyburn knew there was only one way to hide his own involvement.

The heavy doors hissed open and the group started into the airlocks.

"Weyburn? The mission is complete, let's go."

Instead of following them through, Weyburn hit the panel, causing the doors to begin to close. Just before they shut, he tossed in a grenade. As the airlocks started to cycle, the men inside were powerless to open the door. He saw the clicks of bullets chipping at the glass in desperation, but in a few seconds they were simply cracked viewports into the fires of the sun.

* * *

Director Auburns let out a pent-up breath as he settled his weight ungracefully into the seat behind his personal desk. It had been a torrent of nonstop communications within the UWC, and the meetings with the other governments of the world seemed to last about as long as the blasted information run on Mars. He touched a hand to his visor to switch the standard feed shown in the multiple displays about his office to more relevant information and images of the shuttles landing at the orbital staging facilities.

Auburns put a foot up on his desk, even though he knew it would only be minutes before something else demanded his attention. A deep rumble sounded in the room as a reporter halfway across the globe gestured to a massive ship touching down on a dock. The pings of several messages sounded from his visor as he watched the worried looks of the people hurrying off the craft amidst a storm.

"Security Advisory, Communication Suspension, Drake Discovery Complex."

He waved the alert away, having already put a team to investigate it. The other message asked advisement on a timeframe for evacuating the city floor. Starscrapers were designed to be easy to coordinate for an evacuation, but the sprawl of the cities around them had overgrown their efficiency, much like the forest reserves engulfing abandoned roadways. Auburns sent out a notification stating that no timeframe for the launch of the orbital fleet had been determined. He had not yet made that decision.

"What are your thoughts concerning the evacuation?" the reporter shouted to an older man as a security transport flew past them in the heavy rain.

He held a hand to one side of his face to shield against the wind. "We are all confused about the reasons," he yelled back over the rumble of the craft. "There is no good answer of why we have to go through this, but it is better than getting left behind!"

Auburns touched his visor, using his clearance to listen in on the conversation between the Council's transmissions lead and the public information systems administrator. They were discussing the final stages of the release of the Council's informational warning to the public regarding the evacuations. He precleared the global transmission, knowing that seconds of delay could mean thousands of people across the UWC deciding to ignore the evacuation preparation orders. Minutes could mean millions would not be ready for the launch. "Outreach Systems will be demanding a refund for the time we've diverted away from their lease for the informational run about Mars," Auburns heard the systems administrator say in the private transmission.

"Run it for a few hours," the transmissions lead replied. "Anyone still refusing to evacuate after that likely will not leave without forceful intervention."

Auburns agreed with the decision, though giving back even a year's lease of global transmissions time would mean little in cost compared to an evacuation. The economy of the UWC would be hit by trillions, if not more, and an actual launch of the Orbital Armistice Fleet would mean a massive shift from daily revenue to extended maintenance teams.

"I am ready to broadcast the transmission," the systems administrator said. "As soon as we have confirmation from one of the heads . . . never mind that, the director has already signed off. Ready for transmission?"

"Just one moment," the Council transmissions lead said. "I need to take this connection."

Auburns disconnected from their communications and started looking through the non-aired views from the camera crews and mounted observation arrays at the orbital facilities. It was first over the shoulders of a crowd in an OSF that he saw the release of Council's informational warning.

"To the citizens of the UWC, this is the People's Ambassador of Section-K, Jance Lorège."

The director jerked his feet from the desk and sat up straight in his chair.

"A direct address to the Council would be proper procedure; however, I fear what I have to say would simply be covered up in the process. The information I have is troubling, and it has nearly cost me my life on multiple occasions."

Auburns raised his hand to his visor as the crowd at the orbital facility began to murmur in excitement and confusion. Just as he was about to block her transmission, a blip on his visor stopped him. If it had been anyone else—even Chancellor Malcom, Ambassador Hoffsted, or the SRA Representative Lao Weijing—Auburns would have ignored it. But this was from Avery Thorne.

"Charon incident. The Tech-5 Quantum Recalibration Project. Mars Contract initial timeline. Core reactor analysis team. Kannei killed by Weyburn. Hale killed by Weyburn. Kannei suspected Hoffsted of the order."

Director Auburns let his hand fall from his visor. It had said nothing about Jance Lorège, but based on the timing he could only assume she was still with the sectator.

"I do not have the luxury of time to explain everything," the ambassador continued on displays throughout the entire world. "I call for the investigation of Ambassador Hoffsted and for his immediate suspension during the process. This investigation should extend its scope to the Mars Contract and the actions of the major companies involved, namely the applicant selection process of EMA-GO."

Auburns looked from the displays back to his visor. Hundreds of messages were logged and more were piling in. One marked as a priority above the rest was from Chancellor Malcom. It called for a suspension of Ambassador Lorège's Council clearance.

"It was not the Last Edict that murdered Logistician Kannei. The investigation will reveal the source of the command, however the—"

Just as suddenly as it had been transmitted to the world, the message went blank. Auburns had not cut the transmission, and a quick check into its status simply said the connection ended abruptly. No encoded stop was received.

The director pushed himself to his feet and started working as quickly as he could. His first order was to revoke the open confirmation he had given to the information systems administrator. Next, he accepted the chancellor's request and put a temporary halt on Ambassador Hoffsted's top-level authority. He then disabled the displays around the room and started for the door.

He had just about as many questions as he had messages backlogging on the edge of his visor. Auburns immediately started thinking about the ripple effect this earthquake of events would have across the entire globe. The blame for the first attack had seemed balanced between the Last Edict and the SRA, but with Jance now ruling the Last Edict out, he was sure they would see chaos across the world unlike any since the conflicts that prompted the founding of the United World Coalition.

As he stepped into the back halls of the Council, his next order was to initiate a three-day timeframe for the launch of the Orbital Armistice Fleet.

* * *

As the connection failed, the lights around the room started to flicker. Avery stepped back as Director Rulari's desk sunk unevenly toward the floor. Even the suspended ring in the ice sculpture clicked as it fell against the other sections. Jance watched through the frayed display of her visor as the security lights on the door to the director's office faded. Suddenly, a suspended slab of rock in one of the displays smashed through the glass case and splintered across the floor. Ralena jumped in surprise.

"This is just like the disconnects with the ground teams and the blackout in the archives, isn't it?" Ralena asked.

"Avery," Jance said, ignoring the woman's question, "how can we stop Hoffsted's men?"

"I just need to adjust the distortion generator," he said. He knelt on the ground and began working with the device on top of the now collapsed desk. "If the controls are immune to the distortion effects, perhaps I can disable the other field."

"How much time do you need for that?" Jance asked. There was a heavy thud and the door edged open an inch.

"Perhaps longer than we have."

"Where are you going?" Ralena asked as Jance started away. The woman glanced at the director staring out the window before she moved to follow Jance. "Ambassador?"

Jance picked up a chunk of the broken stone slab before making her way down the steps. Another loud hit sounded outside, but thankfully the gap did not widen. "I am going to stall them or get them to drop the field."

"Wait," Ralena said, catching Jance by the arm. "I signaled for security. They should be here any moment to deal with . . ."

Jance shook her head as the pounding on the door continued. "If they are not here now, they will not be. The field that scatters your visor will disrupt the elevators as well." As she passed the darkened showcases and empty display platforms, the door wedged open another inch.

She put her back to the door and motioned Ralena to stay to the side.

"Stop this!" Jance yelled. "It is over! I contacted the Council, pulled a favor, and transmitted everything to the entire UWC!"

"It was on the display," a voice on the other side rattled. "In the elevator. You said nothing about me before I cut you off." Weyburn gave the open gap of the door another kick.

"You think you can hide during the investigation of Hoffsted, Weyburn? You are his personal pilot!"

The loud crack of a shot from a pistol jarred her senses as the sparks bounced through the frame.

"That was a lie!" Weyburn kicked at the door, causing a muffled screech as the door moved again. "I was assigned to Kannei, but he was untraceable after he left the emergency Council meeting early. You were his primary contact, so Hoffsted tried to see if you would reveal anything useful." Another heavy hit caused the door to bounce open another inch. "You were clueless, Ambassador! Contacting you in person was the only mistake I needed from Kannei."

Weyburn gave a fluid-filled cough as he continued to kick at the door and hit at it with the butt of his weapon.

With teary redness swelling her eyes, Jance clenched the piece of rock in her hand as tightly as she could. "What use comes of getting rid of me when the entire complex will be after you? We did not just contact the world. Security has been signaled. You are just as trapped as we are."

"How many are in there with you?" He stopped to cough for a moment. "I heard another scared voice, and I can only imagine the director is still there as well. And what of your sectator?" Weyburn shouted loud enough for Avery to hear. "He has no mech to break through the window this time! No weapons. I found his in the elevator, and a smear of his blood with it. Seems as if nobody is going to fight for you this time, Ambassador!"

Weyburn gripped the crack and began to push with both hands. His undersuit was burnt back from his fingers thanks to his previous fight with Avery. Jance felt a mix of burning hatred and fear ripple down her spine as the door began to inch farther open. She raised the chunk above her head and smashed the rock as hard as she could down into his hands. Weyburn let out a yell as it crushed his fingers into the unyielding steel. He pulled back and another series of shots rang out against the metal.

"Finished!" Avery yelled. Suddenly throughout room a static of momentary pinpoints of light appeared, suspended mid-air as the fields interacted. Without a moment's pause, several more shots blasted through the crack toward Avery, forcing him to drop for cover.

Jance noticed that none of the lights had come back on in the room.

"I think has to get closer, Jance!" Avery yelled from behind the half wall on the rise. The rattle of more shots caused the glass to collapse under Avery's weight and he fell, landing hard on his side next to a blank display. He let out a shout and grabbed at his wounded arm.

Jance threw the stone into the gap to interrupt Weyburn's aim, and the next few shots sparked on the ground a few feet from Avery. Avery pushed himself to his feet and grabbed the disk as he stumbled to get to the side of the room. The flickering static between the fields increased as he neared.

"How much closer?" Jance yelled back.

Instead of Weyburn throwing the stone back through, a grenade bounced across the floor, stopping about ten feet in front of the door. "Go ahead! Drop the fields, Avery!" Weyburn called through.

In the next few moments, Avery limped over to the door opposite from Jance and Ralena. The floating pinpoints of lights from the conflicting fields turned into flickering tendrils several inches long. Ralena yelped as one of the suspended flashes of light hissed against her arm. Avery braced his back against the wall and slid down.

"Avery, are you okay?" Jance asked. It seemed as if the hasty seal on the suit had shifted, and he was bleeding profusely again.

Avery let out a pained breath. "If this goes right, the fields should cancel out."

"No! You can't do that!" Ralena shouted. She stopped flinching away from distortion field static and pointed to the grenade. "Jance, tell your sectator that he is going to get us all killed!"

Jance forced Ralena to an arm's length away and looked closely at Avery. He pointed to himself twice and motioned with the disk toward the door. He then pointed to Jance twice and signaled from the grenade to the door. Weyburn kicked the door once more and it jerked open several inches. She took a breath and nodded, hoping she understood what Avery had planned.

Jance put a heel against the wall, preparing to make a run for the grenade as Avery slowly worked himself to his feet. He activated the disk and spun his whole body with his arm to throw it through the gap. There was a harsh flash on the other side as the distortion generators screeched, and Jance started running toward the grenade. The lights of the room flashed back on and the static stopped as the fields ended. Just as she reached to grab it, a piece of rock rolled underneath her foot, tripping her to the ground with a now flashing ball in her hand.

She pushed it forward toward the door with both hands as Weyburn uncovered his eyes. The lights on the doorway flashed and one half of the door started to pull open as the grenade slipped through. Weyburn raised the pistol toward Jance, but Avery stepped in the way. Jance shouted as two loud shots rang out. Ralena slammed a fist on the panel and the door snapped shut. Avery took two steps to the side before falling to the ground. Several seconds later, the blast on the other side bent the door inward. Smoke poured in through the gap and Jance rushed to Avery.

"Avery!" she shouted, pulling him onto his back. "No, don't let it be like this, Avery!" The two wounds were in his lower chest. He gasped and seized forward at the pain. He gripped Jance's hand tightly, moving his other slowly up to his visor.

"Now," he said weakly.

"Now?" Jance asked. "Now what?" She looked up to Ralena. "Call for medical help!"

Ralena jolted out of her shock and started relaying orders through her visor as quickly as she could.

"Avery," Jance said again. "Hold on. Keep your eyes open. You may think you need to give everything for your mission, but that does not mean you have to die. You still mean something. Avery, you mean something to me. Do not give up!"

"They are on their way," Ralena said. "But we will have to get him to a better facility soon. Our advanced medical equipment has not been used since the beginning of the mission. Observation reports an incoming UWC ship that may be better equipped."

Jance watched in fear as Avery slowly moved his lips, though no sound came out. All she could do was hold his hand and hope that he did not let go. The next half minute of waiting felt like hours. Just as the UWC arrived outside the door in force, a rumbling sounded outside the tower. Massive torrents of wind ripped against the building, knocking free sheets of ice as the repulsors of the dreadnought slowed to hover next to the complex, nearly matching it in size.

"Assistant Director Ralena! If you can hear me," a voice shouted through the bent form of the door, "the entrance is not functioning!"

"Call for a maintenance crew!" she shouted back. "Hurry or we may lose him!"

Jance gave Avery a confused look as the corners of his lips twitched up into as much of a smile as he could manage. Just as she was about to ask, there was a large cracking and scattering of glass from behind. She turned to see a transport pushing against the large window and Rulari stepping backward.

A chilling wind tore into the room as the back of the transport shoved through, causing long cracks to reach across the immense curve of the window. The loading ramp dented the floor as it pushed down. A second later a figure in a temperature regulation suit rushed out the back.

Only when they neared did she recognize the voice as Welnn's.

"Dammit Avery!" Welnn shouted over the howling of the wind. "You two, get the one by the window and get in the transport. I will carry Avery!" The transport popped more ice loose and grated against the floor as the winds pushed against it. "Hurry! Lance is fighting to keep it still!"

They all wasted no time in pushing to seek cover from the torrent of cold, and even Rulari was pulled from his trance. Jance helped to lay Avery down on the floor between a few crates, then Welnn hit the panel to lift the loading ramp. It was still miserably cold in the transport, but Jance hardly noticed with her racing heartbeat.

"What happened?" Welnn asked, taking off his helmet to reveal his usual pale skin and scars. He had a layer of dried blood on one side of his face.

"Weyburn caught up to us." Jance looked down to Avery as he stared blankly upward, only occasionally blinking. She looked up to the other sectator. He held a loop on the ceiling to keep steady and stared just about as blankly as Avery did toward the front of the craft. "Where is Feyn?" Jance asked.

"We had to leave her. She was just as bad off as Avery."

Jance looked back down, feeling a jolt of sorrow, just the same as with Kannei. She rubbed a hand on Avery's shoulder as he started to shiver.

"We have clearance to dock. Brace for approach," Lance said through the ship to their visors. "The turbulence coming off those repulsors is as bad as a storm."

As the ship began to twist from one side to another under the disturbance of the gigantic gravity repulsor engines, Jance could feel the reverberations that made the thunderous drone. It was only when they lifted up through the airlocks of the dreadnought that the noise was muffled. As they bumped down to sit on a landing pad inside the hangar, Lance spoke again.

"Welcome to the *Nemesis Tide*."

* * *

Maylee tapped her fingers absentmindedly above her head where her hair splayed out on the floor. Her feet waved in a similar boredom up above the back of the long bench as she watched more massive transports continuing to arrive upside down at the orbital staging facility. It was equally strange watching from her inverted position as the people walked around on the ceiling.

The area that had been relatively empty and only filled with the halves of families waiting to be reunited was now packed with a steadily moving crowd. They were all waiting for their turn to enter the *Solstice Dawn*. It was mindboggling at first seeing the amount of people being fit into one ship, but after a while of watching the crowds move past, Maylee had grown numb to both the numbers and the waiting.

"Sit up straight," her mother said, giving her a poke in the ribs. "Or at least the right way up."

Maylee sighed and swung her feet around to the floor, feeling the rush of blood leaving her face as she righted herself. After a few more minutes of her mother stopping the tapping of Maylee's shoes, the rhythmic scratching of her small game figure across the seat, and the drawn out popping of knuckles, Maylee finally leaned into cupped hands with her elbows on her knees. She looked up as the display shifted from arrival information for incoming transports to a news report.

"Five wounded, two dead, and three in critical condition as the events continue to unfold in the far reaches of the UWC. It is unclear if the UWC ambassador is amongst that number or not, but the arrival of the UWC fleet hints at a level of alarm from the heads of the UWC military."

"A level of alarm?" Maylee murmured through her pushed up cheeks. She let her feet slide forward and slouched over farther. As if the evacuation of nearly the entire UWC was not enough to figure that out. The only meaningful information that they had aired was what Jance herself had said. "Why do they not show Ms. Lorège's message again?"

She felt her mother's fingernails scratch comfortingly across her back. "There are things happening that we do not know. I imagine that the Council is deliberating on what she said, and once they bring up more evidence, they will share it."

"You mean, try to get rid of it." Once the words slipped out, she wished she could pull them back before her mother heard. However, instead of the scolding she expected for speaking out against the Council, Agatha merely watched as a group of UWC security walked past.

"We will just have to wait. There is nothing more for it."

Maylee pushed off her knees and slouched into the padding of the bench as another wave of people moved into the area. Just as she was about to close her eyes, the stances of all the other people crowding the room caught her attention; they were all looking toward the displays. She stood up on the bench to see over their heads.

"A resolution to the situation in Arctica has been reached, and the People's Ambassador of Sector: K has been confirmed safely aboard a UWC warship. In the wake of this news, UWC Director Auburns has issued a three-day timeframe for the launch of the Orbital Armistice Fleet. We are told specific departure times will be posted in the staging facilities. Though there is much confusion as to why the director has issued the order with the ambassador now safe, we expect further information to come."

For the rest of the people in the facility, the news of the safe return of the ambassador was hardly enough to hold off the new wave of concern many felt knowing that the fleet was in fact going to launch. Even still, Maylee tugged at her mother's arm and they quietly hugged in their happiness to hear Ms. Lorège was safe. However, even that brief bit of comfort was replaced with worry over the uncertainty of her father's transfer forms. More than anytime during the wait so far, Maylee realized that they might be leaving Earth without him. She squeezed her mother tighter.

It was then that a military hauler landed on the pad just outside. She normally would not have thought twice about it with all the extraordinary circumstances of late, but there was no missing her mother pulling away and staring intently into her visor.

"What is it?"

"Sweetheart," Agatha started in a soft tone that could only mean trouble, "I am going to have to leave you to enter the orbital ship on your own. That ship that just landed is here for me."

"Why can't I stay with you?" Maylee asked. She gripped her mother's hand tight. "And what about waiting for father?"

"You must go. Do not wait for me, or for your father." She gave Maylee's hand one last squeeze. "No more questions. Stay strong, little one."

Just when Maylee did not think her world could turn over any more, her mother stood up and disappeared into the crowd without another look back. She would have run after her, but her mother's tone had been much the same as when Jance was first taken. As Maylee watched the ship lift off the pad into the night, she pulled her knees up close and squeezed the game piece tight in her hand. She then realized what the small figure of the knight must feel, kneeling on the ground, gripping a broken shaft sticking from his ribs and holding a shield up against more arrows undoubtedly to follow. At the moment, her only protection was the small metal figure and the place to hide her face between her knees and chest.

Chapter 14: Cryo

Kenneth woke up for perhaps the fifth time since the cryogenesis sequence had been started. Just as the other times, he bolted straight up and rushed to the pod as if to put out a fire. His hurried footsteps woke the tech hunters next to it. Randin simply turned over, raked bits of rubble away with a sweep of his arm, and rolled over into the clear space. Comar looked at him sharply for a moment with the silver ring in his eyes before pulling his hood lower. That left only Kara watching as Kenneth carefully looked over the mess of cables running into the side of the pod.

"You'll pull something loose worrying over it like that," Kara said. She leaned forward from her spot sleeping against the glass of the pod itself and looked up at the control panel to check the remaining time. Nearly an hour to go. She then looked toward the entrance to the large chamber where a hint of morning light poured in through the hanging dust.

"I cannot make it go any faster," Kenneth interrupted just as she opened her mouth. "If I could, I probably would risk it just to get moving before anything has the chance to go wrong."

Kara covered a long yawn with the edge of her hood "What do you think it is going to be like when it comes out? Will it know how long it was under for? Will it wake up just as tired as when it stepped in?"

Kenneth stepped closer and leaned from one side to the other, trying to see in as far as he could. The fog had thinned from the last time he'd checked on it, but he could still only see the blurred hand pressed against the ice. "I'm sure Draken would not object if you wanted to get in afterward. You could see firsthand what it was like."

"And trust you to get me out?" She nodded with a scoff to the wires strewn about. "There would be two feet prying against the inside if that was so, not just a hand."

"You could wait just the same. Someone better suited to cracking pods than I might show up in a couple of hundred years to get you out."

Kara shifted to the side a bit and Kenneth slid down with his back against the glass to sit on the ground next to the pod. He was surprised at the heat coming off it. He'd thought Kara was just being protective of the mission, but the warmth was a welcome contrast to the dull chill of the morning.

"Even given that many years, I think I would be pressing my luck in finding a replacement." Kara held up a small wristband with a flickering display. "And I know I can't leave you on your own to get out of this alive. Probably try to detonate a power pack again, or die from a swarm of rubble mites."

She tossed the band up just enough to flip it over. It was the same one that he had almost finished fixing before the mercenary caught him in Kamriek's Grove. She handed it over to him without a word and Kenneth popped off the back. After using one of the tools that came with the gloves, the screen stabilized for the most part. He clicked the back into place and held it out to her.

She smiled and shook her head. "And you said it was scrap." She plucked it from his fingers.

"It's still scrap. Useless, but you are welcome to it." He shot her a teasing glance. "Something to remember me by, once this is all over."

He expected a snappy remark in return, but there was a moment of hesitation. Kenneth tried to catch the look on her face, but Kara simply stared off into the dark, flipping the band over idly. Perhaps she had seen something.

Kara shot a quick glance at Kenneth before looking down. "What do you think is going to happen then? When this is over."

Kenneth shrugged. "I think the Overlord will get the Cryo, but he will have to keep it hidden somewhere that Silas will not find it. The mines will attempt to help the administrators, but only in secret because Olana Nuand will no doubt fear the knowledge of the Cryo. And once the Kessians find that we went on their land for something as big as this, they will start raids on the outskirts of the Rift Hills, not as a threat, but to try and coax out any information on new weapons that Norclave—"

"That's not what I mean, Kenneth. I was asking about you. You have said nothing about what you want to happen. You will have the means to go anywhere you want."

"I can never see myself . . ." Kenneth rubbed his hands together uneasily. "I can never see myself, not when I think about the future." He paused for a long moment. "I will just have to wait and see where I fit in."

"Sometimes you just have to pick a path and convince yourself that it was the right one somewhere along the way."

Kenneth nodded, though it was infinitely more difficult to dull his thoughts enough to simply accept blind chance. In reality though, it would likely mean that unless he was asked to do something else by whoever had control of the Rift Hills in the end, he would continue to fix riftwalkers at the Rift Outpost as if nothing had ever happened.

"What about you, Kara? Same question. How should things go in your mind?"

She gave a pause surprisingly similar to his own before speaking. "Return to see family, or at least what I consider to be family. I grew up as a cousin to Randin in the northeast of Reclaim. A small settlement in the center of the Ash Flats. He was the one who eventually got me to start exploring the surrounding ruins, years ago."

"What are they like? Your family?"

"Two sisters, three brothers. Of course, no actual relation, just connection. As for parents, I never quite took to them as such. They just fit in with the other aunts and uncles that had part claim to me throughout the town." Kara tucked the band into a pouch and looked over to him. "What about you? Anyone you are close to?"

Kenneth thought for a moment. Most of the people he knew either hated him or were trying to collect a debt. "Just the odd association about Norclave," he explained. "Only some vague, early memories of family, more so what I had to do to survive on my own afterward. I was taken by a Norclave patrol early on and put to work for the Overlord."

"You fit the mold of a tech hunter better than I do." She shook her head and started to say something, but she stopped when they heard a low rumble of a transport echo in through the entrance. Draken started shouting orders to the soldiers while Comar and Randin took off to the side.

Kenneth glanced over to Kara as she started to double-check her weapons. "Looks as if we will have to continue this later," he said.

"Just do not do anything stupid, Kenneth." She gave him a grim look. "I'm not looking to hear any last words. We both will make it out of here alive."

* * *

"Set charges on those transports!" Branon yelled over the boots landing in the dirt and the crackling heat of the repulsors. A few of the Nuand mercenaries made their way over to the Norclave transport and the one stolen from Kamriek's Grove. As Branon pointed for their own transport to land off toward another direction, he adjusted his visor again. Distortion from the engines aside, the visor had not worked the same since Draken had nearly broken it while threatening him to keep the technician alive. The burns on his face were enough to know he should not have followed the order.

"Iren, set up that cannon just on the edge of that trench!"

At Branon's command, the mercenary led two others carrying a pulse cannon from Kamriek. It was far larger than any he had seen before; the kind of weapon almost as dangerous to reveal as to use. Keeping the other regions afraid of the unknown was the best deterrent for invasion, though it seemed that with a prize like a Cryo, nobody was following the standard rules.

"Be ready," he said, moving to the first group of ten soldiers lined up under the thick disk of concrete at the edge of the massive entrance. Even with nearly twenty well-armed mercenaries, he knew it was going to be a mess. Draken and the tech hunters had been set up for at least an entire night. Branon motioned forward with two fingers and the first group started in slowly. Almost immediately into the shadowed chamber they had to begin sifting their way amongst bent and twisted containers. His eyes flicked nervously every time a light sparked on somewhere amongst the ruins.

"Contact!" one of the mercenaries shouted toward the head of the column. A bright flash came from the side and hit the man near his shoulder. He let out a scream and fell to the ground as the searing ejection from the pulse cannon melted through his Kamriek flight armor.

"Take cover!" Branon shouted as another few shots broke from the darkness. The group had already started to break apart to get away from the other shots sending molten chunks of stone spiraling through the air like the embers of a fire. Branon lifted the target-locking rifle he had been given and scattered a round of shots off into the dark. He ducked back as a narrow round from a focused pulse shot made a searing puddle in the metal floor just in front of him. Another spark of a bullet ricocheting from behind showed that they had walked right into the trap.

He crouched behind the bent-in container and watched as a soft glow came from behind a jut of concrete. He tapped his visor, linking it to his rifle, and stared as his visor highlighted the man behind the glowing weapon. He jerked the rifle to his shoulder and the barrel automatically shifted in the weapon's frame, letting off a precise flurry of shots. The weapon dropped to the ground in the dark and he turned to find another target with his visor. Just down the slope of the chamber ahead he saw two bolts of heat fly toward their group.

"Iren!" he yelled into his visor above the raging echo of pulse cannons and gunshots. "Fire toward my signal!" Branon pulled a small canister off his shoulder and threw it toward an uneven row of pods. When the canister cracked against the twists of steel, it let off several pulses of white light and bursts of hissing smoke. It was not enough to stop the tech hunters from firing into his mercenaries, but it did serve to help aim the cannon. The air seemed to pull sharply in toward the intense pulse. His visor display scattered as the entire chamber flashed as if in near daylight. As the shot hit like a flare from the sun, it ripped apart the twisted steel and sent a superheated web of metal back over the tech hunters.

"Give another shot just to the right!" he yelled. His visor flickered again as the giant pulse cannon blast ripped through the room a second time. In the wake of the distortion, Branon's visor attempted to lock onto the flickering form of a hooded figure off to his side. He raised his weapon and fired, but his recovering visor lost its lock when the figure disappeared behind some sort of light distortion.

Suddenly he jerked as two metal spikes pierced through his chest piece. Branon fell back against the crate as the figure appeared again off to the side. The tech hunter held an arm forward and had another spike ready in his opposite hand to feed through the magnetic rail. Branon tried to lift his weapon up, but instead the edges of his vision pulled in. The last thing he saw was a pair of silvery eyes beneath a hood and a hand unclipping the half-bent visor from his head.

* * *

Comar tucked away the visor he'd pulled from the commander and stepped back into the light distortion field with his weapon before any of the others noticed. With the battle raging on, Comar knew he could easily eliminate a few more of the mercenaries. He could fight to the death if he wanted to, but a hell of a lot of good that would do for him.

Worst case scenario, if everything fell apart, he would disappear into the world and discover later if anyone else had kept themselves alive. Comar picked up the generator from the ground and stepped back into the shadows. Caution was every bit as important as skill, and it was his every intention to take to the high ground and let everything play out. Perhaps he would step in if a precise strike could make a difference, but even with the Cryo on the line, this was not his fight.

The sharp echoes from a pair of explosions in the distance reverberated loudly within the rubble. He entered the same hole in the wall that he'd spotted the Kessian spy entering while making for the transports. He started to place the light distortion generator on the ground, but stopped with a stiff jolt of fear. Another small light on the edge of his hood meant his sensors had picked up motion. He could see nothing but worn panels on the walls and the lights shining across the parts of the room that had not caved in. He then heard a faint noise over the chaos he had left behind; it was just a slight shuffle of what could have been a boot scraping against the floor on the opposite side of a pile of rubble. Comar put a hand on his knife.

At the edge of his hearing, almost as if it were the toying growl of a beast, a deep voice gave a gruff hum. Comar's first instinct was to spin and reach for a weapon, but if he was not dead already, a sharp movement would make sure of it. If it were anyone else waiting, Comar might have chanced it. Instead, he pulled in a steady breath, knowing he was at the mercy of Mallec.

"Never lost, I see. Always know which way to run." The rogue tech hunter tossed a light onto the ground, casting a pale white against his dark and scarred skin. From behind the pile of rubble another brute of a man stepped out of the shadows. Comar figured the large man was normally sure of where he stood if from nothing but his size alone, but he was not the one that worried Comar, especially with how he rolled a comms device nervously in his hands.

"That was smart work with that device I gave you," Mallec continued. "Was that how you killed Zac, or are you still telling the others that was me?"

"What do you want, Mallec?" he growled.

"Perhaps I'm here to set the record straight."

"There is nothing straight about it. You played him against us." Comar felt a deeply rooted anger spilling up, and though he knew he was simply playing into Mallec's hand he continued furiously, "That soon, after Grace was killed by the war mech, Zac would have done anything. It was you that put the idea of raiding the Kessian expedition in his head. He would not back down. All he shouted about was how I should have been the first one in the tunnel, not her. If I had known at that moment that you were slaughtering the researchers to sell their tech to Reclaim, I would have killed you instead."

Mallec gave an amused chuckle. "That is why I never gave you the choice. Zac had your attention; there was nothing you could have done differently."

Just then, another round of shouts echoed into the room. If the battle had partially died down with the commander's death, now it had resumed in force. Another shot from the massive pulse cannon tore through, causing a layer of dust to fall onto Comar's shoulders. The large man sent a nervous look toward the battle. He'd obviously found himself in more trouble than he had bargained for.

"So, are you going to make your move," Mallec started, "or are you going to listen to what I have to say?"

"I can already guarantee I will tell you to go to hell," Comar said, "but feel free to waste your breath."

"I followed Draken to get to you. And there is no doubt the First Administrator's men followed the commander you just put two bolts into. That commander may have been working for the mines, but you know as well as I that he was no mercenary. It is a guarantee, as you know, that Silas Konrev is watching."

As Comar narrowed his eyes, his lenses automatically refined their focus.

Mallec continued. "The mercenaries torched your transports. And from the sound of the new fighting, the administrator's men have now arrived. Unless you plan on running on foot to Norclave before the Kessians take notice of the war breaking out within their borders, you need me. You need my transport."

Comar hesitated, hating that he found sense in the man's words.

Mallec continued after Comar gave no reply. "Karzon will go with you and signal back once the tech is ready for extraction. I will then let him know where to regroup, and I will be there with the transport."

"If I do get control of the Cryo," Comar said as he turned to face the weathered tech hunter, "what is to say I am not simply the distraction, just as you had Zac do to me? How can I trust you after the weeks we spent with the Kessians on our heels when you disappeared?"

"There is no trust. Not out here. Anyone foolish enough to trust should be dead already. I expect you to try to cross me any chance you get. But when you are ankle deep in the blood of those you that you led into the wrong choice, I want you to remember that I could have gotten all of you out."

* * *

"Not so tight!" Marice complained as Kara jerked the cable around her wrists after having dragged her farther from the fighting. Kara made another loop of the thin line before dropping the tether to the ground. If it had been a normal cable, the soldier would have had a near-impossible time undoing it on her own, and the spark popping when Kara touched the cable against the steel floor beneath the layer of moss only ensured that she would be going nowhere. The Kessian informant was every bit as helpless as when Kara had used the construction binding to stop Karzon.

"Just be thankful I convinced Draken to let you live." Kara tucked the cable back under her cloak and turned back to where Kenneth, Sora, and Aarol were looking over the pod.

"Fifteen minutes," Aarol said, motioning pointedly to the display. "We should be able to just pull it out now! The Cryo could very well be fully restored and just going through a waking cycle."

Sora stepped in between him and the pod. "Or its heart could need to be started still!"

"We could deal with that," Kenneth said. "But we do have to remember that this sequence was meant for a different person. Feel how warm the glass is compared to before, and look at the ice still on it. The temperature shock alone could kill it if we stop now."

Aarol ducked as pieces of rubble fell from the wall. "You really think the two tech hunters and our few soldiers can hold for that long?" Just then, another area in the distance lit up from a fiery explosion. "Kenneth, we have to do something."

Sora moved to the side and picked up one of the data pads scattered on the ground next to her large bag. "There could be multiple reasons why the records imply that the oldest pods were near-guaranteed failures. It could very well all hinge on the sequence completing. Freezing someone solid cannot be enough."

Kenneth started looking over the cables running out of the pod's side and tried to consider what was going on behind the glass. He had bet everything on forcing the sequence to run on its own, not on comprehending what was happening inside. He should have looked harder at the other pods. Even if he did not figure out exactly what the process was, he would have had a better idea. It was an oversight that could very well cost them everything.

Kara turned around moments before Draken slid over the edge. Draken wiped the blood from his forehead as he glanced back. "The administrators are here. For now they are fighting against Kamriek, but it is only a matter of minutes until one side wins out. I am not going to be here when that happens."

"We cannot take the Cryo out now," Sora said. "It is simply too much of a risk."

The tracker scowled. "I will not allow it to get into anyone's hands but the Overlord's." Draken looked to Kenneth for a definitive answer. "Can it be taken out?"

Kenneth gave a final glance to the hand pressing into the thawing ice. There was no way to be sure. He had no information to base a decision on. If they waited the full time, they could very well be turning the Cryo over to Olana Nuand, the First Administrator, or even eventually the Kessians. But the risk of a failed retrieval could mean watching the answers from a nearly forgotten past just simply die at their feet.

It was not an easy decision, but Kenneth turned back to Draken. "The sequence has to be completed."

Aarol let a curse out in a breath and Sora nodded in relief. But before even Kara had time to react, Draken raised a pistol. The two shots that rang out felt as if they'd slammed into Kenneth's own head. Pieces of glass splintered forward and bounced off Kenneth's shoulder, and it was not until several long moments later that the shards stopped tinkling across the floor. They all stood stunned as Draken turned and started walking away.

"No!" Sora screamed, breaking the silence that even the battle above could not. She started forward toward the pod, but Aarol caught her by the shoulders and pulled her back. She sank to her knees with a disbelieving sob. Kenneth turned slowly. The two shots had broken a chunk out of the front just a few inches over from where the hand now slowly shifted down through the thawing ice. Cold steam billowed out of the gap, a touch of frost against Kenneth's bloodless cheeks.

"What happened?" Comar yelled from the side. Kenneth looked over, and even seeing the familiar face of Karzon could not shock him any more than he already was. There was no hesitation. It was an instant reaction on Draken's part, as if he had already made that choice. Perhaps, like so many others, he did not think of the Cryo as anything more than a container holding information and tech. But that did not change what he had done. Just like that, the Cryo they had fought so hard over was gone. A single instant.

"Draken . . ." Kara said quietly in reply. Comar looked around, but the tracker was nowhere to be seen.

"Change of plans," Karzon said into a small communications device. He gave a long look around at the faces of the group before speaking into the device again. "The Cryo is dead."

Chapter 15: Connection and Divergence

Jance stood alone, looking through the observation window at the Council City in the dark of the morning; not that any of the billions of lights ever truly let the mixed glow overhead fade to night. She slid her hands over the clean uniform she had been given. The other set had been ruined in taking off her temperature regulation suit covered in Avery's blood.

Jance pressed a hand against the window as the rivers of transports shifted throughout the city. They reminded her of something Kannei had told her when she first took the position of ambassador. Jance believed she could have gone all her life without realizing that most of the supply shipments occurred throughout the night. Even with all the access in the world, it was a small bit of information she never would have thought to look for had he not told her. Just as she would have never thought to look for why the Drake Discovery mission was cut short, or how Hale's failed experiment led to the funding of the Mars Contract.

Jance held a hand to her forehead and closed her eyes. But what if Kannei had missed something? What if there was no grand conspiracy?

Jance let out a breath and checked her visor for any messages, though it was only out of habit. Her clearance had been temporarily pulled out of caution regarding Avery's brief access to her. More than that, her own contact with the world outside had been halted. No messages in or out, and despite her insistence, there was no contact with Avery either. She was left ignorant of his condition and made to guess that both Lance and Welnn had been confined somewhere under much stricter conditions than herself. It was even less clear if Feyn had ever made it aboard, alive or not.

The door behind her opened and a soldier stepped in. He did not wear any flight armor, just the undersuit uniform. The white stripe over his shoulder marked him as a support worker. "Is there anything I can get you, Ms. Lorège? We are serving the first shift now, though I can bring your meal here."

"No, I am fine as it is. Thank you."

He nodded, hovering a moment as if wondering whether he should salute or not. They would have informed relevant crew about her revoked clearance, though there was perhaps some confusion if that also translated to her position on the Council. He finally gave a quick gesture of a fist crossing his chest and stepped out of the room. She caught a glimpse of the two soldiers standing guard outside before the door clasped shut again.

Jance rubbed her wrist. Even with the various scrapes and bruises, the feeling that pulled her attention most was the absence of the alert band. Every member in the higher levels within the UWC wore one day and night, and even though the weight of the band was minimal to start with, its absence was noticeable. It had been taken along with her security clearance at the order of the *Nemesis Tide* command.

She shook her wrist to get the thought out of her mind as she aimlessly moved about the tables and chairs in the room. The accommodations here were replicated many times over on the same level, and a quick check on her visor had shown that she was on the emissary deck. The flagship of the UWC was equipped for the many noncombat roles it was expected to perform, and in this case, that meant holding a people's ambassador captive—or near enough to it, as far as she was concerned.

Jance expanded the directions and started out the door. She had been given free leave of the entire level, though the two pairs of boots following behind reminded her of just how free her leave was. She walked, but she had no plan. There was nothing more to do; the matter of the corruption was now in the hands of the Council, but it was perhaps the number of close calls and recent disregard for regulations that made Jance feel as if she was supposed to keep moving.

After several anxious laps about the quarter-mile-long deck, the soldiers standing guard were no doubt pleased to receive a new order to take her back to the original room for a mental health screening. It was a routine procedure, mandatory for Council members on a regular basis, though Jance could not help but worry about the real purpose behind it. Having no contact in or out also meant that she had no way of knowing if the Council had actually taken her recommendation to investigate Jonithan Hoffsted for what he did to Kannei and Hale. For all she knew, this meeting could be a setup by the military ambassador himself. A poor mental health report could be the easiest way to discredit everything she had said.

An officer and several medical technicians were waiting outside the room. Jance felt surprised at how steady her nerves were. They could already have orders to say she'd failed the test, but she managed to stand strong.

Jance stepped up to the door and it slid open. She immediately recognized the counselor looking out the window and had to contain her excitement at seeing Agatha Sharpes. When she had been expecting a nameless face under shady orders, seeing the person she trusted most was more than a relief. Even still, Jance stayed on the side of caution.

"Counselor Sharpes, it is good to see you. Our last meeting was cut short." There would be no overlooking the outwardly cold tone she took, especially from someone as attentive to signals as Agatha.

Agatha turned around and gave a small nod. Her eyes were puffy and red but she managed a weak smile. "Ms. Lorège, it is a relief to see you back in UWC hands. Now, as I am sure you expect," Agatha continued while giving a signal by pointing to her eye, "the UWC would like a full report on your mental health."

Full report. Agatha pointing to her eye. She realized it was a reference to the lenses neither of them had on. Kannei had them take them out for fear of being watched, and this was no different.

Agatha set an area recording device on a table next to a tray of food that she had not touched. The device was used in just about every session to review body language, but Jance took special notice that she did not turn the device on as she sat down.

"As per usual, this session will be recorded for analysis purposes only. Everything will remain confidential, though I assume a committee amongst the Council will take part in the review as well." Agatha dipped her finger into the dressing for the salad and began making marks on the table.

"It is to be expected," Jance replied. "I understand the need for the Council to look at this matter closely."

Jance pulled up a chair and sat next to Agatha. Written on the top of the table were the words: *"Maylee hidden. Fear UWC."*

"Now, I must ask about your transmission that bypassed the Council and addressed the civilian population," Agatha said as Jance dipped the back end of a fork into the tray. "In the transmission, you said the Last Edict was not responsible for the attack involving Morris

Kannei. Do you believe the Last Edict are actually trying to help the world by going against the UWC?"

"Of course not," Jance replied. She paused a moment as she wrestled with her new doubt of a larger conspiracy before writing *"Yes"* on the table. "I was not directly forced to support the Edict in the transmission, mind you, but I needed some way to get a step ahead of the sectator. Now, if you do not mind me asking, have there been any attacks since I was taken?" As she spoke, she wrote *"Hoffsted status?"*

"I cannot provide you with any information," Agatha replied with a shrug.

"Any concern from the Council about preventing more attacks?" Jance asked, tapping a finger on the table as the written question about Hoffsted started to leak toward the edge.

"I cannot say either way what the Council has planned in regards to the matter."

* * *

Klemmeth Auburns looked over the preliminary report from the Council committee responsible for overseeing and determining if the investigation regarding Hoffsted should be started. It was apparent that there was great interest in looking into it; however, the idea of removing the military ambassador when tensions with the SRA were continuing to rise was also met with opposition. It was a bloody mess.

He shifted his vision from his visor to glance about the small meeting room. It was still empty save for the few aids that had arrived before their counterparts. The scheduled briefing was with intelligence officers and archive analysts. He looked back to the findings document as well as his own unanswered messages to the chancellor. Malcom was likely seeking independent counsel on the matter of the military ambassador's clearance.

The director nearly pulled his visor free out of frustration at the inconclusive determination of the report. The matter of investigating the military ambassador was so unprecedented that everyone was trying to tread lightly, but they needed swift actions to counter any possible shifts that would occur long before everything could be analyzed.

On top of that, he was still working his way through the list that Avery had transmitted to him. That was also the real reason behind the meeting he'd called. It would be about the Last Edict in part, but there were more questions he needed answers to since the death of Morris

Kannei. One of them being where in the world the engineers' notes for the Core Reactor Report had gotten mislogged to. The report he had included thousands of pages of diagnostic information and data readouts, but there should have been the notes from the engineers themselves somewhere.

And then there was the matter of an information citation addressed to an unknown server system. It occurred at the same time Jance gave her big speech to the world. Some entity had gathered intelligence on where a particular set of information was stored. The archive analysts would hopefully be able to track the reference and see if that data section had been accessed yet. His gut feeling was that Ambassador Lorège had given the location of the information to the Last Edict, whether she knew it or not. And if the Edict could get a supplies coordinator to speak with the director of the UWC, Auburns knew they could have someone on the inside in a position to retrieve whatever data they were targeting.

He ran his hands over his eyes and dragged his fingers heavily down his face. He had come so close to uncovering a pattern within the Edict, and it was beyond frustrating to have his search bouncing between their involvement and Hoffsted's. Of the brief list of key facts Avery had sent regarding Kannei's findings, he trusted they were both real and vital, but there was also the feeling that he was being played against the UWC by being pointed toward their own secrets. If it meant uncovering whatever dangerous activities Hoffsted was hiding, the strike against corruption would be valuable. However, his original purpose of learning the secrets of the Last Edict seemed to have been purposefully twisted away.

Eventually the other sides of the table filed with the advisors and heads that Auburns had requested attend. He began by asking the archive specialists about the potential threat of data loss. The next minutes were spent assuring him that they had narrowed down the security leak to being a pass at gravity repulsion technology. The analysts insisted that the more crucial data was kept securely within Tech-5 Industries' archives, though it possibly pointed to Avery trying to get the Last Edict information needed to create a makeshift weapon. Or perhaps where next to target.

"And what information do you have about this Drake Discovery incident?"

It was only after several minutes of the intelligence personnel reciting vague information or standard facts that Auburns finally pushed for more answers. When he voiced concern over the military ambassador's involvement, the room fell silent. It was as if he were grabbing them by the heads and forcing them to look at an issue they had actively been trying to avoid. Just as the director was about to break down and start asking for specifics on a question-by-question basis, one younger man finally decided to speak up. He fidgeted, passing his fingers in front of the projectors on the data pad as he explained that the *Nemesis Tide* had set course directly for Arctica, hours before the disruption in communications with the complex. Furthermore, there was a communication between the military ambassador and the commanding general aboard the vessel minutes before the attack in Sector: K.

Auburns drew in a breath. It was nothing conclusive, but it was hopefully something to bring to the Council to get them to issue a halt on Hoffsted's clearance. Perhaps the connection would even be enough to get Chancellor Malcom to move decisively for once.

* * *

Avery felt himself slipping into consciousness. It was a sluggish motion, dulled by untold amounts of chemicals and customized formulas, though they were not nearly enough to hide the constant pain that spread across the middle of his torso. Every breath, forcibly triggered by the equipment he was hooked to, felt like having the two shots rattle through him once again. His senses were numbed to the point that he had no way of reacting but to lie still and stare up at the soft blue lights above. They were supposed to be soothing, but the small attempt at comfort almost made him furious.

Moments later, or perhaps hours, the lights above slowly brightened as the lock to the room cycled. He heard footsteps but had no drive to raise his head to see who entered. It was likely one of the medical personnel tasked with keeping him alive long enough to get some answers. Not that they would find anything, of course. Even if he told them everything he knew, the UWC would gain no ground in tracking any other active affiliates of the Last Edict. He had burnt ties to all his individual contacts when he started his mission, and he doubted their ability to trace the information citation he had sent. Jance herself did not even know she had helped him to point other sectators toward valuable information.

Hell, even if he talked about the meetings with the director, it would be a simple matter for Klemmeth Auburns to deny his words as the ravings of a man on the brink of death.

Out of the corner of his eye, Avery could see the flickering lights of the med-tech working at a terminal to the side. The person had said nothing. Perhaps he did not realize Avery was awake. Avery glanced to where charts and diagrams of his own medical status were displayed. Showing boldly on one panel was his state of consciousness. Any worker in the entire wing could see whether he was awake or not . . . if it displayed the correct information. According to the system, he was still deep in a sustained coma.

Avery felt the forced impulses to breathe fade away as he was transitioned to his own painful life support. It was difficult to make himself pull in the next lungful of fire.

Eventually, Avery felt in control enough to try speaking. "Does that mean I am as good as dead?"

"I am sorry," the man said apologetically. He stepped away from the terminal and moved to look over Avery. Avery did not recognize the round face and short jawline of the medical technician. "You are more alive than you should be, actually. I pulled you out days before you were scheduled."

Avery clenched his teeth as the muscles in his back started to pull tight from the pain. "Are you one of Hoffsted's men?"

"No." The man reached into a pocket of his uniform and stopped for just a moment. "I was contacted several years ago," he said, "by a man sent from the Last Edict. I was too hesitant to be of much use; far from how I imagine you acted, to be assigned such a task."

Just as Avery was about to work up the nerve to speak past the pain again, the man clipped a visor onto the side of Avery's head. He was surprised to find it was his own, though it took several moments before it recognized his impaired neural patterns.

"Now that the time has come, I am finally going to make a stand, in my own way." He tapped the side of the visor to get it to extend its display in front of Avery's eyes. "I can give you about five minutes to make contact. It will take time to get you back under."

Avery started to pull his hand to the visor, but the encryption sequence started before he had his hand even halfway there. Eventually, the connection went through, and he could see Director Klemmeth Auburns glancing off to the side.

"This is interrupting a very important meeting," Auburns said. Avery could hear a set of doors cycle, and the light changed on the director's face. "But something tells me you can give me more answers than my people on what the Edict was after with Lorège's clearance."

"Just listen," Avery said. He hardly felt able to address any problems the man might be having. "Jance needs to be reinstated. No one else will push Hoffsted as hard as she will. You know this."

"She is completing her evaluation now. The committee will make a decision once they review it. Same with Hoffsted."

Avery shook his head, feeling a stiffness that continued high up into his neck. "It will be too late then. Even the Edict will not be able to move quickly enough. There is information missing."

"You are speaking to me from within the medical brig of the flagship of the UWC. Something tells me the Edict is resourceful enough. We also know you used the Ambassador's clearance to point them toward information. It may be because of your actions that she is not reinstated. Avery, it is simply too dangerous for me to intervene and help any further."

"Help?" Avery growled. "What have you done to stop the unnatural and needless end of all of humanity? We told you exactly where to start looking within the UWC. If you would have stopped hiding behind walls of security and looked for yourself at what Hoffsted was doing, the Edict would not have had to go as far as it will now."

Auburns squared his jaw and looked around the empty hall. "I gave you more than enough trust. You are nothing but murderers, and yet I was fooled briefly into believing that you existed for the purpose you claim."

"Murderers?" Avery shook with anger, and perhaps from the pain of being woken earlier than he should have been. "You call us murderers? We are fighting a war. It was you that hid in the dark, feeding Morris Kannei all the information you needed to get him searching. You watched as he unknowingly took your risks upon his shoulders. You used him to make the connections that you could have made months ago, and when it went too far and his life was at risk, it was *me* that you sent to get him out. Before you call me a murderer, ask yourself: Who was really trying to keep Kannei alive? Ask yourself: Who really cared if he was eventually silenced? No, ask yourself, Klemmeth: Who is to blame that Morris Kannei did not know he was risking his life to *almost* save every life that would have continued on after his own was taken?"

The director stood for a moment in silence as Avery fought against the redoubled pain. Without another word, the transmission was canceled. Avery knew gaining support from the director would never happen after Auburns had started funneling Edict information to Kannei. It was a bold move to go after one of the heads of the UWC, and Avery should have been more forceful about his unease after their first couple of encounters. Klemmeth Auburns was simply too far ingrained in his thinking to fully see the solution the Last Edict demanded. It was not perfect; far from it. It demanded sacrifice. To orchestrate the grand scheme, it had to be hidden so there could be no countermeasures put in place. Often, targets were picked at random so there could be no pattern to the real movements. It was something Avery could not have done, and something that he knew Welnn kept hanging above his head during peaceless nights.

But it all could have been different had he swayed the director. The technologies and weapons that were capable of bringing absolute annihilation could have been uncovered, without need for this war. He'd read books—actual binding of papers kept by the SRA—about what had been narrowly avoided in the history of the Earth. He could settle with nuclear war, genetic warfare, and even the prion gasses. The Last Edict were not trying to prevent the world from falling into waste. They were trying to prevent humanity's complete and permanent annihilation.

"That is all the time I can spare," the med-tech said. Avery continued his blank stare upward as the man removed the visor. He said something else, but the words were distorted in Avery's ears as the system shifted back to normal function. He felt a sharp jerk as his breathing was forced to continue in line with the neural compulsions. Before Avery could even complete his thoughts on the strangeness of the feeling, he fell deep into unconsciousness.

* * *

At the forward command bridge of the *Nemesis Tide*, procedures continued at emergency levels. A full staff of control officers ensured that near 90 percent of the stations about the large multistory room were filled. Their orders put the officers in a state of high preparedness, watching tensely over the Council City for any threat. Here, the voices of operators coordinating fighter teams throughout the city echoed up through the various levels and overhead walkways.

In the center of the room, Admiral Brakka stood in command of the dreadnought, looking over the incoming information and location marks of other UWC ships displayed on the ring of projections around the platform. Just past him, at the head of the ship, was a large window giving a bold view out over the city and to the starscraper rising miles above the starry shadows clinging to the darker sides of the surrounding buildings.

The main airlock into the room made shifting noises as the gas was vented and replaced. Any personnel not at their station turned to salute the incoming general. His footsteps were heavy against the steel floor.

General Garneth Obrourke was always armed for battle and currently wore full heavy tactical gear. Many of the other ranking UWC military found it odd, but it was something they were told to not ask about. The inset piston rails and hydraulics that aided motion at the joints were designed to help soldiers lift far more than a person normally could. In the case of the general, it was a tightly kept secret that the suit was to help combat the effects of a degenerative disease.

General Obrourke nodded to the soldiers saluting and continued past quickly. Anyone looking to his roughly chiseled jaw or at the sharp inspection he gave around the bridge would have no way to tell he was anything but a hardened soldier who had worked his way into the command of interior defense.

"Admiral Brakka," General Obrourke said bluntly. It was not in greeting, but to pull the admiral's attention. The general expected no salute and gave none in return.

"If you are looking for commendations on leading us to the ambassador, Obrourke," the time-hardened admiral said, "you can tell your source of the information that I will be glad to give it to them."

Brakka had felt undercut in the operation. He was a proud man, and being told where to send his ship without giving him the source of the information was just the same—in his eyes—as telling him how to command.

"Ambassador Lorège is to be transferred to the Council Starscraper," Obrourke said.

"Give me the order from the Council, and I will see it done." It was a pointed mark of resistance from the older admiral.

"At Jonithan Hoffsted's orders," the general stated.

"I understand that Hoffsted kept you in the military, transferring you up when your situation should have disqualified you. But do you really think following that order is wise, considering?"

Standing nearly a foot above the admiral and wearing a full suit of armor fitted with movement systems, Obrourke gave a scowl that would have made most men think twice about questioning him. "Hoffsted is the ambassador between the Council and us. They have not removed him as of yet, meaning his order has the Council's approval. Unless, of course, you want to deal with the aftereffects of ignoring a direct order when the entire UWC is in a heightened state of alert. I would suggest you give me the location of the ambassador so I may personally see the transfer through."

Admiral Brakka narrowed his eyes. "Not really a direct order, now is it?" He smirked and slowly moved over to the console. "There. Her transfer to the Council is set up. Nothing more you or Hoffsted have to worry about doing yourselves. Now get off my command bridge."

* * *

Obrourke stood for a moment before turning away without another word. It was not ideal, though he had never expected to get a straight solution out of the admiral. He had fought against him on a number of occasions, namely during his quick ascent to the head of interior defense. Obrourke had heard many long speeches about needing to live as part of the system for years before stepping up to control it, but it was that type of thinking that only ensured the continuation of the same losing ideas and stagnant strategy.

He flicked his visor across both eyes and followed the displayed pathway toward the hangars. There were hundreds of launch points to choose from. Had Admiral Brakka thought harder about hiding the departure location of the ambassador, he could have picked any one at random. It was the same formality that forced the admiral into predictability. The old man held the Council in the highest regards, and thus would reserve only Hangar Lock A-001 for the ambassador.

As Obrourke stepped past the security into the elevator, he just hoped Ambassador Hoffsted would stay instated long enough to hold up his end of the bargain. Obrourke's son, Samuel, had barely made it to a transmissions post with Outreach Systems; he'd almost gotten held back because of his genetic history. The only way Obrourke stood a chance to get past the EMA-GO screening was to have Hoffsted convince them to look the other way. That meant finishing his task.

* * *

". . . and check that the straps are secure. Just like that, good."

Jance tugged on the strap over her shoulder and the soldier gave her a thumbs up as the repulsors started to whir on with a low rumble. They were finishing the final preparations for departure to the Council Starscraper. After she had concluded the meeting with Agatha, she had been given back her wristband and told her clearance would be reinstated in full once she appeared before the Council. It was a huge relief, even if there was no word on Hoffsted's status.

She looked out at the crews working in the hangar as the man who had been giving her instructions stepped out of the back. If she moved quickly enough, Jance knew she could keep conflict from spreading between the UWC and the SRA. And perhaps the Last Edict would start to fade away if she could convince the rest of the Council to work further restrictions onto whatever Hoffsted was trying to hide. Perhaps she could even speak with Director Auburns to delay the launch of the Orbital Armistice Fleet.

Deep in her thoughts, Jance almost did not notice the figure stepping up the ramp into the transport. When she finally looked up, she wondered how she had been that distracted. The man almost had to duck as he stepped in, and the mechanical suit he wore had the look of serious business. He did not make eye contact with her, even as the door to the transport started to close. Perhaps he was a personal guard assigned by Admiral Brakka. Jance almost rolled her eyes at how quickly she had gotten used to not knowing all the details over the past days. She pulled her visor across her eyes and saw his name: General Obrourke.

The UWC General of Interior Defense did not take a seat as the transport lifted off the ground; instead, he simply grabbed a handle on the ceiling and his suit made a series of clicks as if locking in place. Jance watched him curiously. Perhaps there was worry even from within about her safety because of Hoffsted's corruption. It seemed as if her message to the world had made an impact.

The lack of conversation as they hummed over the city felt strange, but the only person that she had really spoken with after leaving through the window of Rulari's office was Agatha, and even that had been stiffly false. Perhaps the silence was a precaution. Either way, Jance knew for sure that there would be no speaking with Avery. At least, not for a long while.

Several minutes passed until the pitch of the engines started to shift and they began a descent.

"Why are we going down?" Jance asked, though the man did not acknowledge her at all.

From the window of the emissary deck, she would have sworn the Council airlocks were either level with the *Nemesis Tide* or perhaps even above it. Jance pulled in a breath and forced herself to calm her nerves. She had created a strong defense against action from Hoffsted by calling him out directly. She was safe from his reach. Anything that happened to her would reflect immediately back on the military ambassador, meaning he could not risk employing another agent to come after her and still be able to hide from the fact. His primary focus at this point would be to sway the Council against her recommended investigation.

Her insides felt as if they were trying to continue downward as the craft touched down. The reinforced armor of General Obrourke hissed as it moved for the first time since he'd stepped in. The ramp dropped down and the warm city air flowed in. Jance stepped out onto the large, circular landing pad and looked up at the massive structure rising above.

"Where are we?" Jance asked. She looked over her shoulder past the other two military gunships that had touched down to either side of her transport. Jance gasped as she noticed smoke billowing out of the Council Starscraper in the distance.

A swarm of emergency vessels approached the face of the Council Starscraper, and when she pulled her visor again, she was immediately hit by warnings and caution advisories. The *Nemesis Tide* filled the air with a chopping rumble as it moved to position itself closer to the starscraper and the source of the damage. It looked as if multiple levels had been ripped out just below the Council Chambers.

She started to search for any reports on what had just happened, but she was quickly ushered into the building. They immediately started for the lower levels, pushing her past the checkpoints of SorrCom Industries' security.

"I need a report on what is happening," Jance demanded as Obrourke motioned for the few soldiers to stand outside the pressurized lock to the next room. "Why are we in SorrCom? Who attacked the Council Starscraper?"

"Ambassador Lorège, there was a detonation within the Council airlocks. It could have been a failed repulsor, or it could have been an attack by the Last Edict or SRA." He waved a wrist over a second layer of authorization inside the airlock to continue the sequence. "I am making use of improvised tactics to ensure your safety."

Jance narrowed her eyes as she watched the display flicker for a moment before continuing with the sequence. "The corporations within the UWC have their own security classifications. How is it that you came by access to a SorrCom facility?"

"They have allowed us usage of their facility for the duration of the crisis. This way, Ambassador."

As soon as the doors closed behind her, she knew she should have never stepped forward. The large room was several stories high, and smaller doors around the levels led off to many side rooms. There were sections in the center for computer terminals and data storage, as well as tables with inset places for a variety of tools. Lining the edges of the room for several levels up were hundreds of cryopods. Just like the guards of the various checkpoints, the SorrCom technicians inside the labs gave them confused looks.

"What is this?" Jance spit as she pulled to a stop.

Obrourke looked sideways over his shoulder. "An opportunity. For both of us. We get to escape this war."

One of the workers approached. He wore a grey undersuit accented by white bands and plates along with the half diamond and crescent symbol of SorrCom. "You cannot be in here, this is a private SorrCom storage facility. Any applicants for cryogenic . . ." the man trailed off in surprise when he recognized Jance.

"The ambassador is here to enter cryostasis," Obrourke said.

"I am not!" Jance bit back. "I will not hide from a war when I have the power to stop it."

"We . . . we cannot just place a person in as it is," the worker said. "There are extensive medical scans that have to be—" he stopped again. This time however, he was looking intently at the pistol Obrourke was holding on him. The general then took Jance's shoulder with a grip of iron. As the general nodded for the worker to move, Jance was sure that the only reason she was left walking in front of Obrourke was that he held his arm close enough to the ground for her feet to touch.

She tried to pry his hand away, but it felt like the grip of a caretaker unit. She looked around as the other workers in the room watched in alarm through their visors. A number were calling for security, though she knew the soldiers outside would hold them off for the time being.

"I reiterate," the man said as he nervously walked backward, almost stumbling in front of Obrourke's heavy steps, "we cannot just put her in. While the pods are equipped with the basic equipment, she needs a preliminary scan."

As they reached the end of the room, Obrourke motioned to the wall of pods. "Open one."

While most of them were empty, Jance noticed the inside of one was covered in ice. The maintenance symbol on the display showed it was running a self-diagnostic. The worker gave a nervous glance around before putting a code into the terminal of the pod next to it. The front glass of the pod split along the metal seams, causing the lower third to sink into the base while the rest slid up and back. Jance caught herself against the standing seat inside the pod as Obrourke shoved her forward. She turned just as the general shoved the man out of the way and signaled the doors to close.

"Initiating SorrCom Industries Cryostasis Systems," a voice inside the pod said. Jance pounded a fist against the glass as Obrourke shouted at the man. "Please remain calm while SorrCom technicians or other authorized personnel complete the user data inputs."

"We have to assign a name!" Jance heard the technician shout from outside.

"The process will begin momentarily, A. Zero. One." Jance cursed at the system. If she was going to be forced into becoming an ice cube, it could at least try to give her a real name.

"Hoffsted," the general said into his visor above the protests of the technician, "the ambassador is secured. I will await your final orders."

As Jance started to look around the interior for some way to cancel the sequence, her wristband lit up and a communication request flared on her visor.

"Tell me your position."

"Avery?" Jance exclaimed in excitement. "How are . . . ?"

"You can thank Director Auburns," he said. "I am entering the SorrCom building now. Where are you at?"

"Lowest level. We passed several security points on the way in," Jance warned. She heard a faint echo as a person near Avery told him to continue through.

"Security is not a problem. How full were those transports you arrived in?"

"At least five soldiers are just outside the entrance to the labs. General Obrourke is just outside my pod, heavily armored, though I do not believe he has a helmet." Jance coughed as a wave of cold air flooded into the compartment with a hiss. "The cryostasis sequence is starting. We may lose contact any moment. The name on my pod is A01."

"That is a lovely touch," Avery said. "Better than naming you traitor, I suppose. Or even pain in the ass."

"Is that what Hoffsted would say, or you?"

"It depends on how many more times I get shot this week."

Jance wrapped her arms tight around herself as the cold air continued to flood in. "Avery, just . . . just be careful."

He started to say something, but the transmission cut with the partial crack of a firearm nearby. Jance leaned forward as a thin coat of ice started to form on the surface of the glass.

* * *

"Hold it there! UWC orders!" the soldier shouted from the end of the hall.

Avery held his hand to his chest, though the pressure would not help any more than the tight-fitting SorrCom suit he had on. They believed he was corporate security with the uniform and baton on his hip.

"I am ordering you to stop!"

The other UWC soldiers started to ready their weapons.

Avery tossed a canister forward, and it burst into a cloud of enveloping dust and smoke. Avery closed his eyes and held his breath as he lunged to the side. He was almost immediately deafened by the shots skipping down the center of the hallway. Even the heavy dose of pain inhibitors he'd taken were not enough to completely cut the fire that flared in his arm and chest as he impacted sharply against the wall.

He wasted no time in rushing forward. The chalky dust gave him visual cover, and the flecks of metal specially designed by SorrCom to skirt the edge of the Inhibition Protocols scattered any sensor readings the soldiers may have tried to rely on.

Avery used the sound of the last ringing shots to determine when he was close. He pulled the baton from his hip, and it hummed heavily in his hand as the end charged. A quick press of a button set the baton to a wide dispersal pattern. He started raking the weapon across any flight armor he could and the men began dropping to the floor. The armor diverted most of the shock away, but a longer press with the wide pattern eventually seized up their muscles. Feeling around on the ground, he picked up one of their rifles.

It was only when the air was cycled in the airlock that he finally took a breath. He shook his head, making more of a cloud of dust to be pulled away into the filters. It was a simple matter to bypass the security of the second doors into the lab with the code Klemmeth Auburns provided. Avery had been beyond surprised when the director had ordered his transfer, though this whole thing would have been a hell of a lot easier had he decided to help before Hoffsted got a hold of Jance.

He was forced to immediately dive for cover behind a table as shots sparked off the opening doors. Avery groaned in pain as he rolled up against the front desk. It also would have been that much easier if Auburns could have managed the transfers of Lance and Welnn as well.

Avery took a breath and gripped the UWC weapon tight. The red of the display on the side showed it still had its fire orders. All he needed was one perfect shot.

Avery cycled three slow breaths and raised the weapon over the desk. With Obrourke clearly in the sights, Avery pulled the trigger.

Nothing happened.

As he attempted a second pull, two shots blew into the top of the desk and he dropped back down. Blood streamed down his face from the debris fragments and he let the weapon fall to the side. The display showed a friendly fire override.

"Jance," Avery said quietly, brushing the blood from his cheek and readying another SorrCom canister. "You still there? I need your help to get past this guy."

* * *

Obrourke missed for the fourth time as the sectator moved through the layers of smoke at an angle he did not expect. He cursed and pounded a fist against his arm. Even if the man equipped as a security guard showed himself for only a half second, the suit should have automatically positioned the pistol for a perfect shot.

As a hand reached up from behind one of the worktables, Obrourke pulled the pistol forward and fired manually, missing only by a few inches. He cursed.

It was almost as if the sensors were being forced to ignore the target. Likely some rudimentary form of nanite developed in SorrCom, dispersed in the smoke. To him, the tech seemed in conflict with the Inhibition Protocols. There was a flicker from the side he had not been watching as the man moved up another layer of the desks.

"Thorne!" Obrourke called out. "It is no use! We already know your contact!" When there was no reply from within the clouded room, Obrourke continued looking for where he would appear next. "It was Hoffsted that ordered you brought out of your coma in the first place. The man who woke you was ours!"

"That is the kind of lie that led to this!" the sectator shouted, followed by a cough.

"Not every recruit believes in your vision of chaos! The spy was hesitant. He came forward to the UWC some time ago, did you know that?" Obrourke held the pistol ready for when Avery finally showed his face. "We allowed the Edict to plant him aboard the *Nemesis Tide* just before it set off to retrieve the ambassador. It was a risk that paid off."

There was a rattle from one side as another canister hissed its contents up into the large room.

"You contacted Director Klemmeth Auburns," Obrourke continued. "He was the one who told you to kill Logistician Kannei. And the one who sent you here, to kill Ambassador Lorège." Obrourke waited through another pause of silence as the smoke thinned in the room. Hoping to stir Thorne out, he started forward, just as prepared to finally shoot the man as to crush him underfoot.

Obrourke neared the workstation, dug his fingers into the metal, and flipped it forward. Just then the leg of his suit froze up with a static crackle. He ducked forward, narrowly dodging the sectator's attempt to crack a large metal fusing tool against the back of his head. Instead it sparked against the shoulder of his suit. Obrourke swung an arm around, missing the sectator by only a few inches but knocking the tool some thirty foot away. He pulled the pistol forward, but the SorrCom stun baton pressed into his forearm, locking the system momentarily.

Avery rolled over the last row of desks as the general raked the pistol upward with a series of shots. He growled, feeling the baton messing with the systems of the suit.

Despite his frustration, Obrourke managed a smile as Avery reached the pods along the wall. In the sectator's rush, he started to access the wrong one. The frozen glass opened, spilling waves of murky air out over the floor. Avery then started working to open Jance's pod. Obrourke holstered the pistol and flexed the joints of the suit to ensure they were working properly again. He started forward through the new layers of rolling fog.

* * *

"Avery, watch out!" Jance shouted as Obrourke rushed forward with the extra two hundred pounds of weight of his armor. Avery turned and gave a shout, jumping to the side. She felt a jolt as Obrourke slammed into the closed pod next to hers, busting the glass out across the floor. She pressed against the glass, trying to get sight of Avery.

"I have a transport to Mars waiting for me!" Obrourke's muffled yell echoed louder through Avery's comms than through the freezing glass. "I find no need to suffer here with the rest of the world through the war you started!"

Jance gasped as she saw Avery thrown through the billowing fog and back to the other side of her distorted view. Obrourke rushed forward and Avery struck up with the stun baton, momentarily crippling one of Obrourke's arms.

"If you can't even stop me with that suit," Avery said as he ducked a quick jab, "how can you expect the EMA-GO to accept you?" The baton sparked as Avery smacked it three times into Obrourke's ribs. "Hoffsted's paying your way?"

Obrourke snapped a hand forward and caught Avery on the shoulder. Avery screamed and only a quick flick of the baton kept his arm from being crushed loose from his shoulder. Obrourke lunged forward again as Avery slipped out of his grip. Avery stumbled to the side, just out of Obrourke's reach.

"Hoffsted will clear my path once I make sure the ambassador is safe in cryostasis!" He planted a boot on top of Avery's foot and shoved forward with both hands. Avery could not catch himself as he slammed backward into the fog rolling over the floor. Obrourke dove forward with an overhead punch that landed like a transport crashing into the edges of an airlock.

Jance could not see anything but the punches and flashes of light popping frantically within the fog like a thunderstorm. Eventually Obrourke stood up out of the waves, holding Avery by arm. The baton was in Avery's immobilized hand. Obrourke drew back his other fist to finish it.

Avery let go of the baton and caught it with his other hand. He made a swift strike into the general's exposed neck, and Obrourke's head fell limply back against the metal shoulders of the suit. Obrourke tried to move, but everything was functioning as if he were half conscious. Avery wrenched his arm free of the suit's grip and slipped to the floor. With final one rush, Avery lunged forward with a shoulder and continued pushing, forcing the suit and a dazed Garneth Obrourke to reel backward. There was a loud thud as the general fell into the open pod. Avery strode forward with the baton.

A second later, Jance could just see Avery step back as he watched the paralyzed general unable to move. Avery turned the baton off. He then reached forward, and the glass of the other pod closed as Obrourke's own cryogenic sequence began.

Avery held a hand over his chest as he stumbled over to Jance. The chest piece of his suit had cracks spanning across it, and his shoulder looked just as bad as the chest. "Glad that is over," Avery pushed out.

Jance gasped, not from the encircling cold, but from the connection that she'd just made. "Avery, that gives it away!" Her lips seemed to lag from the temperature.

"What does?" he asked, grunting through the pain. He put a hand against the glass to stabilize himself and looked to the floor. "Gives what away?"

"What Obrourke said. About an opportunity for both me and him to escape the war. He thought I wouldn't see it because I would be locked in here. But Hoffsted was sending him to the Mars colony. That is the connection." She took a sharp breath through the cold. "The colonies can survive no matter what kind of force the UWC uses on Earth. That is the threat Hoffsted intends to leverage against the SRA."

"Are you certain about this?"

She pressed her hand up to Avery's and felt the ice slowly beginning to form between her fingers. "We can stop him now, before this goes too far."

"Jance . . ." He looked up, but she could now barely see him through the ice. "Not this time."

"What do you mean?" She tried to look into his eyes. "Avery?"

"If what you are saying is true, Hoffsted will not be looking for a war. He means to recreate the failure of Alexandar Hale's experiment here on Earth. He intends for the Mars colonies to continue alone."

"But . . ."

He took a step back, leaving her hand alone, pressed up against the encasing film. "I am sorry." Avery spoke quietly through the comms. "If there is a world left, I will come back for you."

Jance watched in surprise as Avery stepped back, turning into nothing more than a shadow through the layers of ice. She gradually felt the cold take a deep hold in her as a new mix of gasses were filtered into the pod, bringing numbness and slowing her breathing. Even against the last echoing recommendations of the automated system to remain standing, Jance let her knees buckle beneath her, let her head droop low, and left a mournful hand pressed against the edge of the world she had just now come to understand.

Chapter 16: Rust and Ashes

Sora shook her head once again and adjusted her feet on top of her large bag of data devices. "I still cannot believe he did it. Draken actually killed a Cryo. Two shots, head high, into the glass."

There was a bump in the back of the transport as one of the repulsors spurted a bit. There was no reaction to Sora from anyone else in the back. Aarol sat next to her with a blank stare, Kenneth sat across on the floor with an arm propped on a crate, and Karzon held onto a handle near the exit as if ready to jump. Kenneth normally would have felt the same urge to escape as the brute of a man, but the shock of everything had left him without the motivation to even think. The transport was heading to Norclave, piloted by the First Administrator's men.

Some time after the Kamriek mercenaries had all but scattered, the administrator's soldiers called through the ruins for Kenneth and the others they had not yet captured to give themselves up. Kara was ready to make a stand by herself, but Kenneth was not going to let her anger about the Cryo get her killed. He knew then, hiding behind the rubble, that it was all over. And he knew he had nothing left to keep running for. Kenneth had told Kara to stay hidden as he stood.

"Why did he do it, though?" Sora continued, mostly to herself. For her, losing the Cryo was a failure after years of preparation.

"So he burned some tech," Karzon said in a sneer. "What did you expect? The Overlord could not risk it falling into the First Administrator's hands. Like we are now."

Kenneth rolled his head far back against the rusted seat and watched the ceiling of the transport. They simply had to wait and see what would happen. The soldiers claimed Silas had questions for them. After that, there was a strong possibility they would all be sent to the Cells. In Kenneth's mind, it was better to have walked willingly than to let Kara be found. Silas had no interest in the tech hunters anyway. They were simply rogue pieces; his main goal was to take control of Norclave.

"I shouldn't even be here," Karzon said in a quieter tone. He looked to Kenneth. "I came all the way out here just to get even with you, you know that? Now look at me."

Kenneth pulled his head back up. "That is a hell of a distance to go for a few missing tokens."

Karzon held up a hand. He had long scabbed strips running around them from where he had struggled against the cable. "When you and that tech hunter of yours left me tied up in the corridors, I was sure I would kill you the next time I saw you." He looked to the wounds on his hands, which would end up as deep scars. "But I suppose that would only make you worth as much as the Cryo is now."

Kenneth took hold of the sack Draken had given back to him and tossed it over to Karzon's feet. "Consider everything paid then. Even all your other debts, if you do not feel like keeping them as trophies."

Karzon gave Kenneth a suspicious look and nudged the bag with a foot. "What is it?"

"Nothing you would be smart enough to use. Just sell them." Kenneth scratched at a bit of dust in the corner of his eye. "Just do not take them to a man by the name of Mackelry Norton. He is expecting them back."

Karzon picked the bag up and sat it on a crate next to him, though he grumbled about being caught in the middle of something else.

Kenneth shuffled around again before finding a position comfortable enough to close his eyes. The occasional jolt in the craft was more than enough to keep him from getting anything close to sleep, but after everything that had happened, it was worth a try. It very well could be the last chance for anything.

* * *

Hours after the administrator's soldiers left with Kenneth and the last of Draken's group, Kara sat with her feet over the edge, watching the chilling fog roll out of the hole in the cryopod. It settled out over the floor, much like mist at the bottom of a valley. The Kessian informant was still bound by the cables down below, and while the woman complained that the haze was freezing, Kara felt no urge to move her. Both Randin and Comar had voted to leave her for the Kessians to find.

They had also voiced their desire to leave hours ago, around the same time the soldiers had taken Kenneth. If the technician had not gone with the administrator's men on his own accord, she had no doubt that she would have gotten herself killed in the process of resisting them. Kara flicked her thumb back and forth through the glowing projection on the wrist band.

She slipped the band over her hand and pulled it onto her wrist. She had said she would protect him, would get him out of this alive. She had not sworn to it, but breaking her word felt wrong just the same, especially when she realized that the band he had joked about really was all she had left of him. The other two tech hunters had plenty to scavenge through after the battle, but she knew nothing else would catch her eye.

"Tech hunter?" the woman down below called up. "Kara?" Marice asked nervously.

"Your ties coming loose?" Kara knew they would only hold tight for perhaps another hour. She thought for a moment about going down and redoing the cable, but Kara actually found it hard to blame her. Despite the transport beacon the woman had activated, in the end it was Draken who had ultimately sabotaged the recovery of the Cryo. The same man Kenneth had told her not to trust . . .

"It is not that," the soldier said, turning to the thinning trail of fog leaking out of the holes in the glass. Every two seconds or so the fog was illuminated by the red glow of the repeating *"Critical Failure"* message. "I think you should come down here."

Kara narrowed her eyes as she searched for any hidden weapon Marice might be thinking to use. It was only when the pulsing red of the terminal panel flicked to a solid green that Kara dropped down off the ledge. She immediately felt the cold swells of the fog boiling over the tops of her boots, as if she were standing in a pool of water.

"I swear I saw something move inside," Marice said.

Kara moved slowly, measuring her steps with caution and keeping her balance ready for anything. For the most part, the gap in the glass was no longer heavily spouting out the chilling vapor. There was a deep shift and the glass of the pod started to separate. Kara crouched low and held a hand close to her knife. A heavy wave of cold spilled out as the top section of the glass lifted up. The bottom half lowered down but caught on one side, causing a crack to spread across the surface as it tilted at an angle.

Kara felt her skin prickle as she heard a gasp come from inside. When the heavy flow of the vapor thinned, she saw the slender hand pressed forward and, for the first time, she saw the figure sitting low to the bottom of the pod.

"Draken missed!" Marice exclaimed. "He missed the Cryo!"

Kara stood up as the figure inside started coughing.

"Damned SorrCom technology," a woman's voice said from between coughs. "What is the year?"

An automated voice in the pod replied. "No authenticated connections. Internal systems date: 3551. A01, it is recommended you wait for authorized personnel before exiting the pod."

"You do not even know my name, how do you expect me to believe it has been five hundred and fifty-seven years?" The woman stepped out of the pod and stumbled, catching herself with a hand on the edge of the pod before she collapsed all the way to the ground. She coughed several more times, and with each a puff of the same vapor came out of her mouth. Kara started to think that it was not cold air, but some other form of preservation gases.

The woman pulled herself up and straightened her uniform, brushing the dust from around the bottom of her leggings. She was surprised to see the resemblance to Olana Nuand's outfit. The angled cut on the bottom went from a few inches above one knee to a few below the other, and the sweep of the offset layer of color brushed up to the opposite shoulder. She also had a thin wire wrapping from just over her temple to over her eye, much the same as the Overlord and the administrators.

The Cryo blinked a few times and wiped away a foamy liquid that clung to the edges of her eyes. It was only after she took a step forward onto the glass shards atop the rubble and dirt that she began to look around. Her gaze wandered across the hazy floor, then, in confused horror, she looked up and around at the wide-open chamber. The woman finally looked to Kara. "Where is this? Was I transferred out of the SorrCom building?"

Kara said nothing in reply for the moment.

The Cryo gave Kara a confused look before glancing over to Marice. "Your uniform . . . that stripe is UWC, but the rest of it . . ." she turned back to Kara. "What is going on? What happened to this place?"

"We were hoping you could tell us," Kara replied, unsure of how much the cryogenic process may have clouded the woman's memory. When the Cryo started looking around again through an image displayed on her visor, Kara decided simple questions would be best to start with. "Your pod, it labeled you as A01. Is that your name?"

The Cryo looked back with confusion and gave a half-laugh. "Of course not. My . . ." She trailed off as she glanced back behind her to the pod; no doubt the holes in the glass caught her attention. The Cryo stepped over to the side and looked at all the wires and cables sticking out of the pod. "Was the pod damaged? Is this mess how you got me out?" She moved to the side and ran her hand over the crushed steel where another pod would have been. After a moment, she turned back to Kara. "I am sorry. You deserve an introduction at least. I am the People's Ambassador of Sector: K and a member of the UWC Council. Jance Lorège."

As the Cryo stuck a hand forward, Kara stepped back. The Cryo gave her a surprised look and glanced over to Marice as if in question.

"Forgive her, she is a tech hunter," the soldier said. She nodded to her tied hands. "Untrusting at the best of times."

"A tech *hunter*?" the Cryo gave Kara a more considering look. "Do you work for the Last Edict? Did Avery send you to pull me out after SorrCom headquarters were destroyed?"

Kara gave no reply and instead left the question to hang in the air, much like the dissipating fog as its last tendrils drifted out of the cryopod. Kara knew it would be best if the woman pieced it together on her own. She had to believe it to understand.

After a long moment, it was as if a heavy realization had finally set in on the Cryo. Her eyes opened wide and she pulled in a slow breath, now glancing around the room a second time. Her attention caught just at the top of the ridge, where Comar and Randin were now watching silently.

"3551 . . ." The Cryo held shaking fingers up to her lips. "Hale was right."

* * *

The First Administrator sat in silence as he tried to wrap his head around the report. The tech that the Overlord was after was a Cryo. And yet Draken destroyed it while it was still in the pod? But that was not even the half of it. While the Overlord had denied him an incredible tool to strengthen his position once he took Norclave, what concerned Silas the most was Olana Nuand's actions. She had used one of his own commanders, a man so prone to failure that Silas had come to expect it, to guide her mercenaries to the site.

The tenuous treaties between the zones normally led to skirmishes between patrols and small lists of casualties from posturing, but this was different. He shook his head over the report on his desk.

For years to come, there would be separate claims as to who fired the first shot, but he could not ignore the stance Nuand had taken.

For the greater portion of a year, she had secretly provided a large amount of his funding. The extremely low prices the mines charged allowed him to bolster Norclave's garrison with men loyal to him, but recent events showed that Olana had her own motives beyond a profit after the upheaval. He was leery of addressing the matter with complete certainty, but he knew she had grabbed at the chance to seize Norclave for herself.

He held a hand up to his visor. When it flicked on, he tried to get it to connect to one of his administrators. When it failed to mimic his discordant thoughts, he used the data pad to establish the link.

"Yes, Administrator Silas?" the man replied from his post on the far side of the city.

"Secure the docks and the first level gates."

He began spreading orders for his men to take Norclave with full force. Trade center docks, pumping station, South Corridor entrances, seventh level hangars, defensive cannons, and the garrison posts were the primary targets. The remaining soldiers that were either unaware of what was going on or who were still loyal to the Overlord would soon see the scale of the operation. Defecting from the Overlord would quickly become the sound choice. The last matter of the process was the elimination of the Overlord himself. Once that was done, Norclave would be his, and then he could address the Nuand threat.

* * *

Marice pulled at the ties around her hands as subtly as she could while the tech hunters talked amongst themselves. They were not exactly trying to hide what they were saying. It was clear that besides them, and the Cryo of course, that she was the only other person that knew the truth. The thin wire broke away from the steel down by her feet. If she moved quickly, Marice knew she could pop her hands free even now.

"What do you think the Kessians would have done had she got the signal through to them?" the hotheaded tech hunter growled. "I can tell you that they would not be near as lenient as the administrator's men. She would have cost us our heads."

"I can retie the bands, Randin," the red-haired woman replied. Kara was the only one of them even partially on her side.

"And then what?" Randin replied.

Marice froze as the hooded one turned the silvery rims of his eyes toward her. "The new ties will loosen just the same, Kara. Unless we take the Cryo to them, we will be forced to watch our backs for Kessian daggers. Unless, of course, they never receive her signal. You know where I stand, Kara."

Marice felt a hard knot form in her throat. Draken had warned them to not trust the tech hunters, but after he had shot the Cryo, she had partially let down her guard. It shouldn't have surprised her that she best served them dead.

"What about the pod?" Kara asked, seeing that she was outnumbered. "Say we put the Kessian informant in. That would give us enough time to get to Norclave, easy. And if it doesn't work, we can say we tried."

Marice gave a nervous look to where the Cryo stood off to the side, staring blankly into the distance with her arms crossed over her chest. Another glance back at the shattered glass and the spread of cables on the ground did nothing ease Marice's apprehension. They did not even know if it would still work with the holes Draken had made and the crack caused from opening.

Before she could even look up at the sound of quiet footsteps, there was a numbing pulse on one side of her head that wrapped around the inside of her skull, pressing against all her senses. She glanced over through crossed eyes as Kara lowered a silver square. Marice immediately felt as if she were unable to fully wake from a strong dream. She only felt the hand grabbing her arm nearly a full two seconds after she saw it, and voices seemed to echo long after the moving of lips.

She watched in silence as she was put into the pod. The glass started closing in around her, and moments later she heard the deep hum that accompanied the movement. The vapor started to rise up around her, and only as she started to slip into full unconsciousness did she feel the chilling cold.

* * *

Kara stepped back as the pod closed completely. Before the heavy vapor started up in full, she could see the soldier's eyes slip shut and her head loll to the side. It was almost as if a cool breeze from the mouth of a cavern had come back into the room as the fog began to fill the floor again. Kara turned away and called for the Cryo to follow. They had a long walk back to Norclave ahead of them, and now they would also have to keep a person who was completely clueless about their world alive along the way. It was going to be worse than keeping track of Kenneth.

* * *

A steamy sun hung in the sky as the haze lifted from the landscape. The sun was a heavy orange, almost as if it were still on the horizon, as Jance looked out across the broken lands. There was so much change from what she knew that it was simply too much to completely understand. So much so that she simply looked around without any solid thoughts taking form.

Jance held a hand to shield her eyes from a swell of wind that brought a sheet of dust their way. Every breath felt as if she were in the uppermost levels of an outdated starscraper.

She followed the tech hunters as they picked a path through the maze. Jance paused as she brushed her hand through a clump of dry and dust-covered grasses jutting out from beside a boulder of rubble. She took a moment longer to feel the blades thread between her fingers. It was actually the first time she had touched a wild plant. Any other plants she'd touched had been cultivated in the arboretums or were a part of the decoration in the atriums. Of course, her sister had regularly talked about the uninhabited reserves and the ecological return of . . .

Jance was pulled out of her darkening thoughts as a small bird fluttered by. There were not many that flew anywhere close to the starscrapers with the constant storms that cloaked them. Supposedly, birds inhabited the reserves with a population similar to that of the two to three hundred billion human population.

When they eventually stepped free of the thick cover, Jance finally got a full view of the sky. A large arc of debris stretched from one edge of the horizon up and around to the other. The bright reflections of the sun's light shifted slowly as the pieces continued their gradual drift on the edge of space. She was too stunned to react to the glowing points of gravity repulsor engines and the thin distorted flares they made as they moved through the atmosphere.

"Cryo, do you recognize the wreckage?" Kara asked as they were forced to wait for her yet again. "Was it there in your time?"

"No," Jance said quietly. "Nothing like this. The last I knew, it was two days before the Orbital Armistice Fleet was scheduled to launch."

Randin looked up and frowned. "So they were actually ships. I might have heard that once."

Jance nodded solemnly. "They were supposed to keep the citizens of the UWC away from the conflict."

Maylee would have been on one of those ships. Perhaps Agatha too, though it would depend on the timeline. As she looked upon the floating destruction, she had an odd sense of disconnection. As new of a realization as it was that untold billions of people had died, there was a level of detachment from the emotions, such as when one looked at the wide stretches of graves from centuries before the UWC had permanently banned burials as part of the Land Management Systems Agreement. At some point, the scale became too large and the time too distant that things began to lose their impact. It was now forgotten history.

Jance glanced back down and watched curiously as the tech hunters looked up at the wreckage. She could tell they were looking at it through a different point of view now. There was no doubt they had known the ruins were not natural, but now it was if they were beginning to wonder how the world they lived in came to be.

"Kenneth would have been glad to hear that," Kara finally said, breaking the silence. "He was the one who actually got you out of the pod. Part of the reason he agreed to keep helping was that he wanted to know about the orbital wreckage." She shook her head. "I only ever watched it, caught up in my own thoughts, as one would with the stars."

As they started forward again, making their way between the bent towers rising up all around, Jance began to wonder about what she said. "Where is this Kenneth now? Does his absence have something to do with the woman we left?"

"You need not concern yourself with that," the hooded tech hunter said from behind.

"Perhaps we can help each other out," Jance offered. "I would like to know about this world, and to eventually understand what happened to mine. It . . . it is obvious I failed, but I would like to know more."

"Your world is gone," the one with the hood replied again. "What does it matter what happened?"

For the first time, the full reality of her situation began to set in. Jance wiped at the tears rolling through the dust on her cheeks and pulled in a deep, stinging breath. "To say I am without a purpose . . . I am without a time. Everything I worked for, my whole life—it has been lost to rust and ashes. All that is left to me now is to understand."

"You will have your answers once we get you to the Overlord," Kara said. "The Overlord pays well for tech, and better for information. I am sure that what you are will see that you get the information you seek." The tech hunter shot a pointed glance over to Comar. "And we *will* get you to Norclave."

* * *

"This is crazy," one of the Overlord's archivists said in a borderline frantic tone as he continued scanning through the pile of data pads and terminals that had been ripped out over the years by tech hunters and scavengers alike. "The whole city is falling to the administrators and the Overlord has us back here searching through data? And where the hell is Sora?"

"Tenan, calm down and keep looking." Laila was the only other archivist besides him now left in the Overlord's libraries. "We have been given our orders. Leave Sora to follow hers."

The man scowled and threw the device he had been searching through back into the pile. "Face it, Laila, the Overlord has lost it. And I am not just talking about the city. Anyone with half their sanity left would have seen it would come to this with the administrators."

"Do not say that, Tenan," Laila argued. "The Overlord knows exactly what is going on. He always does."

Tenan scoffed and kicked the edge of the pile with his boot. "If he knows everything, why are we searching through this pile of overpriced scrap? Half of these have no information whatsoever! Look," he said, picking up a glowing panel that flickered from the grime. "This is not even a data device! It could have very well been ripped from a door by a scavenger, sold to a scrapsmith, and then picked up by a tech hunter who knew they could scam the Overlord's men out of some supplies!"

"Remember what Sora said when she first took over Rielek's position?" Laila stood up and waved a small square that could have come from anything. "The most valuable information can come from the least expected places."

Tenan sighed. "If Sora would have come from the parts of the city I did, she would have lost that idealistic nonsense long before the Overlord transferred her here. Besides, who *isn't* here while we wait for the First Administrator's men to kick down the door?" he shook his head. "Sora has left us to die here, just like the Overlord."

"Tenan!" The woman let out a sharp breath and set the piece to the side. "We are not going to die. Even if Norclave does fall out of the Overlord's control, I guarantee you that the First Administrator will keep us. Who else knows where the information is located better than we do?"

"Something tells me you will hit me if I say who."

"First smart thought you have had in a long while," Laila replied. "Now keep at it. We may still find something the Overlord could use to take back the city."

He sighed and started pulling pieces from the scrap pile. He knew arguing further with the woman would do nothing. On the other hand, he had his doubts that the Overlord still even acknowledged that there was a world outside of this library of his.

Chapter 17: The Archives

Avery Thorne stumbled out of the SorrCom Industries building onto one of the many landing pads that should have been filled with UWC soldiers. Even with the morning sky filled with the smoke raging from the side of the Council Starscraper several miles up, the events in the preservation chambers normally would have made world news by now. Instead, the director and military ambassador would be tirelessly attempting to cover the situation, and the attack on the Council Starscraper would serve as the perfect distraction for the time being.

He started forward again, forcing himself to keep drawing in breaths despite the pain. He could feel that most of his ribs had been cracked on one side. Hell, he could even see that plenty of the plates on the SorrCom suit he was wearing had been split. If not for the heavy pain inhibitors that had yet to wear off completely, the grinding in his shoulder would have been enough on its own to send him writhing on the charred landing pad.

He had not escaped putting Obrourke in the cryopod unscathed, and leaving Jance in the cryopod hurt him just about as much. Avery shook his head. There was no need to risk her any further now that he knew Hoffsted was planning on recreating the failed Tech-5 Charon test on Earth. She would simply be targeted like Kannei.

At least, that is what he kept trying to tell himself.

Avery let out a groan of pain as he pulled himself into the one lone transport pod waiting on this level. The glow of metal around the repulsors was enough to let him know it had arrived recently; it had landed only minutes before he exited the building. The transport pod was the last bit of help Director Auburns could give him.

As the windshield closed down over Avery, he pulled open a panel by his elbow and ripped out a section of the computer. The craft shook as the repulsors fired on without sending a signal to the UWC servers.

The bottom line was that Hoffsted knew he had contacted Auburns. The agent in the medical wing had turned against the Edict, and any further help the director was willing to give would be too short-lived to take the risk. And if Avery tried to contact the director again to tell him to run, it would only paint a target on both of them.

As the transport moved off the edge of the platform, Avery leaned back and closed his eyes, though he could not shut out the images that played from memory. He knew she would have been too much of a distraction, placed hesitation in his decisions, and possibly kept him from doing whatever he had to. He knew he should have never stepped between her and Weyburn's shots, but it was all he could do to keep from turning back for her.

Jance had placed her hand opposite his through the glass. She had trusted him. Completely. After what he had done, leaving her, that trust would be entirely shattered. Perhaps, after he finished what Kannei had begun, he could return for . . . Avery slammed his fist against the glass in frustration. He clenched his bleeding knuckles in grief, forcing himself to acknowledge the truth. No matter how much he hated it, Jance was lost to him. The nearest he could ever get was to send someone to bring her out once this was over.

As the transport continued over the lowest levels of the city, Avery was pulled from his state of half-consciousness as the sky suddenly lit up. At first, he thought it was a bomb flashing through the buildings, but as he continued to watch, the glow only grew stronger. He realized that it was the first ship of the Orbital Armistice Fleet departing Earth.

* * *

"I need the committee to move faster!" Director Auburns spoke through his visor to the chancellor. "It is a matter of security to the entire UWC that Hoffsted be removed from his position."

He had to bite his tongue to keep from yelling as Liberty Malcom reminded him that they had experienced a delay out of their control. Of course there was a delay; the whole bloody Council had been evacuated on account of the smoke and fire rolling up through the building. The entirety of the docks were in ruins from the missile that had gotten inside, and he was damned sure that the Edict could not have gotten it past the scanners. Not in the way that it had happened.

"Director Auburns," she continued, "if you would simply amend the proposal to exclude the measure limiting his clearance—"

"What is the good of an investigation if he is allowed full access to everything that would allow him to interfere and cover his tracks?" Auburns slammed the palm of his hand on the table of his temporary office. "Do you really think Ambassador Lorège willingly went into cryostasis without a word to anyone, let alone the world she previously attempted to warn?"

"The Council has not had the time to review Agatha Sharpes's analysis of her mental condition. Lorège may be maneuvering politically to avoid the situation she backed herself into. What better way is there to do that than to wake up in the future? In short, Director Auburns, we simply cannot know either way until we see that report."

Auburns ran a hand over his face. "Take one guess as to who possessed the power to release her before seeing the report was possible."

"A directive from a Council committee, a pre-vote estimate from me of the Council's decision, a security recommendation from Jonithan Hoffsted, or a summons from you, Auburns. You can speculate however much you want, you can raise as many emergency meetings over the workings of the Last Edict as you deem necessary, and you can strain political stability to the greatest extent with the evacuations of the Orbital Armistice Fleet, but what you cannot do is say that we have proof that the order for her transfer originated any higher than Admiral Brakka. As for the transfer of the sectator, that is an entirely different matter, is it not Auburns?"

After a few more wasted minutes trying to cover the reasons leading up to the eventual release of Avery Thorne, Director Auburns finally ended the transmission. There was nothing more he could do. It was only a matter of time before his interactions with the Last Edict came out. He pushed back from the desk and moved to the door at the back of the room. A wave of his hand opened the way out onto the small balcony nearly a mile above the floor of the city. Even from this height, he had to look up at the spires of a few surrounding buildings and the Council Starscraper reaching far higher into the clouds.

The rumble of a thunder greater than any storm caused displays about the entire city to flicker. The controls on his own balcony shifted in and out of their frames as the lights of the UWC fleet rose ever upward into the sky. Like scattered stars lifting up from the planet, a fraction of the billions of lives he was responsible for made the journey toward their safety in orbit. The burning fires of the Council Starscraper miles above and visible throughout the city served as a warning that the planet was no longer safe for them.

The sectator had warned him, had said he could have kept it all from ever happening. Whether that was true or just another lie from the Last Edict, he did not know. Something deep inside told him that this would have never been truly avoided.

"Director," a voice said from behind. The words had a certain rattle even through the external communication unit on the suit. "It is time."

Auburns ducked his head in a last few moments of thought. As soon as he had ordered the transfer of Avery from the *Nemesis Tide*, Auburns knew he was signing for his eventual assassination. "Distortion field? Overlooked by security because of the interference generated by the fleet's launch?" Auburns gripped the balcony rail and nodded in a grim appreciation of the man's work. On the bright side, perhaps this end would not be as bad as the shame he'd endure in a Council inquisition.

"I take it you are the Rigel Weyburn I have heard so much about?" The director turned to face the man. "For being dispensable, I am surprised Hoffsted has not thrown you away yet." Weyburn wore a full temperature regulation suit marked with the Drake Discovery Complex symbol near the shoulder. "I thought you would have died. The medical team that found you outside Rulari's office had similar projections."

"I might as well be. Internal burns. Nearly every bone fractured in some way or another." Weyburn reached for a control on his arm, but his own distortion field blocked him from adding more of the chemicals that kept him walking. "Perhaps it is just the pain speaking, or the dated trauma stabilizers, but Hoffsted has no need to know we ever spoke."

The director narrowed his eyes when the man shook his arm, as if in an attempt to manually make the system work through the distortion.

"What do you want? What could you want?"

"You and I both know Lorège has been taken care of, but we lost contact with General Obrourke as well. As I see it, the sectator is running free."

"That is absurd. Avery Thorne is securely aboard the—"

"We know you spoke with him before his release. Our agent was there for the call."

"Then bring proof to the Council," Auburns said.

"I have no need to turn you in, to the Council or to Hoffsted. I only need the sectator. It is a small price to pay for me leaving without another word."

Auburns shook his head and gave Weyburn a half smile. "I hope he kills you when you find him. Jerusalem Memorial Hospital. I'll leave you to find the room."

* * *

Weyburn immediately turned, feeling his skin crackling like eggshells underneath the suit. Each step was laborious, each breath filled with the same fire the sectator and Lorège had brought upon him. He pounded a fist on the distortion device and a layer of the charred paint crumbled under the carbon weave of his gloves. Shortly after, the displays about the hallway leading from the director's temporary office were freed from the effects of the distortion generator.

He held a hand up to the helmet; his visor had automatically integrated with the onboard system, though the distortion had been blocking it until now.

"Did he tell you?" Hoffsted asked in a hushed voice.

"Auburns gave it," Weyburn said, continuing down the hall.

"Where is the sectator?"

"You will not have it that easy." Weyburn tapped his arm to add more of the bio-stabilant. "I checked the other transport you have waiting at Auburn's building. You had better think twice about detonating another missile before I am out. The information stays with me."

Hoffsted said nothing to refute his claim. Instead, the military ambassador simply paused before speaking. "I intend to stop Avery Thorne, Weyburn. The cost of failure is not an option. He is the last major piece that can jeopardize everything. Your information will have to come to me sometime."

Weyburn would have laughed had the fluid in his lungs not forced him to cough instead. "That is where you are wrong, Hoffsted. I am going after Avery myself."

* * *

The vibrations felt like a magnified version of the earthquakes that sometimes broke past the starscraper stabilization systems. It was as if Maylee stood on the back of a great beast, stretching its muscles before it readied for flight. A heat rose up from the blinding light beneath the *Solstice Dawn* and cast the magnificent ship in distorted waves through the windows of the facility. She watched as even the crews that had made the final checks at points across the three-mile length of the craft prepared to board for the evacuation.

They had tried to get her to follow, but as the last of the frightened and torn families were ushered on along with the few inhabitants of the undercities that had made it to the orbital staging facility, Maylee continued her refusal to board. Her efforts had even gone as far as escaping from the watch of the security agents. She hid, hanging outside the rails between the large windows and the edge of the floor. She only had to wait long enough for the searching security groups to see the other security personnel leaving the facility. No one wanted to be left behind.

A sudden shout from the side pulled her attention. She saw two men fighting over a bag one of them had found abandoned in the facility. She pulled herself under the bench closer toward the window. Something about their grimy, loose-fitting clothes and the way they struggled over the bag made her want to hide. Perhaps it was also the fact that neither had a visor. Maylee glanced down beside her. The rail she leaned against was the only thing between her and a four-story drop alongside the massive window.

"I found it!" one of them yelled in protest. Instead of a reply, the other struck him across the face and jerked the bag away. When he tried running with the bag, the first clawed his hands into the other's back, pulling the old tears in his shirt wide. "Don't you cheat me again! Grines is going to force us to pay the next time they ditch the meds!"

"UWC! Do not move!" another voice echoed from farther down the hall.

Maylee ducked through the rails and lowered herself down over the edge. Her eyes were just above the edge of the floor as she watched the two visorless men scrambled to get to their feet.

"No time," the first argued as the other man tried to hand him the bag. He instead pulled the man with the bag up by the arm. "We just gotta run."

Maylee looked back and saw a squad of UWC soldiers taking chase after them. Without warning, her visor activated itself, nearly startling her enough to cause her to lose her grip.

"Not now!" she whispered as it started accessing the reality shard servers. She knew better than to let go of the railing to turn it off. Her feet dangled almost to the ceiling of the next level.

Maylee ducked her head farther down, hoping to keep the glow of the visor hidden. As the reality shard finished connecting, she could see an ICC patrol arriving in the area. Six constructs. What did not make sense was that she could see them through the floor. The system must have been getting interference from the repulsors of the *Solstice Dawn*, causing it to not recognize that the patrol was not within her line of sight.

It was only when the outlines of three of the ICC patrol started running forward in the same steps as the UWC soldiers that she realized something was completely out of the ordinary. She would have sworn they had reacted to something outside of the system by the way they took off running. Perhaps the ones they were chasing were logged in? She shook her head. Neither had a visor.

She started to pull herself up, but the other three ICC started forward. Out of habit, she reacted as if they were a threat and froze in place. "Stupid," she breathed to herself. There was no need to risk falling only to hide from the program. She'd just started to pull herself up again when a pair of boots shuffled in front of the bench.

"You hear something?"

Maylee pulled one hand from the railing and took hold of a lip on the side of the floor. The outline of the ICC soldier stopped in exactly the same place as the UWC soldier. She shifted her other hand, lowering herself down, and fought against the fire in her fingers to keep holding on.

"Scanner says there is a fourth mark in the area," another man said. A few seconds later she saw through the floor as one of the other ICC soldiers looked down to a pad in his hands. An alert pinged on her visor, showing that her signature had been detected.

"Nothing under here," the closest soldier said. After a several second delay, the projection of the man crouched over to look under the seat.

"Well, that's odd. The signal is gone now."

"Must be the distortions from those thrusters. Probably picking up a false echo from one of our own signals."

Maylee heard the footsteps and then watched through her visor as the soldiers—UWC and ICC—moved off. Once she was sure they had passed, she pulled herself back up with shaking arms and drew in heavy breaths under the bench. Even disregarding the fact that the ICC constructs were perfectly mimicking the real-world soldiers' movements, she should not have been notified that the scan had picked her up, let alone being hidden from the UWC scan seconds later. She glanced down and saw the mostly transparent shape of a new device hovering just a few inches from her leg. The detection masking device was worth several hundred thousand credits. It was clear someone was severely screwing with the system, because nobody would actually spend that kind of money on her, let alone be able to attach the device to her person remotely.

Regardless of the amount of floors between her and the figures moving about, she could still see the outlines of hundreds of soldiers sweeping the area. Maylee rolled out from underneath the bench and looked around. The hall was just as empty as her visor said. That was, until a data pad impossibly dropped out of nowhere onto the floor of the reality shard.

The hair at the back of her neck stood up as she was reminded of the first data pad she had found. Too soon after she happened upon it, her world began to fall apart. With shaking hands, she picked up the device.

"Open the contact request. Ignore that you cannot see it."

Maylee held a hand to her visor and went through the normal actions to open a request, even though there were no prompts shown. It displayed that a connection had been established and she could see the man that had called. He had black hair and sweat rolled down his bruised and bloody face.

"What is this about?" Maylee asked. She looked over her shoulder. "You can't be in the system."

"You are the one who found the data pad I placed? How old are you?"

"You answer me first," Maylee said. She held tight to her anger and confusion. "Or I rip this visor off and throw it away."

The man gave a pause. "My name is Avery. I saw your shots come out of the old ventilation system. I was the one who left the pad and set up the mission."

Maylee held her hand to her forehead as she furiously rethought the situation. "You traced the path I took. To get to Ms. Lorège. You are the sectator, and you saved my mother, didn't you?"

"Saved? How could you possibly . . ." There was a pause. "Your mother?" Another pause. "Jance's counselor? I remember she was there when—"

Maylee turned sharply and looked out the window as the rumble through the floor became stronger than any time in the last few hours. The hundreds of docking ramps were pulling away from the ship in its last moments before takeoff.

"What is it that scared her so much?" Maylee asked. "Why did she leave without another word?"

Avery let out a sigh. "Do not worry about that. You just need to concern yourself with getting into orbit. Your mother and Jance would want you safe."

Maylee shielded her eyes as the repulsors under the *Solstice Dawn* cast a light through the windows brighter than the sun. A few seconds later, the glass of the facility adjusted to a darker shade to make the light bearable.

"I was supposed to be on the orbital ship already. Mother told me to be on it whether she was here or not, but I . . . I know something is wrong. The ship is leaving now."

"There will be more going up. Notify the authorities. Not the military, just to be on the safe side. Find a local official and have them sign for you to board one of the smaller ships."

"Alright, I wi . . ." Maylee stopped just before she agreed. "Why not the military?"

"Never mind that. Just get aboard a ship."

"Why did you contact me?"

"If I had known who you were, I would never have—"

"Stop! Stop, just stop, quit telling me to close my eyes and forget everything and say nothing!" Maylee grabbed a fistful of hair and pulled against her scalp as her long-held frustration finally broke into anger. "I want to understand why this is all happening, and I want to help Jance, and I want to stop whatever is putting me and my mother in danger. You contacted me. Forget who I am, how old I am, and tell me the truth!"

"Maylee, calm down. Think straight. You know what the Edict does, right? You are in over your head. Now get on a ship."

The room was bathed entirely by the piercing light even through the tinted windows, and her visor flickered violently as the *Solstice Dawn* began to lift away from the dock. She adjusted the visor, trying to look past the flickering. "You are desperate. It does not take lessons from my mother to see that. If nothing else, the blood on your face gives it away. That, and you were trying to recruit some random person you saw in an air shaft without so much as a name to go by."

"Maylee . . ."

"Tell me that there is another option, and I will get on the nearest transport off planet."

In response, there was a pause long enough that the orbital ship had started reaching high into the atmosphere. "Dammit," Avery finally said. "You are just as bad as she is, you know? The truth is that I am out of ideas, running low on bio-stabilant, and unsure that I will be able to make it to the hospital without being gunned down by Hoffsted."

"What do you need to happen?"

"I need someone to directly access the archives in the Council Starscraper. I sent the location of the data, but the Edict has not been able to get in remotely."

"Why not send in another sectator?"

"For the first time, I saw one of our people turn against us. That may as well mean that the UWC knows who all our people are. I need someone that they will never see coming."

"What information do you want?"

"Are you sure about this?"

"Are you?"

The man paused to pull in a breath. "I will send you the details. Essentially, I want you to find anything that will prove to the world that Hoffsted will meet me in hell. The two of us have a lot to talk about."

* * *

"Amidst the series of explosions in the UWC, our latest reports show that Ambassador Lorège, recently rescued from the Last Edict, has entered cryostasis to wait out the hostilities." The reporter paused a moment as she looked into her visor, switching the report over from the information sent by the military ambassador before continuing. "Meanwhile, millions more waiting at similar cryogenics facilities across the globe are being turned away as capacities are steadily reached. To make matters worse for those waiting, many SorrCom employees have simply opted to join the evacuations enacted by the director. The director himself has made no comment on if the cryogenics staff must remain, or if the pre-screened applicants of the facilities will be allowed a refund of their cryogenics fees to pay for their own private transit to the orbital fleet."

Jonithan Hoffsted swiped a hand and the display switched feeds. He knew for certain that Director Auburns would never make a comment on the matter. He was a casualty of the one other explosion across the city that was not an act of the Last Edict. The other event, of course, was his attempt to stall the Council committee from revoking his own clearance. It was risky, but blasting the docks out of the Council Starscraper was less likely to evoke a reaction from the Council against him than actually trying to take out the Council members themselves.

The only thing that mattered at this point was ensuring that the allegations against him were not substantiated before a hundred days or so had passed. He rubbed his eyes with a forefinger and thumb. A hundred days was a long time, but if he could pin his actions on the Last Edict, it was possible. He almost had everything sorted into a stable position. Auburns gone, Ambassador Lorège in cryostasis, the Core Reactor Report buried, Kannei and Alexandar Hale dead, the Drake Discovery archives finally stripped as they should have been years ago, and Agatha Sharpes headed offworld and unlikely to bring forward anything believable, as the missing sections in the recording of her meeting with Jance could easily be held against the counselor if necessary. Sharpes had also been warned to not draw any unnecessary attention onto her daughter, though he doubted he would need to use the girl for further leverage. The threat would be more than enough, even with her beside her mother aboard an orbital ship.

However, even with all of he had accomplished in the past few weeks, there was still one major problem. More than the entirety of the Last Edict operation, Hoffsted was most worried about Avery Thorne. Had Weyburn not wounded the sectator, forcing him into UWC custody, Hoffsted was sure Thorne and Lorège would have broken the whole conspiracy open. What made the matter all the more irritating was that there was too much of a risk of exposure to start another large-scale hunt for the sectator, and Weyburn was the only one who knew what the sectator was going to do next.

Hoffsted rubbed his forehead, still fighting the splitting headache despite the many counteraction meds he'd taken since the moment Lorège spoke to the entire UWC. She would have eventually won the Council over with that.

Hoffsted pulled up a live view of the Council Starscraper. While only a thick smoke could be seen before, now the bared steel within the airlocks was partially visible. The fire teams worked closely with maintenance crews to slowly regain control of the situation. Caretaker units crawled over the twisted expanse, attempting to rescue any survivors.

As a small transport pod descend into the chaos, possibly being used as a makeshift shuttle for equipment or survivors, Hoffsted checked in on the preparations of the reserve team he'd ordered to shift some of the more sensitive information out of the Council Starscraper archives. They would arrive at the empty checkpoint within the hour to recover a number of specific files he would need when it finally came time for him to move offworld.

* * *

Maylee set the transport down within the fires and smoke of the Council airlocks with enough force to crack the front glass. Her hands were shaking as she pulled them back from the controls. For a first flight, it could have been worse. The only instructions Avery had given her in flying was how to hack into the system to keep from being tracked. She was on her own when it came to using the controls overlaid with her visor to operate the craft. At least finding the destination was easy enough. Go to the tallest building and fly into the fire.

A tap signaled the canopy to open. She gave a short scream as the glass shattered and fell inward on top of her. Maylee was immediately hit by a wave of hot air and suffocating fumes. Coughing, she pulled herself up and out onto the bent walkways. She brushed her hands together to dust out the bits of glass that had buried into her skin. She had a feeling she would be roughed up enough to look like she'd survived the initial explosion before she made it out.

Search lights behind her hunted for survivors through the heavy haze of the ruins. Maylee pulled walking navigations across both eyes and was immediately met with a swarm of warnings. Seeing the recommended path guide her toward the previous location of the walkway, nearly five feet above her head and at a hard angle away from where she stood, made her think about getting back in the transport, shattered glass and all. With a screeching pop, the walkway she stood on dropped several inches. She stumbled back as the last section of the path folded and sent her transport toppling down through the mess of steel and broken ships.

Maylee hurried as fast as she could while also being sure of her footing. The height above the fires did not bother her as much as the shifting pieces around the massive room. She had climbed over drops not quite as severe with only her back pressed against one side of a vent; however, making her way through the room as pieces fell from her walkway as well as the walkways high above was an entirely different matter.

Shadows flicked around in the sporadic glow of the low fires eating at the bits of transports scattered about. Her heart almost stopped as her foot sank into a dark splotch hanging near the edge of one walkway. Her first instinct was to think it was part of one of the poor souls that had been in the room, but after jumping against the opposite rail, she noticed it had a color much too green. She glanced around in confusion, now noticing more of the spots clinging to surfaces all around her. She sighed in relief when she noticed a crate torn in half. The misaligned display read *"Boiled Spinach: E-04 Variant."*

As she tiptoed around the last of the piles, some of which seeped trails of dark and pungent smoke, her visor lit up with a series of figures along the far wall. Maylee could see where the UWC soldiers were guarding the entrances to the Council docks. She stepped over an unattached rail and held a hand over her mouth as a docked transport pod continued to burn a hole in the metal with its sparking repulsors.

It was almost astounding to think that Avery could change the positions of the ICC to fit with the real-world soldiers. That, as well as make objects appear in the reality shard without going through the purchasing system. After a moment of thought, she realized that it might be possible the Last Edict were the ones who kept it running in the first place. Using a decommissioned military strategy simulation as the core for a reality shard . . . mix that in with the large sums of money individuals were willing to pay to equip soldiers to fight for virtual sections of real territory, and it quickly became a recipe for funding the Last Edict.

It was only a short way ahead to a pair of the soldiers on the opposite side of an exit. Their location at least told her the passage was functional.

Maylee glanced down to make sure she still had the detection masking device in the reality shard before she realized that she was instinctively holding her pistol. It seemed that the shard also served as a grounds for training and recruitment. Maylee forced herself to holster the virtual weapon at the same time she unconsciously pulled the small game figure out of her pocket and held it tight.

Maylee stepped up to the door. Through the shattered windows, she could see a spread of plastic pinned up to keep some of the smoke from leaking through the level into the rest of the starscraper. Maylee hit the panel on the door and the two soldiers obscured behind the sheet spun around in surprise. They had been set here to stop anyone from entering the docks and likely had not thought about someone coming out the same way.

"Help," Maylee said weakly. She bent down and scraped some of the spinach and dust from the side of her shoe and quickly swiped it from her forehead down across her face. Hopefully it would help make stumbling out of the docks more believable.

As the soldiers started ripping down the plastic, Maylee pulled her visor free and hid it between her arms, cradling one like it had been injured.

"Do not worry!" one of the soldiers said as the other pulled the sheeting completely out of the way. He took note of her arm. "We will get you to the medical station. What is your name?"

"Reela." Without checking against the visor she was hiding, they would have no way to know differently.

"Do we need to call for a medical team?" the other asked.

"I can walk," Maylee assured them. "It is just my arm."

"Okay, let's go," the first said. "I'll contact the control and tell them why we are moving off post."

Maylee stopped as both soldiers started forward. She looked back as smoke billowed away from the positive pressure of the starscraper. "Nobody needs to wander into that." She looked back to the soldiers. "I just need someone to show me the way."

The two looked to each other for a moment before nodding. Without any hesitation they split and one began to show Maylee toward the medical station. She had to remind herself not to smile at how well she'd played that. Now she just had to do something about the one guard.

* * *

Avery stepped out of the transport into the shadowed layer of the undercity. It was the Council City's forgotten ground floor, left behind by a society that had long since taken to transportation in the air far above. Many of the places of the undercity only received actual daylight when the sun was directly overhead, and that was when not clouded by the storms from the Council Starscraper. There had been a recent effort to bring up the quality of life in the worst parts of the city, but those living outside the system were for the most part ignored for simplicity's sake.

"Look at this one," a gruff man said as Avery neared the garbage exit. Near on twenty people had found places to wait amongst the discarded crates and grimy edges of structures. The walls down here were covered in the thick smog buildup prevalent several hundred years ago, before Solstice Consolidated had begun re-terraforming the atmosphere. Whereas the rest of the city had undergone extensive renewal since then, this far down was left to rot. But it was not all to blame on the UWC; the inhabitants that now gave Avery wary looks were more likely to refuse aid than to give up their own ways of living.

"Newcomer," the same man said. He looked Avery up and down in a way only a ringleader sizing up competition would. "Where are you from?" The man reached forward and felt over the cracked plates in Avery's suit with curiosity.

"That is none of your business." Avery pushed his hand away. Not hard enough to stir a fight, but just to let him know his boundaries.

The man grunted and rolled his shoulders. All the other lowlifes seemed to edge closer out of interest. "Seeing as you look like you have been dumped from a transport, I will lay it out easy for you." He spit to the side. "This is my ground you walk on."

"I am here to speak with Grines," Avery said bluntly.

"Aren't we all," he gave a grin lacking a fair number of teeth. An agreeing chuckle passed around several in the surrounding group. "But what makes you special, eh? We have already been sorted into our order. Grines talks to me, I talks to Wikit, Tames, and Mudjal," he said, pointing to specific people in the crowd. "The rest of this lot gets what meds are left for a price. Now," he continued in a lower tone, "you are the newcomer, yet to have a place. We don't know what funds you can bring in, so we cannot trust you to not come back begging next time, see? But by the look in your eyes I would say you might be willing to pay extra to get some meds this time. You know, to part with what you have."

"I want nothing with your garbage medical supplies," Avery replied. "I am here to see *him*."

"Is that so?" the man motioned for the three he'd pointed to earlier. "Without my say?"

Avery quickly picked out which of the backup held bits of steel for weapons. There were a few more in the crowd also looking to jump in, though Avery still made no move for the baton on his leg.

"Now look," Avery warned, "I do not want to scare away Grines, your man on the inside, and I am sure you do not want an entire shipment to actually go to disposal as it should."

That turned some faces amongst the crowd. Some of them looked as if they had been waiting outside the door since the last time Maaned Grines had delivered the medical supplies. Avery had heard about him some time back as a possible contact for the Last Edict. It took no closer of a look than Avery had now of the people he dealt with to see that the Grines would end up much like the contact that had given Klemmeth Auburns away. Long term trust was mandatory in the Last Edict, but Avery knew he was not here to make a friend.

"You think you can frighten Grines? How do you figure?" the group leader asked.

The man in front of him was not particularly intimidating on his own, but being outnumbered did have Avery worried. Not that he was dumb enough to let them know that.

"If he comes out ready to make the deal and sees the greater half of you lying on the ground, he might just run back inside."

At first the man looked ready for the fight, but a few questioning glances from his henchmen made him lose the edge. "You with the UWC?"

"Last Edict."

Between the pause and the quick looks around, Avery knew he had already won.

"Just let him take what he needs," the one called Mudjal finally spoke up. "We can deal with what is left over."

Just then, the red highlight around the door flicked to white. As per their usual operation, the three rushed to keep the rabble away from the shipment. Avery shouldered past the leader and started through the moving crowd. A short man shouted at them to get back from the cart, which he pushed to the edge of the door. The trays were filled with bottles and vials, all weeks past their expiration dates. Most would be perfectly viable, and even needed; Avery saw at least one person with a bandage around their arm that could use strong antibiotics, even if they were legally out-of-date by a few development cycles. Now, whether or not they would purchase what they actually needed was an entirely different question.

"Hold on! Just wait, you vermin!" Grines shouted. "The monitor stepped out for a restroom break! I got more than usual!" His words only served to make the crowd more eager.

Avery made his way through the layers of people pushing against the strong-arms. He stepped past them and moved right up to the disposal cart.

"Who is this?" Grines asked to the three keeping the crowd back.

"Avery Thorne," he introduced himself. "I'm making myself your acquaintance." Avery flipped the cart over into the crowd and grabbed the scuzzy man by the shoulder. "Let's talk, Maaned." He shoved the janitor back into the opening and shut the door behind them both.

"What are you doing!" Grines rushed back to the door and watched out the window as a brawl started outside over the medical supplies. "That was nearly twice the pay for the week!"

Avery jerked the man away from the door by the collar of his uniform. "You can get back to it next week if you help me. But I give anyone one word of this and you get slapped with lifelong fines and put into rehabilitation. That, and intensive monitoring."

"This is not right!" he whined. He glanced at the red rimming Avery's eyes. "I just take some of the stores when they are sent to be destroyed. What do you expect of me? How do you think I can help?"

"You've gotten me into the building. That is step one."

* * *

Maylee put her visor back on as the elevator doors started to close. The confused soldier shouted after her, but by the time he had gotten over the unexpectedness of her sprinting down the opposite turn in the hall, she was as good as gone. Maylee began looking down through the building as the elevator dropped. It soon became clear that there was a strong military presence. Far more than even these abnormal circumstances would permit.

She set her destination for the nearest atrium. Avery had warned against searching directly for the location of the archives, so she figured on using a holographic map similar to the one back on Atrium: 447. It should be untraceable. Hopefully.

When the elevator slowed to a stop, Maylee was almost shocked to find out how closely similar this atrium was to the one she had grown up near. The only differences she could immediately tell were the types of floral decorations along the edges, and instead of the letters *"K-8a"* that were normally replicated about the room, this area used the marking *"UWC Council."*

To be precise, it was on the same level of the building. Even the railings were of the same silver and glass. It just went to show that the unique, local community she lived in was built just the same as someone—or everyone—else's.

"Are you all right, dear?"

Maylee turned to see an elderly woman looking at her intently. Maylee then remembered the smear on her face and marks on her hands. She wiped away some of the sweat from the heat of the fires and quickly reassured the woman before rushing off toward the map. It was only a few steps later when she forced herself to slow down and rethink what she was doing. Standing out. That was one thing.

Several years of training herself should have made this come as habit. She could not let anyone think that she could be using a reality shard. There had been many public warnings against sporadic actions, emotions that seemed out of place with the environment, and, most importantly, looking through a full visor.

She pulled the visor just to project over one eye and gave the room a slow look around. She could immediately tell there were a few people who had already taken notice of her. With the attack on this very building, the search for reality shard users would be far from their minds, but the events had also put everyone on edge. She would have to make it quick.

The projection of the Council Starscraper hovered over the platform on the ground, slowly rotating to appear as a form of decoration. To most, that is simply what it was: a decoration. Growing up, she'd often wondered what the purpose was of knowing where in the building you were if your visor simply told you how to get to your next destination. For most, the floor level was all the additional information anyone could want. She motioned in front of the projection and the sensors picked up her gestures, expanding the image and causing much of the building to drop out of the display range. Out of four miles of height, it would have taken far too long to look manually through the hundreds of thousands of non-habitation sections. Before the projection finished pulling all the way in, a tag displayed close to the side. *"583-Council."* Close to where she had left the airlocks in the first place.

The map showed the levels did not match up with the standard building grid. However, it made sense, as the actual Council Chambers and the surrounding sub-rooms for the heads of the UWC were contained in an isolated shell—the Council grid—within the building. She needed to get into the Council grid before she could find the archives, though it would be much easier said than done. Just like the airlocks, the whole area would be under a heavy guard.

Moments later, Maylee looked up determinedly in the elevator as it sped up through the building. She looked up in part to see if there were any thinner concentrations of the soldiers, but also to avoid eye contact with the few other people in the same lift. Maylee added a new stop at the Council levels and received quiet, confused looks.

"That part is closed off," one of the people finally edged up the nerve to say. Maylee gave no response as she stepped out into the large hallway. There were quite a few supply crates set up, and the barrier equipment was deployed to ensure the entrance was blocked. The soldiers at the post had their helmets closed off completely. The smell of smoke was prevalent and the lights in the area cast long beams through the thick air.

"Get those purifiers set up!" The order echoed from ahead. One of the systems pulled in smoke and put out a heavy torrent of clean air. Several soldiers worked to pull another purifier out of the line of similar crates.

Maylee quickly looked through the one eye of her visor and saw that a few entrances over appeared to have only two figures stationed there. With the amount of precautions they had taken here, even going so far as to set up a projection of a security line, it was a bit surprising to see one undermanned. She started off to the left along the long outer arc of the hallway and passed by several smaller but heavily manned checkpoints at entrances into the Council grid.

The same system of supply crates and barricades had been set up at the entrance she had picked. However, as she moved past the corner and looked into the alcove of the entrance, she immediately noticed something was very wrong with the two soldiers. They were not there.

Maylee pulled her visor all the way over her eyes just to confirm it. It appeared that they only existed in the system. It was possible the reality shard had an error in syncing up with the real-world military monitoring systems in the UWC servers, but the more likely reason was that Hoffsted had faked the UWC soldiers' positions.

She walked cautiously past the unmoving ICC and found that the door was partially opened. That alone should have signaled someone to check it. Not that the maintenance crews would have time for a small malfunction with the airlocks still burning, but the other soldiers should have known. Maylee turned sideways and slipped through into the emptied Council Chambers.

Met with the grand structure of the room, Maylee slowed to a stop. It was no mystery as to what it looked like; she had seen it hundreds of times through the Council transmissions. Yet, as she took in the glare of lights set around the balconies for the councilors and saw the massive UWC seal with its holographic overlay blurring in the waves of smoke, Maylee was stunned.

Opposite the side she entered, the massive window along the majority of the outer arc of the room gave a view out to the confusion of the world. Several more orbital ships pulled away from a landscape now dotted with fires burning elsewhere throughout the city. When she'd asked Avery about the attacks as she exited the orbital staging facility, he simply said to use the shadows cast by the light of the fire. She now understood the fires were the distraction, though it definitely was not just for her.

The last thought spurred Maylee back into a sense of urgency. She crossed through the emptiness of the Council Chambers and climbed up over the long desk that the heads of the UWC used. She glanced over to Jonithan Hoffsted's seat before continuing through the back. Maylee started through the motionless hallways until her path turned into a balcony overlooking an elaborate waiting area. The fluid level design made for various seating recesses between floral displays and artistic waterfalls. What caught her attention more than the elaborate design of the room was a particular display on a wall below. It was a map showing the interior of the Council grid. After leaning over the rail to get a better look, Maylee pushed off the rail and started down the passage directly behind her.

The elevator leading up to the fourth level of the isolated grid normally would have been locked under specific clearance levels; it should have been even beyond Jance's ability to access the archives. Instead, the alert lights of the door simply flashed a bright red and proceeded to open. Maylee stepped into another large room, left mostly in the dark. To her, the rows of servers almost reminded her of the historical archives on 211. Of course, the blocks were not the sealed cases of books that the system would actively scan and display. The room was filled with traditional data storage all the way back to where a slanted window gave a view of the top of the Council Chambers.

"I am in," Maylee said into her visor.

"Search the index," Avery said, his voice twisted with pain. "Use the references I gave you. We are looking for what ties everything together."

Maylee took a breath and activated a terminal tied directly into the rows of information storage. A message displayed boldly that the security protocols for a physical activation had been dropped. Maylee glanced around, knowing that it had not been dropped for her. After a moment, she turned back and initiated the search.

"If that does not work," Avery gasped, "narrow it down. We have to find a connection between everything, even if it is just another lead to follow for now."

Maylee could not help the smile spreading across her face. "One collection matches all the search parameters. It is titled 'Crystal Slate.'" After taking a pause to jump in celebration, Maylee opened it with the tap of a finger.

Chapter 18: Walking Memories

As they began over the top of the starscraper ruins, Kenneth could immediately feel the nervousness and uncertainty from the First Administrator's men. There was a constant stream of chatter from the comms in the front of the craft, and though he could not hear what was being said, the glances backward from the armed soldiers gave enough away. Things were not going quite as planned.

Kenneth called forward to them. "You had better double check! Are they sure the defensive battery of the city is under the First Administrator's control? I would hate to be hit by the hellfire those cannons can unleash if the Overlord wants to stop us from landing."

The two soldiers on either side of the cockpit gave each other nervous glances. Kenneth watched as they exchanged a few words and he had to hide the small bit of humor he found as one turned to speak with the pilots. If the Overlord wanted to, he could bring anything out of the sky from the south face of the starscraper to nearly the Rift Outpost. The key being, if he wanted. With Silas's men knocking on his door, bringing a few unidentified transports down would be the least of his concerns.

Sora gave him a nervous look from the other side of the transport. "The Overlord would not do that, would he?"

"Of course not," Aarol said with a shake of his head. "That is just Kenneth being himself. Can't even step up to the Cells without trying to get under someone's skin."

"At least I am trying to make it there," Kenneth said. "You just want to burn up before we hit the ground."

Aarol clenched his fists and leaned forward on the edge of his seat. "We would not even be here if you had just showed up. Had I known it was *you* we were waiting for, I could have just told Draken to forget it."

Sora put a hand on his shoulder, but the Overlord's technician shrugged it off.

"Aarol," she said, "there is nothing we could have done. If Kenneth had tried to get to the Overlord, I am sure he would have been captured."

Aarol bit his teeth. "Perhaps you are right. But you could have told me, Sora. My own choice would have kept me out of this mess had you let me decide."

"The Overlord was very specific!" Sora retaliated. "No information could get out, anywhere."

Aarol scoffed. "And yet we let the tech hunters run free and leave a trail of fire for the administrators to follow."

Kenneth started to say something, but this time Karzon weighed in. "Your transport made a good enough trail on its own." Karzon lifted up the sack. "Followed the trace on these gloves."

Sora looked at Karzon for a moment before she turned to Kenneth. "I'm surprised you didn't check for a trace or something as soon as Draken handed you the gloves."

"Why should I have looked? Because I didn't trust Draken? You can keep hunting for someone to blame all this on, but I didn't make him kill the Cryo," Kenneth said.

"Really?" Aarol crossed his arms and leaned back in the seat. "As I remember, you were the one who agreed with Sora. Said there was no way we could take it out early. The more I think about it, the less I blame Draken for what he did to keep the Cryo out of Silas Konrev's hands!"

"Aarol!" Sora gasped. "It was a person in that pod!"

"And there are thousands more in Norclave," he said. Aarol slowly shook his head. "There will be many more that will die at the First Administrator's command, but at least it will not be with the tech we helped him get."

"Karzon?" Kenneth asked quietly as he stretched his neck from one side to the other. Mention of the trace had sparked an idea. He grabbed the wall behind him and started to stretch his back, and even though it did still feel a bit stiff from before Kamriek's Grove, he was mostly using the motion to face away from the watching soldiers. "Do you still have that transmitter, and can you think of any way we can bribe your tech hunter to get us out of this?"

Karzon looked at the sack for a moment before shaking his head. "I dropped it back at the pod."

The craft started down rapidly, causing the usual twist in the stomach. One of the soldiers shouted for them to brace as they were coming down to the landing platforms. Kenneth held on to the handle near his shoulder as they touched down with a lack of finesse. Karzon hit the button on the door, possibly hoping for some sort of escape, but it soon became clear that would not be an option.

The administrators had set up a strong line on the pad. Soldiers were ready at stations behind barricades of crates and metal panels. As Kenneth stepped out to see how many weapons were trained on him, he noticed that the other docks sticking out from the starscraper were similarly controlled.

"Hands up and open!" one of the soldiers said loudly as Sora and Aarol were made to stand in line. Kenneth ignored the order until one of the soldiers grabbed his wrists and forced his arms up. He glanced over to see others were cooperating.

"Check that bag," the commander of the group ordered. Just like the others along the dock, his red stripe of Norclave had been replaced by a slash of greyish teal, and an additional stripe had been added along the forearm.

"Sir, how many soldiers do we need to assign to escort them to the First Administrator?" The man asking had the look of being hired off the street to strengthen their numbers. The stripe had simply been painted across his shirt, and the one on his arm was painted on a cloth tied around it.

Kenneth looked sharply into Norclave as a burst of gunfire echoed through the structure. It was met by a low thrum of a pulse cannon and more repeated shots farther in.

"It is not safe to move them through the city. Reports say a couple of the posts have been hit already."

The hired hand saluted, causing the stripe on his arm wrappings to cross perpendicular to the mark on his chest before he moved off.

The commander shook his head and Kenneth raised an eyebrow. It seemed this whole transition was not going as smoothly as they had hoped.

* * *

Silas Konrev clasped one fist tightly with the other and propped his elbows on the table as he looked down at the data pad. They had quickly taken the docks, and the rest of the Overlord's complex soon followed. The brawl as Silas's men tried to secure the South Corridors had forced progress on that end to be halted, and while he feared the cesspit of criminal trade would be the perfect place for the Overlord to disappear into, all the connections many of the temporary recruits had with those living in the South Corridors made it simply not possible to control the situation at the moment. And he was not about to send actual soldiers in while the Norclave defensive weapons were still out of his reach.

A ping on his visor showed a report stating that the seventh level hangars had been fully taken. It looked as if there were casualties, a number being the technicians of the Overlord's hangars. One transport had been shot down attempting to leave. Silas remembered the loud noise echoing throughout the city.

Another ping showed a reinforcement request to the defensive stations. That was the second time since this started. Silas hated to pull soldiers away from the trade center out of fear of more of the random raids the resistance was conducting throughout the city, but the defensive stations were the position of the greatest resistance. He tapped his knuckles against his forehead as he continued to look down at the data pad. The worst part of it all, there had been no sighting of the Overlord himself. They did not even know if the man had given orders for any of the resistance or if it was all just individuals throughout the city working on their own.

He needed the trade centers. Trade was what kept Norclave alive, and they would need as much help in that area as they could get after this. Silas narrowed his eyes as he thought. After a moment, he put a couple of fingers to the visor.

"I need you and your men up on the seventh level."

"Sir, we cannot afford anyone. We have had two attacks on the docks by the Overlord's men in the last half hour."

"I do not care if we lose the docks," Silas said firmly, "the defense cannons control the skies. We need them."

"Yes sir," the man replied. "And what about the Overlord's Cryo team? We have been holding them here."

Silas rapped his knuckles on the table as he thought it through. "All they can do is solve curiosity. The Cryo is dead, and Draken is the only one who would have had direct contact with the Overlord. Report your numbers when you move, and tell the technician I will put another mark on his arm when I have the time."

Silas cut the transmission and made a note on the data pad. He hated to abandon a position as necessary as the docks, but a sobering realization had forced his hand. He was not afraid for the safety of inbound transports; the Overlord had yet to stop the administrators' returning search parties from landing. What Silas was afraid of was the one desperate move he saw that the Overlord had left. Things would get very bloody if he turned the guns in and started blasting the city to pieces.

* * *

"Are you actually saying that hill in the distance, that starscraper . . . you are saying that used to stand four miles in the air?" Randin gave the Cryo a disbelieving look.

Kara watched as the Cryo frowned. "If the ruins you pulled me out of were actually the SorrCom facility, then yes. I was in the Council Starscraper just a few days . . ." the woman paused. "Well, I was there. You know how long ago."

Kara gave the building on the horizon a second glance as they neared the border chasm. Fragmented videos and pictures were one thing, but just looking at it . . . it was hard to imagine it ever being upright. She had never seen it any different, never even heard anyone talk about it being different. The earliest settlements in the Rift Hills had appeared some time after the forests had grown, and the starscraper had fallen long before that.

Soon they were walking along the crest of a hill where one edge sloped gently down with sparse woods mixing in with the steel while the other side cut sharply off in a thirty-foot cliff. It gave them a good look at the building that formed the heart of the rise, and a break in the trees gave a clear view of the Northern Rift. The great rip in the land stretched miles in either direction, making a nearly quarter-mile-wide barrier between the Kessian lands and the heart of the Rift Hills.

"What is this?" Jance asked as Kara continued to lead the way along the ridge.

"It is called the Northern Rift River," Randin replied. "And the Northern Rift, the Kessian Scar, and any other combination of rip, tear, fissure, or crack people could think of for the past two hundred years or so."

"You going to tell me this is new as well?" Kara asked the Cryo as she started on a trail leading down the steep sloping side of the hill.

Randin laughed. "I just want to hear about the kind of weapon that would cause it."

"I have an idea," the Cryo said, "but none of these buildings should have been left standing."

For a time, she and the other two tech hunters were left thinking over what the Cryo had grimly said. As much as Kara wanted to hear more, she also could see that she shared the same feelings as the others. There was little use a tech hunter could find in leveling cities.

As she led the way further down a small trail edging along the steep face of the hill, Kara decided to switch the topic away from destruction for a bit. "In the center of the starscraper, there is a massive disk of metal. I thought nothing of it more than being a landmark to keep the path, but when Kenneth asked about the markings, we realized they were the letters *U*, *W*, and *C*. I have often seen the markings elsewhere, but what do they mean?"

A bit of loose dirt slid off the edge as the Cryo stumbled. Comar caught her by the shoulder to keep her upright.

"Are you sure that is what it said?" Jance asked. "How big was it? The disk?"

Kara thought back for a moment. "The raised letters were about knee high."

Kara glanced back as Jance gave an amused giggle. Gradually, as they neared the bottom of the ridge, whatever thought had caught the attention of the Cryo eventually built into full laughter.

"What is it?" Randin asked with a confused look. Kara turned around and watched as Jance put a hand against the cliff face to hold herself up. Eventually, the last laughs were mixed with shaking breaths, almost as if Jance would have burst into sobs had she not also found humor in whatever it was about the metal disk.

"Knee high," Jance said quietly to herself with a shake of her head. She looked up to the others and straightened her uniform and wiped the tears rimming her eyes as she fought to regain her composure. "I suppose you will never understand how absurd that image is to me. The symbol of the United World Coalition, always seen above the Council Chambers as a grand statement of the command and purpose with which we represented the people of Earth . . . and you walked on it."

"It is the marker for the old path between New Solace and Norclave," Kara explained.

Jance nodded. "Well, at least it is good for something these days. And this Kenneth you keep mentioning, it sounds like he looks at everything in a different way."

Kara nodded as they continued toward the rift. "He asked simple questions without answers, mostly." She pointed forward to where a large building lay as it had fallen across the top of the rift, or perhaps the rift had formed under it. Besides being bent in an arc and a majority of its outer paneling ripped off, it was one of the more complete buildings in the immediate area. Had it not been located on a violent border known for Norclave and Kessian skirmishes, Kara expected it would have had a decent population, if not actually in the building itself, perhaps on either end for trade.

"That is our way across," Kara told Jance. "It is not smooth enough for ground transports to make it over, but on foot it can save many miles compared to going around the rift."

"I wonder what building that was." Jance wondered quietly. "A smaller class, definitely. It would not have taken any repulsors to keep it standing."

"We going through the center?" Randin asked.

Before Kara could say otherwise, Comar put in his vote for going over the top. "Nobody will be looking for us as it is," he said. "It would be safer for the Cryo as well."

"Alright," Kara agreed. The last thing they needed was Jance failing to see one of the many dangers to be had within an interior. "Just keep your light distortion generator ready. I do not want to be seen by any transports if we can help it."

* * *

"Are we sure this is safe?" Jance asked as she took hold of Kara's calloused hand. She gripped tight, and the tech hunter helped to pull her up the ledge. They were climbing up through the fallen building, supposedly on a path the tech hunters knew about.

"You are the only one who tells me this has not been here forever," the woman replied. "I see no reason for it to fall now."

Jance looked at the rip in her sleeve for a moment before following the others up the steep slope of a beam. When she reached the top, Randin offered her a tube of medi-seal. Besides the thought of the ointment being older than the Mars colonies, Jance politely refused on the account that it was a surface scratch at most.

"The rest of the way across should be easy," Kara explained. She was looking out over the quarter-mile span of the bridge. "Nothing to fall from above, and no live cables hanging down. Just follow my steps and avoid slipping near the edges."

The surface of the building looked as if it had been pummeled by falling debris long ago, probably before the wreckage of the orbital fleet had fully stabilized. Besides that, heavy stretches of rust had caused much of the outer paneling to sheer off, providing a view into the heart of the building.

"Still a lot of good tech to find in there," Randin commented as they walked along one strut that was open to either side. Jance was hardly afraid, considering that the path was nearly ten feet wide.

"It is a lot easier to walk across a building," Jance commented when they were forced to pass near the outward edge of the structure. "One time of sliding down the side was enough for me."

"Now that sounds like a story," Randin commented as he picked up a large bolt and threw it just to hear it bounce down through the structure.

"I escaped out of a starscraper, with the help of a sectator and a caretaker exosuit. We broke out of a window at least two miles up and slid down the outside to an airlock."

"What for?" he asked.

Jance sighed, stopping to look harder at the wide gouge of the rift they were crossing. "I thought it was to stop this. Now I have no idea."

The land looked as if it had been pulled apart like cracked mud in the nature habitats. All along the sides of the rift were places where the underground levels of the city had been ripped apart. Some of them stretched out a ways from the sides, and others left huge entrances like caves.

"It would have been incredible to see, your world," Kara said. "But I do not think I could have lived there."

"What do you mean?" Jance asked, staring out into the desolation.

"I find it hard enough to stay in one place as it is, let alone stay where it is crowded with people." Kara moved closer to Jance. "In your time, humans were everywhere. What would there be to explore? To find? What unknown mysteries were there to be discovered?"

Jance shook her head. There was simply no way to describe it. These tech hunters were accustomed to risking their lives every day just to survive, whereas the UWC had cultivated an environment to ensure individuals did not have to struggle to live or find a purpose. There were problems, that was no question. The Last Edict, the disagreements with the SRA, and most of all, the darker motives that floated at the highest levels. But this, this wasteland the tech hunters tried to call home . . . Jance did not know if she could even call this Earth.

"Come now, we have to keep moving."

Jance felt a gentle pull on her shoulder, and soon after felt her feet plodding along over the layers of steel and the rusty powder that coated the surface. Her mind felt numb again, much like the first overwhelming minutes after stepping out of the cryopod. Everything she'd talked about, every detail and strategy used to improve life and every effort to keep it that way . . . it meant nothing. They were just meaningless words within memories. Thoughts that had no place in this time.

"Transport," Randin said, pointing in the distance. "Headed this way."

"Comar, the generator." When the man made no move, Kara looked down from the approaching glow in the sky to the hooded tech hunter. "Comar?"

"Not this time." Comar ducked his head and pulled his hood low. Jance could immediately see the inner conflict on his face. He held a personal communications device in his hand, the kind only used in the SRA. They were particularly dangerous, allowing person to person communication without going through a server.

"What are you talking about?" Randin said, turning a look wavering between confusion and distrust on Comar.

Comar slipped the device into a pocket. "I am not going to throw my life away by going to the Overlord. Even the Kessian informant knew it was too dangerous to take the Cryo to Norclave. I had to do something."

Randin started unwrapping his club and let the cloth fall to the surface of the building. "You think you can sell us out? After all we have done for you?"

"I am returning the favor by keeping you alive, whether you like it or not."

Randin hit the club against his palm. "I should crack your skull for even thinking you are doing this for us."

Kara gave Comar a glare that could have cut through the windows of a starscraper. "If you are so afraid of going back to Norclave, why not just walk away?"

"I put just as much effort into this as either of you!" Comar argued. "Why should I lose out on my share of the fortune just because you do not care if you get the Cryo killed or not?"

Jance let her gaze drop to her feet as they continued to argue. In their eyes, she was nothing more than a bargaining piece.

"How dare you say that," Kara said. "I am taking Jance to the Overlord so that we can understand something about this world, not so that we can learn to fear the new weapons and war tech any other leader would demand."

"He is in the middle of an uprising!" Comar glanced over his shoulder to the nearing transport. "What makes you think he is strong enough, or sane enough, to remain in control without using the Cryo to unlock the weapons of the past? Kara, there are no heroes here. Norclave is finished, and it does not matter who takes control afterward."

In a flash, Kara had out a weapon and sharp pops of electricity bounced around her arm. "If there are no heroes, Comar, then just walk away."

Comar slowly lifted a spike from the pouch on his hip and held it close to the rails on his arm. "You knock me down, Mallec will not hesitate to burn us all from the face of this bridge."

Randin dropped the club and produced a pistol of his own. The wires and cables on it reminded Jance of the one Welnn had stripped open. "It might still be worth it," he growled. "How long have you been planning to trap us out in the open on top of this blasted thing?"

"Ever since I found out the Cryo was still alive."

A long minute passed before a hot wind swept over the top of the steel as the repulsor engines finally touched down, opposite the side Comar stood. Kara spun to face the newcomer while Randin kept facing off against their traitor. The design of the transport was old, even in Jance's time. It almost resembled the single person pods used so often for getting around the cities, though it was elongated to have two seats.

The pilot of the craft stood up through the long-broken canopy of the ship with his SRA battle rifle ready. He was an intimidating man. His dark skin was covered in scars and the fit of his dusty clothes, much like the other tech hunters, could hold any number of nasty tools, either scavenged from the wastes or created in more recent years.

"Exactly the warm welcome I had hoped for," Mallec said in a deep and dangerous tone. He stepped forward off the transport. The cloth hanging from his shoulders whipped about as the repulsor engines continued to stir up eddies of dust. "Just keep an eye on the thickheaded one, Comar. Shoot him before he does something stupid if you have to." Mallec took a slow step forward, watching Kara for a reaction.

"No closer," Kara warned as he started into another step.

"You never did know when you could trust someone, did you Kara?" Mallec made his stride flow seamlessly into a sideways motion, akin to a beast weighing up its prey. "But I suppose keeping your guard up for so long, only to let it down at the wrong time . . ."

"Back off, Mallec."

From behind them, Comar pleaded for her to lower her weapon. "There is no reason to get anyone killed here," he said.

"I can think of quite a few reasons to end him now," Kara hissed, "and very few require me to explain myself."

Mallec slowly started back from the edge of the support beam. "Then listen. I do not want you dead, despite what you may think. Call it sentiment, call it business, I have my reasons. For now, all I want is to keep the Cryo a secret. At least long enough to make a deal far better than the one you are thinking. Whatever the Overlord offered you, I guarantee you it is not as much as I can get."

"He is lying, Kara!" Randin said without taking his eyes off Comar. "We were offered any transport and however much it could carry from the Norclave libraries."

"Blind as ever," Mallec sneered. "Allow me to think on Randin's behalf. Norclave is weak, divided, and fighting amongst itself. At any time, any one of the surrounding factions could step in and claim the city if they do not fear being invaded themselves. But no one would dare move against anyone who has a Cryo for the fear of retaliation with new, unheard-of tech. We sell the Cryo, we sell all of Norclave."

"'We' sell?" Randin gave a dry laugh. "Did either of you two hear him say anything other than 'I am going to put a knife in your back?' Or did he also tell us to turn around?"

Jance turned to look out in the distance and into the rift stretching out from below the building they stood on. Mallec knew nothing about her, nor did he care. It did not even matter what she actually knew. Her value was in the superstitious fear that surrounded a Cryo . . . for being something no one in this time fully understood.

Kara gripped the shocklance as if she were ready to fire at any moment. "I will not let you start a war in Norclave. Jance stays with me."

Mallec stopped moving and carefully watched the wild look in Kara's eyes. "You are fooling nobody. You could care less about the city. Finding this Cryo, it was never about saving the Overlord."

Jance started to lose track of the shadowy tones behind every word as she continued to look out into the rift. The massive split cut its way through the thin forests and ruined spears of steel. It was a wasteland, nothing more. Great thunderclouds met with winds of rust in the far distance, and the ever-present wreckage slowly moved where it littered the edge of space. Jance found herself sinking even deeper into the emotional shroud, devoid of purpose and meaning. It seemed the nightmare she and Avery had fought so hard against had truly come to fruition, sending the world into nothing more than ashes.

"Dammit," Randin said under his breath as he was forced to see the other side of the situation. "Kara, perhaps we should think about this. Not so much about the reward as much as the fact that we do not even know if the Overlord will be alive by the time we get there."

"I . . ." Kara said as frustration mixed with her fury. Her eyes began to water, though she did not dare take her hands away from the weapon. "I have to get to Norclave."

"Kara . . ." Randin said in an apologetic tone. "We have to let it go." He slowly lowered his weapon. Comar gave a nod of approval and mirrored the motion. "Just play along."

Jance looked back from the wide expanse to where now only Kara and Mallec were ready for a fight. She saw a determination in Kara similar to that which she herself had left back with Avery and the rest of her world long ago, though Jance could not immediately see the reason behind the tech hunter's drive. Jance let out a breath, sympathizing with the feeling of being forced to let go of what you had set your mind to for so long. Jance stepped closer, moving past Comar to get a better look at her. Jance felt a tingle go down her spine and suddenly felt as if she were looking into a mirror.

Anger and confusion caused Kara's jaw to tremble ever so slightly as the electricity continued to pop around her hands and reflect back into her glassy eyes. The scrape crossing the bridge of her thin nose and the dust on her chin only accented the uncertainty the tech hunter was clearly feeling.

Jance stepped squarely in front of Kara as she finally figured it out.

"What are you doing?" Kara asked quietly.

"The same thing I would have for myself, if I could step back in time." At that, Jance spun on her heel and confronted the look of confusion on Mallec's face with a firm stance. "I am going to Norclave to speak with the Overlord."

"What?" Mallec asked. When he tried to step to the side to get a clear angle on Kara, Jance matched his pacing. "Get out of the way, Cryo," he growled. "You owe this world nothing."

Jance could only give a solemn smile. "That is where you are wrong. My world is not buried as deep as I was led to think."

He squared his jaw but Jance simply stood her ground, matching the anger in his gaze with a highly practiced and collected composure. After what she had already been through, the weapon in the tech hunter's hands and the scars crossing his face did little to scare her.

The silence of the tense moment was only broken by the shifting winds as Mallec looked into his own memory as much as her eyes. Jance could see the options running through his head, and she set her hands confidently on her hips. Slowly, the look of strength began to fade as the fables of the Cryos started to resemble what now stood before him.

"But you are not like the other Cryo I saw," Mallec said. "He was something to be afraid of. You are just . . ." Mallec stood there with his weapon ready, but the thoughts of his buried past continued to well up.

"Where?" Jance said, almost as a command.

"New Solace." He said the name in a quiet tone even Jance knew was uncharacteristic of him. "I was too young to get in his way after they woke him. There were not enough survivors remaining to work the city into a graveyard. We just left it how it was."

Jance took a slow step forward and set two fingers on the barrel of the weapon, knowing that he had killed people before. The tech hunters would not have feared him so much otherwise.

Mallec had a look of hatred on his face. "You are a fool to think I will let something like you slip away."

Jance could see that the fear put into him at a young age with whatever happened in New Solace was beyond his control. She knew she could exploit that. After all, she was a Cryo.

Jance slowly pushed down his weapon, keeping her eyes on him as he finally gave into the fear of something he understood so very little about.

"I should kill you now . . ." he sneered.

Jance just gave him another smile. "You cannot kill a ghost." She slowly stepped to the side.

The last thing he would have felt was a bright flash of heat washing over him as Kara unleashed a sudden swarm of electricity. Mallec jolted backward and fell stiffly onto the hard steel.

After looking in wonder upon the motionless man for a few short seconds, Jance glanced back to the other tech hunters. They had looks of utter surprise, and the other two beside Kara almost looked as if they were thinking about raising their weapons again.

Honestly, she was surprised it had even worked.

Jance flicked a finger from her visor back to the transport. "If all this talk about Norclave and war is as bad as it sounds, we have no time to waste, Kara." The control overlay of the transport synced with her visor, to her great relief. "If your Kenneth is anything like Avery, he will be trying to take them all on by himself."

As Jance turned to the transport, she paused to take in a breath. As it turned out, speaking with the Overlord was their only hope of figuring out how Kenneth and Avery's idea of taking on the world by themselves had worked for either of them.

Chapter 19: The Warden

Avery grunted as Maaned Grines helped him out of the elevator and into the maintenance hallway. Rather than the clean white halls of the rest of the medical facility, this particular area was designed to allow for drone access along the various pipes and cables for repair.

"This should lead out near the secondary response lab," Grines said as they started down the long hall. The lights from below the grating turned on as they approached. Avery glanced behind them and saw that the lights were also shutting out where not needed.

"Your whole scheme will be turned over and buried if you are leading me on," Avery warned.

"Yes, you have made that clear. Med-tech Narka is on her way to open the lab. She will be the only one there."

Avery nodded and touched his visor. "Alright Maylee, talk to me. What are you seeing in this Crystal Slate?"

"I do not even know where to start," the girl said from the Council archives. "There is so much."

"Just start with something." Avery caught himself on the railing as he stumbled. "Try the Charon tests," he managed to get out as he forced himself to keep moving forward with Grines.

"Research lab based on Charon. Testing was a success. Surviving scientists evacuated 2835.

"Wait, the test was successful?" Avery thought back to what they found in the Drake Discovery archives. "Hale said it was a failure. The logs showed that Emil Forge shut the Quantum Recalibration Project down after they destroyed the facility on Charon. Their funding was redirected to start the Mars Contract."

"No, not according to this. There was heavy damage to the station's systems, but only a handful of people were killed."

"Then what happened?"

"It says there was an error in separating the target's gravitational mass from Charon's gravitational field as a whole. But they . . . Oh wow, instead of moving the test object, they actually moved the entire planetoid! The test trial took, once initiated, fifteen point four five blah blah seconds, and resulted in an estimated shift in Charon's location up to a hundred miles."

"A hundred miles?"

"Avery, if they could move something that large, and that quickly . . ."

"Then they could move something much smaller, much faster. A faster than light projectile."

"I was going to say interstellar travel, but that could also lead to weaponry, I suppose."

Avery nodded. That is what Hale's project was trying to accomplish. That was Hale's big theory. He had set the groundwork for technology that could finally send the human race into the stars.

"Huh," Maylee said. "I don't think they ever solved the problem of separating one gravitational mass from another. One theory suggests building a deep-space station, independent of any celestial body, for continued tests without other gravitational masses. At least, that's what part of the incredibly long title of the document suggests."

"Is there reference to the construction of that station?"

"Capable of the tests? Charon is it. And after the evacuations, no one went back. The project was put on hold."

Avery frowned. "But why was it put on hold? Why not continue research? Why did Emil Forge settle for letting Outreach Systems colonize Mars instead of continuing Hale's work to reach another star system?"

"It was the UWC that stopped them from going back."

Avery coughed and caught hold of the railing in the passage. If they never overcame Hale's setbacks, and the never created a station to base his project as a weapon, how did Hoffsted plan on using the experiment? Avery pushed against the railing and continued walking.

"Any ideas of where to look?" Maylee asked. "Oh, how about this. No, those are just the specifications for the research. That's useless."

Avery would have laughed had he not been so focused on moving forward past the pain. What Maylee called useless was the actual data regarding the process of sending an object through space at faster than light speeds. It was what Avery feared could be a weapon capable of causing too much damage for the planet to survive, though he now doubted it could be used to such an effect without further research.

"Skip, skip, skip, enough with the formalities. Okay, Mr. Director, tell me. What is the big plan?"

"What is the date on the files?" Avery asked as he and Grines took a turn at a cross section in the hallway.

"2839. A long time ago. The director at the time said that the world was too unstable for such advancement as the project would allow."

"So the UWC shut the project down because they were scared of its potential."

"He says that it would be too dangerous while the UWC lacks control of the entire world, etcetera, etcetera. Sounds about the same as now, actually. The SRA is the entity blocking our expansion into the galaxy, according to him. And he sounds like a jerk to me, Avery. More than that, he talks like someone is pushing up on his nose."

"Maylee, focus."

"Right. The other guy speaking with him mentions the Mars Contract. Another is complaining about the pace of the research of the colonies. Something about a design problem with the energy systems, and also having no adequate test of the oxygen storage. Skipping," Maylee chirped. "Oh, he said Crystal Slate, moving back. Okay, talking about eliminating the SRA."

"Pay attention to this part," Avery advised.

"'Our victory can only be complete, no matter the losses to our own. The greatness, and continuation, of humanity rests entirely on this. We have to work as one mind. One people. One government. One planet. An unblemished Crystal Slate on which the foundation of interstellar colonization will stand. We must erase our past in order to gaze forward into infinity.' Now what the hell does that mean?" Maylee asked at the end.

"It means that the UWC founded Crystal Slate after canceling Tech-5's Quantum Recalibration Project. They decided then that Earth was not intended to be that foundation. 2839 was the year the Mars Contract was announced and the colonization started. But that still doesn't tell me how Hoffsted plans to eliminate Earth from the equation."

Avery followed Grines through an exit and stepped into the regular halls of the hospital. *Our victory can only be complete, no matter the losses to our own.* That line said everything Avery needed to finish the connection. "Search for the last mention in the entire archives of Archa Thompson and Marke Reyson."

"It is an empty report. The only word is 'Eliminated.'"

"Go back one. Look up their last report on the core reactors. Not the data, but the recommendation of those two individuals. That is the piece Morris Kannei was looking for."

Maylee cleared her throat. "All readouts on the system are within parameters, though we have come to fear those parameters given to us are not sufficient. The increasing frequency of earthquakes over the past hundred years around the structural points of the core reactors are evidence of a greater instability. Early projections of the system as a whole are classified, giving us no comparative baseline on the expected error threshold, and any attempts to attain access by either Mr. Reyson or I have been blocked. Furthermore, Mr. Reyson's detailed review of the containment fields—the details of which have been left out of our report for specific security reasons—shows a scenario in which the system can be forced to shut down by certain high-ranking UWC clearances if the supports are subjected to specific stresses. I affirm to the Council: the core reactors cannot be shut down under any circumstance. The consequence would be truly immeasurable to the planet. Both of these matters need to be looked into with the full attention of the UWC."

"Maylee, I need you to do something very important. Delete the quantum recalibration files and send the rest anywhere you can."

"What about this transfer request? It shows Hoffsted is cleared for transport to Mars through the EMA-GO."

"Hoffsted does not matter in this. Not anymore. The Council will see to that."

"Alright." She paused for a moment. "Just give me a second, this shouldn't take long."

Avery let out a breath of relief through a great deal of pain. It would be too late for Hoffsted to react now. He would learn about this through the Council, and they would strip him of his clearance, counteracting his efforts to shut down the core reactors and isolate Mars. It was all as good as over. The only thing that was left now was to pull Jance out of cryo and watch Hoffsted's alarms go off. He would finally be powerless to do anything more.

"Is this him?" a woman said as Grines led Avery to the door of a closed medical lab.

"What do you think, Narka?" Grines snapped. "You think I brought the wrong guy here?"

"If I get penalized for this . . ." she started.

"You will get worse than that if we do not help him. I do not want him telling the authorities about our deal, and I definitely do not want to try to hide a body from them if he bleeds out."

"Alright." She used her visor to access the door to the lab. "Bring him in."

Avery groaned as Grines pushed him forward in a hurry, eager to get the door closed behind them. Narka started turning on a portion of the lights, giving a view of the various stations of medical equipment. This section was only open part of the time, mostly reserved for any overflow requiring intense care after a disaster. It should have been at full capacity after the bombing of the Council airlocks, but the evacuations had left the entire building greatly understaffed.

"We will have to put you under," she said to Avery.

He grabbed her wrist and moved the small, silvery square away from the side of his head. He could not say if his resistance was out of habit or something else, but he suddenly felt the unyielding urge that he might need to be awake. Perhaps it was something Hale said. About it being gone the moment he looked away.

"Just do what you can. I still may have to move soon."

* * *

Maylee tucked her small metal game figure back in a pocket as she finished her own bit of business and started to locate all the data on the Quantum Recalibration Project. She left references, but she took anything that looked as if it could be used to recreate the project from the system.

"I have gotten rid of a good portion of the data you mentioned. I just need a few more minutes to get the rest."

She glanced over her shoulder into the dark room. The glow from the archive systems themselves were the only source of light aside from the wide window at the other end. Just before she turned back to the control terminal, she heard the quiet shift of the elevator rising up to the archive level.

"Avery, someone is coming!" she said, holding both hands to the one side of her visor in panic. "I guarantee those are Hoffsted's men, sent after the same thing we were after. There will be no time to send the information, but if I stay until the end, I can get rid of everything on quantum recalibration."

"Dammit," Avery growled. He let out a yell of pain before continuing. "Just get out. Maylee, just run!"

"No, I have to stay and—"

"I can work with what you found. You have done all you can, and I cannot ask you to give any more. Now go," Avery said, his voice tight from pain. "Get to the orbital fleet!"

She hesitated a moment but ultimately shifted off into the shadows as the door at the end opened. Maylee moved as quietly as she could, seeing the lights turning on down the corridors as the group of soldiers moved farther into the room.

"Someone has been here!" one of the men called out to the others. He was looking at the terminal she had left activated. "They were deleting sections of the information."

Maylee ducked to the side between the long rows of machines. She could feel the heat coming out through the metal even with the cooling systems humming inside.

"No time to waste," another said. "Hoffsted's transport is leaving for Mars in a few hours. Grab whatever data is left and finish cleaning it from the archive. And someone check for signatures."

"Not getting any readings, but it could be because of these servers."

Maylee tapped her visor, hoping the glow would not give her away. She quickly sent a message to Avery, relaying what she overheard the soldier say about Hoffsted leaving Earth in only a few hours.

Maylee shuffled quickly to another row as the order for a manual sweep went out. Her heart raced quicker than it ever had when hiding from the ICC patrols. She quickly pulled her visor free to hide the glow as lights flicked at her heels. In the tight corridors, it seemed as if every inch counted in hiding from the lights affixed to their weapons. On one occasion, she nearly bumped into a man as she peeked around a corner.

Too close! She thought to herself quietly, not even allowing her thoughts to make too loud of a noise above the hum of the data servers. She moved away and caught a glimpse of the terminal she had been at. They had a direct cable linked into a data pad, pulling the massive amount of information that was still left. Maylee wasted no time in darting off into the darkness.

On several occasions, she edged past just as a light flicked down the path she had been on. Slowly, she made her way to the entrance of the room. There was one man standing in front of the elevator in completely black UWC armor. The formal red stripe of their military was nowhere to be seen. She glanced around, trying desperately to think of what to do. Being sent by Hoffsted, she figured this man was just as likely to shoot at any movement as to think twice.

But perhaps that could work in her favor.

From the shadows, Maylee looked at the small metal figure that she held tight in her hand. She ran her thumb over the word *"Warden"* inscribed on the base of the figure. It almost seemed a shame to have to use it as a distraction, but she could think of nothing else that would work. Just as she was about to throw the figure off to the side and make a run for the elevator, she thought of a second option. There was no need for it after all. Maylee removed her visor. She then flicked the thin silver band up and over the servers on the other side, causing a slight clicking as it skittered across the floor.

The soldier raised the weapon to his shoulder and pointed down the hall with his light. He took a few steps forward. When he realized his error, he spun around and shot several rounds, which did nothing more than splinter the glass Maylee waved at him through. One tap of the panel caused her to drop down out of his view. From there, she started toward the nearest exit of the Council grid.

* * *

"Every bit of the regeneration and mending has torn itself free," Med-tech Narka said as she looked over Avery's chest. Grines turned a shoulder and held a fist to his mouth as she peeled away the undersuit of the SorrCom uniform. "Even without a scan I can see that the shoulder is broken. I hope you know this requires far more attention than you are willing to receive. You need a fully operational medical lab, staffed by more than just me."

"I tried the one on the *Nemesis Tide*. It didn't suit me."

She shook her head and started applying a layer of medi-seal. "I am not sure what you are expecting me to do. You will be counting your hours if you continue to refuse a stabilizing chamber."

Avery winced as Grines pulled off the pieces of the shattered plate on his arm at her orders. Just like the two holes through his chest, the one in his arm was now a large red patch of inflamed skin. His short time on the *Nemesis Tide* had sealed it over, but he could feel that the weakened tissue had begun to separate within his arm.

The truth was that the Council would have never acted quick enough, even had Maylee gotten the information to them, if what she had said about Hoffsted's planned evacuation was true. His next few hours could mean all the difference in the world.

"Get me something to cut the pain."

"I have already given you all I can without knowing what you have had already," she said, rubbing the paste over his arm. "The only other way is to put you under."

"No time for that. I am leaving."

They both gave him confused looks. "What do you mean, leaving?" Grines asked. "Why come in here just to refuse any treatment that will really help?"

Avery grabbed the edge of Grines's shirt and pulled himself upright. He swung his legs off the table and fought against his shaking knees to stand.

"Things changed. I thought it was over. I thought I had time." He let out a groan as he pulled the undersuit back over his shoulders. Although he knew it would do little to help, he went ahead and clasped the splintered sections of the armor back onto his chest. For the most part, it was in a show of determination to himself. There was no other choice. He had to stop Hoffsted's final move, no matter what happened to him. He had to get to the Power Relay Station of the core reactors.

* * *

The command bridge of the *Nemesis Tide* functioned at full capacity as the deployed ground teams and fighter crews all across the city were met with incident after incident. Admiral Brakka had the displays around his circular balcony showing live feeds from above the various buildings about the city that had been scarred in the attacks. Though the Council Starscraper had only now stopped smoking, he had received positive confirmation that Director Auburns had been at the site of another blast, confirmed dead. All security feeds before the attack were distorted beyond recognition. An initial analysis from the soldiers on the ground put the launch of the Orbital Armistice Fleet as the source of the distortions, though the ground team did not have the clearance to know any better.

Out of two UWC transports that had landed, only one was reported to have been caught in the detonation. The other had simply disappeared. Add that on top of everything Director Auburns had told him just before the attack, and Admiral Brakka was left with nothing but suspicion.

"Rear bridge, take command." He tapped a command through the displays around his station and the information returned to normal system specifications. Nearly half of their fighter craft and soldiers had been deployed in one capacity or another. He backed away and turned toward the main airlock into the room.

Leaving the dreadnought with the secondary command would normally have been the last thing the admiral would do in such a tense environment, but after what Director Auburns had personally told him about the military ambassador, he was not entirely sure he wanted to make any further decisions. At least not without more answers than he had been given.

"Admiral." The officer saluted on the other side of the airlock.

As the man started to point to a few of his soldiers for an escort, Brakka waved him off. "Leave me."

As if signing for the failed transfer of Sectator Avery Thorne was not bad enough, Brakka did not want any more people than was necessary to know he was going to speak with the other prisoners.

While Auburns may have given in to the sectator and Ambassador Lorège, Brakka was not entirely convinced who was behind the particular explosion that had resulted in Director Auburn's death. Releasing Avery Thorne at the director's recommendation could either have been a victory for the Last Edict against the UWC, or a punch against Hoffsted's possible corruption.

The doors swung open and he stepped out onto one of the lower levels. He passed several security checkpoints as he finally neared the holding cells. He entered the first room. It was split in half, separated by a thick panel of glass that was just as strong as the reinforced steel it was bracketed into. In the portion of the room he stepped into, there were a few chairs as well as a small table. The other side, with its own lock system, was the quarters of Lance Gyven, the pilot who had helped Avery and Jance escape out of both the starscraper in Sector: K and the Drake Discovery Complex.

The man leaned forward from where he was lying down on the unaccommodating bed with his socks pressed against the glass partition. He shifted his feet to the floor.

"You could have knocked," he said. He popped his neck to either side as if it were part of his morning routine. "So, what is it?"

"I am Admiral James Brakka of the UWC *Nemesis Tide*. I am looking for answers regarding the Last Edict."

Lance ruffled a hand through his hair. "I'll tell you what I told your men. I am not a sectator. Not actually even part of the Edict."

"Explain your ties to Avery Thorne, in that case." The admiral motioned from his visor to the glass and a series of displays appeared. He flicked a hand to invert them so the man could see properly. "We have two positive connections. One linking you to the caretaker unit we found clinging to the side of the starscraper, and the other in which you requested to dock on my ship. A possible third instance connecting you and Thorne some years back is being retraced, thanks to a surprising tip from the SRA."

"How about you tell me something about him, then. Is Avery alive? Or did he finally pay the price for protecting you, and bloody everybody else!" Lance stood, knocking his one chair down in front of the glass. After a moment of letting his temper burn, he looked from the information displayed by Admiral Brakka. "You tell me, Admiral, or I have nothing to say."

"I can only assume he is still alive. Director Auburns ordered for his release. After that, Avery disappeared."

"His release?" Lance used his foot to scoop the back of the chair up to his hand and slid it back into place. "What are you talking about?"

"What is Thorne looking for? What were his orders from the Last Edict?"

Lance rubbed the back of his neck as he paced to the side. "He would not have orders. Not new ones."

"How do you know?"

The man sat back down on the bed and clasped his hands together. He was obviously conflicted about giving information. "The Edict only gives orders once. At least, that is what he told me before he joined. I helped him track down a corruption ring, way back." He motioned to the oldest piece of data displayed along the glass barrier. "He wanted to attract the Edict's attention. I moved him around under the radar, and he gathered all of the information needed to put every single one of the political backstabbers into a lockup like this." He glanced around his own cell. "Needless to say, the Edict was impressed at how he had managed to uncover some of their people in the process. At least I assume they were impressed. Years later, Avery was given the mission. All I was told is that he was to be an intermediary for some high-ranking official. Set up a trade of information between the Edict and the UWC."

"The director."

"It would seem so." Lance gave a long glance up at the caretaker on the second of the displays. "Something changed. I expect he got close to the information the Edict had been looking for all along. His UWC contact gave him an order to get Morris Kannei out. I was to pick them up. Instead, Weyburn beat Avery to Kannei, and we left only with a shred of the information and Ambassador Lorège. Everything after that was Avery's personal mission."

"Kannei's information led you to the Drake Discovery archives."

"And what a confusing mess that turned out to be. Not even sure if we found anything. I guess that is what happens when you have a batch of washed-up agents trying to work on their own. We just about lost Avery, and Feyn . . . I don't suppose you know how she ended up?"

Brakka held a hand to his visor. "Medical logs." After a quick scan of the information, he continued, "She is still under observation. Projections on her outcome look grim."

"If you try to talk to Welnn, well, first of all good luck getting anything out of him, but if you do try, break that info to him lightly." Lance tapped on the glass that was easily half a foot thick. "Not sure this would be enough."

"The information Avery found in Arctica," the admiral said, keeping him on track, "it led him to the Council archives. There was a security breach shortly after he departed. Do you have any idea where his findings in the Council archives would have led him?"

Lance shrugged. "You would have to follow the trail yourself. You are not going to find Avery just by looking. And this far in, I doubt that he has so much as touched a traceable contact."

"Is there another way to contact him? Does the Last Edict have a way?"

Lance gave a short laugh. "That is a bit too blunt of a question, don't you think? Even if I did know, I would not tell you something like that. Everything Avery has done, that is on him. But that? That would be a swift blow to the entire Edict."

Brakka crossed his arms. "I could not give a damn about stopping the Last Edict at the moment. I do not trust them, but as you said, Avery has been acting on his own. I need to speak with him directly to get an explanation for all of this. Maybe then I can decide if I should be taking a side."

"I'll tell you what," Lance said, standing up from the bed and moving toward the center of his cell. "If you want to get hold of Avery, you need to speak with Welnn. He was a sectator. He would know if there is any way to contact him."

"You know he will not talk."

Lance nodded but gave the admiral a conniving look. "Not in a cell he won't."

* * *

"Transport is all ready, sir."

The military ambassador pushed past the soldier with a hard bump of the shoulder as he stepped from the exterior docks of the Tech-5 launch facility up into the side of the gunship. His shadow squad stood at attention on the inside, having just arrived from the Council archives. None of them dared make eye contact with him as they stood like statues. After all, it was their fault that the girl in the archives had managed to slip past them.

Hoffsted gave a stern look down the line before giving the signal to lift off. Instead of boarding the Tech-5 interplanetary shuttle as planned, he now had to travel by gunship to the Power Relay Station of the core reactors to oversee it personally. The absence of General Obrourke had seen to that.

"Send a message to General Dravis. Give him one hour to begin."

"Begin what, Ambassador?"

"He already knows."

The side doors closed as the repulsors flared in a wave of heat. As soon as Dravis received the order, it would become all that much more important that Hoffsted arrive back here to the shuttle. There was no telling what decisions would be made in the wake of the sheer chaos and ruin to come.

Chapter 20: The Overlord

Kenneth looked out over the thick forests between Norclave and the Rift Outpost. The scattered echoes of firefights sounded behind him as the First Administrator's soldiers headed back into the city. He had heard something about a final push on the defensive weapons of Norclave, and could see a steady flow of transports moving out of Norclave, obviously taking advantage in the gap of control Silas had left. Once he took the weapons control station, Kenneth knew that everything left in the sky would be shot down.

"What do you see out there?" Sora asked. She sat atop her large bag of data pads behind Kenneth on the abandoned platform. As soon as the soldiers had left, Karzon took off into the city and Aarol found the nearest transport to take him anywhere else.

"Nothing different." Kenneth shook his head. "Same view as ever."

"It's a shame we couldn't bring the Cryo back. I would've loved to be able to look at all of this differently. To know the truth behind it."

"It is for the better." Kenneth glanced over his shoulder before turning back to watch the transports dispersing over the valley. "Our world does not even compare to theirs. We live in the shadow of their ruins. What we see as mountains," he turned around to face into Norclave and the starscraper that loomed overhead, "the Cryo would only know as devastation. That is what I am beginning to see."

"Then why not leave?" She gave him a concerned look. "Why stay in Norclave?"

Kenneth ran a hand through his hair, feeling the grit of dust clinging heavily to his scalp. "Perhaps I'm just holding on to memories. Hardly any good ones, but there is nothing new there. Maybe I am just tired of running, or maybe I finally realized there was no point to it."

"That is awfully grim."

"What about you?" Kenneth asked. "Why not go with Aarol?"

She gave a partial smile. "I've known him for a long time, but that does not mean I can stand him. Besides, I really do believe that the Overlord is going to come out on top of this, despite everything. You can see how much more of a struggle the First Administrator is having than he planned for. Once the lower administrators start switching sides back to the the Overlord, their whole overthrow attempt will collapse."

"Not sure I can see it that way, but you can hope. I'm going for a walk."

Sora simply gave a nod in reply before Kenneth took off into the empty walkways of the city. For a long stretch of aimless turns, there was not even a person to pass on the narrow sets of stairs. The only sign that the city had not been completely abandoned were the few pairs of eyes looking out from the doors of their container pod houses. It seemed that even all the soldiers who should have been patrolling the streets had moved to join the fight up on the seventh level for one side or the other.

He found himself imagining being ambushed by a group of the First Administrator's men, only to have Kara appear out of nowhere and pull him out of the fire yet again. He knew it would not happen, of course. They were just idle musings, though he had to force himself to focus his attention on reality as he swore he saw a flash of reddish hair rounding a corner up ahead.

Kenneth eventually found his path blocked by a group of Norclave soldiers on the edge of the trade center. They were scavenging weapons from those they had killed in the fighting and patching up some wounds of their own. The bodies on the ground had the teal grey stripe painted across their chests.

"Hold there," one of the Norclave soldiers said. "I cannot let you into the trade center. Turn around."

Kenneth simply rolled up his sleeve and held out his arm, showing the spread of marks. Normally it would not have been a wise idea, but if they were still loyal to the Overlord at this point in the fighting, they would have heard about those marks.

The man frowned. "Just come on through," he told Kenneth. "Keep your head down, though. It has not been long since we took the area back."

Kenneth walked forward past the group, noticing some of the others giving him looks of admiration. He shook his head. They were probably looking for a sign of hope that this was going to turn out any other way than complete failure.

He started around the edge of the trade center, noticing small pockets of the Overlord's men set up just inside the buildings. The center walkways seemed to be a no-man's ground, even after the Overlord's men had taken the entire area. Overturned stalls littered the blasted walkways and the docks had several transports that had been reduced to little more than smoke and flames. Kenneth stepped over the rubble of one building, and realized that not long ago he'd seen scrapsmiths working to pull apart a drone there. The pieces appeared to be mixed in with the twisted steel of the shop.

Just beyond that, he noticed a hefty guard of Norclave soldiers on either side of another building. The walkways had been torn apart by whatever blast had happened in the fighting, but a hasty patchwork fix of welds and cables now held them in place. Kenneth glanced around at the front of Mackelry Norton's business. Just as the soldiers started to ready clubs and raise rifles, a familiar voice called from just inside.

"Kenneth, my boy, what a sight you are! You will never believe what showed up before you did." The old scab of a man ducked through the twisted doorframe and waved for Kenneth to enter, glancing up and around at the higher levels of the trade center. "Come in, come in."

Kenneth followed as Mackelry started deeper into the blast area.

"You have to watch the open areas. We had one try to get some shots off without us knowing." He glanced over his shoulder. "That did not work out so well for him. He did not know he was shooting at the Overlord."

"The Overlord is here?" Kenneth asked just before the old merchant stepped through the light distortion field in the back.

"Shhh! Keeping it a secret is part of the whole idea!"

"I thought the administrators had him held up at the defensive battery with all of the trouble they were having taking it."

"Well, good. Maybe if we can fool you, we can keep fooling Silas Konrev." He gave another wave to Kenneth to follow. "The main operation is in here, so stay quiet."

Kenneth followed him through the low tunnel running to the main part of Mackelry's business. When he stood up in the large room full of a wide assortment of illegal tech, Kenneth immediately noticed a number of soldiers wearing as near to full flight armor suits as he had ever seen. In the center of the room, standing with his back to the door and leaning forward onto a table, was a large figure wearing heavy armor and a rough cloak that hung down to his heels. The Overlord of

Norclave in Mackelry Norton's black market storage room. Kenneth never thought he would see the day.

One of the Overlord's personal guards gave him a nod as Mackelry led Kenneth off to the side.

"You'll speak with him soon enough, I am sure. But I have to show you this. Now where did I put 'em. Here they are." Mackelry turned around, holding the same set of gloves that he had given Kenneth at the start. "Some brute of a man came by and dropped them off. I thought you were dead for sure if he had them, but sure enough, here you are."

Kenneth looked at them for a moment. It was beyond him why Karzon would have brought the gloves back here, to the one place Kenneth said he could not sell them. "What did he say?"

"Something about debts. I'll have to remember that. Now, go ahead, take them," Mackelry said, shoving them into Kenneth's hands. "I've lost half of my good stock in supplying any extra men the Overlord could round up. It's an investment, you see. And I am sure the Overlord will have something more for you to do, seeing as you've returned from your secret mission."

Kenneth sent a nervous glance toward the table where the Overlord was discussing the battle plans with his other advisors. When Kenneth had started into the city in his aimless walk, he had never once thought that he would have to explain to the Overlord himself how terribly wrong the entire thing had gone. The Cryo dead, their expedition team crushed. He even felt partially responsible for bringing Olana Nuand into the mix. The only thing in his mind that had come out positively in the entire ordeal was that Kara had come out of it alive, though the Overlord would not care about a tech hunter in the slightest.

"Oh, don't worry. They already know what happened. Draken made contact not too long ago. The Overlord was furious, but eventually he calmed down. It was a tough choice the tracker made, but keeping it away from Silas, the Kessians, even the mines . . . it had to happen."

"Where is Draken?" Kenneth asked. He clenched his jaw, wishing he could use the gloves in his hands to beat the tracker for what he'd done.

"All I overheard was that the Overlord sent him back to the Cryo's location to retrieve something."

"Probably the visor, if he did not damage it," Kenneth grumbled.

"Overlord," one of the Overlord's advisors said, looking at a data pad in his hands. "The defensive station has been overrun by the First Administrator. Commander Murlias, Rein Vasfa, and a few others have been captured or killed."

Kenneth watched as the heavy glove of the Overlord's hand slowly curled, giving a hiss of air from the wrist as the rusted cylinders extended.

"Good. Send your team to secure a platform. We leave for the Rift Outpost shortly. Draken will meet us there."

"Overlord?" the advisor asked in question. "What about the city?"

"The final theory of war: What victory remains, is to the one who survives."

Kenneth felt a chill go down his spine, and it was then that the rumble of the defensive cannons unleashing their thunderous fire shook the city like quakes from the Earth.

* * *

Kara leaned out over the side of the transport as they topped the ridge of the starscraper. "Norclave is just below us!" she yelled forward to Jance.

"What are the landing restrictions?"

She gave a hard look down at the city. Kara could hear the feint echo of firefights throughout the whole of Norclave, though toward the top it sounded as if a heated battle was in progress. "Pick a dock that is not shooting at us and we will be fine." If she remembered right, the area now heavy with fighting was the location of the same cannons that Kenneth had disabled long ago in one of his attempts to escape the city. With all of the transports still flowing away from the starscraper, the defenses had clearly not yet been activated.

"Try for the fourth level," Kara called forward past a strong gust of wind. "My guess is that Kenneth is there. He may know where you can find the Overlord as well."

Jance glanced back as they started their descent. "I just want you know that this transport that Mallec guy found is a piece of crap to fly!"

"Something tells me you have had better experiences than most!"

"Are they all this bad?" Jance asked. "The ones that still work?"

"You kidding? This one is a dream. He probably stole it right off the personal docks of the Prime Elect of Reclaim."

"Well, we will just have to see if he still wants it back after I am finished landing it." Jance spun the transport to face straight back at Norclave. "Now which one?"

"See that, there in front of us? Just to the left? Put us—" Without warning, one of the defensive cannons let out a blinding flare, causing a leaving transport to split in half and erupt in a bright burst of flame. In moments, the sky began to turn into a zone of terror and flying scrap. Kara yelled for Jance to get them down, but instead she jerked the craft hard to the side.

Kara felt a jolt as the transport was set into a quick spiral by the shot that Jance tried to evade. She could immediately see that flames were spitting out of the side of one of the repulsors. Any moment, it would burst, sending them into a shower of scrap just like the other explosions across the southern Norclave sky.

She felt another sharp jolt forward as they crashed down upon a platform. A wave of sparks rolled over her when they screeched to a stop only a few feet from the edge of a hundred-foot drop. As quickly as she could with the throbbing in her head and her vision distorted from the brightness of the shot, Kara crawled up and out of her seat.

"Grip tight!" she yelled, grabbing the back of Jance's shirt and an arm. Her voiced seemed to not carry quite as far as she would have hoped, but the woman understood their situation. Kara lifted as hard as she could, and they both toppled out of the side of the transport.

"Up and moving!" Kara yelled again as she stumbled forward, still dragging Jance. In an instant, Kara felt as if she were walking through a pool of liquid fire as the heat from the repulsor collapsed inward and washed around the transport. She fell next to the edge, watching the world behind her flash as brightly as the cannons roaring above. In a sluggish motion, Kara pulled the strip of burning cloth from her sleeve and dropped it over the edge of the landing platform. The last thing she remembered was watching the flame drift ever downward into darkness.

* * *

"Find the Overlord!" Silas yelled between the near-deafening poundings of the cannons. "Do whatever it takes!" He stepped up to the large windows to watch as the spears of flames shot out over the city. They had needed to give up control over the docks to keep the Overlord from firing at the city itself, and that led to the ruthless action he had been forced to take. Most of the transports were simply people trying to escape the violent conflict, but right now, he could not risk a single one aiding in the escape of the Overlord. He had to take undeniable control. There was no other way.

For well over a minute the bombardment continued, launching devastation out into the sky far beyond the reach of the impact valley. Anything closer than the southern horizon was a target for the defenses. The show of force would help initially in taking the city, but it also could prove problematic later on; such was the nature of revealing the true capacity of any tech. The enemy would not be held back by fear of the unknown, and would instead be armed with the knowledge of what they possessed. And if Norclave appeared as too much of a threat, it could mean an invasion on multiple fronts.

"Enough!" Silas yelled. His men powered down the devastation, leaving the rumble to echo back from the interior of the starscraper long afterward. "Keep watch, though I doubt anyone will dare try to take off after that."

He turned to face where his men were still stripping the weapons from the Norclave soldiers. Arriving here in person before all areas of the structure had been secured was a risk in and of itself, but shutting down the skies was the top priority. By taking out the most heavily fortified area of the Overlord's Norclave, Silas had, in one bloody and costly move, set a sure end to the battle. The weak resistance they found in some of the nonessential parts of the city would be a simple matter to sort out once he gave the orders for his commanders to disperse.

He let out a breath and stepped over to one man who was tied up on the floor and under the watch of four of Silas's men.

"Rein Vasfa, ever vigilant informant to the Overlord," Silas chided. "You turned your nose at me long ago." Silas crouched down to bring himself closer to eye level with the man. "I am willing to forget that, under one condition. Tell me where the Overlord is."

The man gave a reproachful laugh and spit blood from the corner of his mouth at Silas's feet. "I'll tell you alright. He's probably looking. Right now. Where he can see you, Silas. Because you fought your way right into the jaws of a trap."

* * *

As the last of the cannons began to fade into echoes, Kenneth ran as fast as he could through the heart of the trade center. Even the couple of shots clicking around the warped walkways gave him no pause. He jumped over a gap without fear of the massive drop below or the shouts from the Overlord's men behind.

It was during Silas's onslaught that Kenneth overheard the report come in. A transport had crashed on the dock close to the one the Overlord's teams. Mackelry had tried to stop him from butting in, but Kenneth even went so far as to interrupt the Overlord to get a better description. Even with only a few words, Kenneth had no doubt in his mind that it was Kara.

"Hold right there . . ." the same soldier at the checkpoint to the trade center said before Kenneth simply blew past him. The soldier could have been shooting and he would not have stopped.

A million thoughts flew through his mind as he took every shortcut he knew of. How bad was she hurt? What was she doing in Norclave? Could he get to her in time?

Without warning, the city lit up with an orange light filtering through the myriad of walkways, and everything was shaken by a rumbling thunder far deeper than even the cannons. He glanced back over his shoulder only to see what looked like a rolling sun spilling over the seventh level of the city. The blasts from the continuing explosions were enough to cause Kenneth to stumble forward a few steps. It seemed the Overlord had finally given the order. The defensive cannons, and everyone in the control station, were suddenly obliterated by his savage stroke. Just as quickly as the rebellion had begun, it had fallen to a swift end at the hand of the beast of war they should have left sleeping.

Kenneth knew it should not have come to this. Lack of attention on the Overlord's part only gave the administrators more and more reason to assume control. And the rolling tide of fire that now consumed a great portion of the top level of Norclave was nothing more than a tragedy spawned of the same events that had left Kara dying on the docks.

He finally saw the sky, filled with smoke and swirling embers as far as anyone could see. Kenneth looked around and spotted the glowing and twisted half of the craft resting on the edge of the dock. The world seemed to slow down, the smoke consigned to a gentle roll, and the fluttering sparks looked like they were hissing through water.

As he stepped onto the landing pad, he could see through the smoke that Sora was pulling a person away from the craft. Sora gave him a teary look and nodded toward the other side of the transport. The world seemed to fall away as he spotted a figure curled up next to the edge. In one moment, the woman he had seen eager and able to fight off any struggle was left so small in the glow of the fires. He rushed over, though his feet refused to move as quickly as he needed them to. A trail of smoke lifted from Kara, and her hair lay splayed out in a haphazard fan—a far cry from how she always kept it tucked away.

Kenneth knelt down and put a hand on her shoulder. He could see just under the embers of her torn sleeve that there was a glow from the band on her wrist. His heart caught at realizing she had kept it. Kenneth pulled on Kara's shoulder to roll her over. He was left completely and irrevocably stunned at what he saw.

Two eyes, wide open, and an amazed look of joy and dazed surprise that could have cut through any amount of smoke and waving sheets of embers.

"You are alive," Kenneth said quietly as he brushed the ashes from her forehead.

"And you are here," she replied weakly. Kenneth felt her fingers slowly glide up along the scars on his arm as he watched the light of the flames dance along the edges of her eyes.

The few seconds that he knelt over her felt like eternity in a moment. When a wave of falling sparks rolled over Kenneth's shoulders, he reached an arm behind her head and pulled her in to shield her against the shards of the fire. In response, Kara wrapped her arms tight around him. For a long moment they rested there together on the edge of the flames, but they both knew it could not last forever.

"We have to move," Kenneth said with his chin on the top of her head. "The other repulsors could give out at any moment."

"Help me up then."

Kenneth slid his other arm around behind her back and started to stand. A loud burst from behind caused him to flinch, but soon they were edging away from the rolling smoke and twisting fires.

"After Draken killed the Cryo," Kenneth started as they approached Sora and the other woman who was trying to dust off her outfit, "I left to keep you from doing anything to get yourself killed. I had in mind that included coming to Norclave."

Kara looked up at him with an unexpectedly devious smile on her face. "But since I brought the Cryo with me, I say that breaks the deal."

Kenneth gave her a confused look.

"Wait," Sora said, "you are saying this is a . . ."

They all looked over to the woman brushing off her uniform.

"My name is Jance Lorège," the woman said, holding out a scraped and bruised hand to Sora in greeting. "I was the People's

Ambassador of Sector: K, and a member of the UWC Council. And . . . I am now a Cryo."

Sora shook Jance's hand with a look of complete astonishment. She glanced over to Kara for reassurance. "How did . . ."

"There will be time to explain," Kara said. She sent one more glance Kenneth's way before stepping away to test how well she supported her own weight.

Jance glanced from them to the smoke rolling up from the top of the city. "I need to speak with the Overlord."

Kenneth pointed to the dock next to them and up a half level, where Norclave soldiers were moving supplies into a transport. "He is preparing to leave the city."

The Cryo brushed at her uniform again, this time sending embers dancing from the edges. "Then we must move."

* * *

Jance hid a smile as Kara waved off another of Kenneth's offers to help her walk. It almost seemed as if the tech hunter enjoyed refusing help, even when she walked with a limp. On the other hand, Kenneth seemed determined to be of use.

"The Overlord is very direct," Sora advised as they made their way up along the edge of the city. "He likely will not ask a lot of questions, but instead tell you to elaborate. Just keep talking until he interrupts you."

Jance had a strange feeling when the soldiers at the entrance of the dock stopped them for questions. Besides the wear on their uniforms and the assorted weapons, they were very near to the look of UWC soldiers. By the way the red stripe across the chest had been repainted, she started to think that Norclave had adopted it as its own symbol.

"Sora, who are these people?" one of the soldiers asked. He glared at the visor Jance wore before looking back to Sora. "I hope you know what is going on here."

"The Cryo needs to speak with the Overlord."

He stood there for a moment as a murmur shifted about the others. He finally moved to salute, and the others began to follow in an unsure sequence. She could see an intensity grow on their faces as they looked on with a newfound hope and purpose. The first man looked between her and Sora. "The Overlord is just arriving."

When he nodded behind them, Jance turned around and straightened her uniform once more, though it did little to help the rips and burnt patches around the edges. When she looked up, the newly arriving soldiers started to fan out around them. Walking in the center was a titan of a man wearing a heavy suit of mechanical armor and a ragged cloak hanging down to his heels. The suit popped and hissed as he limped along the walkway. His thick jaw was covered in a rough layer of patchy hair ranging from grey to the beginnings of white. It was hard to guess his age, though she could see he had led a long and rough life. One side of his face looked lower than the other, and he had a worn look as he took in his surroundings.

It was when he stopped and turned that familiar look of stone on her that she finally realized who it was. General Garneth Obrourke was the Overlord of Norclave, and from his age, it looked as if he had been so for a number of years.

"My Overlord," Sora explained, "this is the Cryo from the expedition. Her name is . . ."

"Did you know?" Jance said angrily, taking a step forward toward the man. "When you forced me into the pod, did you know this is what would happen?"

He raised a heavy gloved hand as if to make his soldiers stand down, though none had even raised a weapon at her approach.

"It does not matter." The Overlord looked past Jance into the ember-filled sky. "We should never have known the fall. Look above you. Look past the shell of the Council Starscraper, past the wreckage of the orbital fleet, past the dying boundaries of Earth and into the vastness of the solar system. That is where I should have lived the rest of my life. Not here, in this waste."

"Did the Contract even survive? Did they ever make contact?"

Obrourke fell silent.

"You could have stopped it all, General. If you had let me—"

"No!" he yelled, stepping forward suddenly. "You dare not push the blame onto me! You put your trust in the Last Edict blindly! I found out years ago that the sectator ultimately decided to leave you in the pod. All I have done is bring you here, to the world they always sought to create."

Jance took another step and pointed at him furiously. "This is not what the Edict stood for. They tried to keep the possibility of our own destruction out of our hands!"

"You are a blind traitor to the human race." Obrourke gave a signal and a few of the soldiers in full flight armor grabbed her arms and pulled her visor free.

"With your help," the Overlord continued, "I can show you the truth behind the Last Edict. Their solution was to bring us as near to the age of ash as they could, so that we would never again rise to the heights Jonithan Hoffsted envisioned."

With one more signal from Obrourke, Jance was pulled toward a transport warming its repulsor engines.

"Wait!" Kara said, stopping just before she moved in the way of the Overlord. Even she did not dare entirely block his path. "Where are you taking her?"

The Overlord stopped just as he passed her. "Tenan and Laila are still in the Norclave Library. Sora will take you there. Collect whatever you see fit, tech hunter. You are done."

Chapter 21: Existence

Maylee sat silently with her head leaning against the window as the large transport shuttle set out from the Council Starscraper. She heard whispers from the others on the transport. Some were off-duty security personnel and others were from the medical lab she had walked into. At least two of them were wondering if they should try to comfort her, and another suggested answering any questions she might have. The truth was that Maylee was not scared. Not after all she had just been through. And as for questions, at the moment, she knew more than anyone else but Avery Thorne.

The transport banked to the side, giving a view of the long drop along the face of the Council Starscraper. It was easy to make out the gash in the side that still emitted a fog of foul air from the smoldering fires within. It was not too long ago that she had landed a transport in the middle of all that, which made her situation easy to explain to the medical technicians. She did survive the Council docks, her parents had made it to the orbital fleet before her, and she did lose her visor in the process of escaping.

The transport leveled out and started the rapid climb upward. She could hear the vents along the floor adding pressure as they neared the top of the Council Starscraper. Looking out over the city, Maylee could see an assortment of bright flares still lifting up through the sky. The evacuation of billions of people was not a simple process, no matter how much the UWC had prepared. For instances like her own—at least the story she had told—a constant flow of transports would pick up stragglers and deliver them up to the support ships. From there, the mile-long carriers would transport passengers to and from the main ships, often providing pickup points to shift individuals and reunite families separated in the loading.

Maylee glanced down at the data pad she had been given in place of her visor. Her schedule was to transfer to the *Fortuna-8* support vessel, then get off at the second docking and board the *Solstice Dawn*. It was as simple as could be. No piloting transports, no landing on unstable walkways, no fire or smoke, and most of all, no one shooting at her.

Even still, she looked out of the window and wondered if there was something more she could have done. As they continued steadily upward and away from the glow of Earth, she knew she would always carry that thought. She had been willing to stay in the archives long enough to get all the data out, even with Hoffsted's men on the way. The only reason she abandoned the terminal was because Avery said they could work with what she had found. Whether that was true or not, she couldn't say. All she could do now was look down and wonder.

* * *

Avery slung the satchel over his shoulder as he ducked out of the medical lab. The pain relief had yet to kick in, but he feared there would be no time to wait. The news reports displayed in the hallways spoke of rising tensions amidst a series of attacks around the globe, one of which had claimed the life of the director of the UWC Council. Another headline spoke of a breach in security around the evacuated Council Chambers, of which there was no response from the military ambassador. Avery saw no surprise in that.

Just as a headline about the SRA requesting an inspection of the Orbital Armistice Fleet appeared on the screens, the lights of the hallway started to flicker and the displays twisted free of their projection bounds and disappeared into the distortion field. Avery shouldered the maintenance access way and felt a shiver go down his spine as the door did not budge. It was not his generator messing with the systems. The one given to him by the Edict was probably back on the *Nemesis Tide*, if not lost in the Drake Discovery Complex.

Two shots suddenly echoed from the direction of the lab. If Grines and Narka had not been killed, Avery could guarantee at least one of them would immediately give away his direction. In fact, right about now Grines would be explaining how they got into the building. His only option was to beat whoever was after him to the entrance and hope up and down that they did not have forces outside to intercept him.

His hands shook in pain, but he finally wedged the door open enough to slide through. There was no time to consider hiding his tracks by closing the door. If the edge of the distortion field reached the elevator, he would be trapped.

Avery moved as quickly as he could. The lights under the walkways remained dark under the effects of the distortion field, and he was left to navigate by the glowing points of the system function indicators scattered amongst the pipes reaching both high above and far below the passage.

He stopped at another cross section in the dark and had to pause to think. At the time Grines had been leading him through the hall, Avery had been speaking with Maylee as well as fighting against the pain that was just now starting to dull. Avery closed his eyes, trying to remember exactly the path they had taken. Arriving at the wrong part of the undercity would mean failure just the same. Hoffsted's transport from Earth was scheduled for today, meaning there was absolutely no time to waste.

The task Avery had taken upon himself was daunting, to say the least. His every action seemed to stand on only blind luck. There was nothing to guide him but necessity. Nothing but his own thoughts to tell himself what direction was correct.

For a moment, Avery almost gave up right then and there in the crossing paths of darkness. There was no guarantee that any of it could even be stopped, no matter how hard he tried or how much he sacrificed.

Avery took a breath and opened his eyes, hoping for even an instant that he could find relief from the weight of his own decisions. Leaving Jance behind, choosing to not trust the Last Edict for fear of another traitor . . . there were so many choices that could be adding up to his inevitable failure.

"Avery Thorne!" a voice shouted in an echo that bounced through the expanses of the shafts. "No more games! No more hiding!"

He was stunned to hear the voice of Weyburn, even as distorted as it was. As several rage-filled warning shots pierced the darkness, Avery added another item to the list: he had failed to kill Weyburn on every chance he'd been afforded.

But it was then, to the echoes of anger chasing him down the hall, that Avery found the strength to pick a direction. It was not the fear of being killed by another man who should have also been long since dead, nor was it the consequences of failing to stop the final stages of Crystal Slate that now drove his steps. It was the fact that Weyburn, at Hoffsted's orders, was trying to stop him. That in and of itself meant there was something he could do that Hoffsted feared would make a difference. It meant that as long as he could find the fight, it was still there to be won.

Avery started running down the large hallway. The heavy falls of his boots echoed throughout the area, but the lights that started to flicker beneath his feet showed his progress. He glanced behind him, almost able to see the edge of the distortion field by the small points of lights disappearing in a sweeping arc. As long as he could reach the elevator before the edge of the distortion, he would be able to make it down.

"Avery!" Weyburn yelled down the hall in the shadows. The area around the man lit up for a moment as he fired his weapon while surging forward. Avery jerked away from the spark the bullet made as it hit the railing next to his hand. "Do not run from me!"

Just as he was reaching for the controls to the elevator doors, Avery stumbled as a result of the next shot burying into his leg. The impact felt more like a hard kick due to the inhibitors, though he could feel that it had lodged deep into his calf muscle. Avery reached up, causing the doors to start opening.

"If you continue to flee, I will find Ambassador Lorège and end her! She is at SorrCom, is she not? I swear, Thorne, she will never wake up!"

Avery dragged himself into the elevator, but that threat clawed hard at the back of his mind. The thought made him hesitate just long enough that, as he reached for the controls, the display distorted and the hall collapsed into darkness.

* * *

"There is nothing more for you to do, Avery," Weyburn said as he limped forward in the dark, one hand holding the pistol and the other over the unusable controls for the stabilizers. "You are only an empty husk, running from your own failures. You are just the same as me."

As Weyburn stumbled to the side next to the elevator, he tried to work the controls on his arm. Before he ended up falling down or dropping the pistol, Weyburn reached down to the distortion device and turned it off. As the field faded and the lights started on, he desperately added more of the chemicals that kept him upright. The burning feeling in his blood kicked up again and he started to regain focus. Weyburn took in a harsh breath and opened his eyes.

Weyburn stepped forward, holding his pistol ready with both hands as he tried to figure out which side of the doors Avery was hiding on. As the doors started to close, he stepped a foot in to keep them open. Without hesitation, Weyburn stepped around and fired two quick shots in one direction, then pivoted to rattle off another series of shots to the other side.

The sectator was nowhere to be found.

Weyburn looked around the elevator, though he could see no secondary hatch or alternate way out. He froze as he noticed a low hum and blue glow coming from behind. Weyburn flipped around with the same deadly speed and fired a shot along walkway. However, instead of hitting a mark, the static baton flashed upward from down beside the rails, catching him under the chin of the helmet. His vision instantly pulsed a bright white, and the burst of pain in his head made him double over, even with the heavy stabilizers burning through his veins.

As he stood back up, he could make out movement from under the walkway. When Weyburn aimed the pistol, a foot kicked his own leg and shook his already disoriented balance. Weyburn stumbled and barely caught himself from rolling backward over the top of the railing. He looked over his shoulder for a moment, seeing now for the first time in the glow of the lights that it was nearly a hundred-foot drop.

Avery pulled himself up from beneath the walkway, gripping the rail with one hand and under the back of Weyburn's helmet with the other. Weyburn tried to hold on, but as Avery began to pull down on his helmet, Weyburn felt his weight shift backward over the top of the rail.

"No!" he yelled as he scrambled to grab hold of anything to keep from going over. Weyburn tried to kick his feet out to the sides to catch one of the pipes or the walkway supports, but he ultimately only managed to grab hold of the sectator's wrist in an attempt to pry Avery's hand away from his helmet. Weyburn's helmet came off in the struggle and Avery quickly grabbed Weyburn's hand and continued to pull.

"Damn you!" Weyburn shouted, trying to twist his arm around from above his head to one side or the other. His helmet made a loud pop, splitting against a pipe far below.

"That is the idea!" Avery gave one final pull and tipped Weyburn over the edge.

As Weyburn fell backward, he focused everything he had left on digging his glove into the sectator's arm. He barely managed to hold on past the hard bounce that nearly pulled them both off. Immediately after, Avery began trying desperately to twist his arm free.

Weyburn knew he had only one option left and gripped the sectator's arm with both hands.

Weyburn managed to pull himself up a few inches before he dropped sharply down, now trying to pull the sectator down with him.

* * *

Avery felt his hand slip a little more as Weyburn bounced.

"Not this time, sectator," Weyburn wheezed, pulling himself up again.

Avery fought with wide eyes against the drop as Weyburn tried to break his grip from the railing. He had one leg hooked above the platform and his other foot braced against the support braces under the walkway. Avery could feel his bottom leg slowly giving out from the dulled pain where he had been shot.

Avery looked back to Weyburn as he prepared to make another go of pulling him down. Avery violently twisted his arm and managed to get the man to drop one hand free. It was then that he saw his only opportunity. Avery released the railing and strained as hard as he could to keep the one leg hooked on the edge of the platform. Now upside down with one hand free, he accessed the pad on the arm of Weyburn's Drake Discovery suit.

The murderous look of pure hatred on the man's burnt and scarred face shifted into a realization of what Avery was doing. One last press through the projected display caused a hiss as pressure released around the base of the glove. When Avery shook his arm again, Weyburn's hand slipped free, sending him falling away from the glove and down into the deep darkness below.

Avery pulled in a breath and curled back on himself to latch onto the side of the walkway. Just as he grabbed hold of the bottom of the rail, he felt his heel slip a few notches in the grating. It took all he had left to work his way back up. For a moment, he lay on his back looking up into the heights of the room with the relief of finding stable ground. He had brought an end to a man that had given him more wounds than Avery cared to count. More than that though, he knew that as long as he could stop Hoffsted, Jance would be safe.

* * *

"Careful with her!" Welnn said forcefully to the UWC soldiers setting Feyn down inside the back of the transport. Besides the medics, the rest of the entire hangar was empty. The notifications that flashed across any visors in the area warned about maintenance and depressurization, though both were false alerts.

Welnn continued to direct the transfer of Feyn's accompanying systems of medical equipment with the same temperament as herding wolves. To him, he had failed to protect her back in the complex.

"This one is a beauty!" Lance said as he stepped onto the transport through the back and started powering on the systems. It had been a while since he had flown a gunship. He could already tell he was going to love this.

"Bolt that down, we do not need it moving," Welnn continued. It was easy to see that he would not be leaving Feyn's side, even if she told him to.

"Would you just let them work!" Lance yelled back as he activated the straps to pull around him. "And call Avery while you're at it!"

"Only when we are out of the reach of this dreadnought."

"As long as we are somewhere in the general area of the *planet*, we will never be out of her reach." Lance started the repulsors to warming. "I suggest you make sure to play nice with Brakka."

"We'll see," Welnn said, finally taking a seat of his own as Feyn was secured on the stretcher now bolted to the floor. She murmured something to him, though her eyes remained closed.

"Ready for takeoff," Lance yelled back. He had been instructed to stay off communications, seeing as their departure was hardly sanctioned. He felt the wind pulling through the craft as the main hangar doors began to open. When the last of the soldiers stepped out of the gunship, he took hold of the controls and dropped down into the city with an excited laugh.

* * *

"Watch for him!" Hoffsted yelled as he stepped off the pad. "Shoot anything that tries to land!" He pointed for a few of the men to follow him as he started toward the entrance. Just as he was about to step inside, a series of shots rang out from the gunship he'd arrived on. He turned to watch a small transport pod burst into flames and crash higher up into the structure. He gave a nod of approval and turned his back on the city. A second impact resounded through the building as they stepped through a side entrance.

Even if none of the pods were the sectator, he was not about to pull back until he had confirmation that the man was dead. Not that it mattered; this entire area would be nothing but a wasteland once the variables were altered within the containment field.

After he disabled the system locking the elevator, he pulled his visor off. Once he motioned through the display to the lowest level possible, he slipped on the visor his team had recovered in the archives. It had belonged to Maylee Sharpes.

* * *

Avery attempted to apply medi-seal to his leg while threading the transport through the lowest levels of the city. Down this far, most of the structures merged into one another in some form. Much of that was because of older infrastructure designs requiring manual transport within the superstructures, often leading to decommissioned tram systems and walking paths crossing at odd angles a hundred stories up in some cases. He would have to fly nearly another half mile upward from his position to begin to see over the tops of some of the buildings.

Avery dropped the empty tube on the floor of the transport pod and increased the speed. As he got closer to the Power Relay Station, the connections between the buildings started to get thicker and the buildings themselves shrank in size. This was an older section, possibly here long before it was ever designated the Council City. It was definitely here before the starscrapers were ever implemented.

Just as he pulled up over the tops of the buildings to see how much farther the station was, a blip on his visor showed that Maylee was trying to contact him through the reality shard. It was the first time she had tried to do so since the archives.

"Maylee, did you make it to the fleet?"

"I suggest you listen." Hoffsted replied.

Avery's heart sank. "Where is Maylee?"

"I have to say, the girl was tough. But that was expected. She broke into the archives, after all."

"If you have done anything to her I swear I will—"

"Anything that happened was her own fault!" Hoffsted said harshly. "She made her own decisions, regardless of what you told her. Now, if you want the girl to live, do not do anything drastic."

Avery clenched his jaw as if trying to break his own teeth. "This will not end that easily."

"The Last Edict's attempts to send humanity into chaos have already fallen short," the military ambassador said. "You gain nothing by continuing. And neither does she."

"Attempts for chaos? You call survival chaos?"

"Humanity has reached a point where it cannot afford to mindlessly choose to survive." Hoffsted paused a moment. "Survival without restraint or purpose only leads to confusion and disarray. With the inevitability of limitless expansion, we cannot afford that disarray to result in the technology pushing interstellar travel to be used as a weapon. Not before we are widespread enough to withstand it."

"You are planning to use the core reactors to annihilate the entire Earth! That is exactly the kind of weapon you should fear!"

"The Earth is no longer the means for humanity! It will only be the source of conflict that *will* end in our destruction. What will happen to the planet is nothing compared to what would eventually follow."

"That is no justification for what you are planning to do. There is another way."

"You think we can just go back? Quantum recalibration has been discovered. If we bury it, the same things will simply be discovered again. At that point, it will be outside of our control to stop humanity from shaping the universe at a subatomic level into a reality we cannot survive within. We will simply be forced to flee to the edges of the galaxy to escape the wrath we spawned. Unless, Avery, humanity is forced to start anew."

"Such conviction. Such sacrifice demanded for your vision," Avery said disgustedly. He jerked the transport quickly to the side to avoid a string of cables running from a spire of one building to the next. "I know where you will stand when you watch the world burn, Hoffsted. I know of your scheduled transfer to the Mars colonies."

"You see! It is beyond your comprehension to even fathom! This is beyond individual actions or morals. Nothing matters except giving the colonies a chance to grow without being caught in the war about to begin here. This is not about being remembered. This is not about doing the right thing. This is about continued existence."

"Sounds a bit like mindless survival, doesn't it?" Avery neared the power station. It stood out as a large, wide structure amidst the shorter buildings. He switched the view to check the position of Maylee's visor within the reality shard. Hoffsted was deep within the Earth, far below any maps the system contained. He just needed a few more seconds on the connection to save that position.

"And what about her?" Avery continued. "What is to say that you do not just leave Maylee on the planet while you disappear?"

"You want a promise? Fine. I will see that she gets to the orbital fleet, and after that, amongst the first wave of those evacuated to the Contract facility. All you have to do is turn back. That is what the girl is begging for you to do right now. She wants to return to her family. She wishes you had never forced her into this, Avery. Just turn around."

The program finished making a duplicate of Maylee's connection within the servers, ensuring Hoffsted's position would remain even if the connection was severed. Avery let out a breath of relief, both at it finishing, and at the misinformation Hoffsted had let slip about Maylee.

"Just so you know, Ambassador Hoffsted, the only thing I forced her to do was get out before your men arrived at the archives. I told her I had everything I needed, but she proved me wrong again. Now, even if she really was there, I can guarantee you the last thing she would want is for me to give up on hunting you down."

There was a moment of silence. "Avery, stop this. You will never make it inside."

Avery terminated the connection and continued with doubled speed toward the Power Relay Station. A hail of gunfire erupted from the distance, causing him to duck the transport back down into the cover of the buildings. In only a short span he saw several pods very similar to his own erupt into flame and fall down into the city below.

Avery then knew it would be impossible to fly anywhere near; Hoffsted's gunship hovering above the docks to the relay station was covering the entire area. At the moment, his only option would be to enter one of the other buildings and use the interior passages to get as close to the Power Relay Station as he could. The problem with that, besides avoiding all the security that could be there, was that he feared it would take far too long. Hoffsted could be long gone before he ever got inside.

Just then, another connection formed to his visor through the reality shard. It showed Welnn as the contact, though Avery could not imagine how. Perhaps the UWC had finally broken into the Last Edict's systems, with Hoffsted's help. The question was, why bother contacting him again? Avery opened the connection and waited.

"Avery, where are you?" Welnn asked. After receiving no reply, he asked again. "Avery?"

"You are going to have to prove that you are with me. I cannot let Hoffsted or the UWC stop me now."

"Brakka released us. Avery, we can help. Just tell—"

"What was your mission? What did you do for the Edict?"

Avery was met by a long pause. Finally, Welnn replied, "I told you, I am never talking about it again."

"I have to hear you say it."

"Avery, don't make me—"

"Anything else, and I swear, I will sever this connection. For good."

As Avery could see how the world might begin to crumble around them, Welnn finally gave a sigh.

"No, Avery. *Nothing* is worth that."

Avery leaned back in his seat, looking up at the churning sky above. Several drops of rain tapped on the glass and slid down the curve of the window. After Hoffsted's lies about Maylee, it was a tremendous relief to hear the truth only the other sectator could give.

"I am by the Power Relay Station for the core reactors. I'm being blocked by Hoffsted's gunship."

"Lance?" Welnn barked. "You hear that?"

"Yeah, I got you. We just need a few minutes. And I might add, I've been waiting too damned long to see some proper action."

"Lance," Avery said quickly, "you have to be careful. They are not giving any warning shots here."

Lance gave a dangerous chuckle. "Oh-ho, neither are we."

* * *

Lance stepped out of the cockpit into the passenger bay.

Welnn gave him a look. "You sure about this?"

Feyn opened her eyes briefly and gave a dazed half smile. "He had better be."

Lance moved past them and opened the side door, stepping out onto the high edge of the building. The large strut sat at a bit of an angle almost at the top of the structure. More than the high slope and the passing sheets of rain, the heavy winds in the thin air forced Lance to keep one hand on the inside of the door.

Lance held the other hand up to his visor, feeling a wave of hot air roll past as the wind circled around the edge of the repulsor engines. In the distance, he could still see the transport circling above the facility that Avery needed inside. It fired indiscriminately on anything in the area.

Lance sent the connection request.

"James Brakka." He paused for a second in consideration. "I mean admiral. Admiral Brakka. We need a favor."

"Am I safe in assuming that this will not lead me to Thorne, either way?"

"You are correct there." Lance glanced to his left, where he could just barely see through the clouds in the city to where the *Nemesis Tide* hovered next to the starscraper. "Nothing personal, but we are working with a tight schedule. If I agree to get you all the information first, there may not be a city below your feet when this is over."

"Alright, state it. Seems like everything is going to hell no matter which way this goes down."

"I will send you the target data." Lance relayed some numbers through the link with the ship and smiled, taking a breath of the cold, turbulent air. He would enjoy this more than a fair fight any day.

* * *

"Just wait for it," Lance said for a second time. "Keep watching that itty-bitty gunship up there."

Avery rolled his eyes and gave himself another dose of inhibitors. If whatever the man had planned took any longer, he might drop out of the sky on his own accord. What was more infuriating was that Lance had refused to tell him what was going to happen. He just kept on like it was some surprise. Not entirely the attitude Avery wanted for stopping an operation like Crystal Slate.

The entire city suddenly lit up as the *Nemesis Tide* released a tremendous pillar of light miles away. The colossal beam held steady as it connected with the gunship. After a moment of delay, the vessel popped, releasing the beam that would have continued unhindered over the top of the city had the target not been hovering over the docks. Instead, as the massive soundwave from the first impact shook the window of Avery's transport and scattered all the displays inside, it was followed by the explosion of the beam piercing into another building.

"Yes!" Lance shouted excitedly as the beam faded. "Did you see that? Were you watching, Avery?"

The pieces of the transport fell down slowly compared to the heights around them, crashing past the soldiers on the platform as the deep tear in the next building began to boil with flame. Everything the Edict touched was burned by their own blind justification. It was the way with anything uncaring of all but the final goal. Once, he thought he was pushing for some sort of progress, building communication between the director and the Last Edict, though as he watched the destruction in front of him, he wondered if perhaps the Edict simply knew how to play him.

"Clear the landing pad and then get the hell out of here."

"Get out?" Lance asked. "I'll clear the pad, but we can help you. Me and Welnn."

Avery cut the transmission.

He was not going to let it go differently. There was no telling if the entire area would be caught in a blast even if he did make it in time to stop the entire core reactor structure from turning the world into an uninhabitable wasteland. Anything less, and Hoffsted wouldn't think Mars could continue alone. Perhaps more than anything though, Avery needed a clear mind about what he was doing. If he went alone, he would move faster. He would also be guaranteed to not get caught up if someone else was wounded or threatened. His risks would be his own.

As he neared the landing pad, a long spray of bullets rained down from the heights of one of the surrounding buildings. He landed a moment later amongst the ruined soldiers and burning supplies. There was a sharp crackle as he stepped out when some of the ammo magazines gave way in the flames. Avery avoided the holes in the steel beneath his feet and made his way to the door. He picked up the one weapon he could see that was not torn to shreds and slung it over his shoulder. Perhaps he should have told Lance to ease up just a bit.

Avery glanced back to the city, knowing that this would probably be the last time he would see it. There was still a glowing aura from where the bolt of light had burned through the air all the way back toward the Council Starscraper.

All of this.

All the buildings still full of billions of people, all the lights rising up through the air into orbit, everything. That was what this was for. That was the justification. He glanced up to see Lance's military transport launching from the side of a building in the distance before turning off toward the north. At least someone he knew other than Jance and Maylee would live to see what came after.

Avery turned around and began moving through the twisted steel Lance had made of the airlock. A steady flow of air from inside the room fanned the flames as the internal systems of the building continued to attempt to maintain pressure. Avery stepped in with his weapon ready, watching for any possible ambush that might have been left for him. More than likely, the gunship and the team guarding the dock now lying in waste had been expected to stop him, but he also knew Hoffsted was dangerous at best.

Avery glanced down, seeing the small blip of Maylee's visor far below. He stepped into the elevator and immediately began breaking into the system. A few moments later, he began to drop down into the recesses of the Earth. Even with it traveling down as fast as possible while still keeping his feet on the floor, it would take over a minute before the system completed its gradual return to motionlessness at the bottom level.

It was when the pace had slowed considerably that the endless tunnel of steel gave way to an overlook of a massive room. It was nearly a hundred feet from the ceiling to the walkway that extended out from the elevator before widening into a large circle. Avery then noticed the vibrant blue glow of the massive energy transfer tubes below the platform that headed down at a steep angle for many miles into the Earth. The entire room was located inside one of the support struts for the core reactors.

It was all built long ago. Without the system, there never would have been enough power to support the starscrapers or maintain any of the fleets of the world. Every piece of humanity hinged upon this room and the many other subsidiary stations like it around the world.

Avery could see from his descending vantage point that soldiers were lining up behind the terminals of the platform, ready for when he stepped out. He could see there was no way he was going to make it across the walkway; it was barely ten feet wide and devoid of cover. Avery reached down to where he had pulled the panel off and rattled a hand in the wires. Suddenly, the elevator tram jerked to a halt by reversing the electromagnets on the rails.

Being built so long ago, Avery was able to crack through the glass with just a few shots. The soldiers' positions behind the terminals gave them no cover from above. He quickly picked off the first few of Hoffsted's soldiers that he had caught unaware. The retaliation as the rest of the soldiers took aim caused the remaining glass to shatter back into the elevator, and Avery was forced to duck back from the torrent of bullets and glass shards spraying inward.

He took a breath as he readied to lean out for a shot, then cursed as a round sparked off the metal next to his head. The next round did a double flick as it skipped against the inside of the elevator. Avery knew he had to do something quickly or he would more than likely be killed by blind ricochets.

Avery pulled in one last breath before stepping around the edge. He felt a bullet glance off his shoulder and another hit him hard in his thigh, but he dared not let anything pull his focus. A strike to his torso deflecting only partially off the shattered plates; shards of metal bouncing into his face; a sharp strike against the bottom of the weapon into his hand; pieces of another miss bouncing into the back of his arm. He continued to fire, bringing all his fury down onto those who would take this world from him. Sparks rained over him from above as a shot deflected into the lights.

Avery staggered as he fired the last few shots into the wide expanse below. A foot slipped, bringing him to lean next to the edge. He reached over with a shaking hand to activate the panel as the room seemed to dim. When the elevator began to move slowly downward, he realized that it was not his own vision that was faltering, but the very conduits running from the core reactors that were starting to darken.

The silence was almost made more so by the gentle hum coming from deep below. If he had no reason to stand up once the elevator gently came to a stop, Avery could have just closed his eyes then and there. But he knew perfectly well what was at stake. The powering down of the reactors was merely a side effect. He could see that now. While it would cause untold chaos across the Earth when the starscrapers fell and the cities plunged into darkness, that would be nothing compared to the true intention. With the containment fields dropping, even the support structures—standing as mighty as the great room that he pulled himself up to step into—would be overwhelmed as the reactors themselves were pulled and twisted by the core of the Earth, ripping apart the cities above with cataclysmic tectonic activity until the quantum recalibrated matter used in their construction finally gave way, morphing the foundation of the planet into an instability no natural material could ever match. The destruction would be beyond complete; it would burn all humanity on Earth, and likely in its orbit, from existence. Every grief, every sorrow, every lament of tortured souls . . . every shred of happiness, of joy, of hope that had ever occurred—all of it would be destroyed as if it had never happened.

Avery limped, dragging his foot with each step, as he pulled himself onto the center platform.

"Do you see now?"

Hoffsted's voice emitted from the transceivers of every soldier now lying on the ground.

"Do you see the Crystal Slate? The only past that exists now is what we chose to store on the Mars archives. It is a foundation for a greater existence. With the sacrifice of its past, humanity belongs to eternity."

"All I see is loss!" Avery shouted, making his way toward the only terminal that remained on. "All I see is a pointless end!" He stepped over where Maylee's visor lay broken on the ground. Hoffsted must have crushed it underfoot when Avery found his location. Before he fled.

"But it is not an end. It is the beginning." Hoffsted paused. "If only you could see it as I do. I watch, knowing that these very memories forming now, the fires that will rain down from orbit and the retaliation that will soon come against them—these memories will only exist in my mind. I will be the last blemish on the perfect beginning."

"Nothing will ever be that way, Hoffsted. You are blind if you see perfection in anything but our own chaotic reality!"

"There is nothing perfect about this world!" Hoffsted's voice crackled through the comms as he yelled. "It is one disaster after the next, never ending until it will ultimately destroy everything!"

"And what is between those events? What happens during those events?" Avery stumbled in front of the terminal. "Everything perfect about this world. Every bit of humanity."

He pulled himself up and tried to clear his vision by wiping a bloody hand over his eyes. He could see the sequence activated by Hoffsted that was slowly disabling the functions of the reactors far below where he stood. The bright glow of the room faded to a dull red as the power output continued to drop.

"Life will continue, Avery! It will spread across the universe if you just let this happen. I have started what you always strived for! Life eternal, without chance of destruction."

The room slowly began to fall into darkness as the output from the reactors began to fade. He could hear titanic creaking echoing from deep within the Earth as he continued to work.

"And it will continue here as well," Avery said, stumbling back from the terminal. "It will thrive, despite what you have done. It may eventually grow stronger, but it will always continue to be, no matter how many times someone like you desires something more than reality."

As the room plunged into complete darkness, Avery fell back onto the floor. He gasped and held a hand to his chest in pain. For what seemed an eternity, Avery looked up through his visor into the void. Only the great shifting of the Earth could be heard, though he could no longer feel anything.

It was then that the quietest hum began.

A gentle pull from deep below.

A pulse of life from the dark.

Avery gave a smile through the pain as the bottom of the room slowly started to fill with the red glow of energy. He knew there would be desolation to come. The world would erupt into wars like never seen before. There would be chaos and sorrow at the fall of the Orbital Armistice Fleet. There would be unimaginable destruction as the starscrapers fell. Even the sky would darken with the ash of despair.

But at least humanity would exist.

He could find perfection in that.

Chapter 22: Projections

Kara stood at the edge of the platform watching as the Overlord's transport lifted off through the ember-filled southern sky. Kenneth glanced between her and the glow of the repulsor engines, trying to see behind her thoughts. He knew this was not what she had expected. Perhaps she had not actually thought about anything past getting the Cryo to the Overlord.

"She knew him," Kara said as Kenneth stepped up beside her.

He glanced down. The same wind that pulled at the charred edges of Kara's cloak made him nervous of the long fall below.

Kara continued, "And he was the one who she blamed for being put in the pod in the first place. Why would that be a bad thing? What was the Overlord . . . General Obrourke, trying to stop her from doing?"

"Kara," Sora asked from behind, "do you wish me to take you to the Norclave Library?"

"The visors," Kara said as she continued voicing her own thoughts, "the ones all the administrators and the officers wear . . ."

Kenneth nodded. "The Overlord did not discover how to use them. He always knew."

"Then what was the purpose of buying any scrap of information he could find?" Kara asked. She glanced over to Kenneth. "It was not our history he was looking for, was it? If he wanted to know about the Rift Hills and Norclave, nothing like that would be stored on anything from their age."

"What if . . ." Sora started. "Well, your Cryo, she came to Norclave for answers as well. Perhaps they are looking for some sort of closure to what happened."

Kara frowned and looked back toward the city. Kenneth watched closely as she glanced from one side to the other, looking down the huge length of the starscraper.

"What is it?" he asked.

She took a few steps toward the city. "Something Mallec said . . ." Kara turned back with a worried look. "When was the last Overlord of Norclave killed?"

Kenneth paused as he thought back on stories he had heard long ago. Most people were afraid to talk about the late Overlord, Thalen Norclave, fearing the trouble it could bring with the new one. "Before the Overlord brought me to Norclave. Some time after New Solace was destroyed."

Kara then looked past Kenneth, to where the Cryo and the Overlord were fast disappearing into the distance. "Mallec said he was there, at New Solace. Said he watched as they uncovered a Cryo."

"Are you saying that the Overlord was the one to . . . ?" He took a breath at the weight of the thought. "Are you saying that Overlord Obrourke was the thing that destroyed New Solace? The thing that killed my . . . Kara, I thought you were making fun of me when you said it was a Cryo!"

"I was! How was I supposed to know it was the Overlord himself?"

As Kenneth and Kara continued talking, Sora looked down at the repulsor-warped steel of the platform. Her face was pale at the realization. "That cannot be right," she said. "I worked with him for years, sorting through information. You really think he killed all those people?"

Kenneth gave her a grim glance before moving to stand beside Kara. "You saw what he did to the administrators."

Kara put a hand on his shoulder as they looked out toward the south of Norclave. Kenneth could feel what that meant. The way her fingers curled into his shoulder spoke volumes of her intention. Even so soon after he had pulled her away from the fires of the crash, she was still just as ready to set off again.

"You really are going after her? Even knowing what the Overlord is capable of?" Kenneth asked.

Kara nodded. "Especially now that I know. If you expect me to leave Jance to her death and take my reward just the same, you can just—"

Kenneth grabbed her arm as she started to turn away. "Not going to happen. Wherever you go, I go too."

"Kenneth, Jance is not your problem. I would never ask you to do this."

"Good. You would just be wasting your breath. Now come on, I'll get us a transport."

Kara gave him a nod that held a deeper appreciation than she would have been able to find words for.

Together, they made their way through the city, through the waves of heavy smoke and past the confused individuals skirting the edges of the side paths. On several occasions they passed groups of Norclave soldiers stripping the teal paint and sashes from those that had followed the administrators. Kara tried to pull Kenneth down a different path to avoid any attention, but he assured her it would be fine. After all, it was the same group that he had passed twice already.

As they stepped into the open space of the trade center, they could make out the pillar of smoke rising high above, filtering through even the topmost sections of the starscraper. Kenneth had no doubt that the smoke could be seen for many miles around. Likely the Prime Elect of Reclaim and the Grand Marshal of Carvanhold would both be watching it from the balconies of their cities. It would be no surprise if they returned to find that one of them had moved to take control of Norclave. If they ever did return.

"Where are we headed?" Kara asked as she followed him through the edge of the market. He had to move along different paths than his first time through. It seemed the explosion on the top level had scattered large chunks of debris all across Norclave.

"To see if my favors have run out."

It was a short time later when he stepped in front of the shop, this time with Kara in tow. There were no longer Norclave soldiers in the area, leaving only Mackelry's hired arms to stop Kenneth and Kara. Soon after they passed on the message of their arrival, the thin merchant appeared from the back. Mackelry crouched down behind the warped counter and did a quick scan of the trade center.

Kara turned from where she had been watching. "The only people in the area are the Norclave soldiers at the south entrance and a few children up on the fifth level."

"Well then," Mackelry said, standing up and looking both of them up and down, "suppose that makes us safe. Who is this, Kenneth? Is this the one you went running out after?"

Kenneth nodded.

"Looks healthy for being shot out of the sky." He started back over the unshelved wares and gave a wave over his shoulder as he moved deeper into his shop.

They followed the old merchant in under the close watch of his men.

"Now, what brings you back to me?" Mackelry asked.

"We need a transport to go after the Overlord." Kenneth looked over to where Kara walked slowly about the room, running a hand over the mundane supplies Mackelry had here. She stopped, looking straight at the false wall projected by the light distortion generator. Kenneth smiled, noticing all the footprints on top of the pile of steel panels leading up to the hidden entrance.

"The Overlord's gone to the Rift Outpost," Mackelry said. He started to say something to try to distract Kara, but she stepped away from the secret passage on her own. "What do you want with him anyway? Perhaps some of his men could help; they left for the Overlord's complex just now."

"We may have to kill him," Kara said bluntly. "Depending on his intention."

Mackelry gave Kenneth a questioning look. "You and her, you're not with the administrators, are you boy? Surely you were not distracted enough to miss that explosion! Silas's cause was lost with him in those fires."

"Everybody this side of the mountains saw it, if not further," Kenneth said. "Now, between me and you, Draken did not kill the Cryo. Kara brought her here, and the Cryo recognized the Overlord. Called him 'General.'"

"You are saying . . ." As Mackelry let his words trail off, Kenneth nodded.

"What is worse," he continued, "we believe he was the thing that destroyed New Solace."

The old merchant said nothing for a long moment before throwing his hands in the air. "That is nonsense, Kenneth. You really think your parents . . . Did you let her talk you into that? Now, I want you to tell me what happens to Norclave if you kill him. What happens to my business, huh? What happens to all the work I spent in backing the Overlord instead of the administrators?" Just as Kenneth was about to speak, the old merchant held up a hand. "No, I'll tell you what happens. I either am put to the Cells for what I do, or the Kessians or the Steel Valley or whoever steps in confiscates my tech so their own people can sell it!"

"And let me tell you this, the both of you, now." Mackelry gave them each a stern look. "The Overlord is dangerous. Not enough to kill a whole settlement but . . ." he stopped for a moment, likely thinking of how the man had elected to take out the administrators. "Well, either way, you are walking into the impossible. I'll give you the same advice as I have once before, Kenneth. Do not get caught up in the middle of these things. Find a transport and get out of Norclave. For good this time. Nobody is likely to welcome you back, especially with you talking like that about the Overlord. And I might add, he is the one person that kept you from the Cells all these years."

"Fine," Kenneth said. "We will do as you say. Where do we find a transport?"

This time Mackelry was caught with an open mouth and no words to fill it. He knew exactly what Kenneth would do if he found a transport, and it would not include staying out of the matter.

* * *

Jance watched the drab landscape roll by underneath through a rusted gap between the panels of the transport. Once they passed the forested area surrounding much of the Council Starscraper, the land turned into relatively barren patches of rubble with the occasional spire that had managed to survive as a shell of its former image. As empty as it seemed, there were still signs of life. At one point she saw what looked to be several homes. There were worn down paths amongst the containers and a small fire in the center of the cluster, like she had seen in the decommissioned section of the Drake Discovery Complex.

She idly pulled at the ties around her hands, though it only made her wrists feel more uncomfortable than they already were. She looked up to where Garneth Obrourke stood. He had one hand gripping a handle on the ceiling and his suit locked into place, just as it had been in the ride before. Scattered pieces of rust had built up over the long years since he had been pulled from the cryopod, and the seals on the pistons and motors were showing their age as well. The long and ragged cloth hanging from his shoulders did little to hide the small motions in the suit when the craft shifted through the remaining buildings.

"The pod next to mine, in the destroyed SorrCom building, it was covered under a section of the building."

"It would have been better luck if it had still been there." Obrourke did not turn to look at Jance. "I woke amidst the ruins of the Council Starscraper. Nearest I could find, some group of tech hunters moved my pod years before they decided to activate the cryogenesis. Turns out they revere our kind."

"So you imposed yourself as the Overlord?"

"I needed information. I started out working on my own, but I came to see that it would not be enough. I took what meager resources Norclave could spare to continue my search."

"What did you find?" Jance asked. "Anything about what happened?"

"Very few precise details exist, even here in the dead heart of the UWC. With the creation of the Norclave Library, I began to piece together a broader picture. Eventually my search led me to trace my own steps. I leaked out information, and a group of tech hunters picked up on it. Several months later they came back, saying there was an unmarked pod."

"The tech hunter, that was Kara," Jance said as she began to learn her own story.

"Yes, and the damned technician from the outerzones actually fulfilled his purpose, though until you arrived I thought my tracker had set everything off course."

"Kenneth, the technician. Kara told me plenty about him. And the tracker—"

"They simply exist to do a job," Obrourke growled. "You cannot trust any one of them on their own, and not just the hunters. Take my appointed administrators, for example. No loyalty, only lies and betrayal. This entire world is full of nothing but animals fighting to the top of a pile of their own corpses amidst the bones of the UWC."

* * *

As Kenneth and Kara threaded their way back through the city, it became apparent that people were beginning to realize the fighting was coming to an end. Things were secure enough that the population could set foot out on the streets, though a few had to step out of the way of any Norclave soldiers shifting prisoners.

"What is the best way to the third level docks?" Kara asked as they neared a set of narrow stairs.

"This will be as good as any." As far as Kenneth was concerned, there was no best way to anywhere in the city. The only differences came with whether you wanted to risk having your pockets turned in a crowd, or be forced to empty them in a darker pass. Not that he had any fear of that. On his own, a flash of his arm was usually enough, but with Kara there would be no trouble except from the bravest, or dumbest, of the ruffians.

"You are sure he is not setting us up?" Kara asked, echoing Kenneth's thoughts as she stopped at crossing paths. "If things go badly for the Overlord, your merchant loses business."

"It is still our best shot. At the very least, we will not have to search around the docks for one to steal." Kenneth stepped past her, brushing closer than he ever would have dared before.

"Just keep a sharp eye outward," she warned. "Any of Silas's men not caught in the blast will be looking to escape."

Finally, they stepped out past the checkpoint and onto the dock. While Kara watched behind them and the surrounding platforms sticking from the city for any threats, Kenneth saw what they were going to ride in. The transport had three cockpits, each of which gave the impression of having been welded into place. Not a one had more glass than the sharp shards around the edges, and he would not have trusted at least half the repulsors to start consistently. One repulsor, tacked on ungracefully toward the back, looked as if it had been smashed against the side of the dock before it landed.

Kenneth let out a groan. It was the same craft that hauled him to Norclave in the first place. The same one that had nearly killed him along with the pilot, whose metal pipe he'd thrown into a burning tree after the idiot had beaten on that dented repulsor.

"No sign of anybody, let alone our pilot," Kara said. "You want to just steal this one and be on our way?"

"I wouldn't dare."

"Why not?" Kara asked. She turned to give it a second look and frowned. "Well, have a look over it. If you can break a Cryo out of a pod, you should be able to get this in the air."

"Perhaps we should try our luck searching around the docks." He glanced to the sides. The few transports he saw were nothing more than bundles of smoke and twisted flames, much like the one Kara and Jance had come in on. "I'm sure we can find something better than this."

Kara flipped around and aimed a pistol toward the entrance of the dock at the slight shuffle of steps from behind.

"Sorry to keep you waiting!" the man said. He slowed up his hurried pace as he saw Kara staring him down. "I was, uh, well in a locked room, as it were."

Kenneth stepped to Kara's side and motioned for her to lower the weapon. "This is Arlen." He lowered his voice so the man could not hear the next part. "The same idiot who was told to bring me to Norclave in the first place."

"Hello there, tech hunter." He turned to Kenneth and gave a frown. "So, how did it go? Your mission you went on? I assume she was one of the tech hunters the Overlord spoke with?"

"In." Kenneth pointed to the transport. "If you must know, it was nearly a disaster the entire way."

"Right." Arlen nodded before moving toward his transport. It seemed as if he was chewing on a thought that he was not ready to spit out. "Hopefully nothing happened to it in the fighting." Just as he stepped up onto the top step, he glanced above them to the smoke rising up and through the starscraper. "Will you be needing a ride back to Norclave?"

"We'll see." Kenneth wanted to say that if there was any other way, any at all, that he would take it instead, but perhaps it was best to not directly insult the man if he could avoid it.

Kenneth stepped up into the same seat he had used before, being especially careful not to put his hands along the edge of the cockpit. He pulled the straps around him, but as he shifted, one of the latches nearly cracked in half. Kara looked over from the other side, tossing a few bits of metal out of her seat that had come from the other transports exploding overhead. Even with the defensive cannons disabled, Kenneth could easily see them sharing the same fate.

"Sit tight now," Arlen said. "We'll be off in a moment."

The craft creaked and shuddered as he fired on the repulsors. They hit with an inconsistent popping as the engines came on over the span of a couple of seconds. Moments later, they lifted unsteadily off the dock and into the sky, where the last flecks of fire were dispersing with the pulling winds.

They buzzed low over the trees, leaving the eternal structure of the starscraper behind. As the wounded city of Norclave put off a pillar of smoke, Kenneth knew that long after the settlement came to be nothing more than a forgotten location, the bounds of the encapsulating ridge of steel would remain, as it had since the starscraper first fell. He sat back down in the seat and looked forward to where the transport rustled over the tops of the trees in the low valley.

Even as far as the thinning edge of the forest, he could spot downed transports and the smoldering scars ripped in the land from the

Norclave cannons. They would heal, in time. After all, the stretches of trees had risen up from a much greater round of destruction during the fall of the starscraper itself.

Gradually, they began to trace their way back through the thickening straits of rubble. The foliage drastically thinned as a greater spread of twisted spires reached up into the sky. On a number of occasions, Arlen simply flew through the steel titans. It was when they started under an arch made of one tower leaning into the next that Kenneth recognized the spot. Water still poured out of the center of the heights, and long trails of vines hung down from the buildings. At the bottom was the pond that had formed from the endless waterfall. A ring of green surrounded the waters and branched off in a long strip along the stream that trailed off to the side. This time, however, not too far from the edge of the pool, was a section of a broken transport. Several people were gathered around it, either looking for survivors or some parts to scavenge.

Minutes later, the land gave way to another shift as the towers fell out of consistency. However, the green of forests and rolling fields did not take hold here. The area around the Rift Outpost was known for being dull. Kenneth always imagined the drab colors and small hills of rubble were what the impact valley looked like before it was reclaimed by the Norclave forests.

"Reminds me of home," Kara called across to Kenneth. "A bit more on the rough side for walking here, though. Does it get dust storms very bad?"

"Not that I've ever seen," Kenneth replied over the rumbling of the transport and the shifting winds. "The worst is the stiff air that sometimes comes up from the rift. Sometimes it can make breathing difficult. Makes your eyes water at the least." Just ahead in the distance, he could see the long split in the land and the deep glow coming from underneath the edge. "There it is!"

For the most part, the buildings of the Rift Outpost lay north of the split, though there were a few abandoned buildings right up close to the edge. Occasionally a drifter would settle down in one, but any looking for a permanent residence generally wanted to know for sure that the ground they were living on would not cave off and be lost to the tatters of steel clogging the chasm.

"You see any sign of the Overlord?" Kenneth asked.

Kara pointed vaguely. "I believe that is his transport, next to the edge."

Kenneth watched for a moment before calling forward to the pilot, "Set us down close to my shop!" Their direction changed to set down farther along the length of the rift, away from the constant shifting of evacuating transports.

"What are you planning?" Kara asked loudly enough to be heard over the unsteady descent of the craft.

Kenneth paused before responding. "We're going to need a riftwalker."

* * *

Jance was guided roughly out of the back of the transport. She gave a confused look to the surrounding area as the lights of the small settlement flickered on against the distant backdrop of towers and the setting sun. High above, the repulsor engines from the orbital wreckage became more visible, and just behind her, the rift in the Earth glowed from the work lights set up just under the edge.

"Welcome to the Rift Outpost," one of the soldiers said offhandedly as Obrourke started giving orders. The locals in the area were quickly pushed to the side at the shouts of the Norclave soldiers. Moments later, a caretaker exosuit was maneuvered out of a large set of doors. Its lights powered on and illuminated the area. From the strange rattle it made and the heavy grinding that came with each step, Jance was not sure what had worn on it more: being forgotten for hundreds of years, or being put to work for some near-equivalent amount of time afterward.

"Obrourke, what are we doing here?" Jance asked. She tried to move over to where he was inspecting the array of caretakers being lined up near the edge, but she was stopped by a pair of the soldiers in full flight armor.

"What does it look like we are doing?" the soldier said. "We're taking the riftwalkers down into the rift."

"Riftwalkers?" Jance glanced again at the caretaker suits.

The soldier motioned lazily to the machines being powered up. "Locals use them to get down the sheer cliffs and near the ruins in the heart of the rift. There is supposedly a well of energy down there. The merchants trade handsomely for the energy before heading on to Norclave or the Shattered Coast."

"General Obrourke," Jance called past the soldier, "what is down there? I know this is not about looking for energy."

"My Overlord," another soldier said off to the side, pointing in the sky along the direction of the rift. "One of our scouting transports."

"Contact it," Obrourke commanded.

The man reached a hand up to his visor but shook his head. "I'll try again."

Obrourke took the soldier's weapon, a crudely refashioned repulsor. He aimed it at the transport.

"What are you doing?" Jance called to him. "Just because they did not answer—"

She was cut off by the deep thrum of the weapon. Before the first shot closed the distance, the Overlord let loose a second burst. The bright flares coursed through the air until they both impacted with the transport in turn. While the soldiers seemed to either shy back or appreciate his precision, the Overlord simply frowned. Then the transport fired several shots of its own back toward them.

As everyone started running for cover amongst the falling debris, the Overlord ripped a piece off the weapon and raised it again. This time, a torrent of heat ripped out of the weapon in a continuous line. As the feet of Obrourke's suit made a heavy score in the dirt from the force of the weapon, the transport was ripped in half while hundreds of feet in the air.

Finally, the imposing man turned to face her, tossing the overheated and melting weapon to the side. He took a few steps toward her. Each limp of his leg made a harsh grating as it half slid across the ground. "You ask what we are doing here? Do you not recognize this place, Ambassador Lorège? South of the Council, in the older part of the city? This is where the core reactors reach up to the surface. The Power Relay Station has long since collapsed into the rift below, but I am told the heart is still intact."

"Obrourke, you do not strike me as one to reminisce about the past. What is here for you?"

"This is the last location your sectator visited, Lorège. If you can bring yourself to face the truth about Avery Thorne, it will be down in the abyss."

* * *

"All of this is yours?" Kara asked as she followed Kenneth into the chaotic space of the workshop. Shelves piled with assorted parts filled the room, and where the loose system of organization could not contain them, the pieces spilled out into piles on the floor or across various tables.

"For the most part. Some things I have lined up to fix and return." Kenneth brushed a hand along an empty spot on one of the shelves before continuing through to the next room. "Someone has been in here since I left."

Kara stepped through just as he was turning on the lights. As she entered, she had to pick her way through a scattered mess of power nodes. It looked as if they had been knocked from a table.

"That mess was the pilot's fault, though."

"Is that why you told him to leave?" Kara asked, though Kenneth gave no answer.

The rest of the room was filled with parts of transports and piles of mech pieces. It almost had the look of a slaughter yard with the parts of the riftwalkers hanging up and their insides spilled across the floor. Kenneth upended the gloves out of the sack and put them on. "Normally they will bring me two walkers. One will be junk, the other more so. My job is to get one running and the payment is to keep what parts I did not use in fixing it."

Kenneth pulled himself up into the riftwalker hanging from the ceiling by chains. Both legs were separated and on the floor. "Of course, the one for scrap rarely has everything I need. I pull from my own supplies, look around for what I do not have, or order from scrapsmiths if the part is not being sold. Most of the time though, the excess will get used in something else down the line." There was a bright pop as he pulled a piece out from inside the driving seat.

Kara looked around, only seeing a few amongst the batch that even had all the limbs. "Is there actually one here that is functional?"

"No. But that is why they are still here, isn't it?" He tossed the piece into the pile below and started climbing down. "I've put together an extra one, though. I just left out the one part to start it so that it did not walk out on me."

He moved on through the room, past another row of shelves. In the corner was one suit curled up in the standard resting position, making the seat only about chest high from the ground. Kenneth reached over and started plugging in wires, ducking his head to the side at another bright pop.

"That should do it." Kenneth stepped back and clicked the fingers of his gloves together in idle thought as he continued to look at the riftwalker intently. The small illumination disk hovered in and out of the back of his left glove from the motion. "Hope it holds up."

* * *

Jance felt her stomach roll as her caretaker exosuit began to move over the edge as the second to last one in the line. She was in a carrying cage strapped to the front of one, her wrists bound through the bars. They told her that the system was frequently used for hauling down far more than her weight in power cells, but that did little to ease the feeling that she would fall out at any moment. She pushed her arms further through the cage and gripped tight as the caretaker lumbered down along the uneven sides of the split, scraping and churning as it followed behind the rest.

The wide ring of work lights above the rift cast down a bright illumination along the rough walls. While the majority of the path was made from an assortment of metal, there were still large patches of crumbling concrete and dirt that the units could not magnetically lock onto. For the most part, the few dead vines were no trouble, though at one point one of the feet of her caretaker slipped.

"Do we know that this is safe?" Jance called back as it recovered.

"I've been at this for at least twenty years," the pilot of the mech called forward. "That is longer than most, and you can take that to mean whatever you want!"

Jance looked down past the legs of her exosuit to where the other three caretakers shuffled down below, heading toward the edge of the light one step at a time. Norclave soldiers clung to them any way they could, including to the top of her own ride. The only exception was the one second from the front; that one held only General Obrourke on its back.

Minutes later, they made it past a layer of ruins clinging to the edge of the rift. She began to see a spread of rough platforms that had been welded on in more recent years. Many had boxes of supplies, and one even had a caretaker unit that must have malfunctioned before it could make the trek back upward.

"The spots that hold the longest charge are farther down," the operator said. "You still gotta know where to pick, but I can make a round before any of the newer drivers even get back up."

One of the soldiers who had a foot on the exosuit's shoulder and an arm braced against the top of the cab leaned back to look down into the abyss. "Do not rely too much on habit," he said. "We still have quite a ways yet to reach where the Overlord is taking us."

As they continued the nerve-wracking descent into what some murmured was the maw of hell, they soon started to slip out of the range of the work lights. The caretakers continued on their own light as they began to make their way from clinging onto the wall to setting out on top of the twisted ruins toward the center. A short time later, they were back to threading down through the maze of metal sheets and bent supports. The soldiers began to whisper about the red lights visible deep in the darkness.

Without warning, a great flow of hot air swept over them. Jance coughed at the sting in her lungs, and many of the others tried to find some way to cover their faces. Even for the locals who could stand the biting winds, the air of the rift at this proximity was too much.

"You all help me watch," the pilot said. "My eyes are starting to water up."

As the air continued to swell, even the visibility began to decline. For minutes at a time, the line of caretakers below could only be seen as a staggered glow moving through the twists of the wreckage. Just as Jance was beginning to wonder about the stability of all of this material simply resting where it had wedged down in the steel crevasse, one of the soldiers gave a shout, followed by an echoing screech as one of the caretakers below tried to regain its grip.

They watched in horrified silence—each of the other caretakers clinging tight to the walls—as the exosuit spun down and away from any surface. The echoing hits as it smashed time and time again made each of them redouble their grips. For a long moment, they waited motionless as the layers of heated fog came and went. Jance looked up to where the last caretaker in the chain held still, just as they did, fifty feet above and along an inward slope. It was only when the shouts of the Overlord broke through the haunting echoes of the dead caretaker that their chain continued down. It took little observation to see that their march had found a new, slower pace allowing for even more certainty of their grips.

"Watch the cable!" They heard the cry call up faintly as they started off the heavy slope and over an edge. The caretaker had to hold tight to the wall to keep from brushing its back along the thick hanging loop. None of them along the line had wanted to test it for a charge, though simply bumping against it could have brushed a few of the soldiers off just the same.

As they finally scaled down past what had the look of an interior, judging by the design of the walls and the office chair hanging at the edge, Jance could see a few doorways branching off at completely the wrong angles. If one were to try to explore the rooms, they would have to climb through the door and continue up at a steep angle with their feet on the side of the hallway. When she rubbed her eyes the best she could with her shoulder, Jance realized at this point that the entire area was bathed in a deep red glow.

She leaned forward and looked down through the bars on the bottom of her carriage at the immense section of steel that had been ripped open to reveal a large room underneath. As the riftwalkers neared the top of the room, it looked as if the massive cables and tubes, glowing with an eerie red, continued down the slant of the room for thousands of feet. However, it was only when the caretakers started down through the inside of the enormous gash that Jance realized that the steep slope of the room continued much, much farther than she had imagined. From the scale of the tunnel leading down at a steep angle into the Earth, Jance knew it had to be one of the supports for the core reactors.

The staggeringly long tubes, still carrying immense amounts of power, pulsed dully as energy was brought up from deep within the Earth. A good number of the tubes had been completely severed by large cracks similar to the one they had entered through.

As Jance's caretaker continued down next to a broken elevator rail, the first walkers were beginning to unload onto a ledge in front of a long, lighted walkway. The path reaching out over the slope of the structure seemed miniscule in comparison to the surrounding space, but as some of the people stepped out onto the walkway, she could see that it was at least ten feet wide, if not more. At the end, suspended high above the pulsating and fiery glow of the energy tubes, was a round platform lined with an array of walkway lights and terminals.

Jance's unit finally sat down on more solid ground, and the soldiers hanging onto the outside of it began to pile off. Some of them simply lay flat on the ground, and a few had to be gently coaxed down off the side of the exosuit. Jance glanced up as the last caretaker made its way down. Even though she had been tied into a basket welded to the front of the walker, she was just as relieved when it set foot on solid ground.

"Untie her!" Obrourke shouted. "Hurry with it!"

Jance flinched as the glowing edge of the knife sliced through her bonds. Had she not stretched and pulled the cloth in the process of hanging on, the heat might very well have seared her wrists. She was ungracefully pulled from the basket and pushed forward to where Obrourke stood at the front of the walkway. She noticed that a few soldiers staying off to the side seemed uneasy at how roughly the Overlord moved her about.

"This is it," he said as Jance was shoved to the ground behind him. "This is where the world was brought to an end."

Jance pushed herself up and elbowed away the soldiers trying to restrain her. "No. This is where Avery Thorne stopped it from ending."

"Walk with me," Obrourke said. "We shall find out."

* * *

Kenneth drew a breath of bitter relief as he let go of the controls to the riftwalker. It was still fifty feet above the platform, and as far as he could tell, none of the soldiers had noticed they were following behind. He glanced up to where Kara had elected to stand atop the walker on the way down. She was attaching a spooling device onto the arm of the mech.

"What is the plan now?" he asked. "Looks to me like your Cryo is following the Overlord to the center."

"She is as curious as he is." Kara clipped the end of the cable onto the handle and tapped through the back side of the faulty display a few times. "Look at the piles of armor and bones everywhere. There was definitely a fight here in her time."

Kenneth looked again in surprise. He had been so busy eyeing the control stations that he had not noticed the five or six bare remains next to them. It seemed that even the rubble mites dared not venture down this far.

"Take us down farther," Kara said. "You think you can keep them distracted long enough for me to get into position?"

Kenneth took hold of the controls again and started the last bit of the descent. "I am sure I can make something up." When they neared the bottom, Kara slid around on the riftwalker so she was on the opposite side of all who might be watching, though they were hardly paying attention. He stopped near the edge. As he powered down the suit, he could make out the faintest hint of the reel whirring line out.

Kenneth pulled in one last stinging breath of courage before climbing out of the walker. He received a few glances, but most of the soldiers and operators of the riftwalkers were busy recovering themselves.

"Kenneth?" one older man asked, leaning forward from his seat in one of the walkers. "Why didn't I see you before now?"

Kenneth nodded back toward his riftwalker. "I had to bring my own. I've seen these broken too many times to trust them. Oh, and I'll fix that seal I've been meaning to on yours before we head up." The man frowned and glanced back as Kenneth continued on past the perfectly fine machine.

He waved at the other Rift Outpost workers that he recognized, as well as a few other soldiers he knew. Kenneth noticed the questioning looks being passed around, but without any one person stopping him, they all figured that someone else knew about his planned arrival. It was only when he approached the walkway heading out to the center that two men stood in the way. They were the diehard loyalists of the Overlord.

"What are you doing here? The Overlord ordered nobody past this point."

"The way I figure, the Overlord will not be happy when he has to limp all of the way back here just to tell you to send me through."

"Oh really?" the man said in disbelief.

Kenneth rubbed his chin. "Just like anybody else when trying to get a rusted meal pack open in the morning, the Overlord gets angry when he cannot get into something." Kenneth shrugged again and gave an uncaring frown. "But if you want, we can wait here. Eventually he will realize all of those terminals will need to be worked on before he can access them."

The two gave each other a quick glance. One cursed and the other looked over his shoulder to where the Overlord and Cryo were just reaching the other side. Finally, they gave in. "One false move, technician, and the Overlord is likely to throw you off the edge."

Kenneth shook his head as he was roughly pulled forward onto the walkway. When they finally reached the other end, Kenneth glanced to either side at the old bones wrapped in black UWC armor. The Overlord slowly walked around the edge of the platform, stopping briefly to look through the logs on the terminals. In the center, Jance knelt on the ground with her shoulders drooped low. She held a thin visor in her hands.

When the Overlord glanced back, he gave a look of fury to Kenneth and the two soldiers. He almost looked tempted to reach for his weapon.

"What are you doing?" The Overlord stalked over with heavy, laborious steps. "You heard my orders!"

"The technician, my Overlord," one of the soldiers said weakly, "he said you would need help with the terminals."

"Did he?" the Overlord growled as he stepped closer. "Leave us. Now!" He turned to Kenneth when the soldiers started away at a run. "As for you, you have been a fascinating challenge to my patience for years."

Kenneth swallowed through the dryness in his throat. It had been a long time since he had needed to face the Overlord himself. The steel-blue eyes of the beast of war settled into tracking him as he slowly shifted from side to side under their scrutiny. The stress-hardened wrinkles on the aged man's face were split by scars, though his jaw still seemed to be as strong as the iron grip of the suit. The motors in the Overlord's hand hummed quietly as he lifted a clenched fist.

"Never forget that your life belongs to me, technician. I brought you in from the outerzones, and I held off your execution more times than any other."

Kenneth squared his shoulders, knowing that he had to stand up to the Overlord, even if it was just to distract him. "That just makes me all warm and fuzzy on the inside." Kenneth layered in all the sarcastic undertones he could manage. "Why *did* you spare my life?"

The Overlord narrowed his eyes as he weighed Kenneth's question. "What are you talking about?"

"New Solace."

The Overlord nodded. "So you know. You know what happened to your parents."

Kenneth felt his heart racing as he finally came face to face with the past he had tried his entire life to ignore.

"They were worthless tech hunters, scavenging pieces from the wastes of the Council Starscraper. They mattered just as much as anyone else in this world."

Kenneth had to fight a dangerous urge as he balled his fists. "Then why did you let me live? Why take me in?" He held up his arm full of scars and met the Overlord's stare. "Why did you keep sparing my life, no matter what I tried?"

"I left you for dead. One of the tech hunters, they put you in a container, hoping to keep me from finding you. Years later, my scouts found a boy of the outerzones. I then kept you because you proved useful in my endeavors."

"No." Kenneth shook his head. "You felt guilt. You killed an entire settlement, but when faced with putting me down, you froze. And again, when your men found me, then you *had* to be responsible for my life."

The Overlord stepped forward and grabbed the front of Kenneth's shirt. The seals of the exosuit hissed as he squeezed. "You may have been the one weakness this world has inflicted upon me, but do not think that you are safe from me. You can steal transports, disable my weapons, even disobey every order given to you, but if you stand in front of me, I will not stop long enough to make the distinction between you and the path beneath my feet."

Kenneth tried to think of something else to say to keep his attention, but no words came. Instead, the Overlord pushed him away and started toward the center terminal.

Kenneth let out a breath and hurried over to Jance.

"What are you doing here?" she asked him quietly. Her eyes were rimmed with red and at the brink of tears as she clutched the small piece of a broken visor in her hand.

Kenneth watched as the Overlord accessed the terminal. He noticed some of the other terminals were displaying warnings of minor structural damage to the reactors. "We have come to get you out. We figured out who the Overlord really is."

Suddenly the entire area flickered blue with fragmented projections of shapes and distorted images. The Overlord stepped through the flurry of three-dimensional static and held his arms in the air. The left arm began to slowly sink down from leaking seals. "I want you to see this, Jance. I want you to know the pain I felt in looking up at the sky. Each time, I was reminded that I never saw my son again. He was a transmissions officer, personally shifted to Outreach Systems on Mars by Ambassador Hoffsted. My knowledge of him ends with the fact that he is long since dead."

"You should be thankful, Obrourke," Jance said, gripping the halves of the visor tightly. "At least there is a chance he survived the war."

"But the distance I feel is far greater than that of traveling the millions of miles through space. It is the insurmountable grip of time that stands between me and all that I left behind. I would be nothing more than a name to the descendents of my family now. A stranger with a forced semblance of relation. Twenty, maybe thirty generations will have passed as I stood in the dark. My place in the universe has been taken from me, Ambassador."

The blurred images floating around them started to fall into place. Fake displays on the terminals flickered with centuries-old information, but most importantly, a figure lay in the center of the platform, only several feet away from where Jance knelt. She pulled in a gasp as she looked at the man.

Obrourke turned a look of hatred onto Jance. "This is the measure of time greater than eternity. The distance longer than infinity."

"Avery!" Jance cried as she moved a hand, skirting the edge of the face in the projection. The man on the ground gripped his chest and coughed. "Avery, what did you do?"

The Overlord looked up blankly. "He prolonged the grief and agony so many tried to leave behind."

Avery lifted a shaking hand up to his visor. "Jance . . . I'm sorry. If you somehow survive the chaos that I was too late to stop, I am sorry."

"Avery, no!" Jance cried, trying to grab his hand, but her fingers only scattered through the projection.

"I am locking the system in your name," the projection weakly said. "If there is still a UWC left, you are the only one I trust to set things right. If not, the world will simply have to survive on its own. I am sorry that I lied to you. That I never . . . that I never came back. That I never . . ."

His hand dropped from the visor and a blank stare settled upward.

Kenneth put a hand on Jance's shoulder, though he knew there would never be comfort enough for what she had seen. He looked up and noticed the Overlord holding a visor in his hand. It was hers.

"You knew," Jance said with a quiver in her voice. "You knew what happened to Avery."

The Overlord turned his shoulder on them. "Yes. I have watched over every inch of this a hundred times."

Kenneth watched in disbelief as the Overlord set the visor down on the edge of the terminal. The Overlord used her name to bypass a dozen restriction notices as he dug futher into the system.

"You just needed her visor to get in? Everything about putting the group together—to unlock the cryopod and bring her back alive—that was just to show Jance this?"

The Overlord turned sharply away from the terminal and pointed to where the projection lay near motionless on the floor. "If it were my choice, Thorne would be the one standing here, watching everything he cared about fade into six hundred years of darkness! He would be the one who had to understand, that what they did—it did not stop the agony. The Last Edict only ensured that the despair of this cursed world would continue far past its death."

Kenneth kept his eyes locked onto the Overlord's, especially as he could see a hand reaching up over the edge of the platform. "What are you trying to access with her visor? What is in the system?"

"The only thing that can erase the void Thorne created."

"What void?" Jance asked.

The Overlord began to turn back to the terminal as Kara started to silently pull herself up over the edge.

"What void?" she asked again, louder this time.

The Overlord scowled and turned back to her. "You do not feel it? This agony, of existing without purpose? Do you not feel trapped knowing that nothing you do can change anything?"

Jance shook her head. "I feel sorrow. And confusion. When I first looked into this new sky, feeling the stinging winds and grit of rust in the air, I thought I had failed. I thought Avery had failed." She looked down affectionately at the projection and gripped the broken visor tighter. "I could never have been more wrong. The world that you refuse to accept, Obrourke, has shown that even near annihilation cannot stop the most important parts of humanity.

"Your revenge," she continued, "was to show me something that I could not reach, no matter how far I traveled. Something that I could not change, no matter how hard I might try." Jance brushed a hand over Avery's forehead as he closed his eyes. "But I saw myself in a tech hunter. She was willing to risk everything for the one she cared for, just as I was for Avery. In helping her reunite with him, in a way, I have changed what happened. If this is a distance of time greater than eternity, then eternity is not that far."

"It is that easy?" The Overlord bared his teeth. "The hours I spent in grief, watching this projection, wishing I had some way to kill Avery Thorne . . ." He gave a dangerous pause. "I'm glad you have given me the answer."

With a lightning speed slowed only by the wear on the suit, the Overlord pulled the pistol from his hip and aimed it at Kenneth.

The shot rang out.

It echoed hollowly through the massive room.

Kenneth stepped back in shock and slowly raised a hand to his chest in disbelief.

He looked over at Kara with a surprised expression as the pieces of the Overlord's broken weapon began to fall out of his hand.

The Overlord raised one arm to shield his head as Kara resumed firing. Shots sparked off the armor, and even though several managed to pierce through the metal, they did not slow the Overlord's charge. She dove to the side just as the Overlord brought a heavy sweep of the arm in her direction. Several clicks sounded from her emptied weapon and she tossed it to the side. She'd gotten several shots into him because he was distracted, but the Overlord did not miss the throw of her knife from under her collar. He tightened the hand he'd caught the blade with as he continued forward, bending the metal between his fingers until the pieces fell through his fist.

As Jance yelled for Kara to disrupt the suit, gunfire erupted from across the bridge. Several shots sparked near her heels. "Use what you did on Mallec!" she screamed over the noise.

"Here!" Kenneth shouted, watching the pulse rounds rip through the air as the Norclave soldiers fought amongst themselves. He held his hand out as Kara backpedaled away from another thunderous, limping charge. Kenneth caught the shocklance just as the Overlord dislodged a terminal with a vicious swipe, sending the bent shell flying at Kara. She dropped to the ground to avoid being bowled over.

Kenneth fumbled with the weapon, looking for the activation. Kara threw another knife, but the Overlord batted it to the side and off the platform. The Overlord reached down with a grip of crushing steel as Kara tried to scramble backward.

"Kenneth!" Kara shouted.

As soon as Kenneth could manage, he let loose the full fury of the weapon. The Overlord's suit jolted as the tendrils of electricity arced outward. Kara kicked the grasping hand with a foot, though she may as well have kicked the platform itself.

The Overlord let out a guttural growl of pain as he raised an arm to shield himself. He turned and started towards Kenneth in jerking motions through the waves of popping static.

Kara connected a silvery tether between the back of the Overlord's leg and the platform, but even with a hiss and spark of light, the Overlord jerked free of the cable by simply ripping free from a section of his suit.

Kenneth cursed as Kara's shocklance sputtered in a few bright flashes.

Kara threw a loop of the cable forward and dove backward to connect it to the ground. This time the Overlord tried to break the cable itself.

"What now?" Kenneth yelled to Jance through the grating of the Overlord's suit against the metal.

"I don't know!" Jance turned to where the fighting amongst the soldiers had all but died down. "If you are with us, help!"

"I need a knife!" Kenneth yelled, not taking the time to figure out what was happening as the Overlord tried to push back toward Kara as she tossed more cables.

"Last one!" Kara slid the weapon along the ground as the Overlord started to shove through the wire with the strength of a riftwalker. The knife caught on an uneven section of the platform and stopped short, still well within the Overlord's reach.

"If you want it, technician, come and get it!" the Overlord spat, raking his arms against the cables.

"Kenneth, no!" Kara, shouted, as she threw another loop forward and attached the ends of the wire to the floor.

Just as Kenneth was about to ignore Kara and lunge for the knife, Jance put a hand on his shoulder.

"This is my fault. You will not be the one to pay for this, Kenneth."

Jance made a rush for the knife, diving to the ground and flicking it back to Kenneth. The Overlord suddenly arced his arm up and down toward Jance. She let out a scream, and the only thing that stopped Jance from being crushed under the heavy hit was the loop Kara had just barely managed to throw over her.

"Get back you stupid Cryo!" Kara cried as the floor under her buckled from the strain of the attached cables. A light embedded into the surface of the platform by Kara busted as the floor continued to warp.

"I can't, my foot—"

The Overlord lurched down again, forcing through the cables and crushing pieces of the armor in the process.

"Kenneth, hurry!" Kara shouted as she tried to throw a loop around the Overlord's neck. He caught it with a hand and ripped it away before she could attach it to the floor. "I cannot keep up!"

The Overlord thrashed in the steel web as Kenneth ran behind him.

He readied the knife, hoping desperately that the blade had heated enough to slide through the thick metal.

The full force of Kenneth bearing into the back of the armor with the knife was met with a thud, almost as if he had used a bare hand against the Overlord's armored back. He ducked to the side as the Overlord jerked around with an elbow trailing cables. With a desperate second lunge up from Kenneth, the knife finally went through. Kenneth was knocked back toward the edge as the Overlord twisted again. Kenneth landed hard on the ground and watched as the knife sheared off against the cables.

"Worthless!" the Overlord yelled. A heavy grating of ripping metal sent a shower of sparks as the Overlord shattered free of the bindings. He pushed the suit forward toward where Kenneth lay just on the edge of the platform. "Just like your family! It is a favor to send this world into oblivion!" The Overlord lifted a heavy foot over him.

"Kenneth!" Kara screamed. She had a smear of blood on her forehead.

Just as the Overlord began to press down, the suit suddenly seized up. The legs of the suit staggered unevenly, causing the Overlord to screech against the side of the platform as he slipped over the edge.

"Cover your eyes!" Kenneth yelled as Obrourke caught hold of the edge.

The Overlord desperately clawed at the steel with one hand while reaching for Kenneth with the other. The Overlord gave an unexpected surge up and gripped Kenneth by the boot.

As if unleashing the core of the sun, the battery of the suit split open with a searing flash of white. Kenneth jerked his foot free and crawled away from the raw fury of the explosion wrapping up and over the edge. He could feel his skin burning as he blindly shoved away from the heat. Kenneth stopped near the projection in the center as the Overlord fell back, holding on only by his fingers that dug into the metal.

Eventually, the harsh light faded as the Overlord's suit melted in two and dropped the glare of unleashed energy far down below the platform.

Kenneth rolled over onto his back and pulled in a sharp breath. Even the hot air of the rift felt like a cool surprise against the heat of his skin. He blinked. It took several tries before he saw past the heavy glow still gripping his vision.

"You have to stop doing that," Kara said. She was looking down at him with the corner of her mouth pulled up in a knowing smile. "I imagined you had something smarter in mind when you called for my knife."

"Well if I—"

Kenneth was cut short as Kara slid her arms under his neck and pressed her lips heavily against his. Just as he recovered from his surprise and started to return the embrace, she pulled back sharply.

"What is it?" Kenneth asked.

Kara started patting sporadically about his shoulders as he sat up.

"Kara?"

"Hold still!" she said sharply. "Your shirt is on fire."

Kenneth looked down at his shoulder and started helping to brush away the embers that were steadily eating their way through the rough cloth. After the quick, chaotic moment, Kara finally swiped away the last of the smoldering patches.

The sound of multiple footsteps pulled their attention, and Jance held up a hand as a portion of the soldiers started cautiously onto the platform. A few had wounds from their own fight against the Overlord's most loyal. Most of them blinked heavily through the blinding light still within their eyes, and a number even let their weapons fall as they held onto the railings for support.

"What happened?" one finally asked.

Jance looked back to where Kara was taking Kenneth's hand to pull him to his feet. "They just saved our world. Them, and that man lying there, as a projection in the middle.

Chapter 23: Endings

Hoffsted looked out over the city from the launch station. In the distance, the Council Starscraper started to buckle inward. The descent was slow, of course. Even if the structure had suddenly decided to drop, it would be many minutes before the towering height would even hit the ground. The process was slowed even further as the repulsor engines, hidden all over the sides, now flared furiously in vain attempts to stop the building's momentum.

It was like watching a mountain shifting and the Earth spewing great jets of fire in protest. Even the skies lit up with storms of lament as the entire structure emitted shrieks of twisting metal. Fire jutted out of the side as the pipes within began to split open. A bright flash erupted from the bottom, and Hoffsted braced himself. Several long seconds later, the shockwave rolled across the city, toppling the buzzing transports off their paths and pushing him back on his heels. More fires lit up the sky as hundreds of transports smashed into the sides of buildings.

It was only when a spear of light flashed down from the orbital fleet that Hoffsted turned to enter the Tech-5 station. The illegally installed weapons aboard one of the armistice ships now rained down upon the SRA. Hoffsted had made sure that the UWC would have no knowledge of the armament, ensuring that the last desperate attempt of the SRA to avoid the war would fail. They would request information about the weapons that should not be in orbit, and the UWC would have nothing to form a reply with. Given no information on how many weapons there were or which of the massive ships were armed, the SRA would have no choice but to fire on them all.

Hoffsted stepped into the large station. It was nowhere near the size of the staging facilities, but it was at least large enough to launch the last passenger ship of the Mars Contract. He could feel a new rumble through the soles of his shoes. It was not the crumbling starscraper or the core reactors collapsing inward, but instead the engines of the shuttle preparing for a rushed departure. Hoffsted was not worried. The counterattacks on the Council City would come later that day, though perhaps before the starscrapers finished toppling to the ground.

* * *

Maylee sat on a bench in the middle of Departure Section: 43. Normally she would have been bouncing in excitement. After all, this was her first time off the planet. Instead, she had hardly noticed the glow of the cities and the halo of the sky fading as they ascended. Even now, the view through the large window of their approach to the *Solstice Dawn* was not enough to pull her unfocused eyes from her own thoughts.

The hundreds of others began to double-check that their items and possessions were still about them as their visors notified them of their docking status. The information also flashed about the room on the many displays, ranging in size from large overlays along the edges of the windows to strips of lights on the floor.

There were many others who settled further into their seats. The people here would have come from all directions, from the adjacent armistice ships to other sections of the globe. Not all had the same destination as Maylee. She started to glance at the data pad she had been provided, but she simply dropped it on the seat next to her. There was no need to check it again. This was her stop, though she did not stand. It would be minutes before the docking was completed. Whereas her transfer from the first passenger shuttle to the *Fortuna-8* was simply a matter of landing in a pressurized hangar, it was a much more complex task to line up the hundreds of airlocks down the length of the mile-long ship with the side of the *Solstice Dawn*.

The room darkened as they passed into the shadow of the larger ship. Maylee was just about to close her eyes when a sudden flare from the far side of the fleet popped into view. A nervous buzz passed around the room, and Maylee stood up on the seat to look out over the crowd of people. She could see a bright beam slowly making its way down to the planet. It was only when she realized the scale that she knew there was nothing gentle about the pillar of light moving in silence. Just as it collided with the land in a wave of fire, their view was blocked by the ships connecting.

The wide doors started to open on all levels of the room, just as they would in the many other departure sections. There was a nervous panic as people began to sift toward the exits, causing some sections of the crowd to mix with the pathways for entering passengers.

The displays in the room started flicking to images coming from the planet and other sections of the orbital fleet. Maylee sat there as the crowds moved past her, simply watching as the colossal bolt of light dropped down across the displays to impact with the surface again.

"Maylee!"

She turned to where the shout had come from. All she could see was an exchange of crowds from one ship to the next. She frowned, thinking for a moment that she had only heard the sound in her imagination.

"Maylee!" Agatha shouted again as she pushed forward through the people leaving the ship. Maylee was suddenly wrapped in her mother's tight embrace and her feet were lifted off the ground. "Thank god, my baby girl! What happened to you? You are all covered in scratches and dust!"

Maylee felt a sudden burst of the emotions she did not realize she had been holding in and pushed her face hard against her mother's shoulder. She could not hold back the tears or even the sharp hitches in her breathing. For a long moment, the two simply stood there together, surrounded by images of war.

"Follow me, dear," her mother said softly. "We have to get onto the armistice ship."

"No." Maylee lifted her head and looked at the images again through teary eyes. "We have to stay here."

"What? Why?"

"The fleet isn't supposed to have weapons, but that orbital strike, it came from that ship there." She pulled away and pointed to the screen, wiping her eyes with her other hand. "Hoffsted is using the fleet to start a war in order to cover his plans."

Agatha gave her a confused look. "What do you know about Hoffsted?"

"Everything." Maylee grabbed her mother by the hand and started to lead the way as the entire room lit up with warnings of the ship's departure. "But it does not matter now," she said. "We just have to get away from the outside layers of the *Fortuna*. If we can, we need to find pressurization suits. Possibly a ship to escape in."

"Escape to where?" Agatha asked as they passed through the door. "You know we cannot take a transport without a destination."

Maylee simply pushed on through the confusion, pulling her mother and gripping the small metal figure of a knight in her other hand.

"It's not that hard, really."

* * *

Hoffsted made his way through the empty hallways. At this point, even the security had evacuated the facility and started to board the shuttle. He could see the intense light coming from the base of the craft as he neared the inner ring of the structure.

The gravity repulsion tech used on the shuttle was even more advanced than that used by the starscrapers or the UWC fleet. The quantum recalibrated components within the repulsor engines were as close to the edge of advancement prohibited by the Inhibition Protocols, directed by Crystal Slate, as was possible. This would be the quickest flight to Mars yet, though in several hundred more years, even its travel capabilities would seem archaic. The workings of Crystal Slate would ensure Mars could survive long past that day, even if Avery Thorne's removal of data in the Council archives pushed the timeline of Hale's research back several hundred years.

He reached the last boarding dock still open. The security official behind the sealed checkpoint motioned for him to stop.

The military ambassador held his hand up to his visor. "Access request, Jonithan Hoffsted." Luckily Avery Thorne and the Sharpes girl had not managed to delete that information as well. Storing his EMA-GO certification and approval in the archives had turned out to be a greater risk than he had believed. His purpose in doing that had been to ensure that no investigation on Mars could link him with intent to leave the UWC. He knew very well that there was no proof when evidence was unreachable, and with Avery Thorne's failure to stop the shutdown of the reactors, the only person not already on Mars who could know about his departure was a little girl with no say in the world.

"One moment," the man on the inside said. Hoffsted crossed his arms behind his back and waited.

"I know it is in system," Hoffsted said impatiently, "I sent it myself."

"I am sorry. We cannot accept this."

"What the hell do you mean?" Hoffsted moved to face the man through the glass and pounded his fist on it. "They cleared me! That was the deal all along! I am the military ambassador to the United World Coalition Council for god's sake!"

"Your pass to the colonies has been revoked by EMA-GO." The man pushed away from the terminal and started shutting down the systems to the room. He sent one last glance to the news showing the SRA beginning to bombard the orbital fleet. "And a damned good thing they did. I know Ambassador Lorège would have been glad to see you suffer some form of justice."

"That is not possible." Hoffsted hit the window again. "Under what grounds have I been revoked?"

The man grabbed his jacket from the back of his chair. He simply transferred the last open terminal screen in the room to display on the face of the glass as he turned to head out the door toward the shuttle.

Hoffsted took a step back, looking at it in stunned confusion. On the glass were the words *"By order of the Warden."*

* * *

Avery opened his eyes, though he was not sure what woke him from unconsciousness. The harsh pops and churning now echoing up from deep within the Earth had not changed since he began to wait for his own end to finally wash over him. Suddenly, he heard the rapid steps of someone running. He rolled to his side and looked up, feeling toward his hip for a weapon. He had nothing. He sent a quick glance around through his hazy vision, but the only thing nearby was Maylee's broken visor, still sitting where Hoffsted had dropped it before fleeing.

There was a laugh as the steps neared. "Avery Thorne, did you think you could really get off that easy? Just save the world and be done with it?"

"Lance?" Avery tried to get his eyes to focus. "I told you to leave."

"Here is the thing," Lance said, "you can order Welnn and Feyn to just let you die, but I for one am not, nor ever was, a sectator."

Avery shook his head. "It is too late. There is no use."

"I figured you would say that. But if it is too late, then how can it hurt to try? Come on, Avery." Lance grabbed under his arms. "You've already given your life to save everything. Doesn't mean you have to die for it as well. At the very least, not down here in the dark."

* * *

The entire room watched in silence as Jance stood with her hands to her lips, a few silent tears running between her fingertips. The remaining Norclave soldiers and the riftwalker pilots stood to the sides as the projections of both men shuffled slowly out of the bounds of the projection sphere toward the bridge. Kenneth wrapped an arm around Kara's back, and she leaned ever so slightly into him. Whether they saw Avery and Lance as ghosts, or simply moved out of their way out of respect, Kenneth did not know. They all could see that Jance, their Cryo, had known both men in the projection.

Kenneth glanced back to the dead hand of the Overlord, still clinging to the edge of the platform. After a time, Kenneth finally decided to end the moment.

"We fasten the wounded to the caretakers, then?" Jance asked when Kenneth stepped up beside her. The woman looked down the pathway, as if she were still watching them walk away.

"Caretakers?" Kenneth asked.

Kara brushed past him, taking the lead and moving down the pathway. "She means the riftwalkers."

"I suppose that is a more fitting name now," Jance agreed. "Riftwalkers."

"What happens after this, Ambassador?" Kenneth asked. "What are you going to do once we reach the top?"

"The world may have changed, but that does not mean I have to. My plan is to head back to the Council Starscraper, to Norclave, and to help the people from there. Without Obrourke as the Overlord, I am sure Norclave will see a struggle. Left alone, control of the city may very well change hands dozens of times. The process would undoubtedly cause a great deal of grief."

"You want to take his spot as the Overlord?"

"Goodness no," Jance replied. "Much like Obrourke, I would be ignorant to how the politics or people of this time function. However," Jance continued with a sly smile, "I can think of a few reasons why the next leader will be glad take whatever advice I may have to give."

* * *

Over the course of the next few days, Norclave slowly started to stabilize. The looting in the South Corridors had been quelled for the most part, though the city still tentatively shook with the uncertainty to come. News of the Overlord's death had spread quickly, and a number of the darker organizations about the city had tried to take the opportunity to carve out their own territories. At Jance's direction, the remaining Norclave soldiers who had taken it upon themselves to maintain some form of peace now turned a blind eye to the maneuvering of one devious entity.

Kenneth had assured her that the best way to keep the criminal organizations of Norclave in check was to let themselves reestablish their order. After considerable repayment for arming the Overlord's soldiers, a shady merchant by the name of Mackelry Norton began to soften the chaos. Jance met with him personally on several occasions. He was a man of business, and, according to his own account, he stood to make a greater profit breaking the old laws of Norclave than to have his trade legal and in the open. If he could work with the Cryo to maintain control until the next Overlord stepped forward, she was more than willing to let him occupy his own space.

It just so happened that she was waiting for that same merchant to arrive as she stood on the seventh level of Norclave. Kenneth and Kara's share of their promised reward from the library was just enough to fund a range of scrapsmiths and technicians to work setting up some sort of defense to discourage others from attacking the city. The Norclave archivists had immediately begun work on directing the operation using the schematics left by the previous Overlord, Thalen, and those improved upon by Obrourke. Laila was easily convinced by Sora to join the project, but Jance had to speak with Tenan personally before he agreed.

"Did he say who it was?" Sora asked. She stood with a data pad in her hand even though she now wore a visor.

"I would not have known who it was anyways," Jance replied. "I am not expecting a great deal of integrity, considering that Mackelry would not have agreed to this without being able to continue his trade. I just hope for someone reasonable enough to do good by the Norclave people."

Sora tapped her finger nervously on the data pad. "What is going to happen to us? Me and the others?"

"You will stay here. That is my condition they will have to live with. I am sure they will welcome people with knowledge of the city. Control of Norclave will be no small task to undertake, and any who are willing to help will be well-appreciated by whoever is to try."

"There they are," Sora said, nodding forward to the group coming up the stairs. The old merchant bounded up the steps and hurried into a mediating position between them and the incoming group. The escort of soldiers were wearing pieces of flight armor, though the outer coat had been ground down to a gritty shine.

"Ambassador Lorège," Mackelry said as the soldiers fanned out into position, "allow me to introduce Olana Nuand, head of Kamriek's Grove and owner of the Kamriek Mines."

The woman gave a reserved nod. She held herself with an air of authority, made more so by the Council uniform she wore. Funnily enough, it was in better condition than Jance's. It was not marked by the flames of a transport or the scuffs from the long journey by caretaker. Riftwalker.

"I was told to give you this," Jance said, holding out a small cube of glass for Mackelry to hand over, "as a symbol of peaceful beginnings."

Olana took the cube and rolled it in her hands with a surprising familiarity. "Peaceful beginnings . . . and to forgetting things past, it seems."

Jance shook her head and smiled. "What has happened should always be remembered. We just have to know what to do with the knowledge."

* * *

Kenneth sat alone, replacing pieces of the transport inside the Norclave hangars. All the other technicians, many of whom he had aggravated at some point in the past, were helping in the great project Jance had put together. He was not sure if it would help in the long run, but he guessed it was worth the same try as anything else. He tossed a broken piece out from the transport, causing the chunk of metal to skitter across the floor. It had been made abundantly clear that Norclave would need transports if it hoped to keep from a complete collapse. If not, then perhaps he could use this one to flee the city once and for all, especially now that Olana Nuand was due to arrive.

He cursed as a filthy fluid spilled out from the repulsor engine next to the one he was working on. Whoever had tried to fix this one hadn't the faintest idea what they were doing. He shook his arm, though it did little to remove the liquid. He doubted if they had even thought to check if the repulsors were filled with rust. Most of the metal was extremely resistant, but centuries always took their toll. He lifted his elbow and frowned as the streak of filth started to flow down toward his glove. Without any warning, a scrap of cloth dropped down into his hand.

Kenneth looked up behind him to see Kara giving a smile.

"How long have you been there?" he asked.

"Just now." She sat down a small basket that had been crudely woven together of grasses and wire. "There are your parts. Not as exciting just hunting through the trade center for them, though. I know a place to the west where we could have found as many as you could ever need."

"It still took you long enough," Kenneth said, using the cloth to wipe away the liquid from the edges of the glove.

"I stopped to watch Jance meet with Olana. I figured we would want a head start if we needed to escape the city again." Kara turned to lean against the edge of the transport and held up the piece of bread she had picked up along the way. "Especially knowing how long it will take you to get this fixed." She took a bite to hide her smile.

Kenneth shook the gloves loose and found a spot to lean beside her. When he grabbed for the bread, she pulled it away. She reached into a pocket and tossed another piece up for him to catch. Before he took a bite, Kenneth asked if Olana said anything about the gift.

"She said enough," Kara replied. "Not sure how long we will be welcome in Norclave, though."

Kenneth nodded. "My offer still stands. We can set out to wherever you want, whenever you want."

Kara took another bite of the fresh bread and gave him a half smile and a long look. "Not just yet."

To the Reader:

I'd like to express my thanks to you for picking up *Cryogenesis,* the beginning of the the adventures for the characters of the Tech Hunter Trillogy, as well as for me as an author. This book has been an important milestone for me, and I'm thrilled to be able to share it with you.

-Ryan Clark

RyanClarkBooks.com